SCATTER THE BONES

Jigsaw and Margot, Part 3

LOST KINGS MC
BOOK 26

AUTUMN JONES LAKE

COPYRIGHT

ABOUT SCATTER THE BONES

Instead of tearing us apart, our sins have forged a bond no one can break.

Margot's darkness calls to mine, her need for vengeance matches my own, and I'll protect her at any cost.

She never flinched when I admitted I'd scattered the bones of my worst nightmare along the highways.

I finally felt free—until the past showed up wearing a face I never expected to see again.

I thought those demons were buried.

But if I've learned anything in my years with the Lost Kings MC, it's that secrets don't stay dead for long—and the one I swore I left behind just came back to find me.

Scatter the Bones is the 26th book in the Lost Kings MC series by *USA Today* bestselling author Autumn Jones Lake. This is the third book in Jigsaw and Margo's story and must be read after *Twist the Knife* and *Collect the Pieces*.

GLOSSARY OF CHARACTERS AND TERMINOLOGY

The Lost Kings MC™ World © Autumn Jones Lake

The following may contain spoilers if you are not caught up on the series or have skipped books.

Please note, this glossary only pertains to my romantic fictionalized motorcycle club world. It should not be construed as applicable to any other fictional clubs or a real-life motorcycle club.

THE LOST KINGS MC: UPSTATE, NY ("EMPIRE," NY)

President: Rochlan "Rock" North. Leader of the Upstate NY charter of the Lost Kings MC.

Sergeant-at-Arms: Wyatt "Wrath" Ramsey. Protector or enforcer for the club.

Vice President: Blake "Murphy" O'Callaghan. Murphy was the road captain up until *White Lies (Lost Kings MC #15)*

Treasurer: Marcel "Teller" Whelan. Handles the money and investments for the club. In After Glow (Lost Kings MC #11) Rock and Teller discovered they were father and son. In *Reckless Truths (Lost Kings MC #21)* they let the whole club in on their secret.

Road Captain: Dixon "Dex" Watts (newly appointed to the position in White Lies) His books are: *Rust or Ride (Lost Kings MC #22)* and *Agony to Ashes (Lost Kings MC #23)*

THE LOST KINGS MC: DOWNSTATE, NY ("UNION" NY)

President: Angus "Zero" or "Z" Frazier. As of *Zero Apologies* (*Lost Kings MC #14*), Z is the president of the Downstate, NY charter of the Lost Kings MC.

Vice President: Logan "Rooster" Randall: Rooster's story is told in *Swagger Sass* (*Lost Kings MC #14.5*), *Rhythm of the Road* (*Lost Kings MC #16*), *Lyrics on the Wind* (*Lost Kings MC #17*), and *Diamond in the Dust* (*Lost Kings MC #18*)

Sergeant-at-Arms: Grayson "Grinder" Lock as of *Throne of Scars* (*Lost Kings MC #20*) His books are *Crown of Ghosts* (*Lost Kings MC #19*) and *Throne of Scars*.

Treasurer: Hustler (he hasn't gotten a legal name yet!)

Road Captain: Jensen "Jigsaw" Kilgore; Jigsaw, Rooster's best friend from childhood. His books are: *Twist the Knife* (*Lost Kings MC #24*), *Collect the Pieces* (*Lost Kings MC #25*) and *Scatter the Bones* (*Lost Kings MC #26*)

THE LOST KINGS MC: PORT EVERHART, VA

President: Cypress "Ice" Caldwell
Vice President: Farmer
Sergeant-at-Arms: Pants
Treasurer: T-Bone
Road Captain: Boots

THE LOST KINGS MC: DEADBRANCH, TN

President: Squiggy

SAA: Steer from the Downstate NY charter moved to TN in *Throne of Scars*.

Retired President: Digger, we first met him in *Lyrics on the Wind*.

He passed away and the Lost Kings attended his funeral in *Agony to Ashes*

OTHER LOST KINGS MC MEMBERS

Thomas "Ravage" Kane: We've gotten to know Rav and his snarky humor a little bit better in each book. Ravage is a general member who helps out wherever he is needed.

Cronin "Sparky" Petek: Sparky is the mad genius/hippie stoner behind the Lost Kings MC's pot-growing business. He is rarely seen outside of the basement, as he prefers the company of his plants.

Elias "Bricks" Serrano: We have seen Bricks and his girlfriend Winter throughout the series. He's one of the few members who does not live at the clubhouse.

Sam "Stash" Black: Lives in the basement with Sparky and helps with the plants.

Hoot: We've seen glimpses of him since Slow Burn when he was a lowly prospect. He finally got his full patch, but still gets a lot of the grunt work.

Birch: We also met him as a prospect. He's been voted as a full-patch member but shares in a lot of the grunt work with Hoot.

Priest: The Lost Kings MC's national president. We first met him and his wife, Valentina, in After Burn.

Malik: Prospect for the Lost Kings MC. Helps out at Crystal Ball. Owns the Lucky Duck pawnshop in Ironworks.

Sway: Former president of the downstate charter of the Lost Kings MC. We've seen Sway and his wife Tawny off and on in the series since *Strength From Loyalty*, usually annoying Rock in some fashion. After some legal troubles in *Throne of Scars*, Sway disappeared to Florida and has not been seen since.

THE LADIES OF THE LOST KINGS MC

Hope Kendall North, Esq.: Nicknamed First Lady by Murphy in *Corrupting Cinderella (Lost Kings MC #2)*, Hope is the object of Rock's love and obsession. Their daughter is named Grace after Rock's mother.

Trinity Hurst Ramsey: Wrath's angel. Former caretaker of the club. She now has her own photography and graphic design business. She is married to Wrath, fiercely loyal to the club, and best friends with Hope. Although she loves her niblets, **Trinity and Wrath are happily childfree by choice and intend to *stay* that way**.

Heidi "Little Hammer" O'Callaghan: Murphy's wife and Teller's little sister. Heidi just graduated from college and works at Empire

Med. Murphy officially adopted her daughter, Alexa Jade. In *Reckless Truths*, Heidi and Murphy had another daughter, Brittany, affectionately nicknamed "Bit-Bit" by her big sister.

Charlotte Clark, Esq: Teller's sunshine. Often credited with taming the brooding treasurer of the Lost Kings, Teller. As of *Fighting the Forbidden*, she gave birth to twins. In *Collect the Pieces*, we meet Ivy and Ivan.

Lilly Frazier: Z's brave and devoted siren. The new queen of the Lost Kings MC's downstate charter. One of Hope's best friends. Z and Lilly's son is named Chance.

Shelby Morgan: Rooster's sassy little chickadee. Country music singer from Texas. We first met Shelby in *Swagger and Sass*.

Serena Cargill: Former downstate club girl. Abused by Shadow, the former VP of the downstate charter. Found love with her Grinder, her "murder daddy" in *Crown of Ghosts*. She gave birth to their son Lincoln in *Agony to Ashes*.

Emily C. Walker: Engaged to Dex. Serena's best friend. Introduced in *Throne of Scars*. She is the guardian of her teenage sister Libby.

Margot Cedarwood: Daughter of the owner of the Cedarwood Family Funeral Home, a business the Lost Kings MC invested in as of *Reckless Truths*. Jigsaw has had his eye the pretty blonde mortician her since the day they met. She's shy, sweet, and has a dark side.

Liberty Isabel Walker: Libby is Emily's teenage sister. The Walker sisters have no other family. Grinder is protective of them.

Willow: Bartender at Crystal Ball, but once or twice we've caught her sneaking in or out of the basement with Sparky.

Swan: Lost Kings MC club girl and dancer at Crystal Ball. Swan has found a new calling as the yoga teacher for the old ladies of the Lost Kings MC and is slowly moving away from dancing at Crystal Ball.

OTHER RECURRING CHARACTERS IN THE LOST KINGS MC WORLD

Griffin "Stonewall" Royal: Remy's best friend and business

partner. We first meet him in *Renegade Path*. He has been in and out of the series since *Beyond Reason*. He helped Grinder out in *Crown of Ghosts*. In a relationship with Remy's little sister Molly. Their books are *Fighting the Forbidden (Ruthless & Royal #1)* and *Repairing the Wreckage (Ruthless & Royal #2)*.

Roman "Vapor" Hawkins: *Renegade Path* is his story. He is married to Dex's "niece" Juliet. We first see in in *After Burn*.

Remington "Ruthless" Holt: Owns "The Castle" with his best friend, Griff. An underground fighting ring Murphy used to participate in. We've seen him most recently helping out the club in *White Lies, Crown of Ghosts, Agony to Ashes, and Twist the Knife*. Guardian of his younger sister, Molly. Considering forming a support club for the Lost Kings MC with Griff, Eraser, and Vapor.

Easton "Eraser" : Owns Zips, a racetrack near the Lost Kings MC territory. Married to Ella. We first met him in *Renegade Path*, and again in *White Lies*.

Dawson Roads: Famous (fictional) country music singer in the Lost Kings MC world. He's been mentioned here and there since *One Empire Night*, but we didn't officially "meet" him until *Rhythm of the Road* when Shelby was on tour with him. We see him again in *Repairing the Wreckage*.

Carter "Scribbles" Clark: Charlotte's goofy, often inappropriate, younger brother. Most recently rescued by the club in *Reckless Truths*. Given the road name *Scribbles* by Wrath.

Loco: Business associate of the Lost Kings MC. He covers the Ironworks area of the Lost Kings MC's territory. He has appeared throughout the series and become a strong LOKI ally.

Lynn Morgan: Shelby's mother. May or may not have hooked up with Jigsaw or Steer at some point.

Russell "Chaser" Adams: President of the Devil Demons MC in Western NY. (The Hollywood Demons series contains his story.)

Mallory "Little Dove" DeLova-Adams: Chaser's wife. Daughter of mafia boss Anatoly DeLova.

Angelina Adams: Mallory and Chaser's daughter

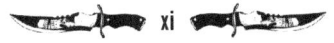

Linden "Stump" Adams: Chaser's father. Former president of the Devil Demons MC.

Sullivan Wallace: Jake's brother, and the owner of Strike Back Fitness. He's a significant character in *Bullets and Bonfires* and has his own book, *Warnings and Wildfires*.

Jake Wallace: One of Wrath's business partners in Furious Fitness. Jake has appeared off and on throughout the series since *Tattered on my Sleeve*. He sometimes holds self-defense classes for the ladies.

The mysterious "Quill" who we met in *Diamond in the Dust* and again in *Crown of Ghosts*.

Anatoly DeLova: Mallory's father. Leader of the Russian mafia. Sometime business associate of the Lost Kings MC.

Stella: Pornographic film actress. The downstate charter is the sole investor in her production company. Ex-girlfriend of Z. Current...something of Sway. Her *Sex in Every City* series sometimes requires members of LOKI to work as bouncers on her film sets.

Inga March: Porn star, and former dancer at Crystal Ball. Sued the whole club for paternity of her son in After Burn (Lost Kings MC #10) We last saw her in *Rust or Ride.*

Tawny: Sway's ol' lady. The former "Queen B" of the downstate charter of the Lost Kings MC.

Anya Regal: Porn princess of the Lost Kings MC, Virginia charter.

Shonda: Club girl from the Lost Kings, MC Virginia charter.

Lala: Club girl from Downstate NY.

Bonnie: Club girl from the Downstate club.

OTHER MCS: FRIENDLY CLUBS:

Devil Demons MC: Based in Western NY. Long-time friend of the Lost Kings MC. Their clubs are intertwined and share a lot of history. More of this is explored in the *Hollywood Demons* series.

Wolf Knights MC: Mostly an ally of the Lost Kings. They used to run Slater County but said they were dissolving their charter in White Lies and turning it over to the Lost Kings. As of *Reckless Truths*, Slater County is officially Lost Kings MC territory.

Iron Bulls MC: (From the Iron Bulls MC series by Phoenyx

Slaughter): Southwestern outlaw club. Meets up and does business with LOKI once in a while.

Savage Dragons MC: (From the Iron Bulls MC series by Phoenyx Slaughter): Texas outlaw club.

ENEMY CLUBS:

Vipers MC: Used to run Ironworks until the Lost Kings took over that territory. Still active in other parts of the country.

South of Satan MC: Vermont MC who has stirred up trouble for LOKI in the past. Last disposed of in *Reckless Truths*.

LOST KINGS MC TERMINOLOGY

LOKI: Short for LOst KIngs. Only to be used by members of the Lost Kings MC.

War room: Where the Lost Kings hold "church."

Property patch: When a member takes a woman as his old lady (wife status), he gives her a vest with a property patch. In my series, the vest has a "Property of Lost Kings MC" patch and the member's road name on the back. The officers also place their patches on the ol' lady's vest as a sign that they always have her back. Her man's patch or club symbol is placed over the heart. Rock's patch is a crown. Wrath's is a star. Murphy's is a four-leaf clover. Teller's is a dollar sign. Z's is the letter Z. Rooster's patch is a rooster wearing a crown. As a joke, Wrath gave Rock and Hope a "product of" patch for baby Grace.

PLACES IN THE LOST KINGS MC WORLD

I use a mix of real and imaginary names to describe the places in my series. Again, I bend and shape geography to my needs as this is a fictional world that I have created.

Empire, NY: The territory run by the Lost Kings MC upstate charter. This is a fictional version of Albany, NY, the capital of New York State. Many of the Lost Kings MC's businesses are located in and around Empire.

Slater, NY: Loosely based on Schenectady County. Until recently it was the Wolf Knights MC's territory.

Ironworks, NY: Loosely based on Rensselaer County (Troy, NY).

At the beginning of the series, it was run by the Vipers MC. It is now considered territory of the Lost Kings MC.

Union, NY: A fictional area two hours south of Empire, NY, where the "downstate" charter is located.

Pine Hollow, NY: Where the Cedarwood Family Funeral Home is located. About an hour west of Empire, NY.

Crystal Ball: The strip club owned by the Lost Kings MC and one of their legitimate businesses. They often refer to it simply as "CB." Located in Empire County.

Furious Fitness: The gym Wrath owns with Murphy and Jake. Often just referred to as "Furious." Located not far from Crystal Ball.

Strike Back: Owned by Sullivan Wallace but members of the Lost Kings MC and Ruthless & Royal have worked and worked out there in the past.

Johnson County/Johnsonville: Fictional area where Heidi grew up. About an hour west of "Empire." Where Strike Back Gym, The Castle, and Zips are located.

Zips: Racetrack owned by Eraser where all the illegal gambling/racing in the area happens.

The Castle: Formerly a juvenile detention center. The building is now used to house the underground fighting ring run by Remy and Griff. Murphy used to fight here. Other LOKI members also blow off steam in the cage here from time to time. Located in the middle of nowhere, NY, it once-upon-a-time housed Griff, Vapor, Eraser, Sully, and possibly Teller during their "troubled youth" days.

Kodack, NY: Another fictional NY area located in Western New York. Somewhere near Buffalo, perhaps. This territory is run by the Devil Demons MC.

Empire Medical Center: Local hospital where all the Kings receive medical treatment. Heidi also works there now.

OTHER MC TERMINOLOGY

Most terminology was obtained through research. However, I have also used some artistic license in applying these terms to my romanticized, fictional version of an outlaw motorcycle club. This is not an exhaustive list.

Cage: A car, truck, van—basically anything other than a motorcycle.

Church: Club meetings all full-patch members must attend. Led by the president of the club, but officers will update the members on the areas they oversee. (Some clubs refer to the meeting room where they hold church as the "chapel." My club refers to it as their "war room."

Citizen/civilian: Anyone not a hardcore biker or belonging to an outlaw club. "Citizen wife" would refer to a spouse kept entirely separate from the club.

Cut: Leather vest worn by outlaw bikers and adorned with patches and artwork displaying the club's unique colors. The Lost Kings' colors are blue and gray. Their logo is a skull with a crown. The Respect Few, Fear None patch is earned by doing time for the club without snitching. Brother's Keeper patches are earned by killing for the club. Loyal Brother is for a brother who's spent more than five years with the club.

Colors: The "uniform" of an outlaw motorcycle gang. A leather vest, with the three-piece club patch on the back, and various other patches relating to their role in the club.

Fly colors: To ride on a motorcycle wearing colors.

Muffler bunny or "bunnies": A girl who hangs around to provide sexual favors to members. Old ladies in my series will sometimes refer to them as "friends of the club," depending on the girl in question. Some clubs refer to them as club whores, patch whores, or cut sluts. These terms are not regularly used in my series. Sometimes simply referred to as a "club girl."

Nomad: A club member who does not belong to any specific charter, yet has privileges in all charters.

Old lady/ol' lady: Wife or steady girlfriend of a club member.

Patched in: When a new member is approved for full membership.

Patch holder: A member who has been vetted through performing duties for the club as a prospect or probate and has earned his three-piece patch.

Road name: Nickname. Usually given by the other members.

Run: A club-sanctioned outing, sometimes with other chapters and/or clubs. Can also refer to a club business run.

I'm sure I'm forgetting something! But this should be enough to get you started!

DEDICATION

To the women who are violence wrapped in sweetness
And the men who would burn the world to protect them.

CHAPTER ONE

JIGSAW

Jensen Killgore, 20 years old.

At a certain point in life, you reach an age when you realize being a man isn't about strength, money, or respect. It's about the awareness of how your actions affect *other* people.

No matter how you try to bury the past, the consequences of our actions—or inactions—often find a way to hunt us down.

More than six years away from my family's farm and I couldn't banish this place from my memory even if I wanted to.

The old white mailbox appears on my left. Rustier now. A little tilted. But still there.

Dread and fury beat against my skin. This isn't a social call. It won't be a warm family reunion.

I'm here for retribution and rescue.

One way or another, my baby sister's leaving with me today.

I'm bigger now. Stronger. I have a little bit of money.

Nope. Don't think about the money or where it came from. Rooster's Aunt Em made it clear on her deathbed, she loved me like a son.

I'd rather have Aunt Em alive and breathing than all the money in the world.

She'd know how to take care of Jezzie. Instead, I plan to take my sister halfway across the country to stay with a woman she probably doesn't even remember.

A woman who once tried to protect my mother from getting involved with my crazy-ass father.

He never hit the girls.

Girls were meant to serve. Be silent. Obedient. He never whipped them or locked them in the basement.

That you know of.

Ruth would've protected Jezzie. The woman who helped me escape. Who promised she'd look after my sister.

I was a kid. Fuck, I'm *still* a damn kid. Rooster's Aunt Em and Uncle Boone saved my life by taking me in after my father's last beating sent me to the hospital.

I owed them everything. After I graduated from high school, I planned to come back for Jezzie.

Then Em got sick. Really sick. I helped Rooster and Boone take care of her until she passed. Peacefully at home. The way she wanted.

Boone was a mess. The man who treated me like his son was lost without his wife. I helped Rooster take care of Boone.

Until Boone had a stroke.

Rooster was dealing with Boone's estate. Learning the ins and outs of the bar and restaurant Boone left us. In a few weeks, I'll return to help him figure it all out.

But now it's time to get my sister. I can't wait any longer. She'll be approaching fourteen now. Getting too close to the age my father thought girls should be married off to start breeding the next generation of the Lord's servants.

Before she passed, Aunt Em tracked down my real aunt. My mother's sister, Angela. Like the mama bear she was, Em hired a PI to learn everything she could about Aunt Angela before giving me the information. She works a normal nine-to-five in a nice small town in Pennsylvania. No children. No husband. No *cult*.

I had a few fond memories of Angela. Her face. Her smile. A yappy dog who always sat on her lap when we visited. How she tried to convince my mother not to move to the other side of the country when my father got his first "vision from the Lord."

Then later how she visited our farm when Jezzie was maybe two or three. The arguments she had with my parents. How she left in a hurry and we never saw or heard from her again.

That's who I was trusting to take care of Jezzie now?

No. If I get any hint that Angela's nuts, I'll keep Jezzie with me.

Where? At Boone's place? Where his motorcycle club buddies drop in to visit with alarming frequency. What's she supposed to do, bring her math homework to the bar after school? So I can help her with equations while I'm busy serving beer to bikers until one in the morning?

While it might be better than living under my father's thumb, it's still not a life for a young girl.

The truck bounces and dips as I steer from the road onto the long driveway leading to the small farm I remember all too well. Dirt and pebbles fly up, pinging against the side of my truck.

What if we need to make a quick getaway?

Slowing down, I jerk the steering wheel, executing a sloppy three-point turn, and stop the truck in the overgrown grass bordering the driveway.

I silently slide out of the truck, my boots barely scraping against the gravel. My gaze travels up the driveway. Who the fuck knows what I'm going to encounter.

Digging under the front seat, I pull out a holster and shrug it over my shoulders. I slide a black case out, flip it over and pull out a 9mm Glock and slap in a full magazine, rack the slide, then tuck it into the side of the holster. A second 9mm rests in the case. I glance up the driveway again.

Fuck it.

I check the second gun and nudge it into place on my other side. Better to be over-prepared than under.

Although, I don't want to put a bullet in my father. Not unless I have to.

No, the fantasy that's played over and over in my head for years—

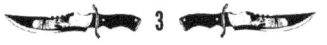

3

chaining him to the wall in the basement and whipping him raw, then just *leaving* him there—is so close I can taste it.

Maybe he gnaws off his arm and escapes. Maybe someone rescues him. Or maybe he slowly starves to death and someone years from now finds his skeleton.

The possibilities are endless.

I stick to the grassy side of the road. Memories of hiking up and down this driveway to or from the school bus return. Dread followed me both ways for different reasons back then. I hated school where I was relentlessly bullied for being "weird," but I feared home—the endless chores, scripture reading, and predictable punishments for any sin.

Weak, pale sunlight spears the gray clouds above but my mood's blacker than midnight.

My footsteps slow as I round the corner and the old white farmhouse comes into view.

Fewer animals and children roam around the yard than I remember. The few pieces of playground equipment have rusted. The grass left to grow so tall, the tops of the merry-go-round bars are barely visible.

Three figures seem to be tending the field at the side of the house. In their white, shapeless garments, silently and slowly moving, they look like ghosts.

Beyond the dilapidated white farmhouse I grew up in, the big, red barn my father used as a "church" seems to be the only building that's had any attention in the last few years. Now, it's a crisp white with a huge wooden cross nailed above the barn doors.

Not an improvement.

Screams from the church pierce the air.

Some things haven't changed.

I turn, scanning the area. The people in the fields continue working.

More screams. High. Girlish.

Fear slams into my chest.

Jezzie. Jezzie. What if that's my sister?

Forget stealth. I sprint through the tall grass, dry blades whipping against my jeans.

Another gasping, desperate scream.

My footsteps slow as I approach the barn doors. They're cracked open wide enough for me to slip through. I grip the Glock tight in one hand. Stale air hits me, dry and suffocating.

Loud splashing echoes from the "altar" at the front of the church.

My father's voice fills the air. "I cast out these demons!"

Memories slice through me like barbed wire as his words slap me in the face.

I close my eyes, forcing the memories of hours of torture away.

Splashing, struggling gasps, and my father's voice splits the air. I open my eyes and edge forward, my eyes slowly adjusting to the gloom.

Only my father's head and shoulders are visible over the rows of benches.

"Submit and repent your wicked ways!" He's bent over a large, white, heavy-duty plastic tub—the thick kind of industrial plastic used for the chemicals used to clean farm equipment.

Now, it's full of what I hope is water. His arm's plunged in up to the elbow and he's holding someone's head below the surface.

Seems the old man's getting more creative with his torture.

"I cast you out, demons!" His voice is harsh and raw with the same violent fanaticism that filled my childhood.

As I approach, thin legs kick, feet thumping against the floor. Pale arms thrash weakly. Small hands desperately clutch the sides of the tub, fingers slipping against slick plastic.

He yanks whoever it is out of the water by a mass of wet black hair.

"You will obey!" His voice thunders through the air.

I have to stop this. *Now.* Before he shoves her under the water again.

The girl gasps and screams, clawing at the air and coughing violently as he yanks her backward.

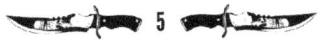

Water cascades over his arms, splashing onto the wood floor. "Are you ready to repent, Jezebel?"

Jezzie. No, no, no.

"Stop!" A raw, broken shout explodes from my chest. Anything to draw his attention away from my sister.

My father's body jerks at the sound of my voice. He releases Jezzie so fast, her arms splash into the water. Her panicked gaze bounces between our father and me as she scuttles away from the tub.

Across the distance, I meet my father's cruel gaze. Hate's aged him more than I expected. Thinning hair and wrinkled skin drooping from his skull. But I'd still recognize him anywhere. As we stare each other down, indignation flares across his evil face.

My finger strokes the trigger. *No.* A bullet through the heart is too easy. He needs to die much harder.

"Get back here, girl!" he shouts at my sister, pointing to the floor in front of his feet. "You're not finished."

I raise the Glock, aiming at his chest. "Yes, you are." My voice and hold on the gun remain steady despite the panic coursing through my veins.

"Leave her alone."

He tears his gaze away from my sister and stares at me. Surprise flickers over his face, then slowly, recognition seems to wash over him. He stands taller and curls his lips into a familiar sneer.

"And who are you trespassing on my property?"

"You know damn well who I am. Your third son."

"Jensen's dead," he says in a hollow voice.

Choking sobs tear from Jezzie's throat.

"You're going to wish you'd killed me when you had the chance," I promise.

"Jensen?" my sister cries.

"Stay back, Jezzie," I warn.

She shuffles farther away, still coughing and shaking violently.

My father's eyes narrow on me, stubborn rage burning in their dark depths. "You always were corrupt. Defiant. A devil."

"Yeah, yeah," I groan, tired of the litany of insults I've heard my

whole life. "You never change. Always worried about the thorn in someone else's eye, instead of the plank in yours."

"The Lord's will is always righteous, unchanging. It's *your* rebellious spirit that will face judgment."

"Abusing children is the Lord's will?" I step closer, my gun steady and aimed straight at his heart. "On your knees."

"I won't kneel before Satan's spawn."

I stay back a few feet, wary. Evil or not, my father's quick, cunning, and an expert at handling weapons. One careless move could be fatal to me *and* Jezzie.

"Jezzie," I say in my calmest voice without taking my eyes off my father. "Go into the house and pack all of your things. Anything you want to take with you."

"Don't you dare move, girl!" my father shouts, his voice booming with self-righteous fury. "You will obey your father. Not this heathen who's been corrupted by outsiders."

Jezzie stands, her nervous gaze darting between us. "Jensen? It's really you?"

"It's me." I glance briefly toward her, heart twisting painfully at the sight. The wet, shapeless white dress clings to her, accentuating her fragile, emaciated form. Anger boils hotter within me. "Please, Jezzie. Get your things quickly. Don't speak to anyone. You're leaving with me."

She bursts into tears. "Okay."

Guilt threatens to choke me.

No, there's time for that later.

Jezzie bolts through the side door without another word and doesn't look back.

"Destined to be a harlot," my father mutters. "If you take her from here, you condemn her soul to eternal fire."

"How many lost souls are following your twisted gospel now?" I ask, eyes narrowed. "How many people are you taking advantage of here on the farm?"

My father puffs out his chest and returns my glare, defiant and unyielding.

"You still torture kids in the basement?" I wave the gun toward the house. "Still claiming it's discipline?"

"You were a stubborn, evil child," he spits back. "I did my best to cleanse your soul." His tone shifts to a lower, poor, pitiful me tone. "But some demons are too strong, and I am just a flawed human."

"Maybe it was *your* soul that needed cleansing?" My voice hardens, memories of that dark basement flooding my mind—chains, bloodstains, echoes of desperate prayers. "You're nothing but a sick, twisted old man who gets off on torturing women and children."

"Blasphemer!" he shouts.

"Hit a nerve, did I?" I taunt. "Let's see how righteous you're feeling while you take your punishment."

"The Lord will protect me." His chin lifts in defiance but uncertainty flickers in his eyes.

"Great. Let's test that theory out. Maybe you'll get lucky, and the Lord will strike me dead." My tone's mocking, the smile stretched across my face deranged.

Unease crawls through me. Jezzie could be doing what I asked. Or she could run and warn the others. I need to move fast.

I step closer, jerking the gun toward the house. "Move."

His jaw tightens. Resistance vibrates through every tense line of his body, but he slowly moves toward the same door Jezzie used.

Several men used to live here on the farm. In outbuildings my father converted to "guest houses." Their wives were often allowed to stay in the main house. Were those men still here, ready to defend the homestead? Or had my father driven them away and kept their wives?

"Move," I order again.

His steps are slow, his body rigid as he shuffles toward the house.

"No, use the side door to the basement," I warn as he turns toward the front porch.

The door screeches as he pulls it open. He hesitates at the threshold of the basement steps, his body stiff.

"Down you go." I press the tip of the gun between his shoulder blades.

Our feet scuff over the dusty, old stone steps. I turn and close the

door behind us. The air grows heavier, suffocating as we descend into the darkness.

Every heartbeat thumps a painful reminder of the past. The days and nights I spent alone locked up in one of the rooms down here.

At the bottom of the steps, he opens another door.

The familiar sickening scent of rust and decay fills my lungs. Underneath it something chemical and unpleasant burns my nostrils.

I reach up and tug on the string dangling from a single naked light bulb. Harsh, yellow glare bounces around the makeshift dungeon.

For a second, I can't breathe or move. I'm a kid again, terrified of whatever punishment my father's come up with.

Nope. Not today.

"To the wall," I order, keeping my voice cold and steady.

He turns slowly, extending his arms in a mocking gesture of martyrdom. "Just shoot me."

"A bullet's too good for you." I jerk the gun toward the iron shackles embedded in the stone wall. Dark stains trickle over the bumpy stones—proof of the years of suffering that's happened in this room. "Strip off your shirt."

He slowly works the buttons loose. I can't even take pleasure in the shaking of his hands. I just want this over with.

I've dreamed about this day. Planned it. Obsessed over it. Fantasized about it every day since the first time he marched me into this basement and chained me to that wall.

I told myself I'd savor each lash and warm my hands with his blood.

But now?

I wish I'd taken Jezzie and left. I wish I was on the road. At Rooster's place.

Anywhere but here.

No.

I caught him trying to drown my sister. He deserves this.

"God will punish you for this," my father hisses, glaring at me.

I shove him forward. "How do you know he didn't send me here to punish *you*?"

"I'm his loyal, humble servant."

"Loyal and humble are two things you've never been, old man." I lower the gun slowly, aiming first at his left knee, then his right, finally settling at his groin. "Strip off your shirt now. Or I'll put a few holes in you and *then* chain you to the wall. Your choice."

"I should have known the wickedness could never be driven out of you. I should've broken you when I had the chance."

A cold shudder races down my spine, memories exploding through my mind—the burning pain, chains biting into raw wrists, dark isolation, prayers whispered to deaf ears, my baby sister bringing me scraps of food and tending to my injuries.

"I caught you trying to drown my sister," I remind him, my voice cold as steel. "Trying to drown a little girl. That's evil. Stop fucking around and move."

He flinches at the curse. Like most hypocrites, a *word* offends him more than evil acts. My resolve to punish him returns.

Wordlessly, he shuffles toward the wall. His shoulders slump, as if he's accepted his fate.

The quick acceptance triggers my internal alarms.

I step back a second before he whirls around, throwing a fist where my face had been two seconds ago.

The punch arcs wildly, throwing him into a half-spin. I cock my arm back and smash the gun into the side of his head, knocking him to the floor.

"Nice try." I stand over his dazed body. "I'm not a malnourished kid anymore. And I'm not afraid of you."

"You need to fear the Lord."

"I fear nothing," I inform him. "You still have that vault in your office?"

Breathing hard, he raises his eyebrows as if he's surprised I know of its existence.

"Gideon showed it to me when we were little," I explain. Gideon. My big brother who let me tag along on all of his adventures, then one day just *disappeared*.

His jaw drops.

"Is that why you killed him?" I ask, taking a stab in the dark. "He knew about all the money you were hiding?"

His mouth snaps shut and his gaze slides away.

My stomach lurches. Gideon disappeared a long time ago. Father said he chose the devil and left the family. I was so angry at my brother for leaving, I didn't give his departure a lot of thought. I accepted what I was told.

Only later did I wonder.

And now. That guilty look creeping across my father's face seems to confirm my suspicions.

A SOLID WHIPPING LATER, he still won't give up the code to the vault.

Breathing hard, he slowly turns his head and fixes the full weight of his preacher stare on me. "You won't win, son."

"Don't call me *son*." I flick my wrist, cracking the whip over his shoulder blades. Hard enough to sting but not draw more blood. "Boone and Emily treated me more like a son than you ever did."

Why the fuck are *they* gone when this sick bastard's still alive and torturing children?

"Do your worst, Jensen. The Lord will protect me."

"If there was a god, he wouldn't protect a child abuser." I step back, the whip slipping from my numb fingers, disgust churning in my gut. "Especially one who won't admit his sins."

He narrows his eyes and spits out, "Whoever spares the rod hates their children, but the one who loves their children is careful to discipline them."

Brutal flashbacks slam into me as he utters the same words he used to justify torturing me as a kid.

"You know I'm right," he says when I've been quiet for too long. His bitter laughter pulls me from the well of memories I'm slowly sinking into.

Enough of this shit.

I raise the Glock and steady it, aiming for his leg.

His twisted laughter stops. "You wouldn't dare—"

I squeeze the trigger once, cutting him off. A deafening crack echoes off the stone walls. The bullet slams into his thigh. He screams. Eyes wide with disbelief, he stares at the bloody hole.

"Still not gonna give up the code?" I aim for his stomach.

He grits his teeth and glares at me.

"All right." I tuck the gun away and let out a hollow cackle. "Hang tight, I'll be back."

Leaving him alone in the darkness, chained to the wall and bleeding, the way he left me many, many times as a child, feels less like righteous retribution and more like a sick circle finally completed.

Upstairs, the house hasn't changed much.

Not sure how much time I have before one of the disciples comes to investigate all the noise I've been making in the basement, I hurry to my father's office.

No one will call the cops. My father's always managed to instill a fear of law enforcement and government agencies in his people. That doesn't mean I want to deal with their questions.

Nothing's changed in his office either. Same heavy, dark wooden desk with a Bible and telephone. Nothing else to clutter the surface. Same sick, twisted paintings of hell—naked men and women hanging over open flames—on the walls.

The vault's on the far wall, concealed behind a piece of wood paneling. I run my fingers over the slick surface, searching for the groove to reveal the hidden door.

Click. Cheap wood panel scrapes against the thin carpet as I drag it open, revealing a thick steel door with a combination lock.

Fuck.

I grip the Glock and stare at the safe. I don't want to add to my scars or accidentally kill myself if the bullet ricochets off the steel door.

People are simple creatures. Always use a number that's easy to remember. Birthdays, anniversaries, wedding dates. First, I punch in various versions of my father's birthday.

A sharp bleat and flash of red after each number says I'm wrong.

He's not sentimental enough to use my mother's birthday, is he?

I try that anyway.

Nothing.

Should I return to the basement and try a few different torture devices? He used a cane on my bare ass one time. That stung like a motherfucker, and I couldn't sit down for a week.

Whoever spares the rod...

Proverbs 13:24.

My breath steadies as I approach the keypad again. I punch in 1-3-2-4.

The lock beeps twice and a small green light flashes.

Damn, I should've known to start with Biblical numbers.

The heavy vault door swings open with a metallic groan. Gideon and I never went inside when I was a kid. I always envisioned it as a shallow space in the wall where he stored some extra cash. Maybe a weapon or two. My parents never had flashy jewelry or anything else you'd normally stick in a safe.

In reality, it's a walk-in vault the size of a large storm shelter. Maybe it was originally intended to be a safe room for the end of days. I have to duck through the doorway, but once I'm inside I stand tall.

Nope.

While it's big for a safe, it's still an enclosed space. I step out and push the heavy door all the way open, pinning it in place with my father's large, leather office chair.

Reassured I won't accidentally lock myself inside, I return to the hidden room.

Guns line one entire wall. Not a surprise. He taught me to shoot when I was barely old enough to hold a gun. Never knew he had enough weaponry to outfit a small army stashed away, though. Long arms, shotguns, and handguns. Shelves at the back hold boxes and boxes of ammunition.

While I'd love to take this arsenal with me, I can't risk driving across the country with Jezzie, my father's bones, *and* a truck bed full of guns.

And I don't plan to leave this house standing when we go.

The opposite wall holds more shelves and what looks like more personal items. Backpacks, duffle bags, folders, boxes, women's purses.

I start at the far end and open a shoebox.

Stacks of cash.

Now *this* I'll happily take with me. The stacks appear to be hundred-dollar bills. Quick math adds up to at least sixty-thousand dollars in this box alone. *What the fuck?*

I flip the lids off the other shoeboxes and find more stacks of cash. Another holds gold bars.

He made us live like peasants when he had this much money stashed away. Where did it all come from?

Can't get distracted.

I move on to a gray metal box. Thankful it's fastened with a simple clasp, I flick it open and stare. Documents. Identification.

I sort through driver's licenses, Social Security cards, and birth certificates. Some names I recognize. People who lived on the farm for short periods of time.

My father would say they left for the temptations of the outside world. Their hearts weren't pure enough to accept God's salvation or whatever bullshit.

Why would they leave this stuff behind?

Uneasiness crawls through my stomach.

I flip the lid of another gray box on a higher shelf.

The first birth certificate freezes the blood in my veins.

Gideon Killgore.

My older brother. Who ran away without saying goodbye.

I set that one aside and pull out the next.

Joshua Killgore.

My other brother. Who supposedly influenced Gideon to leave. Both gone when Jezzie was so little, I doubt she even remembers them. My father certainly never allowed anyone to utter their names after they left.

A yellow envelope rests at the bottom of the box. With trembling hands, I take it out and set the box back on the shelf.

Fear crackles through my veins as I slide the yellowed certificate out.

Elizabeth Williams.

My mother.

At the bottom of the envelope a few rectangular cards are stuck together. I shake the stiff paper over one of the shelves and the cards flutter and plop onto the metal surface.

My mother's driver's license. Social Security cards for my brothers and mother.

My brothers…I could see them leaving this stuff behind. Especially if they left in a hurry.

I've tried searching for Gideon and Joshua. Aunt Em hired people to search for them. And we never found a trace of my brothers anywhere.

He killed them.

The truth of it rattles my bones.

Maybe my brothers never abandoned me after all.

I was angry they left me behind. Surface anger. Underneath, even as a kid, I suspected they no longer walked the Earth.

That's why when Ruth brought me my papers and encouraged me to leave, I did. Even though it meant leaving Jezzie.

Did he kill all of these other people too?

I pick up one of the ID cards—*James Lamb*. He disagreed with one of my father's sermons. Not long after, he disappeared from the compound, leaving his wife and kid behind. My father said he wasn't committed enough.

As I continue shifting through the documents, I encounter other names—both familiar and unfamiliar. Mr. Lamb's the only person I have a specific memory of.

I stuff my family's documents into one envelope, fold it in thirds, and shove it in my back pocket.

I know what I have to do now.

Barrels of lye. That's what I need. My father stored them behind the barn. Kept them for making soap and other farm chores.

I'm about to use it for a much different purpose. Maybe my father did too.

Maybe I'm more like him than I want to admit.

MY FATHER'S where I left him. Shackled to the wall. Leaning on it for support, cheek against the cold bricks.

"Wake up." I grab the bloody whip from the floor and crack it in the air.

He moans and turns his head, fixing me with a bleary-eyed stare.

I snap the envelope free and pull out Gideon's birth certificate, shoving it right under his nose. "Did you kill Gideon?"

Pain or fear seems to break his stoic expression. He shifts his gaze away. "They were evil, wicked boys. Had the Devil in them."

"Them?" I pull out Joshua's birth certificate and hold it in front of his face. "You're about to find out if there really is a god—although if there is, I suspect you'll be going in the opposite direction—so come clean now. Unburden yourself," I add, fighting hard to keep my tone more grave than sarcastic.

"I've always done God's will," he whispers.

"I'm sure you think so." I shake the birth certificates in my hand, the thin papers rustling in the dank air. "Speak the truth. Did they really run away?"

"They were stubborn and rebellious." His voice rises with conviction.

"So, what'd you do, stone them to death?"

"They dishonored us—your mother and me. The Scripture is clear, boy." His voice trembles with the same righteous indignation that used to spark fear in my chest. "Deuteronomy tells us to purge the evil from our midst. A rebellious son is an abomination in the sight of God. It is my duty as your father to see that His justice is served."

That's probably as close to the truth as I'll ever get out of him.

"What about Mom?" I ask "She didn't just up and die one day. What'd she do to deserve your twisted version of 'justice'?"

Anger ripples over his face. Minutes away from death and he seems to be gaining strength. "The woman who betrays her husband betrays God Himself." The same imperious tone he used for his lengthy sermons fills his voice. "Scripture *demands* death for her sin. 'Both the adulterer and the adulteress must die.' Elizabeth abandoned her duty to God and to me. Her punishment was just."

"Bullshit! She never cheated on you. When would she even have the time? If you weren't working her to death with chores, she couldn't leave the farm without you glued to her side."

"There are many ways a woman can abandon her duty to her husband, son."

"What? What justifies murder? Taking a mother away from her kids? What? She didn't want to fuck you anymore after you started bringing home teenagers to add to your harem? Was that how she 'disobeyed' you?"

He winces as if the curse word is the worst thing about my accusation. "There's more evil coursing through you than ever, boy. Living with those people in the outside world has corrupted you beyond my wildest nightmares."

"Don't you dare say one fucking word about Boone and Em. They treated me more like a son than you ever did." A fist of grief wraps around my throat, but I fight to keep my face blank. I won't give him the satisfaction of knowing Boone and Emily are dead. He'll see it as some sort of sign from God that he's the righteous one. "You killed my brothers. Did you kill my mother too?"

He says nothing. His silence as good as a confirmation for me.

I tilt my head toward the stairs leading into the house. "All those other documents you have in the vault. All those disciples. I remember some of them. They didn't 'leave' like you always told us, did they? The ones who 'failed the Lord.' They challenged you and you killed them, didn't you?"

He glares at me with the confidence of a man who thinks God will send his angels to swoop in and save him at the last minute. "I did what was right to protect my flock."

That's the only confirmation I'll probably ever get from him. The rage and grief I've carried for so long collide, chilling me to the bone. "*Where* did you bury them?"

"They're with the Devil now." He closes his eyes as if he's so meek and pious. "Paying for their sins."

Tired. I'm so fucking tired of his twisted religious shit.

"I really hope Hell is real. That's definitely where you're going." I pull the Glock from my side. "Any last prayers?"

His chin jerks upward, defiant. Still arrogant but a hint of fear shadows his eyes. "You'll break God's heart."

As if he's ever cared about anyone's heart before. "Yeah, well, he never stopped you from tearing out mine over and over in his name, so I guess this will make us even."

"You c-can't," he stutters. "You won't get away with killing me. You'll be locked up."

A heavy ache settles in my chest, warning me not to give him too much information but needing to purge my soul. "I've felt imprisoned my whole life. By you, your god, memories of you, the scars on my back." A bitter laugh catches in my throat. "If it ends up being official, I'm fine with it. As long as *you're* no longer walking the planet."

"God will welcome me with open arms." He tries to wave his hands, his chains scraping and rattling against the stone.

"Doubt it." I raise the Glock, leveling the barrel at his chest.

A glint of gold catches my eye.

I lower the gun.

His fearful expression shifts to relief. "I knew you'd see the light."

But it's not his life I want to spare.

It's the ring on his pinky. A solid gold band—thick, severe, and heavy-looking. The years have dulled its shine and worn the edges smooth, but the symbol at its center is still clear. I remember it well— a sword driven through the spine of a serpent, its coiled body twisted beneath the blade. What he always claimed was a symbol of his dominance over sin.

 18

As if sensing my intention, he curls his fingers into a fist. I pin his wrist to the wall and tug the ring free.

"This sin will haunt you for the rest of your miserable life," he spits out.

"You have no idea how many times I've thought of this. Every time you whipped me. Starved me. Made me bleed." I pull the Glock out again and press the muzzle to his chest. "I promised myself I'd come back one day and show you real sin."

I let that sink in. Watch it register. No one's coming to save him.

"No."

"Yes," I whisper. "You're finally reaping what you sowed all these years."

Slowly, I squeeze the trigger, savoring the final moment—the one I've fantasized about for most of my life.

A single shot echoes violently around us, deafening in the still basement.

He slumps against the chains, the arrogance and false righteousness draining from his body.

The silence rings louder than the shot.

My hands tremble as I stuff the Glock into its holster.

Breathe. Just breathe.

There's still so much more work to do.

Time's tight. Anyone could come down here and see what I've done. Sure, they're more likely to drop to their knees and start praying than call the cops but I'd rather not test out that theory.

There's a slop sink down here and a barrel of lye out back just waiting for—*fuck*.

I glance at the slop sink. Old steel and rusted seams—useless. Lye would eat through it in minutes, spilling him out onto the floor before the skin's even melted off of his carcass.

A slight ringing in my ears remains from the gunshot. But no guilt or remorse weighs me down. No, I can't stop seeing Jezzie's small body fighting under my father's hand. How long has he been using drowning as punishment? Was that the first time he did that to her? The tenth? Hundredth?

It's over now. She's safe.

The tub in the barn. That's a much better vessel. It'll be a pain in the ass to haul my father's body out to the barn but worth the effort.

I hurry through the maze of rooms in the basement and find an old, rough blanket on the floor of one of the cells. My stomach recoils at the traces of blood on the walls, little slashes in patchy dark red—like someone with tiny fingers tried to count how many days she'd been locked down here. Was it Jezzie? Another kid on the farm? One of my father's "wives?"

Are they even still alive?

Forty minutes later, sweat slicking down my back, muscles screaming, I finally heave him into the barn. His lifeless form thuds onto the bench in front of the makeshift pulpit—the very spot he preached hellfire and punishment morning after morning.

The large white tub waits silently for me in the center of the room. Still half-full of the water he used to almost drown my sister.

Her terrified gasps replay in my head as I approach the tub.

A grunt escapes me as I lift one end. Water gushes onto the wood, seeping through cracks and grooves, staining the floor dark. Without a glance at my father's still form, I shake off the chill racing down my spine and stalk to the back of the barn. Fifty-pound bags of lye are stacked right where I remember.

I'm not an expert but three bags should be enough to complete the job. I yank the collar of my shirt up to cover my mouth and nose as I dump the bags into the tub. My eyes sting and my nostrils burn as the fumes sear through the fabric of my makeshift mask.

Behind the stacks of lye, I find the rusty propane heater. A pair of old goggles and a set of ragged gloves rest on top of the heater. Wish I'd seen these earlier. I slip the goggles into place, pull the gloves over raw knuckles, the ragged material tight and itchy against my sweaty skin.

Steam billows around me like thick, suffocating smoke as I pour scalding water into the tub. The goggles help but my nostrils still burn. I cough hard, throat raw, and turn away from the tub.

Prep work complete. Time for the main event.

My muscles strain as I heave his corpse into the tub. His body sinks into the bubbling solution with a thick hissing sound. Violent foam froths over the water, welcoming him into the deadly brew. In a few hours he'll be nothing but bleached, brittle bones.

The acrid smell sears my lungs. Bile rises, scorching the back of my throat.

No prayers. No farewells.

Just chemicals devouring the monster who tortured his children.

The irony hits me—sharp, satisfying. He tried to kill his only daughter in this tub.

Instead, his son will use it to strip his bones clean.

BACK INSIDE THE HOUSE, a fearful group of my father's disciples have gathered in the kitchen and dining room. Wary eyes dart around as if they're in need of direction from someone or they're waiting to be punished. No sign of Jezzie. Ruth is the only person I recognize.

She's aged a lot since I last saw her, and I can only imagine the horrors inflicted on her by my father over the last few years. Especially if he figured out she was the one who helped me escape.

Careful not to attract any attention, I walk up behind her and lean down. "Meet me in my father's office."

She whirls around, the long fabric of her dress rustling around her ankles. A sharp gasp breaks free as her wide eyes lock on my face. Her lower lip trembles like she's staring at a ghost. "Jensen?"

I nod once, then turn away from the dining room and head toward my father's office.

Ruth's soft steps follow behind me. Inside the office, I quickly close the door behind me.

"Jensen? It's really you?" Ruth whispers. "Your father told us you died."

Of course he did.

"He wishes." Or *wished*. "I went to live with a friend's family up north."

She runs her gaze over me. I can only imagine what I look like—splattered with blood and reeking of death. "You've...grown. You look well. They must have taken good care of you."

Throat too tight to speak, I nod. Can't talk about Boone and Emily here. Not now. Not with Ruth.

I open my mouth to change the subject. But Ruth shifts to the side and I realize she brought someone with her. She's holding the hand of a little boy. Maybe seven or eight? Wearing the same too-short hand-me-down black pants, scuffed black shoes, and button-up shirt my parents used to force me to wear to school all the time. The uniform that invited every school bully's commentary.

But the clothes aren't the only similarity. It's his eyes. Wide. Curious. Hopeful. Eyes too similar to the man currently melting in a tub of lye out in the barn. If I'm not careful that look on his face will carve me wide open.

"Jensen," Ruth says, tugging the boy forward, "this is—"

"We don't have a lot of time." I turn and head for the wall safe. Irrationally afraid I wouldn't be able to open it again, I'd left the door open a crack. I push it open wider. "How many people are on the farm now?" I ask without looking over my shoulder.

"Uh, eight adults," she says. "Ten children, including Jezzie and Cain."

Cain. Of course that's what he named his youngest son. A name to let him know he's bound to be cursed.

I clear my throat. "Everyone needs to leave the farm. Can you help me talk to them?"

"Leave?" She rushes up behind me and grabs my shoulder. "And go where?"

"Wherever you want." I gesture toward the shelf with the boxes of money. "Help me sort through these documents and split up this money for everyone."

Confusion clouds her dull blue eyes. "Where's your father?"

"Don't worry about him."

"What did you do?"

I yank two of the boxes off the shelf and carry them into the office,

tossing them on the desk with a hard thud. "Ruth." I snap my fingers to yank her out of her frozen trance. "Help me go through these documents."

"How did you find—"

"It doesn't matter." I cut her off and grit my teeth. "Hurry."

Finally, she accepts the pile of papers I shove at her and starts sorting them into separate stacks. "The kids...Mary's husband left her here with her children. He was supposed to—"

"He's probably dead." I stare at the papers in her hand. "How many kids are hers?"

"Five."

"How many vehicles are still on the property?"

She shakes her head slowly. "The old truck. The Keesee's car. A van..."

"Enough for each family to leave?"

"I think so."

"Good." I return to the vault and grab two of the shoeboxes of cash. At my father's desk, I crouch down, searching the drawers. I find a stack of long, yellow envelopes in the bottom drawer and grab a handful.

Ruth's eyes bug when I flip the lid off one of the boxes, revealing the neat bundles of hundred-dollar bills. "Where did that come from?"

"No idea." I lift my chin toward the door while shoving stacks of cash into envelopes. I try to split it evenly. Except for the woman with five kids to support. I step into the vault again and grab another box to fill her envelope. "They can use it to start a new life, join another cult, I don't really fucking care."

"What about you?"

"Don't worry about me." I don't want to tell her how much cash is actually in the vault. "Did you find your documents? Your son's?"

She shakes her head. "They're not here."

Fuck. "Okay." I grab the stacks of birth certificates and driver's licenses, shoving them in the correct envelopes, and use a Sharpie to scribble the names on the front. "Pass these out and help them pack. I'll keep looking for your papers."

"Jensen, what am I supposed to tell everyone?"

"Tell them my father ran off and you found these packages on his desk." I stare her dead in the eyes. "Or tell them I found him trying to drown my sister out in the barn and punished him accordingly. I really don't give a fuck what story you give. Just get rid of them."

She recoils in fear, like a dog wary after being kicked in the ribs too many times. Regret pokes at me. I shouldn't be so harsh with her.

Painfully aware how much bigger I am than her now, I take a breath. I left a scrawny kid and returned a man. I tower over her by a lot. I force some calm into my lowered voice. "Please?"

She nods slowly and backs away, clutching the envelopes to her chest. Her gaze drops. "Stay here with Jensen."

I lean over the desk and find Cain sitting cross-legged on the floor, staring at the wall. Scared, bored, indifferent—I can't tell what's going on in the kid's head but at least he's quiet. He briefly glances in Ruth's direction and nods.

Ignoring both of them, I return to the vault and start tearing through the other boxes. I can't decipher any pattern to how my father stored things. Nothing's filed alphabetically or by date, just stacks of envelopes and a mixture of boxes. The system probably made sense to him but it's frustrating as fuck for me—the person trying to find anything of value in a hurry.

Finally, I locate Jezzie's birth certificate, Social Security card, and a bunch of progress reports from school. Those might help Angela get Jezzie enrolled in school. I add them to my pile.

I move to the shelf closest to the door and pull a green file folder into my hands. It flips open and papers flutter to the ground.

Ruth and Cain's papers. Birth certificates. A high school diploma. The last piece stops me cold—a marriage license signed by what must be Ruth's father, giving her permission to marry my father when she was a teenager. My stomach heaves with disgust. She's younger than I thought. Only two years older than me. What kind of sick fucking parents did she have who'd let her marry *my* father?

It doesn't matter. She's free now and not my problem.

I grab two more shoeboxes and carry them into the office.

Cain's standing right outside the door, still staring at me with those wide, blank eyes.

I shift the boxes to one arm and gently ruff my hand over the top of his head. "You go to school, little man?"

He nods slowly.

Still watching him, I drop my armload on the desk. "You like it?"

He shrugs, then nods again.

"You know how to talk?"

His serious little face screws into a scowl. He's got some Killgore fire in him after all. "Yes."

"Good." I return to the vault and pull two of the metal boxes off the shelves. I dump the papers on the desk and transfer the cash into one of the sturdier boxes. Then stack everything for Ruth on the corner of the desk.

Footsteps pound over the floor above me and I glance up. Hope that means people are moving their asses and packing their shit, not grabbing their guns and coming for me.

No. Ruth wouldn't have left her son here if she planned to get the whole compound to take me out.

Outside a car engine rumbles to life.

I blow out a sigh of relief.

I search every drawer of my father's desk—Bibles, keys, coins, scraps of paper with half-written verses or angry, ranting sermon notes. Most of it, I toss aside.

The bottom drawer sticks.

I yank harder. It gives with a light squeak, revealing several stacks of small, black leather-bound notebooks. Each one identical in size and thickness. The only difference is the year marked on each spine.

Intrigued, I set them on top of the desk and open the oldest notebook.

Rows and rows of neatly written names, numbers, infractions, and punishments.

A ledger of my father's brutality.

Most of my childhood memories are fuzzy but he must have started keeping this notebook the year after we moved here.

The earliest entries are deceptively mild.

Joshua—talked back to mother—two hours of silence.

Gideon—disobeyed father—write ten commandments ten times.

Jensen—neglected chores—Memorize and recite Romans 6:23.

Elizabeth—denied husband—10 lashes with belt.

Even my mother didn't escape his punishments. My throat tightens. The implications of her entry turn my stomach.

I continue flipping pages. On and on the lists go.

After a while, other names pop up—people who must've stayed at the farm from time to time.

Sarah—refused to share with the community—stripped of bedding and warmth for three days.

Eli—coveted Sarah—three days of fasting and prayer. No contact with women for a week.

Lydia—questioned headship—Copy Ephesians 5:22 one hundred times.

Naomi—seen alone with Eli—confined to room. Hair cut to shoulder length.

Eli—whipped five times—Confined to barn for three nights.

The entries are cruel. Clinical. My father's devotion to God twisted into justification for torturing people. I pick up another notebook and the insane ledger continues.

Thomas—stole bread—twenty lashes. Public apology before breakfast.

Leah—skipped chores—Forced to walk barefoot through fields.

Jensen—talked back—ruler to knuckles.

Gideon—interfered with Jensen's correction. Must repent for idolizing family above God—seven lashes, two days of solitude.

My brother tried to protect me?

I glance down at my hands. Why can't I remember that incident?

Joshua—caught sneaking bread to Gideon—fourteen lashes, confined to barn for two nights.

And my other brother tried to feed Gideon.

Jensen—failed to complete Psalm assignment—kneel on stones for four hours. No supper.

Christ, I can still feel the ache of those stones digging into my

tender knees. Forcing myself to be still and not cry or he'd make me stay there even longer.

Gideon—caught sneaking bread to Jensen—ten lashes, four days of solitude.

I blink, my eyes burning. My brother still tried to feed me even after he'd been punished for trying to protect me before.

Not long after that entry Gideon and Joshua's names disappear from the notebook entirely.

No final notation about what led to their departure. Did they actually escape? Or did he kill them?

I should have tortured him longer.

Until he gave me an answer.

I don't have time to relive the horrors contained in these books, but I can't seem to stop.

Jensen—disruptive in school—no supper, sleep on floor.

Jezebel—disobeyed mother. Sang during nap time—confined to room. No supper.

Jensen—interfered with Jezebel's punishment—four lashes. No breakfast.

Jezebel—cried during morning worship—placed in silent pen. No contact with other children for one day.

Some of *these* memories return. Fuzzy and jumbled. Jezzie was so little. I didn't understand how she could be expected to follow our father's insane rules. But at least he never *physically* punished her.

I toss the book on the desk in disgust and pick up another one. I want to burn the whole stack. Another part of me wants them as a sick keepsake.

And maybe to use in my defense if I'm ever arrested for the death of my father.

A soft knock breaks the silence. I snap the book shut and lift my head. Ruth eases the door open, shoulders hunched like she expects me to throw a Bible at her.

Cain, now quietly sitting by the vault door, glances at her but the stoic expression on his little face doesn't change.

"They're gone," Ruth says. "Everyone took the money, their

belongings, and left without question. I didn't mention your presence."

"Good." That's better than I expected. As my father's wife, Ruth must've held some power over the others. Enough for them to obey her.

She crosses the room slowly, eyeing everything I've laid out on the desk but not saying a word.

I clear my throat and nod to the corner of the desk. "That pile is for you. Cash and your papers." I gesture vaguely at Cain.

Her eyes widen, but she doesn't reach for the stuff. "Jensen...where am I supposed to go?"

I press my hands against the desk and lean forward. "Start over. Somewhere far away. Where you'll be safe." I pull the marriage certificate out. "I wouldn't go back to your family. They obviously have poor judgment."

It was supposed to be a weak attempt at a joke, but it comes out harsh.

Tears fill her eyes, but she snaps the paper out of my hand. "What about Jezzie? You can't raise her by yourself."

"Don't worry about my sister. We have family on the East Coast. She'll be safe." I shouldn't have told her even that much. I don't want Jezzie to have any reminders of this place and that includes Ruth.

"What about you?" she asks.

"What about me?"

"Where will—"

"Don't." I cut her off. "I appreciate what you did for me when I was a kid and I hope you didn't suffer for it, but we part ways here." I nod to the box. "There should be enough to keep you and your son comfortable while you figure things out."

"He's your—"

"Keep him safe. Don't let anyone put their hands on him."

"What am I supposed to tell people?"

"About what?" I spread my hands wide. "Say your husband ran off and left you. Just another deadbeat dad. No one should ask. You'll be far away where no one even knows you."

She opens her mouth again. Maybe to argue or say thank you. Whatever it is, I don't let her get out the words.

"Go. Hurry."

Ruth swallows hard, then holds out her hand for Cain. "Let's go pack our things."

Fuck, I'd hoped she was already packed. I can't shake this sense of urgency. The need to get my sister as far away from this place as possible as soon as I can.

There's also the issue of the body melting out in the barn I don't want anyone to find accidentally.

Once they're gone, I return to the vault, searching for anything that might be important. The items I'm planning to take, I gather into piles on one side. I find another box stuffed with even more cash. Smaller bills this time. I set half aside for Ruth. It won't make up for snapping at her but it's all I've got.

"Jensen?" Ruth's soft voice pulls me out of the vault. "We're ready."

She pushes the office door open wide. Jezzie and Cain are both with her. Red blurs around the edges of my vision. I wanted Jezzie to stay upstairs. If Ruth thinks she's taking my sister anywhere she's out of her fucking—

"Jensen?" Jezzie breaks away from them and slowly approaches. Her hair's still damp, hanging in loose, stringy, uneven strands around her shoulders. She's changed into what's probably her "church" dress. An ankle-length, shapeless white dress with a brown floral pattern. We'll have to stop and buy her new clothes along the way.

Where the fuck am I supposed to go shopping for a teenage girl?

"It's really you?" Jezzie bursts into tears as she wraps her arms around me and squeezes tight. Her whole body shakes with the force of the hug. "He...he said you were dead." She hiccups a breath. "He told all of us the Lord struck you down for your wickedness." Her fingers clutch tighter at my back. "I missed you so much. I used to pray every night you were out there and you'd come back for me."

Those final words almost break me. I'd done the same thing after my brothers disappeared. Tears burn my eyes, and I curl my arms around her. I should've come for her sooner. I knew how twisted my father was.

"I'm here." I swallow hard. "I didn't know. I thought you were...safe."

"Ruth said we're leaving?" She pulls back and stares up at me with hopeful eyes.

"Yes. You're coming with me."

She hugs me again. "Praise be."

Well, at least I won't have to drag her away kicking and screaming.

Outside an engine roars and gravel crunches under tires. *Fuck.* Did one of them come back? Or did they go to the cops after all?

Not sure what I'll be dealing with, I return to the vault and grab a shotgun. It's already loaded and ready to go.

Ruth frowns but doesn't seem surprised by the gun. "Who is it?"

"No idea." I nod to the chair in the corner. "Stay here."

I hurry through the house, all of my attention focused on the front door.

The engine cuts off. I throw the door open and tighten my grip on the gun, keeping it pointed at the ground.

I recognize the battered blue Ford truck immediately. "What the fuck?" I mutter, hurrying down the steps, gun at my side.

Logan throws his door open and flashes a grim smile. At least it looks grim under that dumb beard he's started growing since his uncle died.

"What the fuck are you doing here?" Gravel flies in every direction as I hurry to meet him.

He shrugs and adjusts the ballcap he's wearing. "Your phone keeps going right to voicemail. I was worried about you."

"It's in the truck." I can't decide if I'm relieved or annoyed that he's here.

"You all right?" His gaze drops to the gun. "Were you going to shoot me?"

"Yeah, maybe." I lift my chin toward the driveway leading off the farm. "Heard the truck. Thought it might be his people coming back."

"Sorry." He blows out a breath. "How's..." His voice trails off like he can't find the words to ask how killing my father went.

"He's cooking in the barn."

Logan nods once, face blank. He knows almost all of my darkest secrets and what my plans were for my father. He won't press for details.

"What can I do?" he asks.

"A woman and her son are still here. If you can help me move them along, that'd be great. The rest of them left."

"You got it." He slaps my shoulder, quick and reassuring. "Jezzie okay?"

"No, but she will be once I get her away from here."

Inside, it's silent.

"They should be in my father's office." I jerk my head to the side, silently asking him to follow.

Logan doesn't waste time gawking at the frozen-in-time house I grew up in. He'd been inside at least once before he moved up north.

The office door is closed. I knock twice and push it open.

"It's just me."

Ruth's standing in the middle of the room and slowly lowers her arms to her sides as we enter—as if she'd been trying to protect the kids from intruders.

Jezzie peeks out from behind the desk. She scowls at Logan, then recognition seems to sink in. "Logan?"

"Hey, Jezzie."

Cain's sitting in a chair in the corner, hugging a small, overstuffed backpack to his chest, ignoring all of us.

Ruth watches both of us with concerned eyes. I hold up my hands. "I didn't know he was coming. He's just here to check on me."

She nods once and slowly edges toward her son.

Logan leans closer to me. "I can wait outside."

"Jensen, there are a few things I'd like to take from the house, if that's okay," Ruth says, staring at the ground like my father probably trained her to do when speaking to him. "We're taking the van."

"Yeah." Relief floods through me. Anything to get her going. *Take*

the whole fucking house, lady. I'm planning to burn it down anyway.
"Whatever you want."

"I'll help her load it up," Logan offers.

ANOTHER HOUR LATER, Logan has the van backed up to the front porch with the doors open wide. Dust from the gravel drive floats in the air, mixing with the scent of old wood, fresh grass, and exhaust fumes. Inside the van, a few pieces of furniture are strapped down—an old wooden rocking chair, a few suitcases, a weathered cedar chest, a heavy antique sewing machine, and a box of cast iron pans.

"All right, Cain, say goodbye," Ruth says, her voice tight but steady.

"No!" Cain bolts toward Jezzie and throws his arms around her. She hugs him back, bends down, and whispers something in his ear. Whatever she says makes him shake his head violently, tears streaking down his cheeks.

It's the first real emotion I've seen from him all day.

The first sliver of doubt needles its way inside me.

But I don't know what else to do.

My aunt agreed to take care of Jezzie—her niece. Showing up with my father's widow and her kid in *addition* to Jezzie isn't an option.

"Cain, it's okay," Ruth says gently, holding out her hand. "We'll call Jensen when we're settled."

That'll be hard to do without my number.

Something brushes against my conscience. Guilt, probably. Or the faint echo of a soul. I've just ripped this kid from his home, his family, and maybe a father who hadn't started showing him the business end of a bullwhip yet.

I pull the ring I took off my father's finger out of my pocket and crouch down in front of Cain. "Be good for your mom, okay? Don't take shit from anyone."

He drops his gaze to the ring and frowns. "The monster wears that."

"Not anymore." I hold it out to him. "You keep it, so the monsters stay away."

His eyes widen and he plucks the ring from my palm and holds it up with both hands and stares at it. After a few seconds, he slips the ring on his thumb and closes his fist around it.

Without another word, he joins his mother in the van.

Logan, Jezzie, and I stand on the porch in silence as the van rattles down the driveway and disappears behind the trees.

Jezzie glances up at me. "I don't have a lot of stuff."

"Pack whatever you want." I gesture toward the front door. "Anything you think you might need or want from this place. We'll stop and get you some new stuff but take what matters."

She nods and hurries inside, the hard soles of her shoes thudding lightly on the floorboards.

Logan stands beside me, arms crossed. He knows better than to ask about Cain or Ruth or anything else. He just waits.

"What can I do?" he finally asks.

"Help Jezzie pack. Load her stuff in the back of my truck."

He holds out his hand. "Give me your keys."

I drop them into his palm. "Just keep her away from the barn. I've got some things I need to take care of out there."

I head for the barn alone, the late afternoon sun casting long, crooked shadows across the yard.

Inside, the stink hits first—smoke, chemicals, decay, and something deeper, something older.

I roll up my sleeves.

Time to collect what's left of the man who made me a monster.

Piece by piece.

I'll scatter his bones across the country—coast to coast. Drop a bit of him at every truck stop, every ditch and dumpster between here and Pennsylvania. A puzzle no one will ever piece together again.

Then maybe I'll find peace.

CHAPTER TWO

JIGSAW

PRESENT DAY

Some ghosts haunt you. Others show up out of nowhere and fuck up your night.

As I wind my way through the back roads leading into Empire, my lungs tighten. Instead of calming me, this ride sends dread crawling over my skin with every mile.

How did Cain find me? Why'd he go to Crystal Ball of all places? On paper, my income comes from the laundromat *and* Crystal Ball. Cain can't be more than seventeen or eighteen. Tracking me down at a strip club probably seemed like the fun choice.

Why did he have to choose *tonight*, when my president's the one managing Crystal Ball? Any other night, Dex would've been there. Dex—who's a lot more understanding and asks fewer questions.

What's Cain been doing for the last decade?

Did Ruth drag him into another religious cult? Or was he able to grow up like a normal kid? Is he here to extract justice for his dead father and messed-up childhood?

The road can't give me any of these answers.

I twist the throttle, taking the back roads faster than wise.

Margot knew something was wrong. We were just about to...fuck, my balls still hurt. Cain's a cock-blocking little fucker. I had to leave Margot unsatisfied after mumbling some excuse about Z needing an extra set of hands at the club. She frowned, asked if everything was okay. I don't think she was worried about me going to the strip club. No. By now she *has* to know I'm so motherfucking obsessed with her I can't think straight. Staring at strippers for a few hours isn't a temptation, it's torture.

How the fuck will I explain to her that I've known about Cain all along?

I've had a little half-brother out there all this time and wanted nothing to do with him.

To someone as sweet and compassionate as Margot, I'll sound like a monster.

Killed the kid's dad, evicted him from his home, handed his mother a box of cash, then shoved them out into the big, bad world all by themselves.

Then I did what I do best.

Buried the truth.

Forgot his name. His face. Went on about my life as if he didn't exist.

And now, somehow, he's found me.

Why?

Closure? Family connection?

Or does he want revenge?

CHAPTER THREE

JIGSAW

THE PARKING LOT IN FRONT OF CRYSTAL BALL IS PACKED.

Great. The club's actually busy tonight. Even more reason for Z to be annoyed with me. I pull around to the back of the building. This lot's crowded too. I wedge my bike into the row of employee spots, back tire kissing the rough wall behind it.

As usual, the heavy, gray metal door's propped open with a cinder block. Tonight it feels like it's daring me to walk through and reunite with a past I've tried hard to forget.

Taking my time, I pull off my gloves and unbuckle my helmet, setting them on the seat like the ritual will steady me. My gaze sweeps the lot again. Which car or bike belongs to Cain? Is he planning to stick around? Or is this a hit-and-run where he fucks up my life, then bounces?

The parking lot won't give me any answers.

Get your ass inside, coward!

I trudge into the back hallway. Music throbs through the building and loud, chaotic chatter filters from the dancers' dressing room door. The hallway's empty for the moment. No dancers lingering backstage while they practice some last-minute dance moves tonight. And at least it's not amateur night when there'd be a line out the door and extra security.

The door to Z's office is closed. I take a breath, brace myself for what's on the other side, then punch my knuckles against the wood.

"Come in!" Z shouts.

I crank the tricky knob hard and jerk the door open.

My stomach twists into a painful knot. Z's behind his desk and a relieved smile lifts his cheeks when his gaze lands on me.

Sitting across from Z, a young man in a black hooded sweatshirt slowly turns my way.

My heart slams as our eyes meet.

He stands and faces me. Doesn't move closer. Doesn't say a word.

Neither of us seem to know what to do or say.

Cain's not the same little kid I remember. Now, he's taller, probably about my height. Broader, like he's acquainted with manual labor, but thin. Dark jeans, heavy work boots, messy hair curling over his forehead, shadowed eyes.

Except for his scar-free skin, he looks like a baby-faced version of the guy I see in the mirror every morning.

It's pretty fucking obvious we're related.

"Well, now it looks like we have a matching set." Z claps his hands together and stands like he's trying to break the tension. "You can use my office." He rests his hand on my shoulder as he passes. "Unless you want me to stay?"

I shake my head. If Cain's here to kill me, I don't want Z caught in the crossfire. "I got this. Thanks, Prez."

"No problem." His brow furrows like he's holding back a dozen questions.

Everyone knows I have a younger sister. No one but Rooster knows about my half-brother.

Z closes the door quietly behind him, but it feels like he sealed me inside for my judgment day.

The office hums with silence between the bass beats echoing from the main room. Out in the hallway, girls shriek with laughter. Heels

clack over the floor. A symphony of sound while I face a ghost from my past.

Fidgeting, he clasps his hands together, his thumb and index finger toying with the ring on his pinky. His wary eyes scan my cut, then travel to my face.

It's strange how familiar he feels even though the last time I saw him he was a kid.

Apparently, he's still a quiet little fucker too. I'll have to speak first.

"Cain?" I should ask how he's been. Or what the fuck he wants. But all the words lodge somewhere deep in my throat, too tangled up in guilt and a decade of silence.

"Jensen." His voice is deeper than I expected. Hesitant. Like he's not sure he likes the sound of my name in his mouth.

He holds out one hand. More of an obligation than a greeting.

I take it. Feels more awkward not to. His palm's warm, his grip firm.

A million questions pile up in my mouth.

"You're probably wondering why I'm here," he says with a slow, laid-back cadence.

"You could say that." I gesture toward the chairs in front of Z's desk and pull one out, turning it to fully face the other one.

After a moment of hesitation, Cain settles into his chair and rests his hands on his legs.

"How'd you find me?" I ask, trying to keep the accusatory tone out of my voice.

"Wasn't easy."

Talking to this kid's like yanking teeth.

Normally, I'd wait him out. Most people rush to fill the silence with chatter. Not this kid.

"How's your mother?" I ask.

A flash of pain crosses his solemn expression. He laces his fingers together like he's praying or trying to contain himself. "She passed away recently."

"Shit. I'm sorry." She couldn't have been more than thirty-two or thirty-three. "How?"

Maybe that's rude but I'm not really known for my tact.

"Ovarian cancer." His left hand strays to his side. "She fought hard, but doctors all caught it too late."

Poor Ruth. She didn't deserve such a miserable, early ending.

"She made me promise to find you," he says, voice ragged. "After she was gone."

The finality in his tone hits harder than I'm ready for.

Fucking hell. Cain and I reuniting was Ruth's dying wish? What the fuck am I supposed to say to that? I should've asked Margot to come with me. She'd know all the right words.

Cain draws in a slow, measured breath, like he's holding onto his pain and fury with both hands.

Feels like I'm sitting next to a grenade, the pin already halfway out —and I'm the one who pulled it.

"Where were you living?" I ask.

He glances toward the door. "We moved to New Mexico, after…"

You killed my dad and kicked us out of our home.

He doesn't say that, but my guilty conscience hears it loud and clear.

"Did you like it there?"

The first hint of humanity cracks his robotic mannerisms. "Yeah. We settled into a nice place. Mom made pottery." He works his hands in a circle.

A fuzzy memory of Ruth flashes through my mind—her hands caked in gray sludge, laughing while Jezzie tried to spin a crooked lump of clay.

"Sold it at this gallery nearby," he continues. "Met my stepfather there."

So she remarried. To someone normal or another religious zealot? "Was he good to you?"

He cocks his head as if he needs to think on it, then stares me dead in the eyes. "Treated me nicer than our father did."

Maybe he's not here to kill me after all. "That's a low bar."

He scoffs. "You could say that."

"So how'd you find me? And why come *here* of all places?"

He reaches into his hoodie pocket.

My body tenses and I sit up straighter in case he's going for a weapon.

But all he pulls out is a folded-up piece of glossy paper that looks like it was torn out of a magazine.

"Mom really got to love country music after we moved." He unfolds the paper and holds it out to me. "Big fan of Shelby Morgan."

A smile twitches at the corners of my mouth. How about that? Rooster's little songbird is somehow responsible for bringing my half-brother back into my life.

"She saw this in a magazine and recognized you right away."

I take the paper and scan the page.

It's a gossip piece from maybe two years ago when I was on tour with Shelby helping Rooster work security.

There's a full-page picture of Shelby and Rooster wrapped around each other after one of the shows. My scary face is visible in the background to Rooster's left. Both of our cuts with our Lost Kings MC patches on display.

Shelby Morgan parties with bikers after sold-out show.

Dex, Pants, and a few other guys that had also been on tour are also visible in the background but I'm the only one who was dumb enough to be glowering straight at the camera.

"She knew your face." Cain taps his finger over Rooster. "And your friend. She wanted me to keep it and track you down when the time came."

Meaning, after she died.

"Why?"

His expression hardens. "You and Jezzie are the only family I have left." He shrugs. "I don't have anywhere else to go. Thought I'd do some traveling and look you up."

My stomach knots at the mention of my sister. No fucking way is Cain getting near her until I can trust him.

"What about your stepfather?" I ask. What'd the guy do, toss him out after Ruth died?

"What about him?" Cain shrugs. "I said he was better than our

father. I didn't say he was great. He treated my mom good. Tolerated me."

He rubs his hand over his chest and frowns. "She left whatever money, life insurance, and stuff to me. He wasn't so happy about that."

Is that his way of letting me know he's not looking for a handout?

"That's shitty."

He tilts his head and levels a sarcastic stare at me. "I'm used to shitty situations."

I snort. "Yeah, I feel that." I mirror his pose. "You even old enough to be in this place?"

A blush creeps over his cheeks, and he stammers, "I…I didn't really realize what kind of establishment it was until…"

"Where are you staying?" Fuck, I can't bring him back to my place. I can't even let him stay at our clubhouse next door. If he's blushing about stepping foot inside a strip club, he'll probably die at the antics that go on over there after Crystal Ball closes.

"I got a room at a hotel over by that big mall."

I nod, knowing where he's talking about.

He shrugs. "For a few days at least."

"How'd you get here?"

"Rode. Took about a week."

"You ride?" Guess we have more in common than I thought.

He nods. "Stepdad was into motocross. He taught me how to ride. Mom had picked out a Kawasaki Ninja for me for graduation."

"Nice." My back aches just thinking about riding the foreign sport bike that far.

The ache in my chest is worse. What the hell am I supposed to do with this kid?

"How's Jezzie?" he asks as if he's trying to steer the conversation back where he wants it. He frowns at the closed office door. "She doesn't…she doesn't work *here*, does she?"

"Fuck no." What kind of asshole does he think I am? "She's in college. Just talked me into letting her take a part-time job at a pizza shop."

That's not enough info for him to find Jezzie. There have to be

more than two hundred colleges in New York and three times as many pizza places near a campus.

While this little family reunion's been surprisingly non-lethal, he's not getting near my sister, my club, or my girlfriend.

Not until I know what the fuck he's really doing here.

CHAPTER FOUR

MARGOT

DEATH DOESN'T SCARE ME.

Silence does.

Not the silence of the dead. Not the hush of the home I grew up in. Or the prep room where I prepare the dead for one last goodbye from their loved ones. I'm comfortable with all of those variations of silence.

It's the silence from Jigsaw.

The kind that coils around my heart and whispers, *he's not coming back.*

I thought we'd moved past whatever reservations he had about being in a relationship. We've said "I love you." I've spent time with his motorcycle club and gotten along with almost everyone. Or so I thought.

So why did he bolt a few nights ago, muttering something about a work emergency, and disappear? No texts. No calls. Nothing.

I sent a *hope everything's okay* text the next morning.

The only thing keeping me from freaking out that my boyfriend's dead in a ditch somewhere is the brief response he sent back—*Busy but okay.*

What does that even mean?

Should I send Shelby a text? Something casual? *Hey, girl, I know we only send each other the occasional cat meme, but what's up? Happen to know where my boyfriend is?*

No. I shouldn't do that. Should I?

She's engaged to Jigsaw's best friend, so she might know what's going on. Or would contacting her cross a line into psycho girlfriend territory?

Does it matter? I'm actually worried about him.

"Margot?" My father taps his knuckles against the closed door and pushes it open. "We've got a pickup. At the Briarwood Home."

I spin in my desk chair to face him. "Now?"

"Yes. A Mrs. Beckett. Nursing said she passed this afternoon." He leans against the frame. "The family wants a quick turnaround. I know you're busy with Mr. Hall's arrangements but—"

"No, I'll handle it." I'll have to obsess about Jigsaw later.

"Paul will go with you." He gestures toward the hallway. "I'm still working on—"

"No, it's fine. I've got it."

Death doesn't care about my love life.

"Speaking of Mr. Hall," my father says. "Now that we have another event to plan—although I suspect this one will have far less fanfare than the biker's—would you mind checking to see if April has some availability this week? We could use an extra set of hands. And I'd rather give your friend the work before calling in someone else."

"Sure. I'll reach out to her."

I hurry upstairs and change into something more comfortable, but still professional, for a body removal. Stretchy black pants and a black knit top with a dark floral pattern. My goal is to blend in. Once we're there, I'll slip into my protective gear.

Paul's waiting downstairs in a full suit and tie. Neat and polished as always. "Ready?" He holds up the van keys and jingles them in my direction. "I'll drive."

"Fine by me." I eye his suit. "It's after hours. You're making me look underdressed."

He chuckles. "To be honest, I just climbed into the same suit I wore for the Miller consultation this morning."

"Ahhh, efficient laziness," I tease. "Aren't you clever."

He grins, unbothered, and we share a laugh then head into the parking lot.

The drive to Briarwood is short. Paul distracts me with his insistence on singing along to Megadeth's *À tout le monde* over and over. At least his off-key warbling takes my mind off of obsessing about Jigsaw's silence.

"Here we are." Paul shifts the van into Park near the staff entrance and glances over at me. "Ready?"

"Yup."

He holds up a sheaf of paperwork. "All set."

The scent of antiseptic and burnt coffee greets us in the narrow hallway. *Could be worse.* Paul stops to speak to a nurse. As far as nursing homes go, Briarwood is one of the nicer ones in the area. I still can't imagine ever sending my father to a place like this.

"Room 209." The nurse flashes a friendly smile at Paul. "Do you need help?"

"No, we've got it. Thank you, though," Paul says, ever the professional.

"I think she likes you," I whisper as we head toward Mrs. Beckett's room.

He glances over his shoulder. "Yeah? She's cute. Not sure if now's the time to shoot my shot, though."

"Probably not." I steer my end of the stretcher down the wide hallway. Thankfully, it's late. No residents linger in the hallway to watch as we remove their neighbor.

The door to 209 is shut tight. Paul twists the knob and pushes it open. The room's larger than the average hospital room, but not by much. A tall, rectangular window looks out on a shadowy courtyard. A simple hospital bed in the middle.

And a man in blue scrubs looming over the bed with his back toward us.

Paul and I share a look. We both clear our throats.

The man jumps away from the bed, flipping the sheet up as he goes. He bends over slightly...doing heck only knows what before he turns and faces us. He's handsome but creepy, like a waxy Ken doll come to life. Except, unlike a Ken doll, and judging by the tenting of his scrub pants, this guy seems really *excited* to be hanging out with the poor departed Mrs. Beckett.

"I, uh, was just saying goodbye." The man waves his hands behind him. "She was a nice lady."

"Yeaaaah." Paul draws out the word and scowls. "We've got it from here," he says, voice sharp and protective. "You need to go."

The guy blinks and fiddles with his scrub top, but it's not long enough to conceal the evidence of how much he enjoyed his goodbye. What the hell would he have done to Mrs. Beckett if we didn't show up?

Something cold and familiar simmers inside of me. It would be so easy to find out where he lives...maybe pay him a visit. Add a piece of him to my collection.

My fingers twitch at my side.

No. He doesn't fit my criteria. He's vile for sure. But...*no*.

Murder isn't the answer when I'm raw and restless, looking for something to distract me from my personal dilemmas.

Paul stares the man down while he slinks out of the room.

"Fucking creep," he mutters, shaking his head.

I hurry to Mrs. Beckett's side. She's frail and tiny. Maybe no more than eighty pounds. The white facility sheet is tucked under her arms. Her jaw's slightly slack, one hand turned palm-up on top of the blanket.

"I'm sorry about that," I whisper. "We came as soon as we could."

Paul unstraps the cot while I double-check the name on the wrist tag and the whiteboard by the bed. Standard procedure. No mistakes.

"Confirmed," I say softly.

Together, we lift and gently transfer her to the cot. Her limbs shift under the sheet, light as paper. I drape a fresh cover sheet over her, tucking it smoothly around her shoulders. Then I fasten the safety straps—shoulders, waist, and legs. I probably could've done this pickup solo, but after encountering that creep, I'm glad I'm not alone.

As we pass the nurse's station, the woman we spoke to on our way in lifts a hand in a polite wave.

Paul slows the stretcher to a stop. "I'm going to talk to her." He lowers his voice. "Give her a heads-up about Mr. Creepy-pants."

I shudder at the memory. "Go ahead, I'll get her loaded into the van."

"You sure?"

"If not, I'll text you." I hold out my hand for the van keys and he passes them to me without question.

Outside, the air's chillier, more ominous than before. The stretcher rattles as I navigate over the rough pavement.

The back doors of the van squeak as I open them wide. I engage the ramp, then guide the stretcher inside, and lock the wheels in place. I check that she's secure, my fingers lingering on the buckle of one restraint.

"You're in good hands, I promise," I whisper. "My family will take care of you."

I shut the doors and double-check the latch before turning toward the building. The lot's well-lit and silent. No sign of Paul yet.

I pull out my phone and check my texts.

Nothing from Jigsaw.

"You all right?" Paul's voice slices through the quiet.

My body jolts and I shove my phone in my pocket like it's contraband. "Yup. How'd it go?"

He jerks his head toward the van, his footsteps soft against the pavement. His gaze flicks toward the building behind us. Can't blame him for not wanting to broadcast his dating life all over the parking lot.

He glances in the back, gives a small nod, and climbs into the driver's seat without another word. Doesn't double-check the restraints. Doesn't even glance at the straps. Paul knows I did it right.

I slide into the passenger seat and toss him the keys.

"Sooo?" I prompt, buckling in. "Did you ask for her number?"

He starts the engine, his expression unreadable for a second, then a slow smirk tugs at his mouth. "Now that you've found love, you sure are a matchmaker."

Isn't that a kick in the stomach.

I stare straight ahead. "Sure, that must be it," I say, voice flat. "I can't just want to see my cousin happy?"

"I'm kidding, Margot." He reaches over and pats my leg. "Actually, I told her about Happy Pants guy. She was really upset. They've complained about his behavior before, but the owner of the facility doesn't seem to care."

Hmmm, escaping justice is one of my criteria. Maybe I should reconsider putting him on my list after all.

"Figures."

"You know I hate that shit," he grumbles. "The dead can't protect themselves."

We both do. And unfortunately, that wasn't the first time we've walked in on someone treating a body like an object instead of a person.

"I know," I say, my voice quieter than before.

Paul taps his thumb against the steering wheel. "She gave me the owner's number. I'll probably pass it off to your dad—he's got more pull. Maybe it'll actually go somewhere if he's the one to lodge the complaint."

"Let's hope."

"Anyway," he says, easing out of the creepy conversation, "I didn't even have to ask for her number. She gave it to me. We're supposed to get together next week."

"Oh good!" I clap my hands together and bounce in my seat like a child. "This week is nuts. Hopefully things are calmer next week."

"Right? She's a nurse, so I think she understands the hectic schedule."

Grinning like a hopeless romantic, I stare out the window.

"So," Paul says after a beat, "are you almost done with all the Hall family's requests? Think your biker boyfriend and all his buddies are going to show up for the service?"

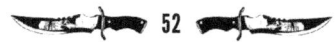

That's enough to wipe the smile from my lips. "I'm not sure."

Jigsaw was helping me locate a Harley Davidson Hearse Funeral Chopper from the list Mr. Hall's daughter gave us. Thank God Jigsaw left his notes so I could finish where he left off.

Almost like he did it intentionally.

Like he planned to vanish from my life.

CHAPTER FIVE

JIGSAW

STILL REELING FROM CAIN'S REAPPEARANCE IN MY LIFE, I NEED distance. The open road. I don't have a particular destination in mind. All I need is my bike, the road, and the engine to drown out my thoughts.

I don't bother telling anyone where I'm headed and don't know how long I'll be gone. I head east, riding until I pass into Massachusetts, then take I-95 north until I cross the Maine state line.

Wind tugs at the edges of my sleeves as I take the roads toward the coast, trading highway fumes for fresh salty air.

Shuttered seafood joints and colorful shops line the streets as I enter a small town. I lean right, down a hill, and finally roll into a small parking lot. The entrance to a public beach straight ahead.

The same beach where I'd recklessly and randomly buried the last pieces of my father years ago, after leaving Jezzie with my aunt.

Have the bones been found by now? Dug up by some dog? That would be poetic since my father treated animals with about the same respect he treated humans.

Or have those pieces of him washed out to sea?

I can't remember the exact spot, but it doesn't matter. I'm not here to collect them.

Only a few cars are parked in between the faintly drawn lines. I lazily circle the lot, then pull into a spot designated for motorcycles. I cut the engine, and the quieter roar of the ocean fills the silence.

Wind whips around my face as I pull my helmet off and stretch my back. Ancient aches awaken from the hours of riding. I roll my shoulders and crack my neck.

Colorful towels hang from balconies of the hotel next door, flapping in the breeze. Off-season or not, a few people must be staying here. Maybe that's where I'll check in later. Find myself a lobster dinner, bring it back to my room, and eat on the balcony while the sun goes down.

I follow the pavement to the sandy edge and stop to unlace my boots, then strip off my socks and roll up my jeans. Sinking my toes into the cool sand, I make my way to the water's edge. Icy water laps at my feet. A larger wave rolls in and slaps my ankles. The icy bite stings but I welcome it—reminds me I'm alive.

Rolled or not, my jeans end up soaked in salt water. I back up a few steps and plop down in the softer sand. Stretching out my legs, I lean back and stare at the blue-gray water. I try to find peace in the roar, but it doesn't come.

Seagulls approach, waddling over the sand, searching for treats. They circle near me, then back off.

"Sorry, guys. I got nothing." I pick up a handful of sand, letting it slide through my fingers. "Don't you dare fucking shit on me," I warn the big, fat, winged rats.

They squawk and fly off.

The sea's rough. Waves relentless. It's too cold for lying out on a towel but people are walking or jogging along the beach. Dogs frolic near the water.

It's peaceful.

But I'm still restless.

Restless and five hours from home.

My mind's churning as hard as the ocean but outside, I'm calm. Still, like the rocks stretching into the sea.

A low grunt to my left is my only warning before a big ball of fur and drool smears a wet, cold nose on my cheek.

"Chewy! No!" a woman shouts.

Hot breath blasts over me and I turn to face a big grinning , fluffy, gray-and-white dog. "Hello to you too."

He pants harder. *Huh. Huh. Huh.*

Since he doesn't seem like he's going to rip my hand off, I reach over and scratch behind his ear, searching for a collar but just finding more layers of fur. "I assume you belong to the woman frantically running over the sand?"

Huh. Huh. Huh.

"You must be well-cared for. You don't stink as much as you look like you would." Unbothered by the back-handed compliment, he closes his eyes, leans into my petting and lets his tongue hang out.

"I'm so sorry," the breathless woman says as she approaches. "Did he bother you?"

"Nope. He's been very polite."

"Polite my ass." She holds up a leash and collar. "He's an escape artist. Sorry. He's a rescue. I've only had him for a few days."

I'm really not in the mood for conversation but Chewy doesn't seem to give a fuck about my need for solitude. The big, fluffy beast stretches out in the sand next to me and rests his chin on my leg.

"Oh my gawwwd," the woman whispers, staring down at me with an open mouth. "The rescue told me he doesn't like men." She lowers her voice as if she doesn't want to offend the pooch. "They think he was abused by a man."

I run my hand over the dog's head. "Is that your story, boy?"

"I'm Jenna." The woman wiggles her fingers at me.

I squint up at her flushed face, hair swept up in a bouncy ponytail, sweatshirt and leggings. "Hi, Jenna."

She doesn't need to know my name.

Jenna frowns when I don't introduce myself. "Is that your bike up there? The Harley?"

Knowing I'd probably end up traveling through another club's territory at some point, I'd stopped home to leave my cut and grab a plain riding jacket and hoodie. Apparently, the jacket still gives me away.

"You ride?" I ask.

She lifts one shoulder and tucks her chin like she's suddenly shy. "Only on the back."

Are you shitting me? I may be avoiding Margot because I can't figure out how to tell her what a piece of shit I am, but I didn't ride all the way up here to fall dick first into the first woman I run into.

"That's my girlfriend's spot," I say, even though I know Margot has no intention of ever sitting there.

She flashes an awkward smile. "Oh. Lucky girl."

Not really. I nod and shrug.

"Come on, Chewy." Jenna dangles the leash at him.

He side-eyes her but doesn't lift his head from my leg.

"He really seems to like you. Do you have a dog?" Jenna asks.

"No, my girlfriend has a cat." I wave my hand over Chewy's head. "With a similar personality, actually."

She laughs and I hold my hand out for the collar. She hands it to me, and I gently slide it around the dog's neck and buckle it a notch tighter than it had been. "Sorry, bud. Can't come with me. I don't have room for a passenger."

Chewy slides a look of betrayal my way, then jumps up and trots to his owner's side.

"So...are you up here vacationing by yourself?" She bites her lip and flicks her gaze toward the parking lot. "Are you staying nearby? A lot of stuff is closed this time of year, but I can suggest some good restaurants or um, show you around. I just need to run Chewy home and..."

I tune out her chatter, considering the intention behind them. A year ago, I would've smoothly accepted her offer to "show me around" and probably been fucking her by now. She could be a nice temporary distraction from all the darkness bubbling in my head.

Who's gonna know? No one's even aware I'm here.

But all I can think about is Margot. Maybe she'll tell me to fuck off once I confess how I treated Cain.

"Can I take a picture of you and Chewy?" Jenna says, pulling me back into the conversation. She holds out her phone. "I want to send it to the rescue and tell them—"

"I'd rather you didn't." I've entertained this chick long enough. I grab my boots and stand. Cain tracking me down from a photo in a magazine weighs on my mind. I don't need Jenna taking my picture and sending it to strangers.

"Nice meeting you, Jenna." I bend down and pat Chewy's head again. "You too." I point down the beach. "I'm going to continue my walk." *Alone.*

"Oh." Jenna turns bright pink. "Sorry. Sorry we bothered you."

"No problem. Good luck with him." I kick my way through the soft sand until my feet hit the wet packed-down stuff closer to the water.

It's time to head home.

CHAPTER SIX

MARGOT

THE NEXT MORNING, A FLURRY OF TEXTS WAKE ME UP.

None of them are from Jigsaw.

Downstairs, I'm mid-yawn, waiting for a callback, when my father finds me in his office.

"Margot, one of the bikers is coming by today."

My ears perk up. *Bikers? Any biker in particular?* "Oh?" I answer in a casual, disinterested tone.

"Something about security. He wants to look around before the Hall funeral." Dad's jaw tightens. "I'm starting to wish we'd never agreed to this. It's turning into a circus."

The urge to defend our client rears up but I also understand what my father means. The animosity between Abby and Ulfric hasn't improved since our consultation. Abby's called or texted me dozens of times. And since Ulfric's footing the bill, I have to call and check in with him each time. Thankfully, he hasn't said no to anything, yet.

"It's a lot," I agree.

"I have a call later with Ulfric about some financial matters," my father says, his lips flattening into a grim line.

Better you than me. That's one thing I'm glad my father doesn't ask me to handle.

"Oh, and we have the custom casket issue sorted. I sent Ulfric a photo and he approved it."

"That's good."

"Paul's in the prep room handling a few things. I have to go into Slater for a meeting with those detectives about Daniel."

"Wait, what?" My voice is sharper than I intended. "Should you go there without a lawyer?"

He rears back and blinks at me as if I tried to tell him the sky is green with purple polka dots. "Why would I need a lawyer? I haven't done anything wrong."

Great, I've offended my dad. "*I* know that. And *you* know that. But I don't trust them. You shouldn't speak to the police without a lawyer. Ever."

"Margot, really? I know almost everyone down there. Unfortunately, I don't have a lot of information to give them. I would never suspect Daniel of such a thing. I can't imagine..." His voice trails off and he stares at me.

I swallow hard and glance away. "He's not a very nice person, but I never would've suspected he murders elderly women for their money, either."

"Margot, come on. It's absurd." He frowns. "What do you mean, *not a nice person?*"

I shrug, uncomfortable talking about my ex with my dad. "He's just a nasty, shallow man. I wish I'd never met him."

"I'm sorry to hear that. I wish you..." He clears his throat and glances away, staring at some of the family photos on the wall. "I wish you'd told me. You never said why you ended the engagement. And I didn't want to...pry."

And I never would've told you.

"It doesn't matter now." I force a quick smile. "I'm much happier." Or at least I *was.*

"That's what I like to hear." He screws his face into a disgusted scowl. "Thank goodness I never invested with Daniel like he was always pestering me to do."

"Yeah, he might've tried to knock you off."

He lets out a derisive snort. "No, a coward like that preys on elderly women with few relatives." Sadness washes over his features. "Or his own grandmother, apparently. How awful."

"Paul and I won't let you get swindled, Dad." A more genuine smile curves my lips, then falters as I realize I forgot to include my brothers. *Ah, too bad.* They're never around anyway.

Dad doesn't seem to notice the omission. He smiles. "I know you won't." He tilts to the side, glancing down the hallway. "I'm not sure what the bikers want to look at for their 'security check' but hopefully they don't want to see Mr. Hall, he's not quite ready for viewing yet."

"I doubt it, but I'll let them know if they ask."

He nods, gaze drifting to the hallway again. "All right. I'll talk to you later." Then he grins. "Or call you to come bail me out," he says, voice light and teasing.

I blink.

Did... did my father just make a joke? About getting arrested?

"That's not funny, Dad."

"Hey, you're the one who mentioned it." He chuckles. "I'll talk to you later and let you know how it went." He walks off, done with our conversation.

"You won't be laughing if they *do* arrest you," I say under my breath.

Less than an hour later, the front doorbell chimes. I glance at the screen for the front porch camera. Two men. One absurdly large and muscular—I recognize Wrath from Jigsaw's club. The other man would be impressively large himself if he wasn't standing next to the guy built like a slab of reinforced concrete in a leather cut. I don't recognize him and he's wearing a hooded sweatshirt, not one of the club's vests.

Setting down my pen, I hurry out of the office and to the front door. I paste on a friendly smile and swing it open.

"Good afternoon, gentlemen."

Wrath's lips quirk. "Hello, Ms. Cedarwood."

"Come on in." I open the door wider, inviting them inside. "Dad said you wanted to come by and take a look before Mr. Hall's funeral?"

"If you don't mind," he says graciously as if this visit is optional. "Margot, this is my friend Jake." Wrath nods to the tall, athletic, dark-haired man beside him. "We were business partners with Whisper for years," he says as if that explains why he's here for this "security inspection."

Jake looks familiar, but I can't place him. Handsome in a way that feels intentional. He's got a cocky aura that sets my instincts on edge. Too smooth, too confident.

His full lips slide into a lazy, but charming, half-smile. "Hello, Margot." He draws out my name to a seductive note.

"Don't." Wrath throws the back of his hand against Jake's chest without looking at him. "She's a friend of the club—and Jigsaw's woman."

I can't decide which title sounds more bizarre. *Friend of the club* or *Jigsaw's woman.*

"Ah, that explains why Jiggy's been popping into Strike Back instead of hitting Furious lately. My brother was starting to worry." Jake throws another flirtatious glance my way. "But now I see why he's been hanging around my neck of the woods so much."

Wrath rolls his eyes.

"Actually," I say, straightening my shoulders and smoothing my tone, "I'm a funeral director here. And the mortuary cosmetologist."

Jake nods, his cocky attitude vanishing. "Pretty sure your family handled my dad's funeral years ago."

"Oh," I say, defaulting to sympathy. "I'm so sorry."

"Don't be. He was a worthless bastard." Jake flashes a quick, too-bright smile, like he reflexively tosses that line out as a shield.

Men. God forbid they allow themselves to experience an emotion.

I gesture toward the viewing room. "You're welcome to take a look. Everything's nearly set up for tomorrow."

Wrath dips his chin. "Thanks, Margot. I'm not sure what Ulfric told you, but there will probably be a lot of different people paying their respects to Whisper."

The way he says "different people" sounds more like *criminal element*. At least he's more subtle than Abby had been. "Ulfric and Mr. Hall's daughter mentioned there would be a number of bikers in attendance." I tilt my head in a small nod of acknowledgment. "He mentioned his club had a good relationship with the dominant club in the area—I assumed that was you...your club, I mean."

Jake chuckles.

"That's true," Wrath says. "Our clubs go way back. There might be a few members from another New York club too."

"As I explained to them, we're used to handling delicate relationships. Awkward family reunions. We've seen it all, I promise you."

"I'm sure you have."

I show him into the sitting room. "We have the whole place reserved for Mr. Hall's funeral. Overflow seating is in here. My dad's called in extra staff, we have the permits sorted out, and I've been coordinating with the cemetery for the final ride."

"That's going to be something," Jake mutters. "Better bring your earplugs."

Wrath scowls in his friend's direction.

"We'll make sure everything goes smoothly." I walk across the hall to the viewing room. "We'll seat immediate family up front. Mr. Hall's daughter has been very...involved in the planning." That's one word for it.

Wrath snorts as if he understands by "involved" I mean Abby has been *relentless and demanding*.

Jake wanders down the hall, while Wrath surveys the viewing room like he's counting all the exits.

"Ulfric and some of his guys will probably assist you with seating," Wrath says, nodding to the chairs.

"Usually we—"

"There'll be multiple clubs and a few other members of other... organizations," Wrath explains. "Everyone should get along, but to be safe, Wolf Knights will want to be visible and direct people to their seats."

I give him a slow once-over, arching a brow. "You're not exactly low-profile."

The corners of his mouth curl up. "I won't take an active role like ushering. I'll hang back. A subtle reminder for folks to behave."

I tilt my head, lips twitching. "No offense, but you're about as subtle as a wrecking ball flying at a stained glass window."

He lets out a deep, hearty laugh. "None taken."

Apparently, I amuse him.

I glance at the hallway. Where'd Jake go? I won't have a better time to ask Wrath this. "Uh, will, ah, Jigsaw be here too? As, you know…a subtle 'behave yourself' reminder? Ulfric did personally invite him." I stumble over my words like an idiot.

A wrinkle forms between Wrath's brows. "I assumed he'd be here to look after *you*."

"Oh." My gaze drops to my shoes. *I should shine them before the funeral.*

"Margot?" Wrath's authoritative tone pulls my attention away from my shoes, forcing me to crane my neck to look up at him again. "What's going on?"

"Nothing. I just…" *Just say it.* "I haven't heard from him in a couple of days. Is he okay?"

Wrath studies me for an uncomfortably long moment, his expression wiped clean. No judgment or pity. "I haven't heard otherwise. But I'll see him at church later today."

Please don't tell him I asked. I plead with my eyes. It's humiliating that I have to ask other people about my boyfriend's whereabouts.

Jake returns and nods at Wrath, saving me from further embarrassing myself.

"I like your place, Margot," Jake says. "Feels nice and homey, instead of…"

"Morbid and creepy?" I offer.

One corner of his mouth slowly slides up. "Well…I didn't want to put it *that* way, but yeah."

"Thank you."

"We'll let you get back to work," Wrath says. "Do you mind if I go out the back door and make my way around?"

"Please, go ahead." I walk them down the hallway, trying not to think of how many times Jigsaw's come in this same way—and straight up to my apartment.

Not now.

"All right. See you at the service," Wrath says.

Jake lifts a hand in farewell. "Nice meeting you, Margot. Hope the rest of your day's less…intense."

"Hope yours is less…morbid."

His lip twitch with amusement. "If you ever want to take self-defense classes, come into Strike Back in downtown Johnsonville. I'll take care of you."

"Jaaake," Wrath warns in a dry tone.

"What?" Jake spreads his hands wide. "I've taught almost all the club's ol' ladies. I don't want to leave Margot out."

"You have?" I ask, trying to keep the shock out of my voice. The guys must trust him.

"Yeah. Sunday mornings my brother hosts a class." He leans in, dropping his voice. "But between you and me—I'm the better teacher."

I raise a hand, putting some space between us. "I'm sure you are."

"All right, charmer." Wrath grips Jake's bicep and hauls him onto the back porch. "Let's go."

Laughing too hard to respond, I just raise my hand in a wave.

"See you at the funeral, Margot," Wrath calls.

I close the door behind them.

And then I'm alone.

With silence.

Way too much silence.

CHAPTER SEVEN

JIGSAW

I MAKE IT BACK EARLY THE NEXT MORNING, RIDING DOWN ROOSTER'S long driveway past the house. Through the kitchen window, Rooster's big head bobs into view like a buoy in choppy water.

Since he's up, I might as well spread some cheer. I park near the back door and don't even bother going downstairs to my place.

"Look who's actually here for once." Rooster opens the back door before I even have a chance to knock. "Where ya been, cock-knocker?"

I yawn and scrub my hand over my face. "It's too early to be so chipper." I lift my chin, scenting the air. "But I smell coffee."

"Help yourself."

I fix a cup and join him at the kitchen table. The rest of the house seems still and too quiet. "Where's our little songbird at?"

"She's down in the city."

"What? Why? By herself?"

He slowly sets his mug on the table and lets out a long sigh. "No," he says with barely hidden restraint. "She's with Angelina and Mallory."

"You let your ol' lady go into another club's territory with the wife of *another* MC's president and his daughter? Are you nuts?"

He cocks his head and glares at me. "They're doing a 'girls' weekend' as civilians. No one's going to bother them."

"Surprised Chaser let them go."

"Let them." He rolls his eyes. "They have a driver taking them everywhere. It's not like they're riding the subway alone or hanging out in dark alleys."

It sounds like he's trying harder to convince himself everything's fine than convince me, so I ease up on the questioning. "You okay?"

He stares at me as if he's having an internal battle. While he's working out whatever he wants to say, I sip my coffee. It's nice to worry about someone else's problems instead of my own for a few minutes.

"If I tell you this, can you please promise to keep it to yourself?" Rooster asks. "Shelby will kill me for telling anyone."

Normally, a statement like that would make me hound him for the info but since I'm keeping a pretty hefty secret of Margot's, I shrug. "Well, maybe you shouldn't, then."

He presses his lips together and frowns.

A new worry hits me. "She's okay, right?"

"She's fine. She just…"

"Wait. *You two* are okay, right?"

"Fuck. Yes, of course." He runs his hand over the back of his neck. "She…there's a therapist in Manhattan who works with celebrities. Very discreet. Understands creatives supposedly."

"Wait, *therapist?*"

He sighs. "All the attention she's getting lately, the album blowing up, the award she just won…the amount of people constantly picking her appearance apart's only gotten worse. More intense. It's getting to her."

"What? How? She's gorgeous and talented. Who cares what a bunch of losers think?"

He taps his phone, sitting on the table between us. "You've helped me comb through her socials. The shit people are comfortable saying behind the safety of their screens is—"

"Brutal. I know, but she doesn't actually *believe* any of it. Besides,

there are more comments praising everything about her than there are nasty ones."

He lifts his shoulders. "I know that. And you know that..."

"Obviously she's hot. For fuck's sake, you never take your hands off of her."

"Yeah," he says in a slow, sarcastic tone. "I don't think having me explain how hard my dick gets every time I catch her scent is the cure for what she's going through."

I curl my upper lip in fake disgust. "I didn't need that image in my head."

"Then stop being dense."

"I'm not trying to be dense." I pause and try to consider my words for once. "I hate that something like that is bothering her so much. That's all."

"So do I, brother. Which is why I'm glad Mallory found this therapist—"

"Wait, so Mallory knows?"

He shrugs. "Shelby and Angelina are tight. I think Angelina asked her mom for some advice since she went through something similar in the nineties."

"Forgot she was on that old show." I tap his phone. "It's way worse now, though. Mallory didn't have the constant stream of vitriol from social media to deal with."

"Exactly." He drills me with a hard stare. "Now, forget I told you any of this."

"Already forgotten, brother." I tilt my head and study my best friend. "You doing all right? After everything you two have been through together, it must be killing you not to track down some of these assholes and beat some manners into them."

He squeezes his hands into fists then releases them. "Big things are happening for her. I'm damn proud of everything she's accomplished, so yeah, I hate that some fuckwad losers get in her head. But she's taking the right steps to deal with it. I'm trying to support her the best way I can." His expression relaxes. "You're right, though. I'm *not* thrilled she's down in the city without me, but I talked to her last night, and she sounded happy."

"Good. When you're ready to track down some of these assholes and fuck them up, let me know."

"Who says I haven't?" He flashes a savage grin. "I can do a lot of damage without even being in the same state as these little trolls."

"There's the ruthless Rooster I know." I slap his arm.

"So, where've you been?" Rooster arches a brow. "I sent you a couple texts last night."

Guilt presses tight against my chest. I turned my phone off yesterday and haven't even bothered to check it yet today. Something about cutting myself off from the world seemed very freeing.

I pull my phone out of my pocket and set it on the table. "I think it's dead. Can I borrow your charger?"

He jerks his thumb over his shoulder toward the counter where he keeps a charging station. It's probably not dead but it felt like a good excuse to avoid explaining my absence. I plug it in and turn it on.

The screen lights up with several notifications. A bunch from Rooster, which I ignore since I'm standing right here in his kitchen talking to him.

Princess PITA: Look!

A picture of Jezzie throwing a wobbly-looking disk of dough in the air follows. Sent yesterday. I type a quick reply.

Me: Good job.

How the hell am I going to tell her about Cain? Maybe I should wait until she's finished with this semester.

Z: All good?

I shoot off a quick yes. The rest is noise—group chats I can barely keep up with even when I'm home. I skim, don't respond.

Margot hasn't sent me anything else since my last short, cold response.

Can't blame her.

My thumb hovers over the screen. I don't even know what to say.

"Why's Shelby asking me where you are?" Rooster sets his phone on the table with a noisy clunk.

I return to my seat and flash an obnoxious grin. "Probably because our little songbird was vibrating with the universe and knew we were together talking about her?"

He glares. "No. Margot texted her. Asked if I knew where you were."

My insides seize. "She did?"

"So, if you weren't at Margot's…" He narrows his eyes. "Where have you been?"

Great, he thinks I was out cheating on Margot. "Not where you're thinking."

"You have no idea what I'm thinking."

I blow out a breath and rub my hands over my face. "I went for a ride up to Maine."

Rooster's brow creases. "Maine? Why?" He leans over and lightly punches my arm. "Why didn't you ask me to go with you?"

I shrug and lean back in my chair. "Needed to clear my head."

His expression morphs into something more sympathetic. "You and Margot have a fight or something?"

"No. Fuck no."

He waits, knowing there's more. He'll find out eventually. And I'll have to tell Margot and the club. So I might as well get used to saying it. "Z called me the other night." I sit up and clear my throat. "My half-brother, Cain, remember him?"

He holds out his hand about three feet above the floor. "The little freckle-faced kid I met when—"

"Yeah," I answer quickly, not wanting to get swallowed up by those memories again. "Only he's not a little kid anymore. He showed up at Crystal Ball looking for me."

Rooster sits back and blinks. *Huh. Look at that. He's too stunned to speak.*

"The fuck is wrong with you?" he finally grumbles. "You let me ramble about Shelby's trip to the city instead of telling me that your half-brother showed up out of nowhere?"

"Uh, I don't consider that *rambling*. Believe it or not, I actually give a shit about what's going on with you two."

His jaw tightens. "Same, brother."

I'm out of excuses, so I shrug. "Maybe I wanted you to take my mind off of it."

"What? The ride to Maine didn't clear your head?"

"Not really."

"Well, continue." He exhales, ready to listen. "What's Cain want?"

"Not sure." I shake my head. "Family? His mom just passed away and she wanted him to find me."

"Shit. Poor kid."

I shoot him a sharp look, hating that he's got more compassion for Cain than I seem to have. "Yeaaah," I answer slow. "I'm not sure if I trust him, though."

"Don't blame you." There's no judgment in his tone at least. "How'd he even find you?"

I roll my eyes and grab my coffee mug, taking a quick sip before I solve that mystery for him. "You'll love this. Ruth—his mom—was apparently a big Shelby Morgan fan. She saw a pic of you and Shelby tongue-fucking each other backstage in some magazine. Unfortunately, my ugly mug was in the background staring right at the camera. She recognized me."

Since his shitty ex-girlfriend tracked him down in similar way and tried to fuck up his relationship with Shelby, he gets it. "Sorry about that. Shit, when I told Priest the publicity might not be good for the organization, I never thought about estranged family coming out of the shadows to find *us*."

"Or unhinged ex-girlfriends."

He flicks an irritated look my way. "Don't try to deflect because you're feeling vulnerable."

"Ooo, such big words, motherclucker."

"Don't get defensive, either."

This is the problem with lifelong friends. They know all your quirks and how to disarm them.

"What are you going to do?" he asks.

I shrug.

"Where is he now?"

"At a hotel in Empire." At the judgmental expression that crosses his face, I raise my hands in surrender. "He was staying there before he found me."

"Shit." He shakes his head. "I'm surprised Z didn't mention it. I'm supposed to be his VP."

I glare at him. "It's *not* club business. I asked him to keep it quiet until I figure shit out." I'm actually kind of surprised Z *didn't* immediately tell Rooster, though. "Cain wants to see Jezzie."

"I can understand that," he says gently. "They grew up together until…"

"Yeah, I know."

"So, what's holding you up? You think he's here for retribution or something?"

He's got Killgore blood running through his veins. "Maybe."

"Why didn't you tell Margot?" He pauses. "Does she know about your dad?"

I throw my thumb over my shoulder, gesturing toward the scars crisscrossing my back. "Just the highlights. And that I scattered his bones from coast to coast."

A grim smile curls his mouth. "Not a dealbreaker, huh?"

"Nope." Normally, I'd crack a joke, but I don't have it in me today.

"Damn, she's so perfect for you. Don't fuck this up. Talk to her."

"Why, you worried you're gonna be saddled with me forever if I don't have an ol' lady?"

"No, dickface." His face screws into something smirky and annoying. "We're already brothers for life. I just want you to be happy." He shrugs. "And I like Margot. I think you're good for her too."

"You barely know her."

"Well, I like that she seems pretty protective of you and that she's not judgmental about the club. That shit with the bunnies at the clubhouse could've been a dealbreaker for *her,* but she took it in stride."

"She took out a *knife.*" I grin like an idiot.

He dips his chin in a show of respect. "And she held her own with

Rav. Pranking him was genius. But she was still somehow…respectful about it?" He shrugs. "I don't know. I just like her."

"I like her too. A lot." I glance down at my coffee cup and swirl the last bits of it around. "I love her."

"Then *talk* to her. She's smart. And it's pretty fucking obvious she loves you too. She'll understand."

What's to understand? I kicked a young mom and her son out of their home, gave them some money, and basically told them to fuck off into the unknown. I don't know how Margot's gonna hear that and think, "yeah, that's someone I want to spend the rest of my life with."

I don't bother saying any of that to Rooster, though. He'll justify my actions because he's my best friend.

My phone vibrates on the counter and I stand, taking my coffee cup with me.

Wrath: Get your ass here for church at 2:00 p.m.

A standard order from Upstate's enforcer.

I leave my cup by the sink, then show my phone to Rooster. "Wrath wants us at the clubhouse."

He chuckles and turns his phone over, checking the screen. "Got the same one."

"Thank fuck." I drop into my chair again. "I'm not special."

"Oh, you're special, lil' buddy." He stretches toward me and rubs his hand over the top of my head.

"Har. Har. Cut that out." I swat his hand away. "You realize we're basically answering to two SAAs now, right?"

He snort-laughs. "Yeah, I know. Two presidents too."

"At least Rock *pretends* he's not ordering us to do shit. Wrath gives zero fucks."

"That's why he's SAA and not prez."

Both of our phones ding again.

Grinder: Church. 2 o'clock. Upstate.

Rooster thumbs out a reply. "Told him we're both headed up there now."

"Thanks." I pull my shirt away from my chest and give it a sniff. "Actually, I'm going to run downstairs, shower and change."

He glances down at his plaid pajama pants. "Yeah, no shit. I wasn't planning to go like this." He cocks his head. "You gonna call Margot?"

"Not now. I want to actually have a conversation with her." I tap my phone. "And obviously, I don't have the time."

He shakes his head and stands. "At least let her know you're all right."

I nod once. It's literally the least I can fucking do. Then, like the dick I love to be, I pick up my phone with exaggerated movements and make a dramatic show of tapping on the screen.

"Whatever." Rooster waves me off and heads upstairs.

Once I'm alone, I send Margot an actual text. It's as inadequate as it is true.

I miss you.

CHAPTER EIGHT

JIGSAW

Rooster and I roll through the gate into Upstate's clubhouse yard just before two. The lot's already full—bikes lined up along the fence, a few trucks and SUVs parked near the garage, and Dex pacing in front of the garage like a junkyard dog looking for an ass to chomp.

After we shut off our bikes, Ravage pops out of the garage. That must explain Dex's pinched expression.

"Look who finally dragged their asses here," Ravage yells when he sees us. "Was starting to think you two joined the circus."

"Not when my favorite clown's right here," I shoot back, flipping off my helmet.

Dex walks over and gives each of us a quick embrace. "Thank fuck you're here. He's encroaching on my territory." He waves one hand toward the garage.

Aw, shit. I should've stopped by Downstate's clubhouse to see if anyone needed anything. At least pretend I'm doing my actual road captain duties.

"I was *helping*," Rav says, joining our circle.

"Welcome back," Rooster says to Dex. "How was your trip?"

"Good. We had fun." His lips quirk. "Libby didn't burn down the house while we were gone."

"Can't ask for more than that." Rooster lifts his chin at the clubhouse. "Everyone inside?"

"Fuck no." Dex laughs. "Rock, Wrath, Z, and Murphy aren't even here yet."

I glance past Dex and run my gaze over the line of SUVs. "Grinder here?"

"Yeah. He's in the dining room with Serena."

Murphy and Teller pop off the path from the woods. Murphy lifts a hand and waves.

"You didn't run your ATV up here?" Rooster shouts to Teller.

Teller shakes his head and jerks his thumb at Murphy. "No, Charlotte and the twins are at his place with Heidi. I drove them up." He nods to a ridiculously oversized blue SUV.

"You went with the Escalade?" Rooster asks him.

Teller nods. "The smaller one. Not the ESV."

"Small?" I snort. "It's the size of a school bus."

Teller cocks his head and inhales a slow, patient breath. Kinda similar to the way Rock does when he's thinking of choking one of us. "Two kids and all their shit take up a lot of space."

"Jiggy doesn't need to worry about that." Rav holds out a fist toward me. "We have a no procreating pact. Right, brother?"

I hold out my own fist and tap his knuckles lightly. "I don't remember agreeing to that, but whatever."

Everyone stops and stares at me.

"Awww, you and Margot would have cute little babies," Murphy jokes with a doofy grin on his ginger-bearded face.

My jaw locks shut. No snarky comeback slips onto my tongue. *Margot's so patient and calm. She'd be such a good mom.*

"Shut your mouth." Rav points a finger in Murphy's face. "Just because you're trying to spawn an entire football team, doesn't mean Jiggy has to abandon his commitments."

Murphy rolls his eyes and slaps Rav's hand away. "Whatever." His gaze lands on me and he frowns. "You all right, Jiggy? You look like you're gonna hurl."

I swallow hard. "I'm fine."

"Oh, shit." Rav's eyes widen. "You didn't knock Margot up already, did you?"

"It's getting really disturbing how obsessed you are with everyone's procreation plans," Dex says.

"I'm not *obsessed*." Ravage tugs on his cut and lifts his chin. "I'm *concerned*."

"It's *weird*," Murphy says.

I clear my throat and gesture toward Teller's new ride. "Does Charlotte like it? Did you make her get rid of that sweet Raptor?"

"Make her?" Teller scoffs. "No. She loves that truck. I wouldn't ask her to trade it in." His shoulders shake with laughter. "She *said* she wanted something bigger, but she hasn't wanted to drive *this* yet. It's 'too big'."

"Why?" Murphy glances at me. "You finally want to upgrade that busted-up 4Runner of yours?"

"Don't talk shit about my truck," I snap. "That ol' girl's got more miles on her than you do."

"Doubt that," Ravage snarks. "What's wrong, Jiggy? Why so touchy today? Margot dump you already?"

"Shut *up*," Rooster growls.

"Wait, hold up." Ravage's gaze swings between Rooster and me. "Did she? I got twenty bucks ridin' on this with Stash."

"For fuck's sake, seriously?" Teller groans.

"Dude." Murphy grimaces. "You're betting on his sex life? That's weirder than you commenting on our family planning."

"No," Rav says defensively. "I'm betting on whether or not he comes to his senses."

"Do you ever stop running your mouth?" Rooster gives Rav a quick shove.

Christ, brother. Could you be more obvious? I shoot Rooster a *knock it off* look.

"Margot's actually a cool chick." Rav touches his fingertips to his chest. "I just don't get what she sees in *Jigsaw*."

That actually pulls a laugh out of me. "You and me both, brother."

At least that finally seems to help everyone move on from my love life.

And to further distance everyone from asking about Margot, I nod to Teller's Escalade again. "So if you needed more room for the kiddos, what made you pick that monstrosity instead of a minivan?"

"Charlotte said *no* to a minivan." Teller rubs a hand over his jaw, eyes glinting with amusement. "Ground clearance isn't high enough."

"Because you do *so* much off-roading?" Rav deadpans.

We all ignore him.

"It's probably overkill." Teller shrugs, smug as hell. "Six hundred eighty-two horses, tows like eight thousand pounds, electronic limited-slip diff. Not exactly a normal grocery-getter."

"No." Dex shakes his head. "It's a souped-up dad-wagon."

"When are you even going to use half that shit?" Rooster asks.

"I didn't even do any mods to it yet," Teller continues, ignoring both of them. "It'll haul a trailer, a double stroller, all the baby gear, and," he tips his chin at me, "still outrun your 4Runner."

"I should hope so." *It probably cost twenty times what my 4Runner's worth.*

"Anyway," Teller says. "It even has a little fridge in the center console. That's Charlotte's favorite thing about it so far. She'll get used to driving it eventually."

"What's the fridge for? To store breast milk?" Ravage asks with a straight face.

Teller whips a glare at him.

"Someone wants to die today," Dex sings under his breath. "Painfully."

"Can you let the grownups talk?" Teller says to Ravage.

Murphy clamps his lips together tight, trying to hold in his laughter. It's useless. His shoulders start shaking.

Teller scowls at him. "What's so funny?"

I glance at Rooster and Dex—both grinning like assholes.

Finally, Murphy can't hold it in any longer. "Wrath's right. You *do* sound exactly like Rock's mini-me."

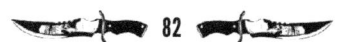

"*Can you let the grownups talk?*" Dex mimics in a deep voice. "Is classic Rock. Just sayin'."

"*What* were you saying?" Rock calls out as he steps out of the woods with Wrath and Z behind him.

Dex flashes an unapologetic smile at his president. "Your son's stepping into the Papa Bear role real nice."

"That right?" Rock hooks his arm around Teller's neck and hugs him to his side. "What were you saying, knucklehead?"

Hell help me. I love when Rock puts Teller in his place.

Rav's slowly tiptoeing away from our group toward the clubhouse.

Wrath catches up to him and slings his arm over his shoulders, spinning him around and back to our group. "Yeah, what was being said, Rav?"

"Uh…" Rav flicks his gaze around the circle, seeking support. Any other day, I might throw him a bone, but the breast milk comment was one too far, even for me, so today I keep my mouth shut.

"Nothing." Rav points to Teller's SUV. "Teller was sharing some details about his new ride. Jiggy wants to buy one."

I raise my eyebrows. "Nah, if I spend that much on a vehicle, it better jack me off and tuck me in at night."

Murphy snorts.

"It's time to upgrade that 4Runner," Wrath says, releasing Rav and sending him stumbling forward.

"Why is everyone picking on my vehicle today?" My eyes widen with outrage, and I hold my arms out wide. "Are we a *motorcycle* club or a *truck* club?"

"No one's picking on your vehicle, Jiggy. We live in an area with brutal winters. You need something reliable," Dex says. "I think that's what Wrath meant."

"No, I meant it's a rust bucket." Wrath shakes his head.

"Well, we can't all be like you guys," I wag a finger at Murphy and Teller, "collecting vehicles like you're gettin' ready to film your own *The Fast and the Furious* spin-off."

Murphy chuckles. "No joke. My car insurance bill's starting to look like another mortgage."

"Well, I'm ready to buy Heidi's little SUV from you whenever you want to sell it," Dex offers.

Murphy nods. "I'll bring it out to the track for her to test drive. Just let me know. It'll be a good car for Libby while she's going to college."

"Wait?" Rav's eyes bug and he frantically slaps Dex's arm. "You're buying a *car* for your ol' lady's little *sister*?"

Dex presses one finger to his lips. "Shhh. Grown-ups are talking."

"All right." Wrath claps his hands together. "If you're done strokin' each other's tailpipes, let's make our way to the table. We have things to discuss."

"Finally," Rock mutters, following Wrath inside, their boots thudding over the wooden steps.

Z stops me at the bottom of the stairs with a hand on my chest. "Everything all right with you?"

"Yeah, why?"

"With your brother?" he asks in a low enough voice not to be overheard.

I could strangle Cain for going to Crystal Ball looking for me. "I think so."

"Where's he staying?"

"At a hotel right now. He hasn't really said if he's planning to stick around or not."

Z studies me for a moment, then flicks his gaze over my shoulder —probably clocking Rooster standing guard at my back. "Look, I don't know your whole family history." His mouth curls like he just bit into something rotten. "I'm sure it's as wholesome as the rest of ours. And I only met him for a few minutes, but he seemed like a good kid. Little lost. But eager to see you."

He got all that from five seconds with Cain?

"Yeah, I just don't know *why*. We...didn't grow up together. I met him once when he was like seven or eight." I clear my throat and glance away. "That's it."

"Maybe that's better." He huffs a bitter laugh. "I got two brothers I grew up with and I wouldn't piss on either of 'em if they were on fire."

That's probably how Cain feels about me. Or *should*.

"I hear you, Prez." I'll say just about anything to appease Z and shut this conversation down. "I think he really wants to see my sister—they *did* live together when they were little. But I'm not sure I trust him, yet. I gotta see what his intentions are before I help them reconnect."

He frowns and stares at me for a few beats. "Yeah, I don't blame you. You need anything, let me know." He pats my shoulder, then bounds up the stairs into the clubhouse.

Rooster and I follow him inside. Everyone's already filing into the war room. No stopping to gab with the ol' ladies today. *Wait.* "Where is everyone?"

"I know as much as you do," Rooster says.

Sparky shuffles over to us, eyes bloodshot and faint smile forever plastered on his lips. "Ol' ladies and kids are down in the dining room or doing yoga." He tilts his head toward the hallway.

"Look at you, so knowledgeable at this hour." I bump my fist against his shoulder.

"I know stuff," he mutters, rubbing the spot and shooting me a scowl. "When you close your mouth and open your mind, you absorb all the things the universe has to offer."

"Greaaat." I widen my eyes and nod slowly.

Even though no one lingered in the living room, it takes a while for the guys to find a seat and Rock to call the meeting to order.

I drop into a chair on the far side of the table, halfway between Rock's end and Z's. Rooster slides into the seat on my left.

Outside, more bikes rumble into the parking area—stragglers.

I'm not sticking around after this, so they better not block me in. I double-check that my phone's off. Just because Wrath didn't collect them today doesn't mean he won't choke us if a phone rings during the meeting.

I lift my head and meet Grinder's eyes across the table. He dips his chin like he's silently thanking me for remembering to shut off my phone.

I send my gaze up and down the table. Of course, it's downstate guys late to the meeting.

Hustler and Suds bust through the door just as Wrath's about to close it. Hustler's grinning like an idiot and holds up a crumpled file folder and nods at Teller.

"All right." Teller holds up his hand for a long-distance high-five across the table.

Hustler stops and says a few words against Z's ear. Z nods quickly, then Hustler drops into the chair next to Z.

I lean left and whisper to Rooster. "Think we're all gettin' raises?"

"Looks like it."

"All right." Rock leans forward, no need to bang his gavel this morning—he already has our attention. "Thanks, everyone, for being here. As always, welcome to our downstate brothers. I know it's a longer ride for you, but we appreciate seeing your faces."

"Not a problem, Rock," Butcher rumbles, waving one of his meaty hands through the air. "You know we never say no to more time in the saddle."

Hustler's practically vibrating in his seat. Teller leans in, murmurs something to Rock, who gives a slight nod.

Rock gestures down the table. "Z, you want to go first?"

Z props his elbows on the table. "Our dirty little cop says we're off their radar—for now."

"Jesus fuck," Suds groans. "About time."

"The break-in at the laundromat was a pain in the ass but since my boys cooperated with their investigation." Z reaches over and slaps Hustler's arm, then points at Rooster and Eazy. "They decided we must be good little law-abiding bikers."

Grinder snorts. "That guy couldn't find his way out of a phone booth with a crowbar."

Dex flashes a sly grin. "I don't think they have phone booths anymore."

"No one asked you," Grinder growls, casting a sideways glance Dex's way. "Keep it up and I'll take you outside and teach you some goddamn respect."

Dex's grin only widens.

"Anyway." Z raises his voice. "Hustler has news."

Hustler grins like a kid who just passed a test he didn't study for—or understand—which kind of sums up his role as Downstate's treasurer. "Thanks to Teller's guidance, we saw a solid jump in our portfolio. Teller recommended we lock in profits on a few positions, so I'll be distributing bonuses to Downstate this week."

"Nice!" Butcher pumps his fist in the air.

"Prospects gettin' a bump too?" Suds asks.

Hustler and Z share a look. "Small, but yeah," Z answers.

Suds scowls. "Prospects didn't get shit back in my day."

Z stares him down for a beat. "We didn't have indoor plumbing back in your day either—doesn't mean we need to shit in a hole out back." His cold, sarcastic tone makes it clear this isn't up for debate.

"Progress is good," Rock says. "We ask a lot of prospects."

"Unbunch your boxers," Hustler mutters at Suds. "He ain't gettin' a full cut. But he takes risks like the rest of us—oughta get something for that."

"Pretty sure all the free pussy is the reward," Eazy mutters, then side-eyes Z. "Just kiddin', Prez. I'm cool."

"Good." Z flicks a hand, passing the floor back to Rock.

"Teller, share your news," Rock says.

Teller gives us all a shit-eating grin. "Same deal. Bonuses will hit by the end of the week." His smug smile slips into something more serious but almost hesitant. "The U.S. market's volatile right now, so I'm looking to reduce our risk by diversifying into some international positions. Nothing wild, just a few high-growth opportunities I think we've been overlooking."

He glances around, picking up on the blank stares and fading attention, then tacks on quickly, "If you want to go over the charts after church, come find me."

Sparky lifts a hand, his eyes still bloodshot but his voice firm. "You're not talking about investing our money in places that use child labor, fund terrorism, or disappear journalists, then gaslight the world about human rights concerns, are you?"

A beat of silence settles over the table.

Teller's grin fades. His voice drops, low and steady. "No. I'm not

touching anything shady. Just a few sectors overseas—clean energy, medical tech. Stuff like that."

"It's all hella shady though, isn't it?" Dex says.

Rock rubs his fingers over his forehead, a clear sign he'd like us to *wrap it the fuck up.*

"To some degree, sure," Teller agrees. "Doesn't mean I don't do what I can to minimize harm." He flashes a quick, easy smile. "But we gotta eat too."

And buy hundred-thousand-dollar SUVs.

Nope, definitely don't add that to the conversation.

"Thanks, Teller," Sparky says.

"I can give you a list, if you want," Teller offers. "You might be more plugged into causes I'm not aware of. If there's something specific you're opposed to, let me know. I can adjust."

"Jesus Christ," Suds mutters. "Hippie Harry over here will have you investing in energy crystals and goat Pilates."

Z narrows his gaze. "It's a valid concern these days."

Sparky lifts his chin at Z.

"Any other questions?" Rock asks in a tone that suggests the answer better be *no.*

Eazy raises his hand and swivels his head between Z and Rock. "This mean we gotta kick up more money to National?"

The strangest hush falls over the table. No, more specifically *Rock's* end of the table. It's brief but noticeable. To me anyway.

I've never wanted to be involved in whatever the fuck it is the treasurer does, but knowing Priest, I bet he has all kinds of questions whenever a charter sends National *more* money than usual. Downstate's never had that problem before. When Sway was our president, we were bleeding money, not gettin' bonuses.

But dealing with National is Teller's problem, and now Hustler's too. Not mine.

After a beat, Teller leans forward, voice smooth as ever. "Yup, we kick up the normal percentage. Mark it down as income."

Eazy frowns. "That don't seem right, since you're the one doin' all

the…" He waves his fingers like he's casting a spell. "Investing wizardry."

"Great." Z claps his hands. "When Rock gets promoted to national prez, you'll be the first one I nominate to be on the committee to change the bylaws."

Everyone chuckles. Even Rock.

"Whoa." Rav throws out his arms, waving like he's guiding a 747 in for a landing. "Rock, you're not threatening to gut him for suggesting you'll be national prez?"

Grinder's normally grumpy mug twists into something closer to savage pride. "Someone must be making peace with his upcoming promotion."

"Knock it off," Rock growls. "I'm not making peace with shit. Priest isn't retiring any time soon."

"That we know of," Wrath says.

"Yet," Dex adds, not missing a beat.

Z raps his knuckles on the table, dragging our focus away from Rock. "Any other questions?"

I'm itching to ask how large our bonuses will be. Enough to buy a new car? Or enough to buy a tank of gas for my current vehicle? Some details would be nice. But I'm not eager to prolong church today to satisfy my curiosity.

When no one bites, Rock turns toward Wrath. "How do you want to handle Whisper's funeral?"

Wrath leans back, brow furrowed. "I've been thinking about this a lot."

"I thought I smelled smoke," Murphy mutters.

Teller elbows him in the ribs.

Ignoring their antics, Wrath continues. "Wolf Knights were friends of the club for years. At least a few of us need to be there to pay our respects." He thumps his palm against his chest. "As much as I didn't get along with Whisper in the end, I need to be there to remind the Wolf Knights their visit has an expiration date."

"Fuck yeah, it does," Z mutters.

"But," Wrath continues, "we need to walk a fine line between showing our respect and whipping out our dicks to remind the Wolf Knights that Lost Kings run Slater County now."

"Agreed," Rock says. "Too many Kings prowling around could be interpreted as disrespectful."

Wrath's gaze narrows on Rock. "*You* need to be there."

Rock slides a slow, sarcastic eye roll Wrath's way. "I didn't say otherwise."

"I'm sitting it out," Z says.

"Same," Grinder adds. "I *knew* of Whisper back in the day but only met him a couple times."

Dex lifts his hand. "I'll be there. Vapor's planning to stop by too. At least for a few minutes."

"Makes sense." Wrath nods.

Bricks glances at Wrath, then Dex. "I'll hold things down at CB. I knew Whisper but not *that* well."

"I'm with Bricks," Ravage adds.

"Sparky, we all know how you feel about funerals," Wrath says. "You can stay home."

"Thanks, big guy." Sparky bobs his head up and down, then mutters, "Wasn't planning to tangle with those dark spirits."

Teller nods to Wrath. "Charlotte and I have to be there."

Wrath flashes a crooked grin Murphy's way. "Whisper hated your ass, so you're free to stay home."

"Oh no," Murphy cries in a dramatic falsetto, "whatever will I do with myself?"

"Probably try to make another baby," Ravage mutters loud enough for everyone to hear.

Ignoring Rav's comment, Wrath focuses on Teller. "You hear anything from Charlotte's uncle? Is Merlin coming?"

Merlin—what a piece of shit. If he bothers to show up, I'd have no problem helping Teller load that dude into the crematorium after the service.

"Haven't heard anything, yet." Teller pulls an annoyed face. "But either way, we're going. Whisper did right by Charlotte. She wants to be there to say goodbye and pay her respects."

Finally, Wrath's gaze lands on me. "I assume you'll be there to look out for your girl."

My blood freezes. Wasn't expecting to be called out. "Yeah, of course. Ulfric extended an invite when I ran into him."

"Let me have a minute with you after church."

What the fuck'd I do now?

When Wrath moves on, I glance at Rooster. He shrugs and mouths, *I don't know.*

I'm on edge for the rest of the meeting, which thankfully doesn't last much longer.

After church wraps and Rock says we can go, I'm ready to bolt with everyone else. There's no way to leave the room without passing by Wrath's seat, though. Rock stays put, Z moves down and stands behind Wrath's chair.

Great, another obstacle.

I stand and push my chair in.

Wrath points at Murphy's now-empty chair. "Park it."

"What's going on?" Rooster asks.

Wrath flicks an exasperated glance at him. "For fuck's sake. Nothing's wrong. I just want to talk to your boy. That all right with you?"

"I'm not his *boy*," I growl. "What the fuck?"

Wrath glances at Rock, then cranes his neck to look at Z still hovering behind him. "I don't need an audience."

"My road captain, my business," Z says.

Somehow that doesn't give me the warm fuzzies.

Rock leans back, arms draped over the sides of his chair like a king settling in to enjoy the show.

"What's on your mind, Wrath?" I finally say in a *let's get this over with* tone.

"I went to visit Cedarwood's today." He pauses, waiting for my reaction.

I lock down my emotions and expression. "Yeah? Why?"

"Getting a layout of the place for the funeral. Margot walked me through their plans."

My breath catches in my throat hearing my girl's name coming out of someone else's mouth.

"Jake came with me," he adds.

All my frozen blood starts to simmer. Jake's reputation with women is worse than mine was. He's sneaky and charming. Margot's too smart to fall for that, though, right? "Yeah, and?"

"Nothing. Just thought I should mention it." He pauses. "Oh, and she asked if you were okay since she hasn't heard from you in a few days."

Teller slowly turns and glares at me.

I swallow hard. "She did?"

"Yup. She tried to play it cool, but she seemed worried."

She really does deserve better than me.

"I, uh, had some personal stuff come up I've been dealing with. I'll call her," I say with all the calm I can harness. "Thanks."

"Okay. Just checking." Wrath pauses. "What personal thing?"

I lift my gaze to Z and raise my eyebrows. *You really gonna let him interrogate me like this?*

"It's cool, bro." Z slaps Wrath's shoulder. "Let it go."

"Everything okay?" Rock asks. At least he sounds concerned, not just nosy like Wrath.

Fuck it. They're all gonna find out anyway. "Yeah, my half-brother showed up outta nowhere looking for me."

For a few seconds, no one says a word. Like they're all trying to figure out what to do with that information.

"Half-brother?" Wrath asks. "I thought you only had a younger sister?"

Since I originally patched-in to our Washington charter, no one in New York really dug deep into my past. Hell, even Washington never asked a lot of questions. I was friends with the nephew of a friend of the club. Uncle Boone's word that I could be trusted was all they needed back then.

Only Rooster knows the goriest details of my childhood. He's of course the one who started the rumor that I killed my father and scattered his bones all over the place, which led to my road name and helped create the unhinged, don't-fuck-with-me reputation I still enjoy today.

"Yeah," I answer slowly. "My father was a pastor turned cult leader. The crazier he got, the more women he pulled into his flock. One was this girl Ruth. She's actually the one who helped me escape. He knocked her up. Married her, I guess. I only met the kid once."

I blow out an exhausted breath knowing this won't be the last time I have to share this story.

I lift my gaze and meet Wrath's curious stare head-on. "When I killed my father and rescued my sister from the sick shit he was doing to her—that's the only time I ever met Cain. Helped him and his mom get out. She died recently. He showed up wanting to reconnect."

Uncomfortable silence descends over the table.

Everyone just stares at me.

Serves you right for poking into my business.

"Well, fuck." Z runs his hands through his hair. "Thanks for the extra context, Jiggy."

Wrath's expression turns more thoughtful. "You don't trust him around your sister?"

"I didn't protect her from our father when she was little." I swallow hard, shame slithering down my throat. "Our relationship's kinda fucked up as it is. I'm not bringing him around her until I know what he's really here for."

"You think he blames you? For killing your father?" Rock asks.

How does he just know shit? "He was little. My father didn't usually start on the real torture until kids were older. All Cain knows is, I showed up, flipped his world upside down, and disappeared with his sister."

"Didn't his mom explain what actually happened?" Z asks.

"I'm not sure what she told him. We didn't get that deep the other night."

"Where's he staying now?" Teller asks.

"Some hotel by the airport." I flick my gaze to Z. "I can't bring him to the clubhouse until I know I can trust him. Same for my place." I gesture over my shoulder at Rooster.

"What do *you* want?" Rock asks. "From him, I mean."

I open my mouth to say *nothing*, but the word sticks in my throat.

"Maybe...make things right? If that's even possible. I don't know if he plans to stick around. We don't have much in common. Crystal Ball seemed to scandalize him and," I grimace, "he rides a fucking *Ninja*."

No one laughs. My attempt at deflection crashes and burns.

"He can't stay in a hotel forever," Teller says. "How old is he?"

"Seventeen or eighteen."

"Eighteen this summer," Z says. "That's why Malik sent him to me when he tried getting in the front door. Kid didn't even try to use a fake id."

"Young to be out on his own," Wrath says.

"*You* were on your own earlier than that," Rock points out. He glances at Teller, then Z. "We all were, more or less."

"Nah." Teller shakes his head. "Murphy and I had *you* to keep us in line." He jerks his chin at Wrath. "And him to terrorize us into submission."

"And look how well you turned out," Wrath says.

"Grinder kept *me* in check," Rock says.

I blow out a breath, guilt slamming into my chest harder than I expect. From what Cain said, it doesn't sound like he has anyone.

"Why don't you have him move into the apartment Dex was using," Teller offers. "He's living with Emily now. The apartment's furnished."

I turn and stare at him. "I just said I'm not sure I trust him. What if he burns your entire building down? You got other tenants living there."

He shrugs, clearly not taking the threat seriously. "It has a sprinkler system."

"What if he trashes the place?"

"I've got insurance. Things can be repaired. Besides, it puts him closer to Margot's place, so you can keep an eye on him..." His voice trails off, like he's silently asking if Margot and I are even still a thing.

"Yeah... I guess that might be easier."

 94

"I can hook him up with a job at Sully's gym," Wrath offers. "He could practically walk to work."

"I can't ask Sully to do that," I protest. "I just told you I don't know a damn thing about the kid."

"I'll pass that along to Sully and let him make up his own mind," Wrath says in a slow, patient tone. "Jake mentioned they're short-handed since Grinder left. Sully can't find anyone who lasts more than a week. If your brother flakes, no harm done. If he sticks around, great."

I shake my head again, already trying to put distance between me and the idea. "I don't know…"

"Talk to Cain and find out what his plans are." Wrath slaps the table like he's finally wrapping up my interrogation. "Let me know."

It really is a generous offer. I need to show my brothers more respect. They could've said "good luck with the reunion" and gone about their business.

"Thanks." I nod at Wrath, then Teller. "I appreciate it. Really."

Finally, I'm dismissed.

Rooster follows me out while the others stay behind and close the door. Loud voices echo from the dining room, and the scent of bacon wafts through the air, but the living room's empty for now.

"Feel better that you have a plan of sorts, now?" Rooster asks.

I stop a few feet away from the front door and turn to face him. "For Cain? Yeah, I guess so."

"Want me to come with you to talk to him?"

Irritation prickles at the back of my neck. For fuck's sake, I'm not scared of the kid. I don't need backup. But Rooster's not questioning me—he's trying to be supportive. Doesn't mean it doesn't rub me the wrong way.

"No. I can handle it."

"Well, if you need help getting him settled in the apartment, text me." He hesitates. "You *can* bring him to the house, you know. You've got your own apartment. You pay fuckin' rent. You can have whoever you want over."

"If it was just you and me there, I would." I shake my head. "But I don't want to take a chance with Shelby. I won't do anything that might make her feel unsafe in her own home."

His frown deepens, and he swallows hard. "I appreciate that."

Great, now he's all choked up.

"Besides," I add, forcing a lighter tone, "Mr. Real Estate has a free apartment sitting empty. Might as well use it, right?"

He chuckles. "Yeah. Maybe if we start getting more bonuses, I'll pick up a rental property or two myself."

A thought from earlier rekindles. I step closer to Rooster and lower my voice. "You ever think Upstate's sittin' on a fuck-ton more money than Downstate?" I ask. "Teller didn't suddenly get good at investing. And he's been treasurer for *years.* Can you imagine the money he's made for them?"

Rooster nods slowly. "Yeah. But it's not a nest I'm gonna stick my beak into."

"That's not what I meant." I blow out a breath. "If Sway hadn't been such an egotistical asshole, trying to drag Rock into a dick-measuring contest all the time, our charter could've been making the same bank. Teller wouldn't have gatekept that knowledge from us."

"Ahhh." Rooster closes his eyes briefly. "You're right. You ever wish we'd kept riding north and patched in here, instead?"

"Yeah, kinda. Took us too long to realize Sway talked a good game but was full of shit and only out for himself."

"Agree." He snorts. "Not much different from some of the guys in Washington. That's probably why it took so long to see it. Felt normal to us."

Laughing, I shake my head. "Pathetically fucking true." I bump his shoulder. "That's why I go where you go."

"Same, brother."

We head for the front door, side by side—like always.

Only difference now?

I've got a blood brother crawling out of the past, and I need to figure out what the hell to do with him.

And that's my cross to drag. Alone.

CHAPTER NINE

MARGOT

GRIEF DOESN'T FOLLOW A DRESS CODE.

The house is packed. Men in leather cuts, dark denim, a few suits, a handful of women in revealing black-and-silver dresses, and a few in more regular funeral attire.

I have to squeeze through groups of loud, boisterous men clustered in the hallway. Their voices bounce off the old walls, lively and hearty despite the occasion. I stop and straighten a flower arrangement that doesn't need fixing. It's me. I need something to do to keep my mind off of Jigsaw.

I feel him.

Feel his presence in the house, even though I haven't actually *seen* him yet. That low, electric hum my body only seems to recognize when he's nearby.

I shouldn't allow myself to get distracted.

There's too much work to do.

But the days of silence from Jigsaw have me questioning everything. And also...*angry*. Something I thought I'd never be with him.

Job. Focus. Be present. These people are here to celebrate Mr. Hall's life. They deserve my full attention.

My gaze lands on Abby, seated in a corner near her father's customized casket. Shiny black lacquer with silver hardware that catches the light streaming in from the windows. The engraved Wolf Knights MC emblem we rush-ordered and added to the casket matches perfectly.

Abby's curled into herself, hands clenched around a crumpled tissue, mascara smeared under her eyes. Alone, in a room full of men who called her father "brother."

Why the hell is she sitting alone?

I grab a fresh box of tissues and thread through the crowd. Leather cuts brush against my arms. Heavy boots thud dully over carpet. Low murmurs. A cough. A stifled sob. And somewhere outside, the constant rumble of Harleys, coming and going.

"Hey," I say softly.

Abby jerks upright like she's just remembered where she is.

I crouch beside her, offer the tissues. She grabs a handful without meeting my eyes.

"Thanks," she whispers, voice raw.

I drag a chair closer to her and sit. "Do you need anything? Water? Coffee?"

She shakes her head. "No. I'm fine." She pauses, then reaches out and takes my hand. Her grip surprises me—tight, needy. "Thank you for everything. I must've driven you crazy with all my calls and texts this week."

"Not at all," I say. "It's what I'm here for."

She gives me a watery smile that slips almost as fast as it appears. Her gaze flicks up and scans the room. Every direction. Not at anyone in particular. Just...the crowd.

And then the smile dies altogether. "Never get involved with a biker, Margot."

Pain squeezes my throat. "I'm sorry?"

She laughs, bitter and sharp. "The club always comes first. No matter what."

Now we're treading into awkward territory. I have dozens of responses memorized for grieving loved ones. For this, I have nothing. It hits too close to home. Is that where Jigsaw's been, doing something for his club? Wrath didn't say that when I spoke to him, but why would he? I'm just the girlfriend of one of his brothers, not someone he'd share club matters with.

Unless they're asking me to cremate someone for the club.

No. I push that thought away. The club's business arrangement with my father and my relationship with Jigsaw have nothing to do with each other.

"I'm sorry it must've felt that way at times," I finally say, then wince. That sounded patronizing.

"Oh, trust me." Her eyes narrow, meeting mine. "It is."

"It must be hard having so many people from the club here, then," I whisper, feeling like a traitor since Ulfric paid all the bills but not wanting to ignore Abby's feelings.

"Yes and no." Her gaze darts around the room and lands on Ulfric standing in a group of men—one I recognize as Rock, the president of the upstate Lost Kings, his son Teller, and a wiry, craggy-looking older man who looks like he rode through a tornado without stopping to be here.

"Ulfric was like an uncle to me when I was little. He was always nice. My father's responsible for his own choices." A faint smile ghosts her lips. "He and my dad owned a drive-in theater when I was a kid. It was one of my favorite places to be in the summers. I have a lot of happy memories there." The smile slides off her face. "But when my mom had enough of his cheating and divorced him, she moved us across the country, and I never really saw him much after that. She didn't want my brother joining the MC too, so she got us as far away as she could."

"Did your brother join them?" I don't even think her brother showed up for the funeral.

"God, no." She sighs and sits up straighter. "My dad could've had visitation with us in the summers, but he only bothered once. Having us around during 'riding season' was an inconvenience, you know?"

So much of Abby's bitterness makes sense now.

"He moved to be closer to me, recently. He wanted to get to know my kids but never wanted to really discuss the past. Own up to it. Apologize. Nothing." She lets out a strained laugh. "Like, how dare I harbor some resentment about him abandoning me for all those years."

This isn't our first client or even the hundredth whose grief rubs against their unprocessed abandonment issues. It's still hard to think of an appropriate response.

"It's hard for some people to own up to their mistakes." That seems like the safest thing to say. "They'd rather pretend it didn't happen and move on. That doesn't mean you're required to do the same."

She frowns as if she's working through my words. I hope I didn't offend her.

"Wow," she breathes out. "Thank you for saying that, Margot."

Her voice is softer now. Less bitter.

I squeeze her hand gently, then stand.

"You sure you don't need anything?" I ask.

She shakes her head. "No. I'm okay. He really wanted this," she says, gesturing toward the casket and the room full of men in leather. "Thank you for working so hard to make it all come together."

"Of course." There's still so much left to do but at least we got this part right.

I step away from Abby and circulate through the room. Different leather vests with various states stitched into the bottom of the back patches—*Montana, Idaho, Nomad.* Huh, that's different. The scent of leather, oil, cologne, smoke, and flowers fills the air—a little grittier than the normal funeral scents.

In the hallway, I bump into my father. "Everything's going well," he says in a low voice, his gaze flicking around. "All the permits are in the glove box."

"Got it." I flick my pen over the checklist on my small clipboard. "We have our escorts and the route ready." I lower my voice. "Ulfric says his men will take care of the few road closures we need, but Slater PD said they want to handle Main Street."

He nods once. "I'll speak to Ulfric about that one."

"Thanks."

"Wrath says they'll assist with a perimeter at the cemetery. It seems like overkill but," he shrugs, "I'm not about to argue with him."

My lips quirk. "No, I suppose not." Does that mean Jigsaw will be there too?

Nope. Not now. I wrap up things with my dad and move on to the refreshment table, dispose of empty paper plates and wadded up napkins.

Someone gently bumps my shoulder, a light, warm presence. "Dear God," April whispers in my ear. "That tall, intense one with the murdery vibe, wearing the dark blue plaid flannel under his leather vest, hasn't taken his eyes off you all morning."

"What are you talking about?" I laugh then quickly smooth my expression into something respectful.

I turn and scan the room. More than half the men in attendance today qualify as "tall, intense, and murdery."

But I don't have to ask who she's referring to. The weight of Jigsaw's gaze weighs heavy on my skin even before our eyes meet.

There he is.

My breath catches.

April's right. Even though he's in a loose circle with three other bikers, his eyes are on me.

Waving like an infatuated teenager would be more than inappropriate. Besides, what I really want to do is throw my clipboard in his face. Ask him where he's been. What the hell's going on.

"Yup. Tall and scary," April murmurs. "My goodness."

"He's not scary," I mutter.

He's a dangerous heartbreak waiting to happen.

"Ohhh," she says under her breath, somehow managing to keep a placid, professional expression in place while subtly teasing me. "He's the guy you're *kind of* seeing?"

I lift one shoulder, afraid to admit all the things I feel for him.

"A biker, huh?" She raises her eyebrows but not her voice. "Did your dad shit a brick?"

"No, he likes him."

"Go, Mr. Cedarwood." She chuckles softly. "Learning how to unclench at his age isn't easy."

"April!" I scold in a harsh whisper.

"I'm teasing. Introduce me to him after the service."

"Not if you're going to call him scary and murdery."

"Ooo." She raises her eyebrows. "I'll try."

"Go refill the guestbook pens before you say something even worse." I give her a light shove.

"On it, boss." She grins and hurries away.

Shaking my head, I finish clearing debris off the table.

A shadow falls over me. My skin prickles from scalp to toes.

"Can I talk to you for second?" Jigsaw's warm breath caresses my cheek. Warm shivers slide down my spine.

"I'm working," I say through clenched teeth.

"Margot."

Just my name. But from his mouth, it's a trigger.

Damn it.

Why can't I resist his raspy, pleading tone?

I turn, slow and deliberate, and stare up at his contrite expression. No. Something more than contrite. Haunted.

"Where have you been?" I ask.

"I'll explain." He glances around. "Later. I promise."

Why, why, why does he have to sound like that—like gravel and regret. All while he stands there looking like sex and apologies wrapped in flannel and leather.

CHAPTER TEN

JIGSAW

As much as I wanted to get here early, Wrath insisted those of us attending Whisper's funeral arrive together. A united front. We rode while Hope and Charlotte drove the new Escalade.

One glimpse of Margot and my lungs forget how to work. Somber. Professional. Fucking heart-stopping.

Her father smiled at me and shook my hand as soon as he saw our contingent. I couldn't tell if he was relieved to see members of my club or actually happy to see *me* specifically. Either way, I caught Teller watching with wide-eyed respect.

See, I told you I wouldn't fuck up the club's relationship with the funeral home.

My *own* relationship—that's a different story.

Margot's working. This is her job. I can't wrap my arms around her waist and drag her upstairs like I want to. She's working.

Still, every time she smiles or talks to a brother wearing a Wolf Knights MC cut, I want to launch myself across the room and empty my Glock into his skull. Doesn't matter that most of them are closer to her father's age than hers. Age doesn't stop them from eye-fondling her, touching her elbow, or worst of all, calling her sweetheart.

I never knew I'd turn out to be such a possessive motherfucker.

Margot's nothing but professional. Pride and awe beat around in my chest. That's *my* woman. She put all of this together. Up until last night she was probably freaking out. Worried everything wouldn't come together in time. But now, she's nothing but poised and calm.

One of the attendants walks up and whispers something in Margot's ear. Then the two of them turn and stare at me.

Fucking hell. The second my eyes lock with Margot's, my heart stutters.

Her gaze narrows, anger simmering over her pretty face for a second before she gives me her back and continues speaking with the other woman.

Yup, I deserve that.

I was going to wait until after the service. Be respectful. Give her space. But I can't take another second of this self-inflicted silent punishment. Every second she refuses to acknowledge my presence scrapes my insides raw. This isn't the time or place to lay out the whole story—but I have to say *something* to her.

Excusing myself from the conversation I'd been barely listening to with a couple of bikers from Idaho, I cross the parlor and come up behind Margot. Part of her hair's caught up in a silver clip, the rest flowing down her back. Desperation to sweep her hair to the side and kiss the side of her neck pulses through me. I curl my hands into fists at my sides.

I step closer and her entire body tenses up as if she senses me looming at her back. The same kind of awareness that's lived in my bones since the first time we touched.

I lean down, close enough to breathe her in. Citrus, vanilla, a hint of incense. "Can I talk to you for a second?" I whisper against her ear.

Her jaw clenches tight enough to crack teeth. "I'm working."

Please, please, please, let me fix this. "Margot."

She drops her head and takes a long, slow breath, then turns to face me.

My face must betray how desperate I am for her. The second our eyes meet, her harsh expression softens. Her fury—which I deserve—

cracks enough for other feelings to flicker over her face. Confusion. Hurt. Concern.

"Where have you been?" Her soft voice comes edged in steel. Like if I lie or give her some weak-ass excuse, she'll never give a shit about my whereabouts again.

Damn. I glance around the room full of bikers loudly reminiscing about past road trips and talking about what a shame it is Whisper died so soon. This isn't the time or place for us to have such a personal conversation. "I'll explain. Later. I promise."

She tilts her head and runs her gaze over me again. I pull my shoulders back and try to dial back the desperation.

"Are you okay?" she asks.

I blow out a breath, my heart thudding like it's been trying to claw its way back to her this whole time. "I am now." I hate how much that sounds like a line when it's one hundred percent true. Even though a funeral's going on around us, the second I stepped into her orbit, the heaviness that's been surrounding me for days lifted.

Why didn't I just come back the other night and tell her what happened?

"Margot?" her dad calls from the doorway. "They're about to start."

She turns and nods. "Okay."

After he leaves, she reaches out and squeezes my arm. "I have to—"

"I know."

"We'll talk later." She raises her eyebrows as if it's a question.

"Thank you."

A small, but genuine smile curves her lips. "I'm happy you're okay."

I don't know how to respond to that. She takes off before I come up with an answer. Should I follow or stay put?

The silence she leaves behind is deafening.

A few seconds later, movement ripples through the room. Everyone starts drifting toward the double doors across the hall.

I need a minute.

I grab a golden cookie off the tray and bite into it. It's dry and flavorless, like sawdust on my tongue. I pour a cup of coffee to wash down the world's worst cookie.

Get it together.

I step into the hallway and slip into the viewing room through the back entrance, the one farthest from the casket.

Wrath's standing against the back wall, arms crossed over his chest, expression unreadable. I take up the empty space next to him and he turns to nod at me.

I turn my attention to the front of the room where Ulfric's speaking.

"Whisper was formed by the grit of the gutter and the dust of the highway." Ulfric glances at the coffin. "Despite his intimidating appearance, he spoke quietly, in a way that commanded your attention and respect. That's how he got his road name…"

News to me. Since many bikers have a twisted since of humor and hand out road names as jokes, I always assumed it was because Whisper was a loudmouth when he was younger.

"He was a stealthy fucker too," Wrath whispers to me. "I think that's *actually* how he got his road name. Could break into buildings without anyone hearing a thing."

"Probably not the best thing to mention at his funeral," I say out of the corner of my mouth.

He snorts. "Give it five minutes. Someone'll bring it up. Probably Merlin."

At the podium, Ulfric steps aside to make room for Whisper's daughter. She sidesteps him, avoiding the embrace he clearly planned to give.

I lean closer to Wrath. "Margot was right about the friction between them."

"Yeah, he didn't talk about his family much. I figured there was some tension there." His gaze scans the room. "That's the difference between us and a lot of other clubs. They make the club their family and ignore their actual family."

"Whereas we suck our loved ones into our vortex until there's no escape?" I question with two innocently raised eyebrows.

Wrath rolls his eyes. "Sure."

One by one, Wolf Knight brothers step up to say a few words

about their ex-president. Then neighbors, friends, and other people who knew him.

While a middle-aged, teary woman's recounting all the ways Whisper helped her reach her fitness goals, one of the brothers slips through the door and stops beside me.

I glance over long enough to clock a vaguely trusted face— Hudson. Around my age. Patched member of the Wolf Knights. Not someone I'd go out of my way to share a beer with.

"You mind if we talk for a sec?" Hudson asks under his breath. "In private."

I *know* Hudson but not well enough for private chats. His urgent tone sets my radar humming. I glance at Wrath but his attention's locked on the woman still speaking.

"Uh, yeah, sure."

We weave in between different guests clustered in the hallway. My gaze ping-pongs, searching for a quieter, less crowded location. I find a spot near the staircase—by the hallway that leads to the prep room. It's far enough from the main rooms to talk without drawing attention, but still visible to anyone walking by. No shadows. No doors. Just enough privacy.

I turn to face him. "What's on your mind?"

"You seem to know the place well." He gestures toward the parlor. "Ulfric mentioned the funeral director's daughter is your ol' lady."

I cross my arms over my chest and stare him down. "Do we know each other well enough for you to be prying into my love life?"

He blinks, then his face settles into granite. "Didn't realize it was a secret."

After the world's shortest staring contest he blows out an annoyed breath. "I wanted to ask if your club's recruiting."

We very much need to grow our numbers but I'm not about to share that with someone wearing another club's patch. "Why? You know someone who wants to prospect?"

"Yeah, *me*."

I let that sit for a beat, then drop my slow, sarcastic gaze to the flash stitched on the patch on his chest—*Road Captain*. I drag my eyes back up to his face. "You already *have* a club."

"I got my president's blessing to ask, so don't think I'm a traitor to my club. Truth is, Wolf Knights are probably disbanding my charter soon. I don't want to move to another state. Again." He sighs, jaw ticking. "Honestly, I'd really like to move back home. I grew up in Slater and even though the winters fucking suck, my mom, my sister and her kids are all here. I'm tired of missing birthdays and holidays with them."

"You grew up in the Wolf Knights, right? That's how you know Teller's ol' lady?"

"Yeah, our dads patched-in at the same time. Charlotte and I hung out a lot when we were kids."

"So, why ask me instead of Teller?"

He tilts his head and widens his eyes to a cocky degree while staring at my own road captain patch. "RC to RC, I guess." He shrugs. "Besides, I don't know if Teller would be cool with it. He seems to be under the impression there's more history between Charlotte and me than there actually is."

"No offense, but I doubt he gives you much thought at all, bro." Teller's way too cocky to see anyone else as competition. "He and Charlotte are tight."

"Glad to hear it," he says in the least joyful tone possible. "Are you guys looking for recruits or not?"

"Maybe." I study him harder. "You really want to jump clubs?"

"Told you, ain't gonna *have* a club pretty soon." He shrugs. "We were always good with Lost Kings. I like your club's structure. You still take riding seriously. Ulfric always had a lot of respect for Rock. Seems like it would be a solid fit."

I'm sure *somewhere* in the history of the Lost Kings MC, someone might have patched-in from another club. I've never heard anyone talk about it, though.

"You know you'd have to scrape your club ink if you jump." With his long-sleeved shirt, no Wolf Knights insignias are visible, but I'd bet my bike he has at least one.

He nods like he expected that and rolls up his left sleeve, revealing a faded black wolf head with *Wolf Knights* scribbled like an afterthought over the wolf's ears. Some truly hideous line work.

"My prez said either way, I gotta do it before I leave. Got this." He pats his arm and then his chest. "And another one incorporated into a larger piece here. I'll probably laser this one and cover the other one."

Makes sense.

"I got no idea if they'll make you prospect the full term or—"

"I don't care," he cuts in fast. "I'm not looking for special favors. I want to earn my full patch same way everyone else does. Want my new club to trust me—not worry that my loyalties might be somewhere else."

That's a good sign. Not a lot of guys who've been officers in a club want to get busted back to prospect.

"All right, yeah. Since we're all here, you want to talk to Wrath?" Wrath knew Hudson's old president pretty well. It makes sense for Upstate's SAA to start Hudson's vetting process.

"You rang?" Wrath's voice booms through the corridor like a cannon.

He walks up, slaps a heavy hand on my shoulder and eyes Hudson for a second. "Was wondering where you disappeared to."

I jerk my chin toward Hudson. "Talking to Hudson."

Wrath nods and shakes his hand. "How've you been? It's been a minute."

Hudson meets Wrath's stare head-on and shakes his hand without wincing. "Can't complain."

You literally just complained that your charter is closing.

"Actually," I say, drawing out the word to grab their attention. "Hudson might be interested in trading in his patch for a skull and crown."

Wrath's whole vibe switches from conversational to hardened enforcer. He crosses his arms, body going still, face hardening into that quiet, lethal calm he's famous for. "That right?"

To his credit, Hudson doesn't flinch under Wrath's scrutiny. Doesn't even blink.

He nods once, then runs through the shorter version of the pitch he gave me. Wrath cocks his head, listening intently or running background checks in real-time behind his cold eyes—who knows.

"Yo, Hudson!" Merlin's voice cuts through the hallway. "Get over here."

"You sticking around for a bit after the funeral?" Wrath asks Hudson.

"Planning to stay with my mom for a few days. Help her out. Hang with my niece and nephew."

Wrath nods once—quick, like he wasn't asking for Hudson's whole itinerary. "Stop by Furious any afternoon. We'll talk more."

"All right." Hudson hold out his hand. "Thanks." He nods at me next. "Thanks, Jigsaw."

"Sure."

Wrath's attention stays locked on Hudson until he's around the corner, then he turns to me. He flicks his gaze to the stairs. "What's up there?"

"Second floor is where her cousin lives. And a kid's playroom I think? I've never really explored it." No, I'm always in a hurry to hide out at Margot's place and get my hands all over her. "Margot's place is up on the third floor."

He glances over his shoulder and must decide this is a secure enough place to talk. "What's your thought?"

"I have lots of thoughts. Be more specific."

His eyes narrow to pissed-off slits. "On Hudson."

"Uh, I barely know him."

"Why'd he come to you, then?"

I tap my patch. "He said RC to RC but I'm not sure."

"We should all sit down for church tomorrow anyway," Wrath says. "Share details we learned here today. We can talk about Hudson then. Get everyone's take."

What details did we learn today? "Yeah, all right."

"You staying here tonight?"

I shift my gaze to the side. "Not sure yet."

Thankfully, he doesn't pick up on my hesitation and ask about my situation with Margot. "I'll tell Rock noon for church?"

No one's ever asked me for scheduling input before. "Whenever you need me. I'll be there."

Wrath's attention shifts to the hallway where a steady stream of guests are moving toward the back doors. "I think they're gettin' ready to head to the cemetery. I told Ulfric Kings would take up last position."

"I didn't expect anything else."

"Good." He claps me on the shoulder and heads off down the hall.

I hang back for a second. Then I make my way toward the front parlor, threading through the stragglers, searching for Margot.

She's standing near the front door by the guest book. Shoulders tight with her warm, professional smile plastered in place as she gently guides the last few guests where they need to go. Ulfric stops to talk to her, resting his hand on her shoulder for a moment.

I close my eyes and force myself not to picture my fist going through his throat. This knee-jerk rage that shoots through me every time another man gets close to Margot should be studied by scientists.

I wait until she's alone, then step into her space.

At least this time she doesn't look like she wants to waterboard some answers out of me. No, she looks tired.

I lean down, keeping my voice low enough for her alone. "I wanted to tell you earlier—you look really pretty today."

Her smile falters for half a second. "You can't fix things with an empty compliment."

Ouch.

"But thank you." There's no bite to her tone this time. Just weariness twisted with affection.

I don't deserve her.

Someone props the back door open, and I catch a glimpse of a black Harley trike with a black carriage behind it. *Fuuuck.* I was supposed to help Margot find that hearse funeral chopper setup and I totally bailed on her.

I shift, uncomfortable now that I've been reminded how badly I dropped the ball on something so simple. "You found one?" I nod toward the parking lot.

She tilts her head, glancing up at me. "Yes, thank you for the notes you left. They were helpful."

If it were anyone else, I'd assume they were being sarcastic, but Margot seems sincere. Grateful even. She's too sweet to tell me what a fuckup I am.

Wait until you tell her about Cain.

I shove that thought aside for the moment.

The hallway's almost empty now. Outside, a motorcycle starts up. "You have earplugs?" I ask.

She slips her hand inside her pocket and pulls out a small, round purple case. "Yup."

"Is the graveside service going to be long?"

"Probably. There were a few additional requests."

I glance at the back door again. "I should probably get out there..." I don't want to leave her side, though.

She leans up on her tiptoes and beckons me closer to whisper, "They asked guests to wear black and gray."

Wolf Knight colors.

I run my gaze over her prim dark gray suit and silver blouse. She's even wearing gray, low-heeled pumps.

"Usually, I would as well," she says. "We try to fit in if the family has a 'theme' or requests certain attire, but it felt wrong when blue and gray are the colors of *my* man's club."

The possessive way she refers to me as "her man" travels straight to my balls. *I'm going straight to hell, not even a pit stop in purgatory.* Even when she's pissed at me, she's worried about something like my club's colors?

"But I didn't want to antagonize a client, either." She lifts her hand, tucking her hair behind her ear, showing off sparkling blue stones set in shiny white gold. "So, I'm wearing my sapphire earrings."

I'm going to bury my face between her legs tonight and lick her clit until I'm drowning in her.

As if she senses exactly where my thoughts ran off to, a devilish smile curls her lips. "And blue undergarments."

Fuuuck me. "Why are you trying to get me hard at a funeral?" I whine like a horny teenager. If we were anywhere else, I'd push the collar of her blouse aside to confirm. "You're a naughty girl."

"Who said they were for you?" she tosses over her shoulder, already walking away.

"You know damn well they're for me," I call after her.

She doesn't turn around, but I swear I catch the faintest shake of her shoulders—like she's laughing.

I hope she keeps that energy for our conversation later.

I hang back a second, then shove my hands in my pockets and head outside.

Rock and Teller are waiting on one end of the porch.

"Everything good?" I ask.

"Yeah." Rock nods and steps away from the railing. "Girls are in the car out front. We're just waitin' up here until they sort out some stuff."

I glance at the parking lot. Wrath and Dex are talking to Ulfric and another guy with a Wolf Knights cut. Mr. Cedarwood's hovering near the trike, inspecting the casket's placement. Margot's nowhere in sight.

Finally, Wrath signals he's ready for us.

The three of us clomp down the stairs.

The sky's overcast and chilly.

I squint up at the clouds. "As long as it doesn't rain, it's a good day to ride."

Rock nods, distracted, his mind clearly somewhere else.

Wrath and Dex catch up to us.

"All good?" I ask Dex.

"Yeah, we offered to help close off one of the roads, but Mr. Cedarwood said it's handled."

"So, we're just following the pack?"

"Pretty much."

"All right, brother." I tap my knuckles against Dex's.

I swing my leg over my bike and settle into the seat. The lot's so full I can barely make out the trike hearse or the black car behind it.

Margot's up there somewhere. Probably in the car with Whisper's daughter. Some of the Wolf Knights' ol' ladies are on the backs of bikes. Hell, a small group of women are riding solo.

That'll never be Margot.

It doesn't matter. Charlotte and Hope are driving to the cemetery, and so are some of the other ol' ladies. It doesn't mean anything. I'll never try to talk her into something that scares her so much, but it doesn't stop me from thinking about having her at my back.

I pull on my helmet and fire up the engine about the same time everyone else does. The sudden, unified rumble drowns out my thoughts, but not the ache in my chest.

CHAPTER ELEVEN

MARGOT

THE SILENCE INSIDE THE HOUSE FEELS HEAVIER THAN IT DID THIS morning. The people my father hired to clean downstairs after the mourners left are gone but the sharp citrus scent of whatever cleanser they used still lingers in the air. After having so many people in and out of the house today, the quiet is a relief.

It's just my father, Paul, and me now, meeting in Dad's office to recap the day's events.

"Thank you, Margot." My father drops his lean frame into the chair behind his desk and lets out a heavy sigh. "You did an excellent job with all the biker details."

That's probably the most enthusiastic praise my father's ever given me.

"And thank you for bringing in and assisting April," he adds. "She was a big help today."

"I didn't need to give her that much assistance," I say, keeping my tone even. "She's been doing this as long as I have. She likes our smaller, more personal setting."

"She definitely has the personality for it." Paul chuckles and takes a seat on the couch next to me. "She's the perfect mix of bubbly and somber."

My lips quirk with amusement. That describes my friend well.

Dad nods once, thoughtful. "Thank you for all the behind-the-scenes stuff you did today, Paul. It was a complicated event and everything ran smoothly."

Paul casts a sideways glance my way. "Of course."

We run over a few more details for tomorrow's much smaller and quieter service. "Mrs. Beckett's family plans to be here early and no trip to the cemetery to coordinate so it should be an easier day," Dad says.

"Why would you jinx us like that?" Paul jokes.

Dad responds with a tight smile.

"Is Jigsaw coming back later?" Paul asks me.

Even though I know they're both aware of the nights Jigsaw spends here, heat still travels over my cheeks. "I'm not sure. I didn't have a chance to talk to him before we left the cemetery."

"The big one, Wrath?" Paul spreads his arms far apart like he's trying to hug a mountain. "He said his club set up a reception at their clubhouse for Ulfric and his guys."

Probably the one in close proximity to their strip club. Is *that* what Jigsaw's doing now? Hanging out with his friends in a place that smells like sweat, dollar bills, and desperation?

"All right," Dad says. "You two get some rest. I have Ken and Bruce on call in case we receive any calls tonight."

I didn't realize Dad trusted those guys so much. But I'm so thankful I'm not on call tonight that I'm not going to question it.

I murmur a goodnight to Paul and my father, then slip out of the office. In my apartment, I toe off my shoes and set them neatly by the door. Gretel comes running and twines herself around my ankles.

"Mraow."

I crouch down to pet her, running my hand over her silky fur until she's purring like a little motorboat and rubbing her chin against my fingers.

"Are you hungry, girl?"

She lets out an irritated, *"Nrrrow,"* and scampers into the kitchen like I've failed her at every level by working all day.

"Well, you're going to have to wait until I change."

"Mraow."

She follows me into my bedroom, expressing her annoyance with a chorus of tiny "Mrrrp" noises.

"I'm going, I'm going." I strip off my suit, unbutton my blouse and pull on my thickest, softest sweatpants and hoodie. Funeral armor off. Comfort armor on.

"All right. Dinnertime."

Gretel leaps into the air and bolts into the hallway.

She lets out a few impatient *"Mrrrows"* as I pop the lid off the can. She vibrates with excitement, practically dancing in place. Her purrs are so loud, it takes a second to register the low, distant rumble outside the window.

My heart jumps.

The sound grows—closer now. Deeper. Familiar.

I set the dish down and Gretel attacks the food with savage *get in my belly* energy, purring and making wet smacking noises with every bite.

Am I nuts, or is that Jigsaw's bike?

I straighten and tilt my head toward the window.

I've heard dozens of Harleys today but this one sounds familiar.

The noise draws closer, then abruptly cuts off.

Normally, I'd be halfway down the stairs by now.

But tonight, I don't feel that same magnetic pull.

Is he coming to see me? Spend the night? What explanation can he possibly have for his silence the last few days? I've been dying to know.

But now I'm afraid to find out.

CHAPTER TWELVE

JIGSAW

I never had the chance to talk to Margot at the cemetery. Right after the service, Wrath pulled me aside—insisting we roll over to Remy's bar with Ulfric and the remaining Wolf Knights.

I stayed long enough to choke down a burger and shoot the shit. When Dex announced they were moving the party to Crystal Ball, I ordered a bag of cookies and a buffalo chicken sandwich to go and said my goodbyes.

I've waited long enough.

Margot needs to hear this from me—tonight.

The Cedarwood home looks completely different now. Parking lot empty. No one lingering outside on the porch or on the sidewalk. Only one light on downstairs and one glowing faintly on the third floor.

I roll into my usual spot and cut the engine. The silence descends over me. After a few seconds, the faint night noises return—wind skimming across the pavement and rattling crumpled leaves on brittle branches, the crackling *tick, tick, tick* of my bike cooling.

When I make it to the back porch, it's empty and dark. She usually meets me by now. Maybe she's asleep? Or hasn't come home yet? I glance at the garage, but the bay doors are all shut—no way to tell if her car's there or not. No warm porch light on tonight, either.

She's given me the code for the back door before, but it feels wrong to use it tonight—like I'd be breaking in.

I pull out my phone and send her a text.

I'm out back.

A second later, the lock gives a low, mechanical hum. I hurry up the steps and slip inside before it re-engages.

Downstairs is quiet and shadowy. Only a faint glow spills from under the door to her dad's office.

Not wanting to run into him, I head straight for the stairs, pulling off my gloves as I go.

I've got the sandwich in one hand, and the cookies tucked under my arm like some kind of pathetic peace offering. *Here's a lukewarm, soggy sandwich and a handful of cookies—sorry I've been such a dick.*

I reach the top step just as her door swings open.

There's my girl. Standing in the bright light of her apartment, she radiates peace, happiness, and every other good thing I never thought I wanted.

I hesitate, feeling like a demon trying to sneak past the pearly gates.

"Are you coming in?" Margot asks.

"Yeah." I hurry and cross the threshold. I push the bags of food into her hands. "I brought you something from Remy's. It's probably cold and soggy by now and the cookies are probably—"

She stares down at the crumpled paper bags in her hands and smiles. "Thank you. I haven't eaten yet." She walks toward the kitchen and sets the bags on the counter, then turns toward me with raised eyebrows.

She's not distracted by the food. Nope, she's waiting for answers. I unlace my boots, toeing them off and setting them next to her shoes, then shrug off my cut and hang it by the closet.

By the time I finally face her, she's got the sandwich on a plate, two glasses of sparkling water poured, and the cookies spread out on a napkin.

"You didn't bring anything for yourself?" She gestures toward the sandwich as she hops up onto one of the bar stools.

"Uh, no. I ate there."

She stares at me for a few beats, then picks up the smooshed sandwich and takes a bite. Her eyes close and her lips gently curve as she slowly chews.

"Still warm." She dabs at her lips with a napkin. "And only a little soggy."

I blow out a breath. "Good."

"I hope you're not here just to talk about the condition of a chicken sandwich, though?"

I love the gentle way she calls me out on my bullshit.

"No."

She takes another bite and side-eyes me while my mind races to put the last few days into words that make sense.

By the time she takes a sip of water and sets her glass down, my tongue's still frozen.

"Okay." She swivels her stool to face me. "Let's start small. Where've you been the last few days?"

"Around. Took a ride to Maine."

"What's in Maine?"

"Ocean. The beach."

Her lips pinch with annoyance. "The closest beach to us is actually in Connecticut. New Jersey, Rhode Island, and Cape Cod are all also closer. While I love Maine, why did *you* go there?"

"To clear my head."

She takes a long, deep, irritated breath. "Okay. Let's try this again. You left here the other night and said Z needed help at Crystal Ball. So what kind of stripper emergency made you cut off contact and ride all the way to Maine to 'clear your head'..." Her voice trails off and she frowns. "Did you discover that you knocked up a stripper or something?"

The idea's so absurd that laughter explodes out of me.

Margot's frown deepens.

Oh, shit. She's seriously worried about that. I reach over and wrap my hand around hers, squeezing gently. "No. Absolutely not."

She sighs. "So, what happened?"

"A...family thing."

"Is Jezzie okay?"

"Yeah, she's fine. Still having fun at her job."

"Good." She picks up a fork and knife, pushes the bun off the sandwich and cuts a small piece of chicken off.

"My half-brother showed up looking for me."

Her fork clatters against the plate.

She turns to fully face me and rests her hand on my thigh. "Why didn't you just tell me?"

I stare into her eyes, ashamed to admit how fucked up Cain's visit has me.

"Because when you asked if I knew whether it was possible that I had other siblings out there, I *lied*."

She blinks as she absorbs the truth.

"The girl who helped me leave," I continue, "was pregnant when I left." I close my eyes in disgust. "She was a kid herself. Only sixteen at the time."

Margot wrinkles her nose.

"Yeah, I know," I say, acknowledging her obvious disgust. "I met him when I went back for Jezzie."

I explain every part of that day in as much detail as I can remember and when I'm finished, Margot doesn't run screaming from her apartment or ask me to leave.

She slides off her stool, pushes her way between my knees and slides her arms around my middle, squeezing me tight without saying a word.

After a second or two, I wrap my arms around her, holding her close. The painful wires that wrapped around my lungs the night Cain showed up slowly unwind and I can finally *breathe*.

"I love you, Jensen," she whispers in my ear.

I shared some of the most evil things I've ever done, and she still loves me.

"Why didn't you just tell me, though?"

"I didn't know how to tell you about Cain." I shrug and shift my gaze to the floor. "I should've just told you before."

"We...haven't been together very long. I don't expect you to disclose every secret in your past to me all at once."

"This was kind of a big one."

"Maybe. But it was wrapped up in a lot of complicated feelings and painful memories."

"Memories?" I let out a bitter laugh. "I don't actually have a lot of those. So much of my childhood's a fucking blur." I squeeze my eyes shut and rub my finger between them as if that might reveal something.

Margot's warm hand wraps around mine and drags it away from my face. "That's because your brain wasn't allowed to make childhood memories. You were trying to survive. Instead of storing memories, you were avoiding danger. You were bracing for impact because you probably never knew what would trigger you father's punishments."

And just like that, Margot has described exactly how I felt as a kid. "Even when I thought I knew what to do to avoid punishment, I'd still do something that needed 'correction.'"

"Because it was never about you or what you did," Margot says. "It was about your father's need for control."

I turn that over in my head. She's right, but it's still hard to accept.

"I wish you'd told me," she adds. "We're both adults, I would have understood."

"Eh." I tilt my head. "Emotionally, I'm basically a teenager in an adult's body."

Shaking her head, she pulls away, but a small smile plays over her lips. "That you're aware of your emotions at all says you're more mature than you realize."

"I did a shitty thing, Margot." I gently squeeze her hand and lift it to my lips, brushing a kiss against her knuckles. "You're the kindest, most compassionate person I know. And I did something so fucking heartless by turning my back on that kid."

"You know me better than that, don't you? I'm always on your side no matter what." She trails her fingers through my hair, gently stroking. "You didn't even know him. You left the farm before he was born. I can understand why you wouldn't feel connected to him. Your dad impregnated a...teenager." Her voice lowers to a conspiratorial whisper. "I can see why you'd have trouble processing that and seeing Cain as a sibling."

I hadn't thought of it quite that way. I nod slowly, letting her words settle.

"You know everything about me," she continues, "and you've never judged or turned away."

"This is different. You kill in defense of the innocent. I hurt someone who *was* innocent."

"Hurt? How?"

Hasn't she been listening? I shrug and glance away. "Tried to forget he existed. Took him away from his sister. Sent him and his mother away instead of—I don't know. Doing more?"

"Jensen." Sympathy and exasperation color her voice. "What were you, nineteen? Twenty? Cain *had* a mother. He *did* have someone to look after him. Seems like you took care of Ruth and her son in the best way you could, given the situation."

She pauses, her eyes searching mine. "Besides, Jezzie and her safety was your priority. I think you did the right thing. Getting her far away from that place and all those bad memories was probably the safest solution."

"That's what I thought at the time too."

"Good." She pats my leg. "So, you already know the answer."

I lean back, letting her words settle into the spaces where guilt has lived for so long. I'm not ready to let go of it, yet.

"Some of the best—and only—memories I have from my childhood that don't involve punishments are with Rooster. Or Rooster's mom."

Margot tilts her head, listening closely.

"She was the kindest woman. Always tried to include me in stuff. I think my dad freaked her out, but she still came to pick me up for trips to the beach, or the fair, or whatever."

"I'm surprised your dad let you go with an 'outsider.'"

"I think he hoped to pull her into his 'flock,' honestly."

"What happened to her?"

Pain knots in my chest, sharp and deep. "I thought Rooster's life was perfect. But home was hell for him too—just in a different way."

She nods once as if that's a sufficient explanation and she won't pry into someone else's story to satisfy her curiosity.

That alone makes me love her even more.

CHAPTER THIRTEEN

"Thank you for listening to all of that." Jigsaw forces a tight smile. "And still saying you love me."

His tone's light. Like he doesn't actually believe it. How could he think he failed anyone when he did more for his sister, brother, and even his father's victims than any other person would?

He thinks I'm some sort of saint for loving him? He couldn't be more wrong.

How do I say this, so he understands and absorbs my words?

"Of course, I still love you. How could I not?" I reach for his hand, curling my fingers lightly around his. "You seem to have mistakenly placed me on a pedestal."

"That's because you're perfect," he says, dragging his gaze over my face.

"No, I'm not." I squeeze his hand gently, urging him to listen to me. "Jensen, please take a breath. Quiet your mind—"

"I don't think mediation is the answer right now." He lets out a humorless laugh.

I tilt my head and give him my sternest stare. "Your cute quips aren't needed right now. I want you to actually *hear* what I'm saying, not sit there churning up excuses to give me when I'm finished speaking."

He closes his eyes and draws in a long breath, then slowly exhales like he's forcing himself to shut out everything else.

"Thank you." I place my hand over his. "I *love* you. You have more courage than anyone I've ever known—"

"Make no mistake, Margot. I went back for my sister. But I went back for revenge too. I was planning to kill him whether I found him hurting Jezzie or not." He swallows hard. "He was a dead man."

"And *you* should know that I understand that better than anyone. However." I take a breath. "If you make a mistake, I have no problem telling you so—"

"So you admit I made a mistake?" A spark of vindication lights his eyes.

"No." I squeeze his earlobe and gently tug. "List-en-ing, remember?"

He snaps his mouth shut. Probably a rare occurrence.

I wait a beat to see if he'll remain quiet.

"Even *if* you make a mistake, I'll still love you. I love you so much that I'll tell you you've made a mistake, *and* I'll try to help you fix it."

He swallows hard and slowly nods.

"But I meant what I said," I continue before he jumps in again. "I *don't* think the way you handled things *when you were a teenager* was a mistake. I think what you did was compassionate and empathetic."

"How?" His eyes widen in disbelief. "How can you say that?"

"Oh, buddy." I let out a weary laugh. "Buckle up because I have a list of reasons for you." I hold up my hand, curling it into a fist and stick out my thumb. "One, you could've *not* gone back for your sister at all. It sounds like you had a good life with Rooster's family."

He opens his mouth—probably to object—but I quickly cut him off with a headshake. "I know things were hard there too. His aunt and uncle sound like they were good people who died way too young. But in the middle of your grief, you still made your sister a priority. *You rescued her*. It sounds like you saved her life. Or saved her from a traumatic injury."

His eyes shine and he closes them, slowly turning his head away.

I won't let him sink into those dark memories. "Stay with me." I squeeze his hand.

He nods but still doesn't look at me.

"You could've just grabbed Jezzie and run," I say. "That would've been the easiest thing. But you didn't."

His jaw tightens, but he says nothing.

"You could've killed your father and left everyone else to rot—but you didn't. Even though someone might've seen you, might've turned you in… you didn't hurt anyone else."

I keep my voice steady. "You could've taken the money and vanished. But instead, you tried to do right by the people your father hurt. You tried to restore his victims in the best way you could."

The enormity of what he actually did catches in my throat. "Your actions were thoughtful and kind at an age where most men only care about getting laid and partying."

He meets my stare head-on. "I did *plenty* of that afterward. I'm not a hero, Margot."

How cute, he thinks he can scare me away with his playboy past. As if I didn't already know. "You're a brother. A good friend. And the *best* boyfriend."

"Such a great boyfriend that I took a joyride to Maine instead of telling you what a fuckup I am?" He raises an eyebrow.

"Your communication skills need improvement." My lips curve into a teasing smile. "But I'm willing to work with you."

He slides his hands over my hips, holding me in place. "You're like this shining light for me. All goodness and warmth. I want to bask in that and keep you away, far away, from the bad things in my life."

"Jensen." I use the most patient, authoritative tone I can muster. "I live in a funeral home. I've been surrounded by death and darkness from birth. It's twisted me in ways you already know." I cup his face, staring into his questioning eyes. "I love you. And I accept all of you. Not just the fun parts."

"Thank you," he rasps.

"But don't do this to me again," I add with a harsher bite to my tone than I intended. "The days of silence. Worrying about you. Not knowing where we stand." My throat tightens. "It was humiliating asking Wrath if you were okay. And I felt like an idiot texting Shelby."

"But you did it."

I can't tell if that's pride or disbelief in his voice.

"Yes. I swallowed my pride and asked because I love you."

The cobwebs of the past entangling him seem to snap. He leans forward and takes my hands. "I'm sorry. I'm not used to having someone worry about me."

"I'm not saying I want to stalk your every move. But you left here abruptly, then nothing. I was worried."

"I know. I won't do it again." He rubs his thumb over the back of my hand. "I'm sorry I made you worry."

Will he be able to keep his promise?

Who knows.

I can't keep raking guilt over him. He's carrying enough.

I take a breath and gently shift the conversation. "When do I get to meet Cain?"

He sits back, a frown creasing his forehead. "I don't know if that's a good idea."

"Why?"

"I don't trust him."

I plant my hand on my hip. "He's a kid."

"So? I just told you what a shitty thing I did to him and his mom." He holds up his hand as if he wants to preemptively cut off any argument. "What you said made me look at the situation differently, but that doesn't mean *he* sees it that way."

"What did he say when you met with him?"

"Not much. He wants to see Jezzie. I told him she's busy with school right now."

"Jensen." I fail at keeping the scolding tone from my voice.

"You don't get it." His voice lowers. "Jezzie was furious with me for years." He swallows hard and glances away. "When I took her away from the farm, she assumed she was coming to live with me."

My stomach sinks. "Oh no."

"She didn't remember our aunt. She was only a baby when we moved out west. I had some money, but I didn't know how to raise a teenage girl, and I didn't have a stable living situation for her."

"Understandable." It's not even remotely the same thing, but as someone who lost her mother young, if my brothers had tried to raise me, that would've been a disaster.

"When we got to my aunt's and Jezzie realized—"

"No! You drove all that way and never explained it to her?"

His eyes narrow. "No, Margot. I didn't know how." His expression softens. "Besides, I told myself if Angela seemed off, or if anything felt wrong, I'd figure out a way to keep Jezzie with me."

Well, that's something. I blow out a breath. "But their reunion went well?"

"Oh yeah. They got along great. Angela set up a really nice room for Jezzie. She never married or had kids. But she actually seemed excited to have her. She was my mom's older sister, and it hurt her when my mom cut off contact. So she welcomed Jezzie into her home. Me, not so much." He lets out a bitter laugh. "I think I reminded her too much of my dad or something."

"That's unfair. Did she know what happened?"

"I never told her. But I'm sure she guessed."

I nod slowly. "And Jezzie? She was happy?"

"Oh yeah. Loved it at first. Angela took her shopping for normal clothes—stuff she'd never had before. She was excited." His jaw tightens. "But when it was time for me to leave, she lost it. Screamed, cried. Wouldn't speak to me for months. Angela kept me updated, but it took a long time for Jezzie to come around."

"She probably felt abandoned," I say gently. "Even if it was the best choice."

"Yeah. She thawed eventually. When I finally moved to the East Coast, I was closer, so I visited more often but as you've witnessed, things are still tense sometimes."

"It had to be hard to stay mad at you for leaving her someplace she was happy."

He shrugs. "That's one way to look at it, yeah. But as prickly as she can be, Jezzie's sensitive. She doesn't like hurting people's feelings. Well, except mine."

I elbow him lightly. "Maybe stop being so stoic and let her know you *have* feelings."

A slight smirk tilts his lips. "Sure, that's an option."

"Does your aunt know about Cain?"

"Good question. I don't know if Jezzie ever mentioned him to Angela or not."

"Do you think Jezzie wants to see him?"

"She rarely mentions him. I'm the one who brought him up last time I saw her."

I bite my lip, unsure I should offer my opinion. "I feel bad for Cain. He has no family." *And no one seems to care about him at all.*

He exhales a long breath, like the weight of that landed hard. "I know. I told you I'm a piece of shit."

"I didn't say that."

He rakes a hand through his hair. "I couldn't protect Jezzie back then. You were right about what my father did to her—he could've killed her or left her with brain damage. I should've been there sooner. That's why I *have* to know Cain's not a threat before I let them near each other again."

I understand that. I love him for it.

But several doubts keep circling in the back of my mind.

What if Jezzie doesn't want to see Cain? What if Jigsaw decides he doesn't want a relationship with him at all? The only brotherhood he seems to need is his club.

Cain came all this way.

Looking for a family that might end up rejecting him.

Again.

CHAPTER FOURTEEN

JIGSAW

SHARING ALL OF THAT WITH MARGOT WASN'T AS AWFUL AS I KEPT telling myself it would be. She listened. Challenged me in that quiet, relentless way of hers. Pushed me into seeing the situation in a different way—something no one else has ever done before.

"So." She strokes her hand over my arm. "How did you leave things with Cain?"

I already sense her protective side stirring. The same instinct she uses to care for the grieving families who walk into the funeral home is now aiming to wrap itself around my half-brother. She's not gonna like my answer. "He's sticking around. Staying at a hotel for now."

"By himself?"

I shrug. "He was already staying there before he found me. The guys offered to help. Teller's got a place open in that building he owns downtown. Said Cain could use it if he wants. And one of Wrath's friends runs a gym nearby—he might be able to hook him up with a job if Cain wants it."

"Wow. That's really generous." Then with a touch too much cheer in her voice, she adds, "Oh, his friend Jake? The one who came by with Wrath yesterday?"

My jaw tightens. "You met him, huh?"

"I did. He was nice." She taps her finger against her bottom lip, eyes sparkling like she senses the jealous beast waking inside me and wants to poke him. "Wrath went out of his way to tell Jake I'm a friend of the club and your ol' lady."

I grin like an asshole. "He did, huh?" I'll have to remember to thank Wrath.

She tilts her head, still playful. "It's weird—I never saw Jake at the funeral. But I guess it was busy. I might've missed a few guests."

More like Jake realized he better keep his distance from my girl.

Her smile fades. Fatigue creeps around the edges of her eyes, the long day catching up with her.

"Hey, let's put this aside for a bit." I glance at the clock in her kitchen. "It's late. You've had a long, grueling day."

She yawns and nods. "I have another funeral tomorrow too."

"Shit, really? And you're letting me keep you up this late?"

"Death doesn't keep a schedule." Her smile fades. "It'll be a much quieter, quicker service."

"Good." I'm so fucking proud of what she accomplished. Her dad and cousin helped too but I sensed Margot's touch in so many small details today. "Hey, you did a really great job on Whisper's funeral. It must've been complicated but everything looked seamless. Ulfric was really pleased. When we were at the bar, he kept talking about how nice you and your dad are and how much you helped Abby."

Margot's eyes glisten and she turns way. "That's really nice to hear. Thank you."

"Hey." I gently grip her chin, encouraging her to face me again. "I wouldn't say it if it wasn't true."

One corner of her mouth tips up and she nods.

I take both of her hands in mine and draw her closer. "Thank you for listening to all of that stuff about my family."

She slips her hands free and wraps her arms around my neck, pressing into me. The weight of her, the way she fits against me— perfect. So fucking perfect.

"You can tell me anything." She turns her head, her hair tickling my neck, and whispers against my ear, "I'm very good at keeping secrets."

"I know you are."

As she pulls back, her earrings catch the light from the kitchen—the blue sapphires she wore to keep one of my club's colors close to her today.

I let my gaze drift over her oversized dark purple sweatshirt and matching sweatpants. A black cat is embroidered on the front, and another peeks around one leg of her pants like it's stalking prey.

I pinch the soft fabric between my fingers. "This is cute. Looks like something Gretel would've picked out for you."

She glances down at the embroidery and smiles. "She *is* a bit of a narcissist, isn't she?"

I tilt to the side, searching behind Margot. "Where is she, anyway?"

"I fed her when I got home. She's probably snoozing her way through a food coma by now."

I smile and squeeze her hips again, loving the feel of her—delicate but solid in all the ways I need. My fingers slip under the hem of her sweatshirt, searching for warm, bare skin.

She twitches. "You're tickling me."

"Hey, I'm grimy from riding all day. Will you come take a shower with me?"

Interest sparks in her eyes. "Sure."

"Excellent." I slide off my stool, curl my hand around hers and pull her toward the hallway.

"Right now?"

"It's only getting later." I stop outside her laundry room and start unbuttoning my flannel.

"You're stripping in my laundry room?" she asks, arching an eyebrow.

"Yeah. I'm all about efficiency, baby."

Her shoulders shake with laughter as she gathers my clothes, tossing each item into the washer.

"I know how to do laundry," I tease. "I ran the club's laundromat downstate for quite a while."

"I'm all about efficiency too, baby." She grins as she tosses my words back at me. "Besides, the sooner you're naked, the better." Her gaze travels over my body, devouring every inch of my bare skin, finally landing on my jeans.

It's such an unexpected thing for Margot to say, but I hold in my laughter. Still watching her face, I slowly pull my belt free and set it on the dryer, then empty my pockets one item at a time.

She sucks in a breath as I pop the top button of my jeans loose and slowly lower the zipper.

"You want to help?" I tease. "Or stand there and watch?"

She continues staring, following the movement of my hands. "You're doing fine on your own."

Holding her gaze, I let the silence stretch as I push my jeans down and kick them off, catching them mid-air. "You sure about that? Because you're still fully dressed, and that seems awfully inefficient."

That earns me a small smile. "You have a point." She holds her arms over her head. "I could use some help though."

"My pleasure." I step closer and hook my fingers into the hem of her sweatshirt. The restraint I display should earn me a medal as I slowly drag the fabric up, revealing her soft curves, pale skin, and finally a blue lace bra. "You really were wearing blue underneath."

"You thought I was lying?" Her words are muffled. Struck dumb by the dark blue lace encasing the heavy curves of her breasts, I stopped before taking her sweatshirt all the way off. I hurry to pull her arms free and toss the shirt aside. She shakes her hair out and the sapphires in her ears catch the light again.

"I want to see if your panties match."

She laughs softly. "Why would I lie?"

I slip my fingers under the waistband of her pants and tug them down her hips, kneeling to kiss her stomach. Matching blue lace comes into view.

I flick my gaze up to hers. "Beautiful."

"Thank you." She runs her fingers through my hair.

I yank her pants off the rest of the way, tossing them aside and run my greedy hands up her calves, up her thighs, straight to her center.

She lets out a needy gasp when I press my lips to the thin material and slowly pull it away with my teeth. "I've been dying to do this all day," I rasp.

"R-really?"

"Yeah." I slide the panties down her legs and help her step out. "It's so pretty on you, but I need the bra off too."

She wiggles out of my hold, turns and pulls her hair to the side, revealing the clasp, silently telling me to do it myself.

Chuckling softly, I sink my teeth into one round cheek, then kiss my way to the base of her spine. "Smart ass."

I rise and work the clasp loose.

She slips the straps off her shoulders and tosses the bra to the side. "Come on." She holds out her hand to me.

"Uh, I had other plans in mind." My mouth protests but my feet follow her around the corner into the bathroom.

"You said you wanted to take a shower."

"I wanted to get you *naked*." I wasn't lying about feeling gritty from the day, though. "But I'm willing to multi-task."

She glances at me over her shoulder as she turns on the shower spray. "In the name of efficiency, right?"

"Brains and beauty. I love you." I mold myself to her back, wrapping my arms tight around her. I don't know what it is about Margot, but I want to give her everything and anything in the world. I want to give her the best version of me even if I don't know what the fuck that is.

She tips her head back, resting it on my chest and stares up at me. "I love you too." She rubs her hand over my arms. "Ready? Oh, let me put my hair up."

I release her and she hurries to the counter to pick up a bright-green claw-shaped thing. She winds her hair into a thick, messy knot and secures it with the clip.

The door lets out a low creak as I open it. Steam billows out and I reach in to adjust the temperature. "Hurry."

She reaches into a cabinet and pulls out two thick yellow towels and hangs them on the hooks outside the shower. "On my way."

I step in and hold out my hand for her.

As soon as she's inside, I lean down and slide my lips over hers. All my blood rushes south as she opens for me. She reaches down and wraps her hands around my cock and strokes.

I hiss in a breath. "Fuck, not yet, Margot."

She pushes out her bottom lip. "But you look like you need some attention."

"You're going to attend to me, don't worry."

She grips me harder, working her soft warm hands over me with quick, firm tugs.

"Fuuuck." My legs shake from how good that feels. She's distracting me from my plans. "Turn around and put your hands against the wall."

She frowns. "Are you sure?" Her hand tightens around me, and she strokes faster. As much as I'm trying to stay in control, my hips jerk in time with her movements. "It doesn't feel like you want me to stop," she adds, voice low and taunting.

"You want to make me come?"

She's staring so intently at my dick, another wave of pleasure shudders through me.

"Yes."

I squeeze my eyes shut. *Maybe I should.* Shooting my load now might help me clear my head so I can focus all of my attention on her. My tongue already tingles with the need to taste her.

"Little harder," I encourage.

She squeezes and gives a quick twist at the end of each stroke.

"Just like that." I pant the words. My pulse pounds through my ears. A long, satisfied groan bursts out of me as my cum shoots all over her stomach and leg.

She's wearing a pleased grin when I lift my gaze to her face.

"You're so naughty. Interfering with my plans." The doofy grin on my face negates the playful scolding I'm trying to give her. "Now put your hands on the wall for me."

"You got it," she says with an extra dose of sass. She turns and presses her palms to the slick tile.

"Oh, fuck, you're gorgeous." With my heart rate back to normal and my head clearer, I'm free to take my time, allowing my gaze to devour every inch of bare, wet skin in front of me.

I pour bodywash into my palm and lather her up, mapping every curve. When I'm done, I wrap my arms around her body, raising my hands to her breasts, kneading them and teasing her nipples. "You're irresistible."

She lets out a happy sigh.

"Don't conk out on me yet," I warn as the water pours over us in a constant stream. "I still have a lot of things I want to do with you tonight."

"I'm looking forward to them."

I slide my hands down to her hips and turn her around, nudging her back against the tile. Steam curls around us, clinging to the air.

"You have any idea how many people I wanted to punch today for staring at you?"

She flicks her gaze to the ceiling. "Be serious."

"I'm dead serious." I trace my fingers along her damp collarbones, then down over the slick tops of her breasts. "But you're all mine."

"Yes, I am."

I lean down and brush a kiss over her lips, trace my tongue against her neck. Warm water glides over her skin, like it's following the path my tongue wants to take. I duck lower and suck her nipple into my mouth. She lets out a small whimper when I slip my fingers between her legs but it's not enough.

Lowering myself to the slippery floor, I kiss her stomach, then grip her thighs. "Open for me."

She slides her foot as far as it can go in the tub. I lift one of her legs, guiding it over my shoulder. A startled noise has me glancing up and she's clawing at the wall, like she's afraid she'll fall.

"I won't let go." I swoop in, flattening my tongue and sweeping from her center to her clit, smiling at how good she tastes. Everything I've wanted all day.

She gasps and spears her fingers through my hair.

"I wanted to bury my face between your legs the second you

showed me those earrings today," I murmur against her wet skin. With the water pounding over us and my face mashed up against her blond curls, I'm not sure if she hears me or not.

She squirms and moans with every lick. When I latch onto her clit and suck hard, she arches her back, pushing herself against my face.

My knees ache from kneeling on the tile but fuck I want to make her come so fucking bad.

Her body jerks and she whimpers, but not in the usual sexy way.

I glance up and she's struggling again.

Water streams in my eyes and up my nose, choking me for a second. I said I wanted to drown in her but not like this.

I reach for the water and shut it off. "Let's move this to the bedroom."

"No." The forlorn but desperate pout on her face tickles an inner sadist I didn't know I had. "I was so close."

"I'll make it worth it." I drop a kiss on her shoulder. "Promise."

Damn she's pretty all surrounded by steam, cheeks rosy from the hot water. I slide the door open and reach for a towel.

"But what if I can't come now?" She wiggles and rubs her thighs together. "I feel like a bottle of champagne you stuffed the cork back into."

Jesus, she's so fucking cute.

"I will dedicate the rest of the night to making sure you come all over my face. Or any other part of me you want." I yank the other towel free and quickly rough it over my body, wrap it around my hips, then take hers and gently pat her dry.

She's silent now. No more twitching either.

"You okay?"

She tugs the towel out of my hands and wraps it around her body. "My thighs are too big, aren't they?" She tips her head toward the shower. "I couldn't give you enough room to work with?"

"What?" I scowl, confused by the question but not liking the direction it's headed. "No." I swipe my hand over my chest and throw on my cockiest smirk. "Look, I know I've got the body of a thirty-year-old Greek god, but I also have the knees of an eighty-year-old linebacker. Kneeling on the tile was killing me."

Would I admit that to anyone else? *Nope.* But I can't have her thinking she's the problem. Not even for a second.

Her anxious frown shifts to playful. "And the humility of a rock star at the top of the charts." Her smile fades. "Sorry, I don't want you in pain."

"My own fault for not being able to control myself." I scoop her into my arms, and she lets out a soft squeak, quickly looping her arms around my neck.

Her skin's still warm from the shower, slick and damp against mine. The bathroom's full of steam and the faint scent of her bodywash clings to both of us. I'm going to need to buy my own bottle of whatever that is to use when we're apart.

I step into the hallway, headed toward her bedroom, which has never seemed farther away. She buries her face against my neck, her breath warm on my skin, her tongue sliding over a sensitive spot I didn't know I had. We may have started out with me giving her some "lessons," but she's taught me just as much.

Halfway to her room, Gretel streaks across the hallway, letting out a yowl as if we've offended her.

Margot shakes with laughter.

The knot on my towel loosens. My hands are too full to fix it. And a second later, it unravels completely and lands on the floor.

"I'll get it later," Margot says, peering over my shoulder. "Don't stop."

"Wasn't planning to." I push the bedroom door open with my foot, then kick it closed after I cross the threshold.

Next to the bed, I stop and set her on her feet.

Margot

My legs shake, too weak to hold me up. Jigsaw doesn't give me a chance to compose myself, though. He tugs at the towel tucked around my body, ripping it free.

"I need you on the bed." He cups my face and brushes a kiss on my cheek. "Right now. We have unfinished business."

"Yes, we do." I sit on the edge of the bed and scoot into the center. "Where do you want me?"

I stare wide-eyed at the glory of Jigsaw's naked body as he stalks to the foot of the bed, all coiled intensity, a predator waiting to pounce on his next meal. Me.

"Right in the middle. Up on the pillows." His voice sharpens, all command and focus—barking orders like he's directing a scene he's already played out a hundred times in his head.

Excited by his intensity, I can't arrange myself in the spot he wants fast enough. I stretch out my legs, crossing them at the ankles.

"Goddamn, you're perfect." He rubs his fingers over his chin.

Fiery sparks race over my exposed skin.

"Feet flat on the bed. You know better."

I bend my legs, keeping them tight together.

Shaking his head, he rests his knee on the mattress and slides his hands between my legs. Palms against my inner thighs, he pries my legs open. "Stay like that for me."

He stretches out on his stomach and hooks his arms around my legs, sliding me to his waiting mouth.

"Look at you." His low, silky murmur travels straight to my center. He dusts small kisses behind my knees, then drags his tongue to the crease of my thigh. "So pretty and wet for me."

"Well," I exhale a shaky breath, "we did just get out of the shower."

He swipes his tongue against me, and I bite my fist to keep from screaming, it feels so good. The empty ache I'd felt in the shower, before we stopped, pulses to life as he lazily slides his tongue along the seam of my lips.

He lets out a long, contented groan. My vision swims but I force myself to focus on him. How much he seems to love pleasing me.

He licks, kisses, and sucks at me with a need so wild it vibrates through his whole body. His arms are locked around my thighs, holding me open, fingers spreading me, tongue teasing me higher and higher. The bed rocks beneath us, jolting with every thrust of his hips against the mattress, matching the rhythm of his tongue. Sensations overwhelm me but watching *his* excitement while using his mouth on me pushes me over the edge.

My vision goes black; I spread my legs impossibly wider and grind myself against him.

"Yes," he mumbles against me, sliding his tongue higher to circle my clit.

My low whimpers twist into sharp screams as he gently sucks.

"Oh." Broken sounds babble from me, and I let out another long moan when he slides a finger inside me, then another, carefully stretching and exploring me.

"I...I..."

"I know," he murmurs, kissing my inner thigh while his fingers keep working their magic. "You're so close, aren't you?"

"Yes," I whine and twist my hips.

"You're soaked. Dripping all over me." He wiggles his tongue against me. "I love it so fucking much."

He shoves his fingers into me harder, shaking my body, and lowers his head again.

Heat races over my skin. He groans and grips one thigh tighter, then curls his fingers inside me, rubbing and rubbing at a spot that sets off a blinding white flash behind my eyes.

He keeps licking and kissing, keeping my body purring and wanting, not allowing me a chance to come down.

"Oh my God," I whimper and try to press my knees together. "I can't."

"Yes, you can." He releases my leg but continues to work his fingers inside me in an erratic rhythm. "You're nice and ready for my cock. Aren't you?"

"So ready."

"Good." His mouth is a hot brand against my skin as he drops kisses over my stomach, up my ribs to the undersides of my breasts. His lips close around my nipple, licking and tugging. A shudder of pleasure rolls through me.

Finally, he settles over me, his damp chest warm against my

breasts, a happy, playful expression on his handsome face. I hook my arm around his neck, dragging him closer and press my lips to his. His chin, his lips, are covered in my scent.

The warm, hard head of his cock nudges against me and I struggle to angle my hips, needing him inside me, letting out a pleading whine.

He smiles against my mouth. "What's wrong, little lady death?" He dips his head and sucks a sensitive spot below my ear. "Want something?"

"Yes." I glare at him, hoping he feels the blazing heat of my eyes.

He slides his hand under my butt, tilting my hips.

"This?" he teases, pushing inside me.

Need strips the smart comeback from my lips. I lift my legs, wrapping them around his waist. I rest my palms against his cheeks and desire locks our gazes together.

His cocky demeanor dissolves, lines of tension cord his neck as he slowly thrusts inside me. White-hot bursts of pleasure spark through me with each inch. The relentless stretch teeters on the edge of pain and pleasure, finally landing on *holy-fucking-amazing.*

"That's my girl," he whispers. "I love being inside you." He withdraws slightly, then thrusts in harder. "Could stay here all night."

I clench around him, and he squeezes his eyes shut.

"I like you on top of me like this," I whisper.

"I'm not squishing you?"

"No." I clamp my legs around him tighter and roll my hips. "You make me feel like a sexy, safe little bundle." I roll my hips again. "And hit something really good at this angle."

Amusement sparks over his expression and he slowly slides out, until only the tip of his cock is inside me. Then he eases inside deeper. Each time a little faster. His arms slide under me, cradling me to him until we're one sweaty, connected ball of pleasure.

All my awareness shatters as he works up to a relentless, pounding rhythm that rattles my bones. My breathy whimpers and his ragged breathing combine, filling the silence.

Wave after wave of warmth unfolds over me. I squeeze my eyes shut and allow the mindless bliss to obliterate me.

"Good girl," he croons against my neck, never slowing down.

Before I have a chance to recover or even open my eyes, he tightens his arms around me and twists our bodies, until I'm on top. Instinctively, my hips keep moving.

"What a beautiful view." He reaches up and brushes my hair out of my eyes.

I rest my hands on his chest and slowly roll my hips. "Are you tired? Need me to take over?" I tease.

A lazy smile curls his lip, and he tucks one hand behind his head. "Yup."

Still watching me, he brings his thumb to my mouth, pushing inside. "Suck for me."

I swirl my tongue around it a few times and he pulls free. "Now lean back."

"I thought this was my show?" It sounds like a protest, but my body's already following his directions. Delightful sensations pulse through me as I rest my hands against his thighs, slowing my movements.

He brings his thumb to my sensitized clit, rubbing gently. His touch still overwhelms me. I let out a yelp but circle my hips faster.

This orgasm rips through me in a brutal, mind-numbing streak. My back arches, my legs shake, bursts of light explode behind my eyelids, and my pulse pounds in my ears.

Heavy hands clamp down on my shoulders and he slams up into me, twisting my orgasm into something entirely new. Sharper. Deeper. I curl my hands around his arms, hanging on for dear life. My breasts bob and jiggle, and I release him to cross my arms over my chest.

"No." He taps my arm. "Either play with your nipples or put your hands back where they were. I want to watch." He shifts his hands to my waist, squeezing and holding me right where he wants.

I curl my fingers around his arms again.

"Good girl." He thrusts harder, lifting his head from the pillows to watch. "Fuck."

I cling to him, dazed from my orgasm but elated that I have the power to make him completely lose control.

Finally, he comes with a long, low groan. Our chests heave and our ragged breathing fills the room. He roughly pulls me down, hugging me to his chest and kisses my forehead. Breathing hard, eyes bright, he pulls away, eyes searching my face. "You kill me in the best way, woman."

"You give the best orgasms." I press a kiss over his heart. "And so many of them."

He rumbles with laughter, his body shaking under me. Unable to get enough of him, I bury my face against his neck and lick the salt from his skin.

He laughs harder. "That tickles."

"What?" I lick him again. "This?"

"Yes." He peppers several stinging smacks to my butt and squeezes one cheek.

A low buzz of excitement surges through me, almost drowning out his next words.

"I love your ass." He pops his hand against the other cheek and bites his lip. "Next time you're wearing one of your cute dresses, I want to find a nice, secluded spot, bend you over, lift your dress and have my way with you."

Desire explodes through me. "I'd like that." I pop another kiss on his cheek and roll to the edge of the bed.

"Where are you going?" He sits up, reaching for my hand.

Heat streaks over my cheek. "Uh, the bathroom."

He frowns and glances down at his body. "Yeah, I need to take care of this too."

I scurry off to do my thing, grabbing his towel off the floor on the way. Mid-pee, he pushes the door open. I blink and stare at him. "What are you doing?"

"Getting rid of this." He drops the spent condom in the trash can next to my sink.

"I'm peeing." *Or I was. I'm stuck and can't finish now.*

His lips twist with amusement. "I'm covered in your fluids, but you're worried about me hearing you pee?"

I guess he has a point. But I can't say that. He's too smug as it is.

He steps by me and leans into the shower, flipping the nozzle on. A hard stream of water patters against the tub. "Does that help?"

I flick my gaze to the ceiling and shake my head.

Laughing, he steps into the shower.

"Let it flow, let it flow," he sings in a high, goofy voice. "Don't hold it back anymoooore. Let it flow, let it *floooow.*"

"Oh my God!" I burst into giggles and finish my business. "Is that your version of..." It takes a moment to recognize the melody. "The song from *Frozen*?"

He rubs a clean spot on the glass and grins at me. "Did it help?"

I step into the shower with him. "Why do you even know that?"

"Uh, the kids watch it at the clubhouse. All. The. Time." He clicks open my bodywash and runs his soapy hands all over me, paying particular attention to my nipples. "I don't think I've ever watched it all the way through, but somehow the song gets stuck in my head."

If that isn't the cutest thing.

I glance down at his hands, still massaging and kneading. "I think my breasts are clean, now."

"I like to be thorough." He turns me toward the water and rinses the suds away.

This shower's quicker, quieter—more about comfort than heat.

When we're done, we towel off and climb into bed, the sheets cool against our still-damp skin.

I curl against him, head resting on his chest, our legs tangled under the covers. "I'm glad you're staying."

"There's nowhere else I'd rather be." His fingers absently rub the top of my head, gently kneading my scalp in a hypnotic way. "I'll have to leave for church in the morning, though."

"Mmmkay," I mumble. "I have to be up early." I pick up my head and find him watching me in the near-dark of my room. "What will you talk about in church? About the funeral and Wolf Knight biker-y stuff?"

He laughs softly, his chest rumbling under me. "You know I can't tell you club stuff. But yeah, probably that." He's quiet for a few minutes and I rest my head on him again.

I'm half-asleep when his chest dips, and he says, "One of the Wolf Knights I talked to today wants to patch over to our club. We're definitely discussing *that.*"

I blink and sit up, fully awake now. "You just said you can't tell me club stuff…then told me club stuff?"

He reaches for me, tugging on the ends of my damp hair. "I trust you. Besides, you already know a hell of a lot more than most ol' ladies."

Why does my skin tingle when he calls me that? I should be insulted. But I'm not. "Will you get in trouble for telling me that?"

He cocks his head, still watching me with that unreadable expression. "No." He hesitates. "But don't tell anyone club business that I share with you. Not even the other women. Every brother decides for himself how much he shares with his ol' lady."

"Okay." I turn that over for a few seconds. "Do the other ol' ladies know *my* role…what I've done to help the club?"

A few beats of silence pass. "Hope probably does."

"Ahhh, that makes sense. I felt like she was trying to see inside my skull at Teller's wedding."

Instead of laughing, he nods at my weak attempt at a joke. "She's a lawyer, so she probably gives Rock advice."

"A biker taking advice from a *woman?*" I tease.

His lips curl but he doesn't even try to deny the sexist reputation MCs have. "The best leaders seek advice from the smartest advisers." He's quiet for a few beats. "Charlotte probably knows a lot too. She's a lawyer but she also grew up in an MC. Grinder's kind of old school, so I don't think he'd involve Serena in club business." He clears his throat and glances away. "Unless he had to. Dex hasn't asked to patch Emily yet, so he probably doesn't share with her." He shrugs. "I don't know. *I* trust *you.*"

"Thank you." I yawn and he rubs the top of my head again. "Let's get some sleep. You have another busy day."

"Oh, are you going to talk to Cain tomorrow? After church?"

His body stiffens, the air shifting around us as if all the lovey, romantic vibes have been sucked out of the room. "I don't know. Maybe."

Danger. I can sense how much he doesn't want to talk about this, but it's too important to retreat now. "I think you should. And I can go with you, if you want. I should be done—"

"No. Not yet." He shifts, slipping his arm out from underneath me and turns on his side. Away from me. "Good night, Margot."

The room falls quiet, except for the random creaks of the old house and the steady rhythm of his breathing.

All right. He's shared so much with me today. Opened up and allowed me into some deep, dark places in his past that he's kept locked away for years.

I'll give him space. This moment of silence.

But I love him too much to let him run from this much longer.

CHAPTER FIFTEEN

JIGSAW

THE COLD MORNING WIND CUTS THROUGH MY FLANNEL AND CUT AS I ride through the quiet streets of Pine Hollow.

Margot was still asleep when I left—one arm flung across the bed, golden light spilling over her shoulder. Part of me wanted to stay. But my asshole side won, and I snuck out of the apartment and out the back door like a burglar.

She knew I had church today so it's not weird that I left. Never mind I'll be four fucking hours early. At least I didn't leave a shitty goodbye on a Post-it Note this time. I've got that going for me.

I slept like shit. Serves me right for shutting down when she asked a simple question about Cain.

Why am I still being such a coward about this?

When she prodded me to go visit my sister, everything turned out fine. Jezzie and I actually had a good day together. Talked to each other like adults.

Margot's never met Cain.

Still, Margot has good instincts. She knows people and understands all sorts of fucked-up family dynamics. Am I actually worried Cain's a threat? Or do I just want to hide from the truth of how I abandoned him?

I roll to a stop. No traffic in either direction. No one behind me either. Right will take me to the highway. Left will take me into the small city of Johnsonville. Wrath said he'd talk to Sully about giving my brother a job, but I'd rather know for sure that Sully's good with it.

I turn left.

Fifteen minutes later, I pull into the lot behind the strip of businesses along Main Street, stopping behind Strike Back Studio. Through the glass door, the place looks dark.

Shit. Are they even open this early?

I kill the engine and get off my bike.

Farther down the parking lot, a family's hauling big black garbage bags and bottles of detergent into the back door of one of the businesses. The scent of dryer sheets drifts in the wind. Another back door is propped open with a large, white trash can.

I pull on the wide metal handle of Strike Back's door and it swings open. That's a good sign.

Cool air and the sharp scent of industrial cleaner mixed with sweat and rubber mats hits me first. Ahhh, the comforting stink of hard work and discipline. Shiny hardwood floors stretch down a long hallway, leading to an open area with the front desk.

Muffled grunts and a repetitive clink of metal echoes from the other side of the wall. Otherwise, it's quiet. No music cranking through the system for motivation or background noise. I continue down the long hallway, stopping outside Sully's office. The door's ajar. I tap my knuckles on it, then push it open. Empty.

Weird. Every time I've stopped by to work out, either Sully, his brother Jake, or Sully's fiancée Aubrey are here. I wander toward the reception desk by the front door and peek around the corner leading into the workout area.

As I pass the men's locker room, the door swings open. Sully steps out, arms full of neatly folded white towels. He stops short when he sees me, surprise flashing across his face.

"Jigsaw? What are you doing here at this hour?" He recovers quickly and jerks his chin toward the front desk. "C'mon."

"I was in the neighborhood. Wanted to talk to you if you've got a minute."

"Yeah, sure." He drops the towels into a basket beside the desk and turns to face me.

The gym's quiet—just one guy across the room grinding out pull-ups, back to me, face tilted toward the ceiling.

"You working solo this morning?" I ask.

He scrubs a hand through his dark brown hair and huffs out a breath. "Yeah, Aubrey's at the house with my mom waiting for a furniture delivery." He casts a quick glance at the front door that looks out on Main Street. "And who knows where Jake is."

"Furniture delivery? You know, like, twenty bikers in the immediate area, why didn't you just ask us for help?"

He huffs a laugh. "It's a whole new bedroom set for my daughter—she's coming to live with us. I thought it'd be easier if the store delivered it but so far, not so much."

He runs his hand through his hair again, clearly stressed. I feel bad wasting his time with this, but I guess Wrath was right and he could use an extra set of hands. "So, what's on your mind?"

"Did Wrath talk to you?"

"About your brother? Yeah." He nods. "As you can see, I need the help."

"Okay. Good. Thanks." To a clean-cut family guy like Sully, what I'm about to say will sound shitty as hell but I need to get it out. "Look, I don't know how much he told you but we're only recently back in touch. I, uh, don't know him that well, yet."

He stares at me for a few beats, no judgment, just calm understanding. "You've met my little brother, right?" He lifts his eyebrows. "Jake's still a handful. I get it."

Our situations aren't even remotely similar, but the thought's nice. And now I've said what needed to be said.

Something buzzes and he slips his cell phone out of his pocket. "It's Aubrey. Let me grab this."

"Yeah, go ahead."

He walks a few steps away toward his office. It's impossible not to

overhear him, though. "What do you mean? Of course, they're supposed to carry it inside. Put him on the phone."

I walk over and tap Sully's shoulder. "You want me to go have a chat with 'em?" I knock my fists together to demonstrate the kind of conversation I have in mind.

He shakes his head quickly, lips twitching like he's not sure if I'm joking.

I glance around the near-empty gym. This isn't all that different from the laundromat, right? I can man the desk. Shouldn't have to talk to too many people.

"Go." I wave toward the back door. "I'll watch the place."

Sully freezes mid-step, eyebrows pulling tight like I offered to babysit his firstborn. "Uhhh…"

"I'm house-trained." I shrug. "I've run our club's businesses."

"Hold on, Aubrey." Sully lowers his phone and studies me. "You sure?"

"How much damage can I do?" I deadpan. His incredulous expression doesn't shift so I drop the dickish attitude. "I'm not gonna torch the place or scare your customers away. Promise."

He watches me for another second, then lifts the phone. "I'll be there in ten minutes, baby. Don't let them leave."

They hang up, and he flashes a relieved smile. "Thank you."

I glance at the clock above the front desk.

"Really, I won't be that long. Jake should be here soon. No classes until eleven, and it's usually quiet," he explains in a rush. "Aubrey's got the desk set up tight. If anyone calls, there's a binder with answers."

Shit. Maybe I'm in over my head. We don't have a binder at the laundromat. "I'll figure it out."

He runs his gaze over my jeans, boots, flannel, and leather cut— not exactly gym gear. "There's a cabinet in my office with clean sweats and stuff. Borrow anything you want. You can hang your cut in there. It'll be safe."

He makes the offer with quiet respect—like he understands I wouldn't hang my club's colors just anywhere. Not because he's uncomfortable having a biker repping his gym.

"Thanks. I got this, really. Go scare the piss out of those delivery guys."

He growls an unhappy sound and rushes out the back door. "Thanks," he calls over his shoulder.

I push my way into his office and hang up my cut on a hook behind the door. I take one look at the stack of nerdy polo shirts with the embroidered Strike Back logo on the chest pocket and decide my jeans and flannel will do just fine.

On my way out, I close the door behind me, then take a slow lap around the place. The guy who'd been busy doing chin-ups before has moved on to knocking out a brutal set of push-ups.

Sully's upgraded some of the equipment in one of the rooms. I check out the new stuff, then return to the front desk.

The quiet's almost suffocating. Allows my brain too much room to gnaw on the fact that I dipped out of Margot's place before she woke up, *and* that I'm avoiding my brother. I have to fix one of those problems before I attempt to repair the other.

I pull out my phone and shoot off a quick text.

Me: Can we get together this afternoon?

He responds right away, like he's been gripping his phone, waiting for me to reach out.

Cain: Yeah. Any time.

I send him a time and offer to meet him at the hotel—figuring I know this area better than he does.

He answers with a thumbs-up emoji.

Typical. Setting aside my annoyance at an emoji response—he's seventeen, after all—I toss my phone on the counter and scrub my hands over my face.

I'm flipping through the local paper and stop at an article on the second page.

Man Wearing Clown Mask Arrested After Jewelry Store Robbery in Johnsonville

Clown mask. I blink. No way that's real.

But it is.

JOHNSONVILLE, NY — A 34-year-old Long Island man was arrested

Thursday afternoon after allegedly robbing Sandfire Family Jewelers while wearing a rubber clown mask.

Police say the suspect entered the store around 2:15 p.m., brandished a hammer, and smashed several display cases before filling a backpack with jewelry. Witnesses reported the suspect fled on foot.

Officers located the man hours later at the Sunset Taproom, less than two blocks away. He was still wearing the same clown mask pushed up on his head, according to multiple witnesses.

"He ordered a drink like nothing was wrong," one bartender said. "We thought he was just a weird dude."

Several pieces of jewelry matching the store's inventory, worth thousands of dollars, were recovered from the suspect's backpack. Police also found multiple baggies containing substances believed to be methamphetamine and fentanyl as well as hundreds of dollars in small bills.

The suspect is currently being held at the Johnson County Jail pending formal charges.

At first, it's amusing—another case of criminals doing dumb shit. But the drugs and cash? Not as amusing.

Sounds like a dealer. And no one should be running that shit through our territory. He's probably just a dumbass, not a major player. But he has to answer to someone.

I tear the article out, fold it into a square, and tuck it in my pocket.

Might as well bring it up at church later.

The front door swishes open, the overhead chime giving an annoyingly cheerful *ding*. I set the paper down and glance up, my gaze landing on Remy in running pants, a sweat-soaked shirt and road-worn sneakers.

Not in the mood to deal with him. "Did you run all the way here?"

He stops short and stares at me. "What are you doing here?"

"Sully needed to run home." I walk around to the front of the desk. "I said I'd watch the place for him." I cross my arms over my chest. "Keep the riffraff out."

He snorts and gives me a pointed look. "Too late."

"Aren't you clever."

He rests his hands on his hips and blows out a breath. "Can you not bust my nuts today? I've already had a shit morning." He points to his sneakers with both fingers. "Molly's pissed at me. Left behind a parting prank before heading back to school. I've been finding wads of paper stuffed in the toes of my sneakers all week long."

Laughter explodes out of me. "I knew I liked that kid."

"She hit literally every pair of shoes I own." He laughs with me. "I had it coming, but still."

"At least you admit it."

"Yeah, to *you*." He taps his chest. "As her big brother, I gotta maintain the illusion that I'm always right."

That lands harder than it should, wiping the last traces of humor off my face.

Jezzie and I will never have a playful, play-pranks-on-each-other kind of relationship.

Cain and I sure won't either. Hell, if we do, it won't be something cute like paper in my shoes. Probably more like shards of glass in my coffee.

As if he senses the shift in my mood, Remy approaches slowly. "I forgot to mention it last night, but I think we're finally having that welcome home party for Griff. I spoke to Wrath, extended an invite to the whole club, but since I ran into you, I wanted to mention it."

"Yeah, about time. He's been home for a while, hasn't he? He doing all right?"

He lifts his shoulders. "Better—"

The front door swishes open again. A gust of cool morning air follows Jake as he hustles inside. His gaze goes straight for the front desk and lands on me. "Hey, Jiggy. Thanks for holding things down."

"Not a problem."

He nods to Remy, then strides over and offers a quick handshake. His other hand is clutching what looks like a breakfast sandwich wrapped in foil. "I got it from here."

I give Jake a quick clap on the shoulder, say goodbye to Remy, collect my stuff and head out the front door. Outside, I stand on the sidewalk and breathe in the morning. Exhaust fumes and fryer grease from the diner two blocks down drift in the breeze. The strip of stores lining each side of the street looks like something from an antique postcard. Swear it feels like a scene straight out of the 1950s. Two- and three-story brick buildings with wide, plate glass windows house a mix of different shops and businesses. Almost looks frozen in time.

Next to Sully's gym, there's a florist. I should really get Margot something since I bounced so early this morning. I glance at my phone. I probably have time to run back to her place and still make it to church on time. Flowers would get trashed on the way there, though.

She doesn't like flowers. Shit. How'd I forget? She deals with flowers all the time for work. They represent death more than romance to her.

I glance across the street. *Steep Dreams.* A colorful tea kettle is painted on the window along with lettering that announces they sell exotic, hard to find teas. Does Margot even like tea that much?

After the florist, there's a women's boutique with a display of long flowery dresses in the window. I *should* buy Margot a new dress and bra to replace the ones I destroyed on our woodland chase and fuck adventure. The memory turns the corners of my mouth up. We need a repeat of that. Soon.

She's never going to let you near her again—in the woods or anywhere else—if you keep shutting her out every time something bothers you.

I glance at the dresses again and second-guess myself. She's sensitive about her body. If I screw up the size, too big or too small, doesn't matter—it'll sting either way.

Hands in my pockets, I keep moving down the sidewalk, searching for something else. A laundromat catches my eye. Black-and-orange For Sale sign in the window. Not sure if it's the machines or the whole damn business, but I stop anyway.

The place looks clean. Bright. Spotless white industrial floors. White walls with colorful posters of jellyfish. Machines aren't brand new, but they've been upgraded within the last few years. Maintained by someone who gave a shit—nothing's leaking, floor's dry, coin boxes aren't janky.

This is something I at least have experience with. I'm starting to feel like a bum not having a real job to go to like normal people. Maybe this is the answer. Club's been wanting to have more of a presence out this way.

I pull the door open, and the bell overhead gives a half-hearted jingle. A guy in his sixties looks up from behind the counter and sets the newspaper in his hands down on the counter.

"Help you with something?" he asks. Friendly tone, but cautious eyes.

I nod toward the window. "The sign. What's for sale? The building? The business?"

His brows lift. "Whole thing. Building, machines, couple steady commercial accounts—the gym next door, local salon, and a few restaurants."

Well, shit. That's better than our place downstate that mostly relies on walk-ins, hopes, and dreams to stay afloat.

"Got two solid employees I'd like to see keep their jobs," he adds.

That might actually work. Club can't spare too many guys anyway. "All right."

I glance around again. Looks even better inside. "Place is in good shape."

"My wife and I spent twenty-two years making sure of it." He shifts his gaze to the window. "She passed and it's too hard being here without her."

Aw, fuck. "I'm so sorry."

He nods stiffly. "Moving to Arizona. Can't take the damn cold and snow anymore."

"I hear that." I walk around a bank of washers. "Machines look newer."

"Swapped 'em out between two and four years ago. Didn't think I'd be... well, anyway. Speed Queens. Solid and easy to fix. I kept the manuals, service logs. Got everything documented."

"You do the maintenance?"

He nods. "Most of it. Called in help when I needed it. But I kept the place running."

I rub the back of my neck, thoughts spinning. "How soon you looking to sell?"

"As soon as someone's serious," he says, studying me. "You serious?"

"Maybe," I answer, then glance back at the sign. "I have to talk to...my people."

He drops his gaze to my patches and lifts an eyebrow. "Your club?"

"Yeah. That a problem?"

"Not with me."

We swap info. He reaches under the counter and pulls out a packet of papers—financials, equipment list, service logs, all neat and organized.

Looks like something I'll be handing to Teller when I get to church.

Excited about the possible new business venture, I ask for a quick tour, and when we're done duck out the back door into the same lot where I left my bike. It's getting late.

I stuff the packet in my saddlebag, swing a leg over my bike and fire it up, the rumble grounding me.

The ride out of Johnsonville gives me too much time to think. Cold wind cuts through my flannel as I open up the throttle, heading for the clubhouse. No traffic, just the hum of my bike and the buzz in my skull.

I roll into the lot and, as I figured, only a few guys from downstate have made it here so far. Z's bike and his wife's SUV are at the far end of the lot. Must mean his family stayed here last night. *Fuck.* Most of the guys probably stayed at the other clubhouse once they wrapped up the funeral after-party. We've only held church down there a handful of times, though. So, I'm in the right place. I park along the fence line.

My gaze drifts to the trail that cuts into the woods.

Instantly, I picture Margot here the night of the bonfire. She held her own with my brothers, didn't flinch when the bunnies hassled her, and was so sweet to my brothers' kids.

She fits so perfectly into my club. Even Wrath said she's good ol' lady material and it usually takes a while to win him over.

What the fuck am I doing? Sneaking out of her place like she's some fling I want to forget, when she's the only future I want? The only peace I've ever felt.

I pull my phone out, lean on my bike, and call her.

CHAPTER SIXTEEN

MARGOT

Jigsaw's communication issues are really starting to piss me off.

I woke up alone. No "goodbye, see ya later" written on a crappy Post-it Note to be found anywhere in my apartment.

I don't have time to be annoyed with him. Not when I have a funeral to prepare. Still, the empty side of the bed gnaws at me while I get dressed and hurry downstairs. My mind races ahead, going over the checklist—flowers, music, seating. All the things I need to do before the family arrives. No time for distractions.

Why'd I have to push him about his brother again last night? I should've let it go. He opened up to me about so many things yesterday. He's probably up in Maine again. Or maybe this time he kept riding. Maybe he's on a fishing boat in Nova Scotia by now.

I'm finishing the floral arrangements when my phone buzzes in my pocket. I wipe my hands on my apron and check the screen.

Jigsaw.

My heart jumps. But my stomach tumbles. My thumb hovers over the green icon on the screen. Should I let it go to voicemail? Let him sweat, thinking that I'm mad at him?

One tap and I'll hear his voice. Make sure he's okay.

"Hey," I answer.

"Hi." He blows out a breath, like he'd been worried I might not answer. "You get up on time?"

"I had my alarm set." I tuck the phone between my cheek and shoulder, rearranging a spray of lilies. "Don't worry, I wasn't counting on you to wake me."

He lets out a short huff of laughter. "I'm sorry. I couldn't sleep. I kept thinking about…stuff."

"You could've woken me up to talk about it." The words come out softer than I mean them to. Too close to pleading.

"I didn't want to unload any more stuff on you. Just needed to clear my head."

"Where'd you end up this time? Canada?" It comes out sharp and I instantly regret it.

"No. I'm at the clubhouse."

Well, at least that's something. Maybe his club brothers can help him sort through things better than I can. It still stings, though.

"Good," I murmur, trying to be supportive and hide my hurt.

"I, uh, thought about what you said. A lot."

My stomach clenches. I said a lot of things. This isn't a goodbye call, is it?

"And I'm meeting up with Cain today. After church. I'll talk to him about the job, apartment, see what his plans are and stuff…"

Relief washes through me so fast I forget to breathe.

I press my hand to my chest, fingers curling into the fabric of my blouse. That couldn't have been easy for him.

He's doing it anyway.

"I'm glad," I say. "Really. That's great. I know it's hard. I… I'm proud of you."

The words are out before I can stop them. God, I wish I could see his face right now. Gauge his reaction.

He's quiet for a second. "Nah, you were right." Another pause. "Thank you."

"For?"

"Everything. Listening to me." He lets out a short, self-deprecating scoff. "Answering the phone now."

My throat tightens, but before I can respond, a dozen motorcycle engines roar to life in the background, drowning out everything else.

"Hang on," he yells. "Let me go in the garage."

"No, it's okay," I say quickly, raising my voice in case he can't hear me. "I have to finish setting up anyway. And I need to talk to my dad about a few things."

The background noise fades a little, like he ducked into a quieter spot. "All right. I'll... I'll catch you later, okay?"

"Yeah. Okay." I hesitate, wishing I could see his face, reach through the line, touch him. "Be careful."

"I will." A breath. "Margot?"

"Yes?"

"I love you."

"I love you too."

The line clicks. Silence wraps around me, thicker than before.

I tuck the phone into my pocket, my chest tight, and force my feet to move.

There's still so much work to do.

It's not until I'm brushing the final touches of blush on Mrs. Beckett's cheeks that it hits me—we never said when we'll see each other again.

CHAPTER SEVENTEEN

JIGSAW

I STARE AT THE SCREEN AFTER THE CALL ENDS. *SHIT.* WHY DIDN'T I SAY more? Promise to come see her tonight. Or at least make a plan for when I'm going to see her again.

I have no idea how long I'll be with Cain this afternoon. That's why. Or what kind of mood I'll be in when we're done. If I act like a dick to her again, she'll probably kick me to the curb for good.

I slip the phone into my pocket and lean against the metal shelving unit bolted to the garage wall.

Something shifts above me.

Clatter.

A box of air filters smacks my shoulder before bouncing off and hitting the floor with a dull thud.

Fan-fucking-tastic. Even the shelves want to punish me for being an asshole.

I pick up the box and stick it on the shelf.

The earth-shattering rumble of a diesel pick-up finally stops, then a bike's engine cuts off.

Pretty sure I know who just showed up, but I walk out to confirm.

Rooster's big diesel pickup sits on one side of my bike.

I walk around it to meet him and find him getting off his bike on the other side.

"Who?" I frown and glance at the truck.

The driver's side opens tentatively and one jean-covered, cowboy-booted foot slides down, toes touching the running board.

"I did it!" Shelby shouts, jumping from the cab of the truck and landing on the pavement with a thud. "Comin' up the driveway and making that turn was a doozy."

Rooster's grinning from ear to ear. "Good job, chickadee." He rounds the bike and scoops her up, planting a sloppy kiss on her cheek.

I clear my throat. "What in the devil's uncut dick is happening here?"

Shelby draws back, eyes wide, and bursts into laughter. "What?"

Rooster sets her down but keeps an arm around her. "Good morning to you, too."

I hold out my hands, palms up, and raise my eyebrows, waiting for an explanation.

"You know I hate driving the truck. It's so dang big." Shelby scowls at Rooster's bike. "But it's colder than a polar bear's balls, so I didn't want to ride. And Rooster had some stuff to haul up here, anyway." She jerks her thumb over her shoulder. "So I wrangled this beast like a badass." She slaps her hand against the side of the truck.

Leave it Shelby to pull laughter out of me when I'm feeling shitty. "Yeah, you did. Good job, songbird."

Rooster squints. "What's up with you? Why so early?"

I shrug and jam my hands in my pockets.

"Brrr." Shelby hugs her arms around herself. "Y'all can gab out here. I'm gonna go inside and get some tea or somethin'."

They engage in yet another long, slow kiss. I turn away, staring at the house.

Something soft touches my arm. "You all right today, Jiggy?" Shelby asks.

I peer down at her and nod.

"Margot come with you?"

I'm not scared of the ass-kicking Shelby threatened to give me if I screwed things up with Margot, as much as I'd like to avoid seeing the disappointment in Shelby's eyes. "No, she's got a funeral today."

"Phew, that must get depressing."

"You fix things there?" Rooster asks.

Thanks a lot, dick.

Shelby's eyes narrow. "Oh, yeah. Why was she lookin' for ya?"

I blow out an irritated breath and glare at Rooster. "I'm surprised you didn't tell her."

"I didn't know if you wanted me to." He shrugs.

Shelby stares up at him, then me, her expression darkening. "Tell me what?"

"Not what you're thinking." I cut that off before she even says it. Christ, how do I put this into words without diving into the entire story? Shelby's had enough ugly things happen in her life; she doesn't need my dark past in her head. "I, uh, have a younger half-brother who showed up, looking to reconnect. Kinda threw me. Still dealing with it."

"Well, shoot. Really?" Her eyes widen. "I didn't know. That's wild. Is he older or younger than Jezzie?"

Shit. I can't have her telling Jezzie before I have a chance to. "Younger. But neither of us have seen him in years. It's complicated. Please don't say anything to her yet. I...I need to figure out what he wants first."

She frowns. "You think he's dangerous?"

"Maybe."

Shelby blinks and stares at me as that sinks in. "Of course I wouldn't go blabbin' your business unless you told me it was okay. I won't say a thing." She swipes her finger over her chest in an X. "Promise, bestie."

A genuine smile tugs at the corners of my mouth. "Thanks."

"When do we get to meet him?" She glances up at Rooster. "Or have you already met him?" There's no venom in her question. No quiet scolding that Rooster knew about this but didn't share the info with her.

Rooster's intense gaze is focused on me, but I can't figure out what message he's trying to burn into my skull. "Just once, years ago," he says.

"Funny story, songbird," I say, ignoring Rooster's mood shift. "Being on tour with *you* is how he found *me*. His mom saw my picture in one of those gossip rags that love publishing pics of you and your biker entourage."

She hoots with laughter. "Well, damn, look at me. The family reunion maker." Her laughter abruptly stops. "Shoot. I sure hope my dad doesn't find me the same way."

Rooster and I have already discussed how we'll handle it if he ever *does* show his face.

"Do ya guys look alike?" she asks.

"Z seemed to think so."

She reaches out and squeezes my arm. "Well, I hope everything works out. If you need help talkin' to Jezzie or something, let me know."

I'm not sure how that would help, but it's a nice offer. "I will, thanks."

"And I hope you're bringing Margot around again, soon?" She glances up at Rooster. "You really should have her over to the house. She hasn't even seen your place yet. Rooster can show off his fancy new grill."

"Yeah, I want to. She's always on call, though. So it's hard to get away."

"You're okay staying there?"

"Yeah, her place is nice." I slap Rooster's arm. "He saw it. She's not keeping me in cold storage or anything."

Shelby's lips turn up slightly. "Okay. Well, we just miss ya."

Behind her, Rooster shakes his head and mouths, *Nah.*

"Thanks, songbird," I say, ignoring Rooster.

Her concerned eyes study me for a few more beats. "Don't disappear on us after church today, okay? Heidi and I are making banana pancakes." She holds her hand up and twists her middle finger over her index. "Prayin' we don't make a big ol' mess."

"I'm sure you won't"

Rooster keeps his eyes on her the whole time she crosses the lot and skips up the steps into the clubhouse, so I don't bother saying anything until the door closes behind her.

"Thanks for keeping that under wraps," I say.

"I don't know why I bother since you tell her everything anyway." The corner of his mouth turns up for a second, then he frowns and fixes his concerned brother eyes on me. "Why so gloomy today?"

The scrutiny feels too heavy, and I take a step away from him. "What're you talking about?"

"No motherclucker jokes." He squints at me. "No devilish gleam in your eyes."

"Jeeezus Christ." I roll my eyes skyward. "You startin' to write songs with Shelby now? Devilish gleam? What the fuck?"

He grins and claps me on the back. "That's better. But seriously, what's wrong?"

"Nothing."

He moves around me and lowers the tailgate of his truck. "Help me unload this. Maybe it'll loosen your tongue."

"Unload what?" I move closer, peering into the bed of the truck.

He flips the hard cover back, revealing neat stacks of white and blue bags. "Salt. Remember the giant pallet I got that deal on? I said I'd bring some up for Z. He's out."

"Already?" I lean in and start dragging the twenty-five-pound bags to the edge of the tailgate. "Uh, I'm not carrying these all the way back there."

"Well, that path isn't big enough. I'm not scratching the shit out of my truck."

"What a drama queen." I jerk my thumb toward the garage. "The UTV's in there, let me get it."

Actually, there's more than one outdoor vehicle in here. If it's parked in the main garage, it's gotta be for any brother to use, right? The labels on each set of keys leads me to believe the answer is yes. Christ, if Dex is maintaining all these additional vehicles for the club, then I've really been slacking on my road captain duties. We only have one old shitty UTV downstate that I change the oil in, maybe rotate the tires—if I remember—like once every six months. Might be time to give it more than a half-assed once-over before someone blows the engine.

I grab the set for a Polaris Ranger and start it up. The bed's small, we'll probably have to make more than one trip. But that beats carrying five hundred pounds of salt through the woods.

I roll the UTV around to the back of Rooster's truck and kill the engine. He has more bags lined up and waiting on the tailgate, and slow claps his hands at me like I'm the one holding up progress.

"You're lucky I like you," I mutter, jumping out and tossing a couple bags into the Ranger's bed.

He snorts. "Nah, I'm lucky you're avoiding whatever's crawling around in your skull today."

I don't take the bait. Just grab another bag, toss it, repeat.

We run out of room in the UTV about halfway through.

"Let's drop this off and come get the rest," he says, climbing into the Ranger.

I slide into the driver's seat and fire it up. The growl of the engine hopefully loud enough to discourage Rooster from talking.

"You fight with Margot?" he asks once I maneuver onto the path in the woods.

I hit the brake hard, throwing him forward. He slams his hand against the dash, turns and glares at me. "I'll take that as a yes."

"Oopsie, didn't want to run over that squirrel."

"Squirrel my ass. What happened? You held it together in front of Shelby but you're being moody as fuck."

"I'm always moody as fuck."

"This is different."

I glance over at him. "I didn't fight with her."

"Okay." He shrugs like it's no big deal, but I know he's not done. "You ghosted her again?"

"No, just left early." I tighten my hands on the steering wheel. "But I called her this morning."

He nods slowly. "And?"

"And what?"

"You clean up the mess you made by sneaking out without a word?"

My silence is answer enough.

Rooster sighs and shakes his head. "Man, you're lucky she puts up with your shit."

"Don't I know it," I mutter, slowing as the path curves to the left before Wrath's house. "You done lecturing me now?"

"Never." He flashes a grin that doesn't quite reach his eyes.

As I clear the turn, a sharp *crack* splits the air.

"The fuck?" I mutter.

Wrath's shirtless body swinging an ax in the air comes into view and it all makes sense.

"Well, that's not something I needed to see first thing in the morning," Rooster says.

I slow the vehicle, stopping by the path leading up to the wide front steps of Wrath and Trinity's log mansion.

Leaning forward so I can see him through the cab's window, I shout, "Are we intruding on some Red Riding Hood/Lumberjack role-play thing you and Trin are doing?"

Rooster strokes his hand over his beard. "Nah, I think he's getting ready for a photoshoot for another book cover. Something like, *Taming the Viking Lumberjack,* maybe?"

Wrath sinks the blade of the ax into a tree stump and stalks over to us, sweat gleaming on his chest.

"Did you oil yourself up to chop wood?" I ask with a straight face.

"You two are full of jokes this morning, huh?" He stops on Rooster's side of the cab, slaps his hand on the roof, and leans in. "The fuck you doing up here riding around this early?"

Rooster jerks his thumb toward the back. "Brought some salt up for Z."

Wrath eyes the bags loaded in the back. "Awww, isn't that sweet of you." He pushes away from the cab and hefts two of the bags into his arms. "Thanks, Culligan Man. We're low too, so I'll help myself to these as your toll for interrupting my morning workout."

"Knock yourself out." Rooster shrugs.

Wrath tosses the bags over his shoulder and heads into the house.

Laughing and shaking his head, Rooster waves his hand in front of him. "Go, before Murphy runs out of his house and jacks us for another two bags."

I ease my foot onto the gas pedal and steer the UTV back onto the main path. "I mean, since we're here and we still have more bags in the truck to unload, we might as well drop some off at everyone's house."

"What're you, the water softener fairy now?" He laughs. "Should I get you a pair of wings?"

"Nah, I already sparkle enough." I grin and toss my head from side to side.

He twists around, counting under his breath. "Fine. Stop at Murphy's. I'll toss two bags on their porch."

We bump and bounce along in the UTV until Murphy's big log cabin comes into view. I veer to the right, stopping at the low stone wall marking off their yard and shift into Park.

Rooster glances over. "You're making *me* drop off the bags?"

"Yeah. I'm the driver." I flip my hand in front of his face, shooing him out of the cab.

He groans but hauls his big ass out, grabs two bags and marches up the walkway to drop them at the foot of the front steps.

"I feel ridiculous," he grumbles as he climbs back into the cab.

"We're almost done." We keep moving, passing the lot Dex chose for the house he's building.

Finally, the cabin Z built tucked into a heavily wooded area of the property comes into view. From the outside, it seems modest, compared to the monstrosities Wrath and Murphy built, but everything inside is high-end.

We stop in front of the house and hop out. I grab two bags and head up the porch steps. The door swings open just as I drop them.

Z stands there in nothing but thin red gym shorts—slung low enough to see way more than I ever wanted.

I groan and slap a hand over my eyes. "Demons save me. No one needs to see that."

"Speak for yourself, Jiggy!" Lilly shouts from somewhere inside.

I lower my arm a fraction, peeking over it to find Z with his arms crossed over his chest, glaring at me. "I should make you run laps carrying those bags, just for being a disrespectful punk."

I heft the bags again, shift them to one arm, and slap Z's stomach as I pass him—immediately regretting it when my knuckles sting. The man's built like a granite countertop.

"If anyone needs to run laps, it's you," I say. "Gettin' a bit of a dad gut there, ol' man."

"The fuck I am," he growls.

Grinning, I turn to face him. "Where do you want these?"

"You can leave them there." He points to a closed door to my right. "I'll bring them downstairs later."

I set them down and Z's dogs run over to me, rumps wagging so hard their feet skitter over the floor. Ziggy sniffs my pants and licks my hand while Zipper dances around my legs, whapping me with his tail. I crouch down and pet both big beasts and accept a few slobbering kisses on the cheek.

"Boys!" Lilly claps her hands. "Stop drooling on Jiggy. Come here."

Ziggy immediately runs to her while Zipper butts his cold nose against my hand one more time, then trots away.

Rooster passes me, dropping his bags next to mine. A few seconds later, Z drops the last two bags in the same spot.

"Shit, Rooster, you didn't need to bring this much," Z protests. "That's enough to last a few months."

Rooster shrugs. "There's more in the truck. Wrath helped himself to a few bags, and while we were at it, we dropped some off at Murphy's place."

"Such a good motherclucker." Z taps his fist against Rooster's shoulder. "Looking out for all your brothers."

"We skipped Rock's place, but I'll get him with the second load."

"Saint Rooster," I sing. "How we love him."

"Do you guys want breakfast? Coffee?" Lilly asks.

My stomach rumbles. I still haven't eaten today. But it feels too much like intruding on Z's family time to plop down at their dining room table and help myself to breakfast.

"Nah, we gotta unload the rest of those bags," I say. "Thank you, though, Lilly."

"I'll help you," Z offers.

"Where's little man?" I ask Lilly.

She points toward Murphy's house. "The kids had a sleepover with Auntie Heidi and Uncle Murphy."

Z circles his arms around his wife's waist and yanks her against him, kissing her cheek. "Yes, they did."

There's a baby-making joke waiting to be born but I don't have it in me at the moment. I roll my eyes Rooster's way. He shrugs and silently jerks his thumb toward the door.

We're almost back to the UTV when Z catches up—still rocking the red shorts, but at least he's added a half-zipped black hoodie and sneakers.

"Where you going? I said I'd help."

"You looked busy, Prez," I say, sliding behind the wheel again.

Rooster offers the passenger seat, but Z jumps into the bed of the UTV and slaps the side.

I follow the path leading back to the clubhouse. Ahead, an overgrown turn-off appears and Rooster points at it. "Can you go back this way?"

"There's no clear trail." I duck, trying to see past Rooster. "That leads out to the stone amphitheater, doesn't it?"

"Yeah," Rooster says with exaggerated patience. "That's why I want to go that way."

"You thinking of having the wedding there?" Z asks.

"Maybe." Rooster shrugs.

"It's a good spot for it." Z rattles off a list of things they did to set up Rock and Hope's wedding out here and I tune most of it out.

While they're talking tulle and tents or whatever, my gaze drifts to the spot in the woods where I finally chased Margot down and had my way with her.

Heat flares low in my gut. There's suddenly a lot less room in my

jeans. Getting hard in a UTV with my prez and best friend inches away seems like a bad idea.

I suck in a slow breath and count back from ten.

Doesn't help.

"You all right, Jiggy?" Z slaps my shoulder.

"Yeah, yeah." I nudge the UTV back onto the trail, and a few minutes later we roll out of the woods and into the parking lot.

We park behind Rooster's truck and the three of us get to work reloading the UTV.

"Go ahead," Z says when we're finished, waving toward the clubhouse. "I got this."

"Prez, I don't mind," Rooster protests.

"Nah, you already went above and beyond. Appreciate it." He pulls Rooster in for a one-armed hug and slaps his back.

"You too." Z pats my cheek, the same way he pats his dog's hind end. "See you at church."

He climbs in and takes off.

Once the UTV disappears into the woods, I turn and stare at Rooster. "When'd you turn into such a brownnoser?"

"What?"

"Prez, I don't mind," I mimic in a high-pitched voice.

"What?" He holds his hands out. "Z's been really patient with me running back and forth to Tennessee all the time. Just trying to help him out."

"Yeah," I say slowly, feeling shitty that never occurred to me. "He's been cool with me hanging out at Margot's all the time too. Relieved me of my duties down at the laundromat."

"True, but you're also working with me on website maintenance, and helping out at Cedarwood's. Even though that's Upstate's action, it's still a club business."

"Bro, we both know the only person I'm helping out there is *myself.*"

"That's not true. Supposedly, the old man gave Rock an earful at the funeral about how much you help out around there. Seems like he appreciates it."

"What? Margot's dad talked to Rock? About me?" How'd I miss that?

'Cause you were stalking Margot all day instead of paying attention to anything else.

"Apparently."

"How do *you* know?"

"Z mentioned it last night. I guess Teller called him and gave him a report of what went on at the funeral."

Not sure how I feel about being mentioned in Teller's "report" of anything.

"And, we want to expand our presence in that area," Rooster continues, "so having you out there helps in that department too."

I *did* walk around downtown Johnsonville in my cut this morning. "Funny you said that. I stopped at Strike Back today and watched the place for Sully so he could run home." I pull the info I'd gotten about the laundromat out and hand it to Rooster. "Found a potential investment. Something to give us a foothold out there. You think it's worth bringing to the table?"

"Hell yeah." He grins and flips open the packet. "Maybe it's something both Upstate and Downstate can invest in, so we have one joint business."

Both charters are good about helping out wherever we're needed, but I get what Rooster's saying. A business we each have a stake in makes sense.

He hands the packet back to me and I stuff it inside my cut.

"I'd bring it up after church. With just the officers for now," he suggests.

"Yeah, okay."

As soon as we step into the clubhouse, the sugary-sweet scent of vanilla and bananas fills the clubhouse. My stomach rumbles.

"You think Shelby will let me grab a pancake early?" I ask Rooster.

He huffs a laugh. "I don't think she'd say no to you."

We head down to the dining room together. The coffee station's set up, but we continue into the kitchen.

Shelby's at one counter cutting fruit while Heidi's flipping pancakes from the griddle to a big platter. Alexa, Chance, and Grace are seated on the other side of the counter, each with their own plate-sized pancake, decorating them with fruit and whipped cream.

Murphy's on the other side of the kitchen at a table with baby Brittany.

"Now I know why the whole clubhouse smells like banana cream dreams," I say, snagging a still-hot pancake from Heidi's platter. "Ow, fuck!"

"Duh, it just came off the griddle, Jiggy." Heidi waves her spatula at me.

I grab a napkin off the counter and toss the pancake on it.

"Do you want a plate like a civilized person?" Shelby asks, waving a paper plate through the air.

"No, it's not going to last that long." I borrow the can of whipped cream from Chance, squirt a big glob of it on the pancake, fold it in half and stuff a big piece in my mouth.

The kids giggle and point at me, so I add a bunch of nom-nom noises, making them laugh harder.

Shelby shakes her head. "Hungry much?"

"Starving," I mumble around the mouthful. "I've been running all over the tri-county area and then your man made me do manual labor."

Rooster grabs the whipped cream and smears some on his own pancake. "I didn't *make* you do anything."

"Lilly said you guys had a sleepover," I say to Heidi. "Looks like everyone had a good time."

"We did." She turns and flashes a wide grin. "We're racking up those babysitting coupons for when Bit-Bit's old enough to join the sleepovers."

"Nooo," Alexa whines. "No Bit-Bit."

"She can too," Grace says.

"You like that solo time, huh, Alexa?" Shelby asks.

"I *need* it." Alexa throws a dramatic stink eye at her baby sister. "She screams. A *lot*."

Murphy cracks up laughing.

"She does, Daddy!" Alexa yells.

"So did you when you were her age."

"No I didn't!"

"Yes, you did," Chance shouts, apparently trying to prove his point with zero evidence or logic, just sheer volume and certainty.

"How would you know?" Alexa shoots back.

Shelby bites her lip, turning toward Rooster and letting out a snort of laughter.

"Well, this seems fun." I sidestep Heidi and grab another pancake. "But I need coffee." The kids are cute and all, but all the racket is starting to make my skin itch.

The kids are still yelling and shouting at each other as I bust through the kitchen doors and sprint across the dining room to the coffee where Dex and Emily are busy filling their cups.

Emily spots me and lights up. "Morning, Jiggy. Is Margot with you?"

"Not today. Work stuff."

Her smile dims. "Oh. Sorry."

I shrug, pouring coffee into a mug. "She works hard."

"I bet." She glances down at her cup. "It must be such a difficult job."

I nod quickly. "She's good at it, though."

"Oh, I know," Emily says quickly, as if she's worried she insulted me. "I mean, I can tell. She seems very kind." Her lips curl into a wicked grin and she lets out a cackle. "And diabolical. I'll never forget the sound of Rav screaming when he found that doll by his bed."

"Absolute gold," Dex agrees.

A wicked grin spreads over my face. "I didn't help her plan that, either. She came prepared all on her own."

"Well, she's smarter than me." Emily flicks a glance at Dex. "Rav still thinks I'm a moron for, you know…" Her cheeks flush red.

Showing up to amateur night at the strip club dressed in your rave outfit?

"Nah," I say, lifting my coffee to my lips. "Takes guts to show up to amateur night looking like a sentient glow stick." Might as well just address the neon elephant in the room.

Dark pinks flares over her cheeks.

Dex narrows his eyes at me.

Too soon?

Cheeks still pink, Emily pulls her shoulders back. "Yes, yes, poor choices were made." She leans up against Dex's side. "Thankfully, Dex was there to pound some sense into me."

Dex chokes on his coffee.

A slow, sadistic smile spreads over my face. I'd be remiss in my brotherly duty if I let that one slide. "So, *that's* what all the noise was, huh? I knew it."

Emily blinks, clearly replaying her words. "Oh shit." Her hand flies to her mouth. "That's not what I meant."

"Jiggy," Dex warns.

"What?" I widen my eyes. "Nothing wrong with giving your girl some enthusiastic...*clarity* against the filing cabinet."

The red on Emily's cheeks deepens and creeps to her forehead and down her neck. Damn, she's kinda fun to tease.

Screeching from the kitchen punches through the walls again, sucking all the fun out of our conversation. That raw, chaotic noise that seems so cheerful to everyone else sends chills crawling over my skin.

I sip my coffee and shudder.

Screaming like that when I was a kid meant severe punishment. My body freezes and I force myself to breathe in and out. No one here would lay a hand on those kids. If anything, Murphy's probably in there egging them on. They're safe.

Dex's expression switches from murderous to concerned. "You okay, Jiggy?"

I force my face into a smirk and tap the side of my head. "Yeah. Just adding *industrial strength condoms* to my mental 'to buy' list."

He snorts. "You sound like Wrath."

Emily shakes with laughter. "I'm kinda with Jigsaw on this one." She lifts her chin, scenting the air. "Although, whatever they're making smells really good."

"Banana pancakes," I say. "They were delicious."

"Hmmm." Her gaze darts to the closed kitchen door. "I'm going to risk it. And I want to say hi to Heidi."

She presses a quick kiss to Dex's cheek and hurries away.

He watches her for a few seconds, then settles his concerned stare on me. "You sure you're all right?" He waves a hand in the air. "And don't give me the condom story again."

I blow out a breath and set my coffee on the table. "Just…feeling some sort of way. Where I grew up, making noise like that got you punished. Starved. Whipped. Locked in a room for days. Depending on how creative my father was feeling and which Bible verse he was using to justify the abuse."

Dex's jaw drops. "I'm sorry, brother."

I shrug, uncomfortable with revealing so much. But I trust Dex. "It's fine. I survived." I let out a bitter laugh. "Obviously."

My gaze shifts to the kitchen. "And I *know* no one here would ever hurt those kids just for…being kids, ya know? Still chilled me for a second."

He stares at me like we're meeting for the first time.

"Yeah," he says quietly. "We never get a warning before our past bites down and rips opens scars we thought we'd healed."

CHAPTER EIGHTEEN

JIGSAW

A󰀏󰀮󰁅󰁆 󰀑 󰀘󰀙󰁃 󰀏󰁅 󰀏󰀙󰀑󰁔󰁔󰀗󰁅 A󰀙󰀈 󰁎󰁅󰀗󰀗󰁔󰀗󰀙󰁎󰁃 󰁑󰀗'󰁅󰀗 󰀃󰀗󰀙A󰀘󰀘󰀩 A󰀘󰀘 󰁃󰀗A󰁔󰀗󰀈 A󰁔 the war room table. Minus Rav and Butcher.

Rock smacks his gavel down, silencing the room.

"Let's make this short today," Rock says.

"Banana pancakes are waiting," Murphy adds.

Ignoring him, Rock turns toward Wrath. "You want to start?"

Wrath's gaze lands on me for some reason. "Jiggy actually has the most interesting news."

All eyes land on me.

I do?

"But I'll go first," Wrath continues. "Things went smoothly yesterday. No issues at the funeral. Ulfric appreciated the support." He glances at Dex. "I hear you had some problems at CB?"

Dex leans forward, clasping his hands on the table. "Eh, it was annoying but understandable. Ulfric took care of it."

"Wait, what was it?" Birch asks.

Dex rolls his eyes and blows out an irritated breath. "Some of Ulfric's guys assumed the after-after-party at CB meant just because the drinks and food were comped, they didn't have to tip any of the dancers. Ulfric took care of it, but it was awkward for—"

"Yeah, no," Z cuts in. "You're being too generous. Whole world knows—even if everything else is on the house, you still tip the girls at a strip club."

"You're telling me Ulfric got jacked up for the funeral and the after-parties?" Grinder scoffs, shaking his head. "And he ain't even prez anymore."

"We footed the bill for the food and drinks at Remy's place," Wrath points out, folding his arms over his chest.

"Goodwill gesture," Rock says. "And hopefully a *final* farewell."

"Amen to that," Wrath mutters, then nods to Teller. "Did Charlotte's uncle vacate the area?"

"Thank fuck, yes," Teller confirms. "Made some noise about wanting to meet the twins, which would've been a hell no from Charlotte. But then he ended up dipping early. Called from the road and said 'next time.'"

"Good riddance," Murphy grumbles.

"Exactly."

"He was the *worst* offender with the non-tipping," Dex says.

Teller points to his blank expression, one eyebrow raised just slightly. "This is my shocked face," he says, voice dry as dust. "He's always been a piece of shit."

Dex snorts. "Well, Rav and Butcher are staying at the other clubhouse until all the Wolf Knights are gone."

"Good call," Rock says, then he focuses on me. "Let's hear your news."

Fuck me sideways, why am I getting so much damn attention lately? "Uh, Hudson approached me at the funeral." I sit forward, resting my elbows on the table. "He's interested in possibly patching over. Stitching a skull and crown on his back."

Rock stares at me.

Teller scowls.

No one at that end of the table seems receptive to this news.

I glance at the other end. Z gives me a wide-eyed, *please continue* look.

"He says Wolf Knights are probably disbanding. Not enough guys in their other charters. He wants to move home anyway. His family's here." I try to give only the facts that Hudson relayed to me. There'll be time to offer my opinions later. "Said he always liked our club and the way we run things. Didn't have a problem with prospecting again. Already knows he'll have to get rid of his Wolf Knight ink and has a plan for it."

Did I cover everything?

"Interesting." Rock glances at Teller. "Thoughts?"

"Oh." I raise my hand to get Rock's attention before Teller shoots this down. "He says he's got approval from his current prez."

"Thank you, Jigsaw," Rock says.

"Why'd he come to you?" Teller asks.

I'd had the same question, so I try to ignore the disbelief dripping from Teller's voice. "Because we're both road captains. That's what he said at first." My lips twist into a smirk. "He was also concerned you think he has the hots for Charlotte, or she wants—"

"Yeah, no." Teller rolls his eyes. "I haven't thought about him at all since the last time we ran into him."

"It's not like we don't need more bodies," Z remarks. "If he doesn't have a problem with prospecting again after serving as an officer, that's a good sign."

"I thought so too," I agree.

"I'll contact his current prez," Wrath offers. "Make sure he's really okay with it. I know another Wolf Knight I'll reach out to and ask about him."

"I'm not calling Merlin to ask," Teller says quickly as if he needs to cut that idea off before it's spoken. "One, I don't trust his opinion on anything. And two, I don't want him to get the idea that patching over is an option for *him*."

"Absolutely-the-fuck-not," Wrath growls.

"I wasn't going to suggest otherwise," Rock replies coolly, fixing his steely eyes on his son. "You have any strong feelings on this?"

Teller shrugs. "Not really. Charlotte knew him when they were kids. Never had anything bad to say about him. He's always been respectful." He lifts his chin at Wrath. "I'll wait to see what the big guy finds out and base my vote on that."

"Anything else?" Rock asks, glancing around the table.

Wrath raises his hand. "Remy's setting up that welcome home party for Griff. I think most of us should at least stop by."

Murphy rubs his hands together like he's conjuring an evil leprechaun. "Can't wait to roast his ass over that fuckin' reality show. Goddamn embarrassing."

"He was just trying to make some coin," Wrath drawls, stroking his chin. "Not all of us have pots o' gold stashed in our wee ginger beards."

Laughter erupts around the table. Even Murphy cracks up.

"Okay, fair." Murphy lifts his hands in surrender. "Hell, I probably would've done it too when I was his age."

"All right, simmer down." Rock knocks his knuckles against the table and glances at Wrath. "Why do you want us there?"

"We need to tag team Griff at the party," Wrath suggests.

Birch raises his hand. "Uh, I don't swing that way."

"No need to take Rav's place in the saying-stupid-shit department just because he's not here," Wrath warns, dismissing him and returning to his original point. "I'm sure Griff plans to train at Sully's gym but I want him at Furious. At least part-time. Get my gym a little shout-out on fight night. Dex, Jigsaw, Rooster, suss out what else he needs."

"He'll *need* more than two people with him in Vegas," Rooster says. "Those fighters roll deep. He's new to that scene. The guy he's going up against is trash. They'll definitely try to fuck with him at the press conferences and stuff. Rattle him before the fight."

Wrath knocks his fists together. "I'd love a motherfucker to test me."

"We don't need anyone getting arrested in Vegas," Rock warns.

Wrath's mouth slides into a smirk. "They'd have to catch me first."

"You *are* incredibly fast for such a big fucker," Z says.

"So." Wrath's gaze drifts down the table. "Who's ready to do some damage in Vegas?"

His eyes stop on me, one eyebrow raised. Pretty sure that's not a question.

"Fuck, yeah. I already said I'm in."

Dex shakes his head. "I hate Vegas. I already told you, I'll watch the bar for Remy while he's gone."

Wrath nods. "Make sure you tell him that."

Bricks leans forward. "I'll cover CB for you."

"Thanks," Dex says.

"As much as I'd like to support the kid," Grinder says. "I'm not comfortable leaving Serena and Lincoln for that long." He hurries to add, "For something that's not strictly club-related."

"Understandable." Wrath nods.

"If I can do something else to help out here, I will," Grinder offers.

Rooster lifts his hand, catching Wrath's attention. "You already know Shelby and I are in."

A chorus of *ooooos* goes around the table.

"Planning to get hitched there?" Dex asks.

"Nooo," Rooster says slowly, barely hiding his irritation. "Shelby still wants to get married *here*." He grits his teeth. "Although, there's apparently talk about having a second 'public' wedding in Tennessee."

Say what? "Talk with who?" I ask.

He cocks his head at me, pure sarcasm in his eyes. "Who do you think?"

"Dawson?" I raise my eyebrows. "What the fuck does he care where you get married?"

"I'm assuming for the publicity," Grinder says in a dry tone.

"Indeed," Rooster agrees.

"Uh." Wrath leans forward. "You realize if you have an event like that in Tennessee, Deadbranch and National will expect an invite."

Rooster nods slowly. "You know Dawson. He doesn't care. He's met a lot of those guys. Likes 'em."

Hustler lets out a belly laugh. "He probably thinks hanging with bikers gives him street cred."

"That part," Rooster agrees, pointing at Hustler. "I don't give a fuck. He's paying for whatever party happens in Tennessee."

I open my mouth to ask if letting Dawson bankroll his wedding makes him feel like a cuck—then snap it shut. That's a question to needle him with when we're alone.

Rooster thinks Dawson's harmless. No doubt the guy's boosted Shelby's career and thrown me a few fat stacks of cash to run security on tour. But I still don't completely trust the guy. He ever does anything to mess with Rooster and Shelby, or hurts her in *any* way, I'm throwing his poser country-boy ass straight into the nearest wood chipper.

"It's not a 'real' wedding," Rooster says, curling his fingers into air quotes. "Just a big party. The part that matters is happening in New York with club and family *only*."

Z nods with approval. "You tryin' to plan this 'party' close to National, so we're not making two runs down south in one year?"

Rooster side-eyes him. "Uh, sure, Prez."

Wrath slides a sneaky gaze Rock's way. "Hopefully, it'll be the *last* run we're making to Mississippi for our National meeting."

Rock glares at him. "Bite your motherfucking tongue."

"What?" Wrath raises two innocent blond eyebrows. "Who said anything about New York? We could be riding to Virginia instead."

Dex ducks his head, his shoulders shaking. "What's wrong, Prez? The other day you were fine with it."

"*Fine* is a stretch," Rock says. "It's the timeline that I object to. We're not ready to take over that responsibility, yet."

"Why not?" Grinder frowns. "We got plenty of places for people to stay. And if you don't want 'em here, there are more than enough hotels in the area. Campgrounds. We can figure it out."

"Thank you," Rock says in the least thankful tone ever. "Since you're so passionate about the subject, I nominate you for the party planning committee."

Grinder's mouth twists into a satisfied smirk. Old man's really itching to have Rock take over as our national prez.

While they debate their plans for the party, my mind's moving on to my meeting with Cain.

Once Rock ends church, I stay seated with some of the other

officers. I lean over and tap the table to get Teller's attention. "I'm going to bring my brother by the apartment later today, if that's still all right with you?"

"Yeah." He grabs a notepad from the center of the table and scratches down some numbers and hands it to me. "Top one will get you in downstairs. Bottom number into the apartment. If you have any issues, call me."

"Thanks." I glance at the numbers, then fold the paper and tuck it in my pocket.

"Is that it?" Rock asks.

"Um, no." I pull the papers for the laundromat out. "I stopped by Sully's gym this morning."

Wrath's mouth twists into a smirk. "My word wasn't good enough?"

"Hey, good thing I went. He needed someone to watch the place for a few minutes so he could run home," I say, sidestepping Wrath's accusation.

"How are things out there?" Rock asks.

"Fine. Gym was slow but I was there early." I unfold the papers and smooth my hand over the wrinkles. "I walked around after. Found a business for sale."

I clear my throat. All eyes are focused on me. Not used to being the center of attention and can't say I'm loving it. "Thought it could be a good investment for the club. Give us a foothold in that area."

Rock raises two interested eyebrows and nods with approval. Z grins and taps his fist against his chest.

Teller, eager little beaver that he is, holds out his hand for the papers.

"It's a laundromat," I explain. "So, something I have experience running already."

"Such an easy way to wash cash," Teller mutters, flipping through the pages.

"Guy's got some employees he wants to keep, so it hopefully wouldn't stretch us too thin," I explain.

Rock and Z share a look.

"Sounds like it might be the perfect business for both New York charters to go in on together," Z says.

"Fuck yeah." Hustler pumps his fist in the air. "Sounds good to me."

Teller nods. "Me too." He glances at me. "You sure you want to be responsible for it?"

"Responsible?" *Don't know if I care for that word.* "I need to do something more productive than just hang out at my girlfriend's and terrorize our support club."

Z shakes with laughter. "You do more than that. You're busy helping Rooster with our porn empire." He cocks his head, like he's daring me to make a snarky comment about his ex, Stella. "And keeping Stella the hell away from me."

I press my palms together, like I'm praying to the magical sky daddy above. "Haven't heard from her since the one-hundred-and-one-man fuckfest proposal."

Everyone groans. Guess Upstate got filled in on all the dirty details at some point.

"Let's hope it stays that way," Rooster says.

Z glances at Hustler. "You've heard from her, right?"

Hustler shoots a glare at me, then Rooster. "Unfortunately. She's plenty pissed we turned that idea down."

"Tough shit," Z snaps.

"She's approaching a big milestone of subscribers on her site," Rooster says.

"Yeah, and?" Z asks.

Hustler and Rooster trade *tag, you're it* looks.

Finally, Hustler sighs. "Once she crosses that threshold, I think we ought to celebrate it. Let her know we appreciate her and all that fat cash that comes pouring into our account every month."

Z blows out a breath, letting it out slowly. "You're right. Let her have a party at the clubhouse. Whatever will keep her happy."

"Thanks," Hustler says.

"I ain't fuckin' goin', though," Z mutters.

"Anyway," Rock says, shaking his head like he wants to knock the mental image of all things Stella out of his head. "Mr. Cedarwood had many complimentary things to say about you yesterday, Jigsaw."

Heat crawls up my neck. The way Rock says it, it sounds less like a client praising an employee—and more like a future father-in-law having a sit-down with my *dad*.

CHAPTER NINETEEN

JIGSAW

A few hours later, I jump out of Rooster's truck, boots landing in the grass with a thud.

"Thanks for the ride." I shut the door with a solid thud. Rooster and I left our bikes upstate, so I hitched a ride back with him and Shelby. From here, I'll grab my truck before heading out to meet Cain. Figured it made more sense to have something with cargo space in case he needs stuff for the apartment.

If he even wants to stick around.

After being cooped up in a cage for so long, I need to stretch my legs and breathe in some fresh air. I walk to the edge of the woods, studying the heavy growth, searching for a trail through the trees.

The crunch of leaves behind me can only be Rooster.

"You ever think of cutting some trails through here? Like they have upstate?" I ask.

"You want to buy some four-wheelers and go tearing through the woods like we used to at Boone's?"

No, I want to chase my girlfriend and mount her like a bear, but I don't think you want to have that conversation.

"Yeah, sure." I glance over at him. "You still have that app that shows the aerial view and property lines?"

"Yup. Why?"

Because I don't want to wander onto someone else's land when I'm stalking my girlfriend and ripping off her clothes. What's with all the questions, brother?

Rooster has a decent amount of acreage here but it's nowhere near the amount Upstate has. "I don't want to end up dropping trees on someone else's land."

He pulls out his phone, slides his finger over the screen until he pulls up the right map, then passes it to me. I study the boundaries and markings, then lift my head, staring at the terrain around us. "Can you send me a few screenshots?"

"The property's marked." He lifts a slow, sarcastic finger and points at the bright orange *POSTED: Private Property* sign nailed to a tree about fifty yards away. "You helped me put up the signs."

"Yeah, but still."

"All right" he mutters, sliding his fingers over the screen. "Why do I get the feeling you're up to something more…nefarious?"

Rooster and I share a lot of things, but I'm not about to explain my newly discovered outdoor sex kink to him.

My phone dings several times. I check the photos. "Thanks."

"You planning to hunt the property?" he asks. "I've caught a few big bucks on the trail camera."

Trail cameras. Fuck. I'll have to make sure we avoid those. "Yeah, maybe." I glance at his phone. "Where do you access the trail camera pics? Your phone?"

He frowns at me. "Yeah, why?"

"Just wondering."

"Are you planning to run naked through my woods or something?"

Or something. I struggle to keep my expression blank.

"Maybe. It's supposed to help you connect with nature and Vitamin D synthesis," I manage to say with a completely straight face.

His jaw drops and his scowl deepens. "What the fuck ever. Deer ticks are everywhere down here. Don't come crying to me when you need one pulled out of your wrinkly ball sack. I ain't doing it."

I double over laughing and rub my crotch. "Jesus Christ. Why'd you have to say *that*. Now I'm gonna have nightmares."

"That's what you get for puttin' the image of you runnin' around with your cock out in my head."

Still shaking with laughter, I can't come up with a response. Finally, I wipe tears from my eyes and tuck my phone away. "Thanks for that."

He glances at his watch. "Are you done stalling? Aren't you supposed to meet your brother? You're going to be late."

That's exactly what I've been doing. Distracting myself. Delaying this meeting. Rooster knows me too well. "Yeah, I need to change and get going."

"If you need me, call." He pats my back, turns and heads toward the house. "Good luck."

I wait until the door shuts behind him before heading around to the side entrance that leads to my apartment. The second I step inside, the silence hits me. All my shit's exactly how I left it—not that Rooster would ever invade my privacy. But something feels...off. Still. Too quiet. Like it doesn't belong to me anymore. Just four walls and a mattress to crash on when I'm passing through.

I strip off my clothes, take the fastest shower known to man, throw on something clean, and hit the road.

I can't avoid this any longer.

Time to meet my brother.

The kid I forgot about for too long.

The one who reminds me of everything I'd rather leave buried.

CHAPTER TWENTY

JIGSAW

THE CLOSER I GET TO THE HOTEL, THE MORE I REGRET SAYING I'D MEET him here. Too exposed. Too public. Too many variables I can't control.

But it's too late to back out now.

I spot him before I even finish turning into the parking lot—pacing the sidewalk like he doesn't want to have this meeting any more than I do. Black hoodie, beat-up jeans, and a backpack slung over one shoulder.

My stomach knots.

I roll into a spot and kill the engine. Sit there a second watching him. He's taller than I remember from our short reunion at Crystal Ball the other night. Restless energy rolls off him—something I recognize all too well.

He seems more than nervous. Untethered. Lost.

I push the door open and climb out, forcing my legs to move.

Cain stops pacing as I approach, eyes flicking to mine, then darting away.

"What're you doing outside?" I ask, tone gruffer than I mean it to be.

He shrugs. "Needed air."

I understand more than he realizes. "You want to go somewhere to talk? Grab lunch? Have you eaten?"

Jesus Christ, why am I so fucking awkward around this kid?

He gives me a half smile. "I could eat."

"All right. There are like a dozen chain restaurants on the mall road."

"I know."

"Anything interest you?"

"The steakhouse?" he asks hopefully.

"Hell yeah, let's do it." I clap my hands, eager to get moving.

Fifteen minutes later, we're tucked into a wide, wooden booth in the corner of a Southwest Steakhouse—country music playing overhead, peanut shells crunching underfoot, and the scent of grilled meat thick in the air. The walls are plastered with vintage rodeo posters and rusted license plates, making it look, feel, and smell exactly like every other Southwest Steakhouse I've ever stepped into.

A pretty—in an ordinary, girl-next-door kind of way—server in jeans, boots, and pigtails drops off glasses of ice water and rattles off the daily specials.

"Order whatever you want," I say, figuring he'll get a cheeseburger and fries.

Cain studies the menu like it's a final exam, his brow furrowed and mouth pressed into a tight line. Then he clears his throat. "Uh, the bone-in ribeye. Medium. With the spicy shrimp, baked potato, and mac and cheese."

Did this little shit just order the most expensive thing on the menu?

I snort under my breath and hand the server my menu. "I'll have the same."

"Everything?" she asks, arching a brow.

"Yup."

"And a Coke," Cain adds, without looking up.

I tap my water glass. "I'm good with this."

After she leaves, Cain leans back in the booth, hands in his lap. He doesn't fidget or reach for his phone, just stares past me in the direction the server went.

"How's the hotel?" I ask, gripping the base of my water glass and giving it a slow spin, condensation slick under my fingertips.

"Okay. Planes are noisy, though."

"Staying there can't be cheap."

He shrugs.

"You been eating enough?"

He crosses his arms over his chest. As if he thinks I'm criticizing his lunch order. "They have a free continental breakfast. I've been making it last all day."

"That's good."

The scent of fresh baked bread and cinnamon hits my nose and a second later, a basket of rolls and a dish of cinnamon butter lands in front of us. I nod a thanks at the server and she hurries away.

Cain's eyes light up for the first time since we sat down. He grabs a roll, tears it in half, and slathers it with butter.

I take one too, tearing it in half and smear butter on one side. It's sweet, warm, and soft. Probably terrible for me, but I don't care right now.

We munch on the rolls in silence for a few minutes. The sound of clinking silverware and a country ballad hum through the background.

"So, what's your plan?" I ask, catching him mid-reach for another roll.

He freezes, then slowly sits back. "Not sure." His gaze meets mine, full of something that might be defiance—or just exhaustion. "I want to see Jezzie."

I hold out a hand, palm down. "We'll get there."

"Mom wanted me to use the money she left me for school." He rolls his eyes. "It's barely enough to pay for a year at a state school."

"What do *you* want to do?" I ask.

He pops a piece of roll in his mouth and chews it slowly. "I think I want to be an electrician. Do a training program and find an apprenticeship."

I nod slowly. I know some people who could probably help him out. "I might be able to help you with that." Actually, I'm almost positive the community college out in Johnsonville has a solid program.

"Really?" His eyes widen, like he's shocked I'd offer to do anything for him.

"Look, you said you and your stepdad aren't close. Are you plannin' to go back to Arizona?"

"New Mexico," he corrects, focusing his attention on the now empty breadbasket. "There's nothing for me there."

"You got any other options?"

"Sure." He spreads his hands wide. "I can go anywhere I want now. Just me and the open road."

"Yeah, you can do that."

"Here we go!" Our server swoops in, placing two massive plates with our steaks on them in front of us. A guy behind her delivers the side dishes.

"I'll grab fresh drinks and bring more rolls," the server chirps. "Be right back."

"Thanks," I murmur.

Cain doesn't wait. He dives into the steak, cutting off a thick bite and closing his eyes as he chews. Like it's the first real meal he's had in days.

I stab my fork into the mac and cheese—gooey, creamy, cheesy—and drop a ball of butter into the steaming crack of my baked potato.

Across from me, Cain keeps eating, fast but not sloppy. Intent.

Unease digs into me. *Is he actually staying at that hotel?*

I slice into my steak and take a bite, chewing while I figure out how to bring it up without making him defensive.

After he's inhaled about a quarter of his meal, I steer the conversation toward his living situation. "I have a friend who owns an apartment building. It's about an hour outside of Empire." I circle my finger through the air to indicate the location we're currently in. "But it's nice. My girlfriend's place isn't far from there, so I'm in the area a lot."

"Yeah, and?" he asks, clearly confused.

"It's yours if you want it."

His cheeks redden. "I don't have enough to rent a place on my own and—"

"No rent. He keeps it for members of the club who need a place to crash. It's empty right now. Guy who was staying there just moved in with his girlfriend. As a favor to *me*, my friend who owns the building is willing to let you stay there."

"Why don't *you* live there?"

"I got a place down in Union. But like I said, I'm up that way a lot."

"Sleeping over at your girlfriend's?" He raises his eyebrows, looking like a scandalized ten-year-old who just learned that sex isn't always about making babies.

"Yeah. And my club has some business interests out that way."

"Your club has businesses?"

"Yes," I say sharply. "But that's not your concern right now." I glance over his too-thin frame. "You ever been inside a gym?"

"No," he scoffs. "Mom believed in chores and nature for exercise."

"Well, a friend of mine owns a gym and he needs someone to help out. Answer phones, stock towels, keep the place clean, shit like that I guess."

He blinks at me. "So?"

Christ. Do I have to spell this out? I hold out one hand. "I got an apartment for you to stay in." I lift the other. "And a job so you can earn some money."

"Wait, what?" His fork clatters against his plate. "An apartment? Like, just for me? A job? How? Why?"

"Why?" I repeat. "You're my brother. And you just told me you're basically homeless. So, if you want to stick around, I can help you with the basics."

His eyes turn glassy. He glances away, swallowing hard and blinking rapidly at the wall. "I thought this was a fuck-off lunch," he mumbles.

"What?" I laugh.

"Like, you just wanted to chat and maybe catch up." He flicks his hand in the air. "And then when your curiosity was satisfied you'd say, off you fuck now, kid."

Instead of laughing, I blow out a weary breath. Yeah, I can understand why he'd think that. "No, I don't want you to fuck off into the sunset, Cain."

He chuckles and sniffles at the same time, wiping the corner of his sleeve under both eyes. "Why can't I stay with you?"

"Like I said, I'm not there a lot. Plus, I live in my friend's apartment. There isn't a lot of extra room."

He fixes me with a sharp, unsettling stare. "And you don't trust me not to rob your friend's place?"

Why lie? The kid's not dumb. "Well, yeah. Kinda."

"But I can stay at your *other* friend's place?"

"It doesn't have any valuables," I say with a straight face.

He snorts, then glances back down at his plate. When he looks up again, the humor's gone. "I don't steal."

"Okay."

"And I don't take handouts."

"Which is why I helped you find the job," I answer, barely holding onto my patience.

He fiddles with his fork, tapping it against the side of his plate until I want to rip it out of his hand. "Mom always said you saved our lives."

I swallow hard. "She did?"

He nods quickly, eyes darting away.

It doesn't seem like the right time to dig into that, but my curiosity overpowers my common sense. "How much do you remember about living on the farm?"

He spears me with a haunted stare full of horror. "Too much. I still have nightmares about it."

"I do too sometimes."

He stabs his fork into the mac and cheese and shovels a huge glob into his mouth.

We eat in silence for a while, the clink of silverware and low murmur of conversations filling the space between us.

"Your mom helped save my life," I finally say. "She...helped me leave. He probably would've ended up killing me, otherwise."

"We tried to leave once."

"Really?" I raise my eyebrows. Surprised Ruth had it in her. The little I knew of her seemed so meek.

"Didn't get far." He pokes at his potato, jaw tight.

"How'd you end up in New Mexico?" I ask.

He shrugs. "We were in southern California for a while, but it was too expensive. She liked the art community there."

"Did you like it?"

"Yeah. It was okay." The corners of his mouth twist up, but there's no joy behind it. "Anywhere I didn't have to sit through four-hour fire-and-brimstone sermons or get my ass beat for blinking at the wrong verse felt like heaven."

"I'm sorry," I say quietly. "You were...young. He didn't start... hitting us and stuff until we were older."

He frowns at me.

"Uh, I had two older brothers...*We* had two older brothers. They were...long gone before your mom came to live there, though."

"Where'd they go?"

I shrug. "I don't have any proof, but I think our father killed them."

His face pales. "I used to think he was a monster sent by the devil himself to test us." He hits his hand against the side of his head a few times, the ring on his pinky glinting under the lights. "He was always screaming about sin, punishment, and how the devil tricks you."

"I remember those lectures."

"He was meanest to Jezzie, though. If I messed up something, he'd take it out on her. I just stopped saying anything after a while so she wouldn't get hurt." He focuses his glassy eyes on me again. "Are you sure she's okay?"

Fuck me. What if he's putting on the performance of a lifetime just to get close and hurt us?

He can't be that diabolical at his age, can he?

"Yeah, she's fine." I pull my phone out of my pocket and search for a photo of her that's a couple years old. I find one with her on the back of my bike, arms raised over her head, laughing. Aunt Angela took the picture and fussed over the short ride. I turn the screen toward him. "She's in school, a couple hours from here. Comes to visit on the weekends sometimes."

He studies the picture like he's searching for proof—something in her eyes, her smile, maybe the way she holds herself—that she's okay. After a few seconds, he nods and hands the phone back without a word.

"How about when we're done here, I'll take you to see the apartment?" I slide my phone back into my pocket. "We can stop by the gym too. If Sully's around, you can meet him."

He nods again, more sure this time. "Okay."

Obviously, he doesn't trust me yet.

Can't blame him.

I'm not sure I trust him either.

But at least it's a start.

CHAPTER TWENTY-ONE

"THAT WAS THE MOST FRUSTRATING MOVIE EVER. I STILL DON'T understand why he didn't just tell her what he saw," April mutters as we step out of the movie theater and into the cool night air. "She would've helped him kill that guy to save her family."

"I think that was the point," I murmur, pulling my coat tighter around me. I should've brought gloves. My fingers are freezing. "Sometimes we worry too much about not making others uncomfortable at the expense of our own safety. And, let's face it, he was weak. Too worried about being polite. Too busy following 'the rules' and waiting for someone to come save them."

April snorts. "Couldn't be me. I would've run that dude over with my car and gotten those kids the hell away from there."

"Same." I smile at her, the ache in my chest easing just a little. Today's funeral was short and simple, and when April texted to meet for dinner and a movie, I didn't hesitate. I needed the distraction. Her company and cheerful chatter. Needed someone who wouldn't ask if I was okay, because I'm not sure how I'd answer right now.

"Want to grab some coffee?" April yawns. "I have a long drive home."

"We could've picked a place closer to you."

"Nah, I love that theater. Totally worth it."

"You can stay at my place tonight, if you want," I offer.

She hesitates, as if she doesn't want to hurt my feelings by saying no. "It's okay. I just need caffeine to keep me awake."

"Fair enough." I push open the door to the café and nod for her to go first. "I'm buying."

"Deal."

Inside, the place is busier than I expected this late. Probably other moviegoers needing a warm drink before heading home. Most of the tables are covered with chairs that have been flipped up for cleaning, so April and I slide onto two stools at the long counter instead.

I order hot chocolate, she gets a coffee. The cranky server drops them off quicker than expected, clinking the mugs against the wooden countertop with a hard *thunk* and a grunt.

As I wrap my hands around the warm ceramic, ready for my first sip, something flickers on the TV mounted above the counter.

Daniel Muldoon—Local Financial Planner Arrested in Suspected Serial Murder Case.

The headline screams across the television beneath a picture of his smug, all-too-familiar face.

My blood turns to ice.

The mug stays hovering near my lips, untouched. The room goes quiet in my head, the news anchor's voice distant and warped, like I'm underwater. The string of suspicious deaths. The elderly women whose bank accounts were wiped clean.

They did it. They actually arrested Daniel.

That means they must have significant evidence against him, right?

April shifts beside me. "Margot?" she asks, her voice low, cautious.

I can't tear my gaze away from the screen.

A sick part of me wants to revel in his downfall. But three—maybe more—women paid the price for Daniel's destruction. I can't take any satisfaction from that.

"Isn't that...?" April gasps. "That's Daniel, isn't it?"

I nod once, still staring at the screen. "The police came to talk to me a few weeks ago. They questioned me about his grandmother's death—"

"Oh my God. Are you serious?"

"Yup, and a few other women. Friends of his grandmother's, I think."

I glance over and take in her shocked expression.

My face twists with disgust. "He held his grandmother's funeral at our place—and referred the other two to us as well," I add in a lower voice.

"You're kidding. Why?"

"I don't know."

"No, why do they think he killed them?"

"For their money?" I shrug, but shame creeps over me, sticky and all too familiar. That I was engaged to Daniel feels like a mistake I'll never stop paying for. "I knew he was cruel. Mean. But murder?" I shake my head. "Stealing from elderly women? I never imagined..."

"I had no idea." She reaches out, resting her hand over mine. "I'm so sorry, Margot. This is awful." She frowns like she's screwing up the courage to say something else. "And I know it's probably pointless to say this now, but...I never liked him. Didn't like the way he talked to you. Or about you."

Great, did Daniel say awful things to my friends about me too?

"I couldn't tell you," she continues, "and risk having you mad at me. It was a feeling more than anything concrete, you know?"

"Sure. He fooled a lot of people." I gesture toward the screen. "Obviously."

Silence settles between us, broken only by the clatter of a dish behind the counter and the quiet chatter of the other patrons.

"Margot." April squeezes my hand. "I'm so glad you didn't marry him."

I nod, staring into my cup and let out a humorless snort. "Me too."

She doesn't say anything else about Daniel. What else can be said?

We sip in silence, the noise of the café swirling around us.

After a moment, she sets her cup down. "You don't think they'll drag your dad or the funeral home into it, do you?"

"God, I hope not. That's all we need." I rub my thumb against the side of my mug, chasing the heat. "I probably shouldn't have told those detectives so much about my relationship with Daniel. They interviewed my dad and me, but I don't think we gave them anything helpful."

"How awful." She finishes her coffee and sets the cup on the counter with a *clunk* that sounds like the end of the conversation. "Forget that monster. Tell me more about that hot biker who kept eyefucking you at the Hall funeral."

"April!" I choke on a laugh and glance around the café, cheeks warming. A couple near the door seems lost in their own conversation, thankfully.

Still a bit miffed at Jigsaw's disappearing act, my smile fades quickly. I'm not in the mood to sing his praises to my friend tonight. I glance up at the television. The news has moved on to the weather—colorful maps and a scrolling alert.

"It's still new," I say. "But he's pretty great." *When he actually communicates with me.* "The complete opposite of Daniel in every single way."

"Good. You deserve that." She beams at me. "You'll have to properly introduce me next time."

If he sticks around. My phone's in my purse, heavy with silence. Not another text or call since this morning. I don't even know if he ended up meeting with his brother or not. I want to call and tell him about Daniel's arrest, but I don't want to bother him.

"Do you want to get out of here?" April asks.

"Sure." I push my cup aside. "Let's go."

We step out into the night. The cool breeze nips at my cheeks. Or maybe that's heat flaring over my face. Every time we pass someone on the sidewalk, I feel like I have a neon sign over my head, announcing that I was once engaged to a murderer.

"You okay?" April asks.

I shake my head. "Ugh, it's just weird. Daniel." I wave toward the coffee shop. "I saw him not that long ago at the funeral for one of the women they think...he..."

"Killed?" she whispers.

"Yes. He was *such* an asshole. Talked about wanting to get back together. Get married because he's 'ready to settle down' now. Ugh, still as condescending as ever. But I never suspected—"

"Why would you? Besides, he probably wanted to get married because it would make him look innocent or something." She frowns. "You're the one who dumped him. How dare he act like he wanted to take *you* back!"

"I know, right?" We share a dark laugh.

She hugs me one more time before heading to her car.

"Text me when you get home?" I call after her.

"I will."

Wrapped in the warmth of my car, my teeth still chatter from the cold. I rub my hand over the dash, grateful for the thin stream of heat. I love this car—but it's not always practical for upstate winters.

I fish my phone out of my purse, thumb hovering over the screen. *Whoops,* I've had it on silent all night.

A flood of notifications blinks at me.

Dad: They arrested Daniel.

I tap out a quick reply. **April and I saw the news report at Busy Beans.**

Paul sent me a similar text and I send him the same reply.

It's late but they're probably both still awake.

Jigsaw: Things good with Cain.

Relief and happiness twist so tight, I forget to breathe for a second. More messages follow in quick succession.

Jigsaw: Took him to see apartment. Likes it.

Jigsaw: Taking him shopping for some stuff.

Jigsaw: Can I stop by later?

Jigsaw: You okay?

Jigsaw: Margot? I'm worried about you.

A sad smile tugs at my lips.

Now you know how I feel when you disappear without a word.

I don't have the energy to be petty by making him wait and worry any longer. Not tonight. Not with him.

Me: I'm okay. Went to movies with April. Forgot my phone was on silent.

He responds right away.

Jigsaw: Worried about you.

It's only getting later, and I just want to go home. I start the car and pull out of the small parking lot. My headlights sweep over shuttered shops and quiet sidewalks. I take it slow through the narrow streets.

I need to look up Daniel's story online when I get home.

Did he make bail?

What else do they have on him?

Will this hurt the business? *Ouch, that's selfish.* But I can't help it. Any suggestion that my father was involved or knew what Daniel was up to could ruin our reputation.

By the time I pull into the parking lot behind our home, I'm eager to get inside and jump on my laptop. The garage door rolls up and the overhead light fills the space with a bright, warm glow but it doesn't do a thing to chase away the dark thoughts that followed me home.

I hit the button to lower the garage door, the motor humming behind me as I cross the lot. My heels tap out a steady rhythm on the pavement, sharp and out of place in the quiet.

A figure shifts near the porch, slipping from shadow into the harsh yellow light as the motion sensor clicks on. Floodlights flare to life, catching the edges of a leather jacket, the outline of a familiar body.

Jigsaw.

"What're you doing here?" I hurry to meet him.

My gaze lands on his SUV parked close to the house. How'd I miss that? "It's freezing. Why are you outside?"

"One thing at a time." He curls his arm around my waist and drags me closer. Chilled leather brushes my cheek. How long has he been out here?

He leans down and seals his lips against mine. He swallows my sharp squeak of surprise and cups the back of my head, holding me in place. Our lips slide together with a firm, delicious pressure that chases the cold out of my body, replacing it with a simmering warmth.

Dizzy from the rise in temperature and change in my evening plans, I pull back and stare up at him.

"I missed you today," he says simply.

Another fraction of my annoyance with him ebbs away. "Come inside," I whisper. "You're freezing."

"I didn't want to startle you and meet you outside the garage." He takes my hand, and we walk up the steps to the back door. He holds open the screen door for me while I unlock the door.

"You could've sent me a text telling me you were here." I glance over my shoulder at him.

His serious expression doesn't change. "I didn't want to risk you telling me to go home."

"I wouldn't have done that." I step into the house with him right behind me. The door closes behind us with a soft click. Most of the lights are off downstairs.

I shrug out of my coat and hang it on a hook by the front door. Jigsaw glances at it and then the stairs.

"You can leave it down here if you want. Your truck's parked right outside," I point out. "Seeing your coat won't shock anyone."

He chuckles and slips it off, pulling out his keys and phone, tucking them in his jeans pockets.

The long day grinds into me, each step up to my apartment heavier than the last. Jigsaw trails behind me, close enough that his breath skims the back of my neck.

As soon as I open the door, Gretel trots over with a chirp, tail high and twitching.

"Let me feed her," I say, stepping inside.

"Can I watch?"

I turn and stare up at him, mouth open. "You want to watch me feed my cat?" I ask slowly.

He shrugs. "In case you ever need me to do it for you?"

"Uh, okay."

Gretel doesn't seem to mind the audience. She dives face-first into her dish the second I set it down, purring like a machine.

"I'm going to change," I mutter, already halfway to my bedroom.

Restless, irritated energy pulses through me. I hurry into my room and into my closet, searching for something cozy.

When I emerge, in my red flannel pajamas, I smack right into Jigsaw's hard chest.

He slips his arms around me and leans in, gaze dropping to my mouth like he's ready to finish what we started outside.

"Oh no you don't." I plant both palms on his chest and push—harder than necessary, but not enough to move him.

"What?" He nuzzles against my neck, inhaling like my scent gives him life.

Everything I've been feeling since I woke up alone this morning explodes out of me in a rush. "You can't keep disappearing on me, then come back and use your magic dick to make it all better. Then do it again. And again."

He draws back, amusement playing over his lips. "Magic, huh?"

I slap his arm. "Of course you focused on *that*."

He sighs and rakes his hands though his hair, leaving it sticking up all over the place. "I told you I wasn't good boyfriend material. Not good at relationships. I'm not...I don't know how. I'm trying."

Misery and frustration fold around him like a cloud.

As annoyed as I am, he has a point. His silences *have* shortened. Heck, he even called a few hours after leaving this morning. For him, that's a big improvement.

Is it enough for me, though?

"You're right," I say.

He tilts his head, like he didn't hear correctly, and I don't even think he's being sarcastic.

"I'm sorry," I continue. "I know you're trying. I want to give you space when you need it—"

"I don't *want* space." He hugs me tight against his body. "I want to permanently attach myself to you. But I think you'd get sick of me fast."

Is that what he's doing? Trying to leave before he gets left? "I never get tired of *you*. I *do* get tired of feeling uncertain about *us*."

"The only thing I'm certain about is how I feel about you." He closes his eyes and exhales a slow breath. When he opens them again, he seems sad or tired. "I don't want you to see me at my worst and bail."

Well, that's something I understand. "You think I don't worry about the same thing?"

"It's different."

"No, it's not," I insist. "You're not as complicated as you think you are." A list of things I know are true come to mind, and I give him each one. "You came from an awful situation. You survived. You righted some wrongs. And you're a good man."

"I'm definitely *not* a good man."

"Strongly disagree." I tap his chest. "We're using *my* metrics here. No one else's."

His lips quirk.

"You're loyal and kind—"

"No, I'm not." He laughs. "I'm grumpy and mean to people all the time."

"Well, people shouldn't be annoying, then." I shrug. "You're loyal to your brothers. You're kind to me. You take care of your sister. A lot of brothers would've told her she's on her own."

"I do that out of *guilt*, Margot."

"That you *feel* guilt at all means you're a decent person. But I don't think you have anything to feel guilty about. And I have a feeling Jezzie would agree with me."

He frowns and his lips part as if he wants to warn me to leave Jezzie out of it.

"I didn't say I'm going to ask her," I say. "That's for you two to work out. But I have a feeling she's not as mad at you as you think."

"Margot—"

I don't want to derail our conversation. "I want you to be yourself with me. That's what love is. Isn't it? Seeing your person at their worst and loving them anyway?"

He frowns. Like this is a novel concept.

"My love isn't conditional. I like you." I poke my finger in his chest. "Who you are today."

"Today, I'm a man who snuck out of your bed early in the morning."

I blow out a long breath. "Yes. And yet here you are tonight."

"I missed you." His voice softens. "It ended up being a good day." He stares at me with such a serious expression, I almost doubt his claim. He taps the side of his head. "I had your voice in here, reminding me to give Cain a chance."

"You did?"

He nods quickly. "And after I left his place, there was no one else I wanted to talk to about how things went."

"Really?"

"Well, yeah." He lifts one shoulder. "You did it."

"What did I do?" I tilt my head, watching him carefully.

"You pushed me to go see him. I would've waited... dragged it out longer if you hadn't." His arms tighten around me, pulling me closer. "So, thank you," he murmurs, his breath warm against my ear.

"You're welcome." I rest my hands on his sides, fingers curling into his T-shirt. "I don't mean to be so pushy."

"Sometimes I need a push."

"I think we all do."

For a long moment, we just breathe together in the quiet.

Jigsaw

Demons give me strength.

I can't believe I said all that mushy shit that's been swirling around in my head out loud.

And she listened to all of it. And she still wants me here.

"Have you eaten?" she asks.

"I can always eat. You know this."

She lightly taps her fist against my stomach. "So unfair. Come on. I'll make you a grilled cheese."

"Won't say no to that." I follow her out of her bedroom. "You mind if I change too?"

She glances over at me. "Not at all. I want you to be comfortable here."

I head down to her laundry room, searching for the black sweats she likes and slip those on. Then grab a T-shirt.

"You know," she calls out, "you can start leaving your stuff in the bedroom instead of the laundry room."

I laugh, tugging the shirt over my head as I make my way back into the kitchen.

She's already at the stove, so I drop onto one of the stools at the counter and rest my elbows on the edge, watching her work. She slaps a thick slice of buttered bread onto the sizzling griddle, layers it with rounds of creamy cheese, and crowns it with another slice.

"Forgot I'd been officially upgraded to closet space," I tease.

Without glancing away from the stove, she smiles. "So, how'd it go?"

While the sandwich sizzles on the griddle, she goes to the fridge and pulls out a bottle of sparkling water.

"It was kinda awkward at first. *Heh.* I discovered he was squatting at the hotel. I guess he stayed one night, then he was like, sleeping in the bathroom after dark, popping out in the morning to nab some food from the breakfast buffet, staying out for the day, then sneaking back in at night."

Margot sets the bottle in front of me and leans against the counter, crossing her arms tight over her chest. "He was squatting at the hotel?" she repeats, her voice soft but edged with disbelief. "Sleeping in a bathroom? That's awful."

"Nah, it's clever." *She and I see things so differently, don't we?* "He said it wasn't that bad."

Her nose wrinkles like she's trying to hold back a wave of emotion. "No one should have to do that. Especially a kid."

"He's not a kid."

"He's still a teenager," she insists.

"He's a survivor."

"It still…shouldn't be that way," she says.

"Well, it's not anymore." I uncap the water and take a sip. "He was *really* excited about the apartment."

"I bet." She hesitates. "Wait, so he's there all alone in a new place now?"

I shrug. "I don't think we're at the sleepover stage of our relationship, yet. One step at a time." I pick up my phone and glance at the screen. A few group chat notifications. Nothing I need to answer now. Nothing from Cain. "He has my number if he needs something."

"Good." A relieved smile spreads over her face. She slides a spatula under the sandwich and lifts it off the griddle, setting it onto a plate and cutting it into quarters with methodical precision.

Why didn't I just listen to her? I didn't have to get so prickly when she just wanted to help.

My mouth waters as she sets the sandwich plate in front of me, cheese spilling out of the sides. I pick up one of the quarters, instantly searing my fingers.

"Ow." I drop it on the plate.

"It's hot." She waves her hand at the stove. "You saw it come off the griddle."

"It looks too good, though."

Laughing, she sets a small bowl of pickles and olives next to my plate. "I don't really have anything else to go with it."

"This is fine. You didn't have to cook for me."

"It's a grilled cheese." She rolls her eyes. "Not a prime rib."

How'd I forget to tell her this part? "Speaking of. He wanted to go to Southwest Steakhouse for lunch."

"Nice. I've only been there a few times, but the food was good from what I remember."

"It was. Little shit ordered the most expensive thing on the menu." I laugh, still amused by his brazenness. "All the extras."

Concern, not humor, lines her expression. "Probably the most he's eaten since he left home."

That wipes the amusement off my face. "Maybe. He told me he

thought it was a 'fuck off' lunch, and later admitted he ordered the big steak to get what he could out of me."

"Awww."

The warmth in her voice sinks into the darkest parts of my heart. "See, I told you he's clever."

"And a survivor." She sips her own water. "What else did you do?"

"Took him shopping for a few things. The apartment's furnished but he needed food—obviously."

"Good call."

"Took him to get a heavier coat, boots, sneakers, and some clothes for work."

"That's really sweet."

"I can't let my brother work at my friend's place looking like a scruffy puppy I found under a bridge."

"Jensen." She drags out my name like a scolding.

"What? It's true." I chew a bite of sandwich and pop an olive in my mouth. "Still need to get his bike registered up here if he's staying. Figure out how to get insurance for that crotch rocket. Gonna cost a fortune."

"He's lucky to have a road captain for a big brother."

"Yeah, I guess," I mutter, making a mental list of phone calls for tomorrow. "He was a little intimidated by the gym. But Sully's a patient guy. His fiancée, Aubrey, is a sweetheart. Unless Cain's a total dumbfuck, he'll be fine there."

I've been running my mouth since I got here. I set my final quarter of the sandwich down and wipe my fingers on a napkin. "Tell me about your night."

She doesn't respond right away. Just nods, eyes on her water bottle. The silence stretches, not uncomfortable, but somehow heavier than before.

"You said you went to the movies with April?" I prod.

She nods slowly. "We saw this frustrating movie. But it was nice to hang out with her."

"April's the one you went to school with?"

She nods quickly. "She was helping out at Whisper's funeral, but it didn't seem like the right time to introduce you." Pink spreads across her cheeks and she ducks her head. "She noticed you watching me, though."

"Couldn't take my eyes off you."

Her lips quirk. "Well, she really wants to meet you now."

Shit, all I've thought about is how to introduce her to my family—my club. Haven't made much of an effort to get to know her cousin or friend. Only ever had like one conversation with her dad. I need to do better. "Sure, whenever you want."

A shy but hopeful smile curves her lips. "I'd like that. She might grill you, though."

"That's okay."

Silence settles over us. I finish the last bite of my grilled cheese.

She twists the water bottle cap on and off a few times. "We stopped to get coffee after..."

Why does she make that sound so ominous? I swallow and take a sip of water.

"The news...we saw a report...uh, Daniel was arrested."

I choke on my water, bubbles shooting up my nose. "What?" I grab a napkin and wipe it over my face. "You let me ramble on about my afternoon—"

"You and your brother are infinitely more important to me than Daniel," she says with a quiet conviction that drives home her point sharper than a knife.

I reach over and rest my hand on her thigh. "I appreciate that. But this is..."

"Crazy? Embarrassing?" She exhales hard. "I know it's not about me, but—ugh. And then April told me she never liked him or the way he treated me, which just made me feel stupid all over again."

The crack in her voice guts me.

I slide off the stool and pull her into my arms. "You're the kindest, fiercest woman I know." I press a kiss to her temple, lingering there. "Sweet doesn't even cover it."

Her breath shudders against my chest, but she doesn't pull away. She slides her arms around my waist and hugs me just as tight.

"I think I wanted to believe it wasn't true," she says quietly. "But I should've known the cops wouldn't have come here to interview me if it was nothing. And they wouldn't have arrested him without some compelling evidence, right?"

"He's a rich, white dude. If they arrested him, I'm going to bet the evidence is *overwhelming*. They wouldn't risk a false arrest on such a *pillar of the community*," I finish with a sneer.

"True." She pulls away, lifting her gaze to mine. "I'm scared of what it means for my dad. For the business. And I feel awful because I know that's selfish."

"No, it's not. You haven't done anything wrong."

"I talked to my dad briefly the other day. There's no way he knew. He seemed surprised when I told him Daniel wasn't very nice to me."

"You told him that?"

"I did." Her brow creases. "He didn't say much. Just seemed surprised. Sad, maybe? He said he didn't want to pry into why I ended the engagement."

Engagement. Just the word in connection to that piece of shit stokes rage in me. I clench my jaw. How could her dad not fucking know? "If you had told your father how badly Daniel treated you, what would he have done?"

"I don't know. I don't want him to blame me if this affects the business for some reason, though."

"That's bullshit." I tighten my arms around her, unwilling to let her mind travel down that path. "You're not responsible for whatever Daniel did."

She nods against my chest but doesn't respond otherwise.

"Your family's run a respected business in Pine Hollow for generations. Someone tries to link Daniel's crimes to your family's business, it will get shut down fast." Probably by my club.

She nods slowly. "You're right. My father knows a lot of people. Has a good reputation."

"What we need to worry about, is if he gets off," I say, hoping she follows my line of thinking. "Does he take a plea that lets him out in five years, or does he get life behind bars where he belongs?"

A tired but warm smile curves her lips. "Don't think I don't know what you're hinting at."

"I'm not *hinting* at anything. I'm outright saying it. He better pray he gets a long prison sentence."

She lets out an exasperated sigh. "You know what? I'm not even going to argue with you."

"Good." I smooth my hand over her back but the fury simmering in my chest doesn't ease. "The system fucks up all the time. If Daniel gets out—"

"He's a walking dead man," she finishes.

I love the way she gets me.

What a twisted kind of relief—knowing I don't have to hide who I am when we're together. I'm free to be my murderous self with her.

How can one woman be so perfect for me?

CHAPTER TWENTY-TWO

MARGOT

AWARENESS OF HEAT FROM THE BIG BODY NESTLED BEHIND ME KEEPS ME under the soft haze of sleep. A soft exhale against my neck. Something hard against my lower back. One big, rough hand cupping the weight of my breast that escaped the confines of my tank top during the night.

Outside the blankets feels unnaturally cold.

I burrow deeper under the covers, closer to Jigsaw's body. His thumb twitches over my nipple and I stifle a gasp.

Still shivering, I blink and stare at my bedroom window. Dull gray light seeps around the edges of the blinds. It's too early for my alarm but something doesn't look right.

I push the covers aside, slide out of Jigsaw's embrace, and sit up, fixing my top as I go.

"Where you going?" Jigsaw murmurs. Behind me, he hooks a finger in the waistband of my sleep shorts and tugs.

"I'm cold."

"I'll warm you up."

I shimmy out of his loose grip and flick the curtain out of my way. White glare sears my vision and I squeeze my eyes shut for a second. "Damn, it looks like it snowed. Not a lot but—"

"You got equipment?" Jigsaw asks. "Shovel, snowblower, whatever?"

"In the garage." I turn and stare at him. It's a big parking lot and then there's the whole front of the house that needs to be cleared. He can't do it all on his own before our first appointment. "My dad has a company that will come clear the lot." I glance at the clock. "They've usually started by now."

"I'll take care of it. If you come greet me properly." He crooks a finger and holds the sheet high.

How can I resist that offer? I dive back into bed and snuggle up tight against his warm, solid body.

"That's better," he murmurs, wrapping his arms around me and resting his chin on my head. "You sleep okay?"

Actually, I did. Talking everything out with him helped. No nightmares about Daniel. For now, he's not my problem. "Yes. Although, I woke up to your hand on my boob."

He stretches his arm out, wiggling his fingers. "Sorry I missed out on that."

Shaking with laughter, I press a kiss to the base of his throat.

"I'm surprised it wasn't somewhere else." He slides one hand down my body. Anticipating where he's headed, I shift back a few inches, then sigh when he dips under my shorts and rubs one finger between my legs.

A low sound somewhere between a groan and a growl vibrates through his chest. "You're soaked."

"I never said...I didn't like waking up with...your hand on my breast," I whisper between choppy breaths.

"What about my mouth?" He nips the fabric of my top between his teeth and tugs on it until one breast pops out. He captures the tip between his lips and sucks hard.

"Oh," I breathe out. "Yes, I like that too."

I roll flat on my back and he follows, licking and sucking at one nipple. I scramble to spread my legs, give him room, and he gently closes his teeth over the tip of my nipple.

"No." He lazily swirls his tongue around the tip. "Stay just like you are. I like my hand trapped between your pretty thighs."

Heat explodes over my skin. Why is that so hot?

He holds me in place and slowly flicks my clit. I can't help it, I arch my back and swivel my hips, chasing the zip of electricity.

"That's it. Show me." He nuzzles closer, sucking at my neck, whispering a mix of sweet and filthy things in my ear.

Sweat mists my forehead and I squeeze my eyes closed. Close. So close.

He rubs faster. My center trembles, tingles racing over my skin. My back bows off the bed. My lips part on a silent scream.

"That's it," he encourages, dragging his fingers through my wetness.

Breathing hard, I lay there dazed for a moment while he keeps pressing little kisses to my cheek, my neck, and my chest.

Something hard prods my hip. I roll toward him, and he jerks his hand out of my shorts.

"Thank you," I whisper. "Your turn."

I reach down and wrap my hand around his erection. Dropping kisses against his chest, I slide lower.

He groans and shifts his body, allowing me more access. "Couldn't help myself."

Another groan slips past his lips as I tug his shorts down and seal my lips over the head of his cock.

"Oh fuck." He rolls flat on his back and lifts his hips.

I release him with a soft pop and pull his shorts off the rest of the way. He stretches and reaches for something, while I take him in my mouth again as far as I can, using my hand to cover what my lips can't.

"That's so good." He sucks in a harsh breath. "Again."

I try taking more of him this time and his loud groans fill the room.

A gold, foil square nudges my hand. "Put this on me. I want to see your tits bounce while you ride my cock. Now."

I moan around him and keep teasing my tongue against the underside of his cock while I rip into the foil.

Once he's sheathed, I wiggle out of my shorts but when I try to take my tank top off the rest of the way, he stops me.

"Leave it like that and come here." He helps me straddle his body and pulls me flat against him. "That's it. Kiss me for a minute."

Our lips meet and tongues slide together. I don't even care about morning breath or anything else. I'm focused on the humming sounds coming from his throat every time our tongues touch and the delicious friction from his cock grazing and sliding against me.

He reaches between us, holding himself steady. I have to sit up, find the right position. He pushes against me. I close my eyes and moan as he slowly fills me.

"Nice and slow," he warns.

Feeling greedy, I ease the rest of the way down, sighing at the delicious stretching sensation.

"That's so good," I whisper.

"Show me how much you like my cock filling your pussy first thing in the morning."

I wiggle my hips, lift my hips, then ease down again. "A lot. I like it a lot," I whisper.

"Lean back," he urges.

I arch and rest my hands on his thighs.

"Yeah," he whispers and cups my breasts. "That's what I wanted to see. God, you're fucking beautiful." He settles his hands at my waist. "Move your hips."

"So bossy this morning."

He chuckles, low and devious. "Only this morning?" His thumb presses against my clit, moving in slow circles.

"Ah." My breath catches. "I like it. Your demanding side," I whisper in between choppy breaths.

I roll my hips, seeking the deep throbbing sensation that will send me over the edge. I'm like an addict chasing a high. Except, every time with him seems better than the last. A revelation. Under his intense stare and full of his worshipful words, I feel so good. So *right.*

Sweat mists my skin by the time the familiar tingle rushes through me again. My eyes roll back, and he urges me to move faster. This orgasm builds quickly and hits hard.

"That's my girl," he encourages. "You're squeezing my cock so fucking good. Come for me." His hands cup my breasts, fingers teasing my nipples.

Breathless, I slow my movements.

And then my world flips. He pushes me to the mattress and sits back on his knees, hooking his arms under my thighs.

"Yes," he growls. "You're so fucking sexy." He thrusts into me at a relentless pace. I squirm and try to adjust, the new angle feeling...interesting.

He lowers my legs and slows his movements. "Am I hurting you?"

"No." My face pinches into a frown as I try to find the right word to describe it. "It's intense. But good."

"Intense. Hmmm." He brings his thumb to my clit, slowly rubbing. "Good intense? Not great?"

"Yes," I gasp. "That's good. Right there."

He lets out a feral grunt and maintains the exact rhythm and pace.

"Do you have any toys?" he asks, glancing at my dresser, his thumb still working circles around my clit.

"No, why?" I gasp.

He lifts his hips, hitting me at a different angle or deeper, dragging his cock over the spot that makes my legs tremble.

I let out a sharp scream and clamp my hand over my mouth.

His lips curve into a wicked smirk. "I'd like to hold a wand to you right here." He applies more pressure to my clit and my eyes roll back from the sharp pleasure. "While I'm fucking you just like this." He thrusts extra hard to paint me a vivid picture.

My soul's ready to leave my body from the excruciating bliss and he wants to add more sensations?

"I don't think. It's necessary." I squeeze my eyes shut. "Oh my God."

"Not necessary. But fun."

I dig my heels into the mattress, lifting my hips and using the leverage to grind myself against him.

"Yes," he groans. "Fuck, I'm gonna come if you keep doing that."

A raw, guttural groan tears from his chest. His hips change rhythm, snapping against me faster and faster as he chases his release.

Then I'm falling off a cliff with him.

Jigsaw

Heart beating at a rapid clip, I thrust one last time. White sears my vision and blood rushes through my ears, dulling every sound but our heavy breathing.

My legs are like jelly as I pull out and collapse over her body. I rest my head on her chest, her heart thudding beneath my ear. She runs her fingers through my hair. Why does every orgasm with this woman shatter my entire universe?

"Give me a sec," I mumble.

"Take all the time you need." She strokes her fingers over my back. "I couldn't move if my life depended on it." Her body shakes with laughter under me.

I kiss the side of her breast and shift my weight off her but keep my hand resting on her stomach.

"Let me clean up, and I'll get started on the snow."

"Mmm." She stretches, eyes still closed. "I want to stay in bed with you all day."

"Nothing I'd rather do more." I press a kiss to her cheek, already regretting the need to move.

The low, incessant whine of a poorly maintained snowblower buzzes faintly from outside, drawing our attention to the window.

Margot props herself up on one elbow and cocks her head. "That must be Paul or my dad."

I lean over and kiss her cheek again. "Let me go help them out. But first, can you check in with your dad about the plow? I'm going to call Remy and see if he can make it over here."

"Why Remy?"

"He has a plow on his old Bronco. Or at least he used to. Hoping he still does."

"Oh." A soft, dreamy expression slides over her face. "You're very resourceful."

"I can be." Fuck, I hate leaving this bed. Especially when she's in it, hair wild, skin flushed, her legs tangled in the sheets. Nothing but pure temptation.

Maybe she senses my hesitation. She rolls to her side and slips out of bed, tugging her top into place as she moves toward her closet. I force myself to turn away and head down the hall, each step more reluctant than the last.

***

Fifteen minutes later, I step onto the back porch and the wind slaps me in the face, cutting through my leather jacket. Yup, I'd really rather be upstairs in bed with Margot.

Soft, weightless flakes pour from the sky in a heavy, steady fall, piling up fast.

Someone cleared off the porch and steps and shoveled a path to the garage, but it's already covered with a fine dusting of snow. A push broom and shovel rest against the house, coated in a soft layer of snow. I take the shovel and carve a narrow path toward my truck—hat and gloves are in there somewhere. No warmer coat, though. Fucking forecast never mentioned this much snow getting dumped on us.

The gloves are old, but warm. I wiggle my hands into them and pull on the knit cap, covering my ears, then continue digging through the SUV.

Blanket, tarp, knife.

Glass cleaner, paper towels.

Another knife.

Empty gas can.

Compact tool kit. Tire repair kit and a portable air compressor.

Jumper cables. Tow straps.

Wire cutters. Zip ties.

Duct tape. Electrical tape.

Another knife.

Bolt cutters.

Ballpeen hammer.

A box cutter—why the fuck am I carrying so many cutting instruments?

Flashlight. Headlamp.

Absolutely nothing useful for snow removal.

"Motherfucker," I grumble, slamming the tailgate shut with an unsatisfying *thud.*

"Morning!"

I turn.

Margot's cousin Paul greets me with an amused smile. "Cold enough for ya?"

So engrossed in searching through all the shit stashed in my ride, I missed the sound of the snowblower cutting out and Paul creeping up on me.

Wrath's right, my situational awareness needs improvement.

"You could say that." My gaze sweeps the driveway. "I thought I heard a snowblower?"

Paul jerks his thumb toward the front of the house. "Died on the sidewalk." His red face scrunches into a sheepish expression. "I think it's out of gas? At least I hope that's what it is."

"I'll run out to get it," I offer. "Is it a two-stroke, or four?"

An embarrassed smile spreads over Paul's face. "It's newer, if that helps."

Be nice. He's Margot's cousin. A mortician, not a mechanic. I couldn't drain a body—he doesn't know what kind of snowblower he has. It's all good.

I nod. "Let me take a look."

Paul leads me to the front, where the Cadillac of snowblowers sits tilted on a patch of snow-covered concrete. Stand-on, rubber track drive, probably a fifty-foot throw distance. Overkill for residential sidewalks. Figures the Cedarwoods would buy the most expensive snowblower and then forget to put gas in it.

At least Paul cleared a portion of the driveway and made it to the front steps before the thing died.

I crouch beside the beast of a machine and remove the gas cap, tilting the whole unit slightly to check the tank.

"Yup. Empty."

Paul squints. "That's bad, right? Did I wreck it?"

"Nah." *It's definitely a four-stroke.* "Just needs some gas."

Relief softens his features. "We haven't used it much. One of the guys usually plows the parking lot, then jumps out and shovels the walkways."

"This'll do the parking lot. It'll just take some time." I pat the frame and stand. "I'll run out and get the gas."

"I, uh, you don't have to do that," he protests.

"My truck's ready to go." I nod toward the slice of driveway he cleared. "Your vehicles are still boxed in."

"Good point." He hooks his thumb toward the right. "There's a gas station a couple miles that way. Otherwise, you'll have to go almost all the way back to the highway."

"Thanks." I turn toward my vehicle. "Be back soon."

My engine turns over without hesitation, but I let it idle for a minute. While it warms up, I shoot off a quick text to Margot so she doesn't worry, then tap Remy's number.

He answers on the second ring. "Jigsaw?" His voice is low and rough. "What's up?"

"Like two feet of snow."

He chuckles, the sound muffled by wind. "Yeah, no shit. Been plowing all morning."

Good. "Think you could swing that plow over to Pine Hollow?"

Silence, except for the wind howling over the line. "What's out there?"

"The Cedarwood Funeral Home."

Another pause. "Oh."

"I'll pay you."

"It's not that," he says quickly. "One of my neighbors is sick. I've been keeping their place clear. Just in case, you know, she needs to call an ambulance. Her husband's...not doing great."

"Shit. Sorry to hear that."

He sighs, heavy and tired. "They were good to my grandparents back in the day. Just trying to return the favor."

Grinder had mentioned Remy helped out most of his elderly neighbors. One of the reasons he's got so much respect for the kid— when Grinder usually dislikes almost everyone. "Yeah, I get it."

"Let me make a call," he says. "I got a buddy out that way who can probably get there faster than I could anyway."

"That's all right. We've got a snowblower."

"That'll take forever to clear their parking lot. Hang tight. I'll call you back."

"Thanks." We hang up, and I shift into Drive, easing onto the slick road, while flakes continue to fall in lazy swirls. At least the snow seems to be slowing.

Half an hour later, I pull back into the Cedarwoods' driveway, sliding into the spot I claimed earlier—close to the house, out of the way of the plow Remy promised should be here in another thirty.

Paul's shoveling in front of the garage. He's actually made a lot of progress in the short amount of time I've been gone.

Snow crunches under my boots as I step out of the truck. The wind hasn't let up, but the flurries have slowed.

Paul stops and waves, hurrying over to me. "That was quick."

I pull the can out of the back. "Didn't stop to browse. Let's get that beast going."

We trudge through the powder to the machine, where I unscrew the cap and tilt the gas can, steady and slow. Fuel splashes into the tank with a satisfying *glug, glug, glug*. Paul stands back, arms folded, watching like I'm performing surgery.

"Think it'll start?" he asks.

"It better." I set the can aside, prime the engine a couple times, then hit the electric start. The machine coughs, sputters, then rumbles to life like a pissed-off dragon. Runs rough. But at least it's chugging along now.

Paul lets out a relieved breath. "Damn. I didn't think it would be that easy."

"Just needed to feed it." I grab the handles. "This thing's barely

broken in." I bet they didn't winterize it last year, either. That's something I can do at the end of the season.

I test the controls, adjusting the chute direction and speed. Tracks grip the snow like tank treads. Yeah, this thing's a beast.

Before I can get started, footsteps crunch behind me. I turn to find Margot's dad bundled up in a winter coat, holding out a pair of tan coveralls in one hand and a broken-in Carhartt jacket in the other.

"Here," he says. "You've got more muscle on you, but I think these might fit."

"Uh." I glance down at my jeans and leather jacket, the cold sinking into my bones.

Pride begs me to refuse the offer, but he's right.

"You'll freeze in that." He pushes the coveralls toward me.

"Okay." I grab the clothes from him. "Thanks."

He nods. "I appreciate the help. I don't know what happened to Henry." His frown deepens. "I hope he's okay."

"Maybe he's stuck in the snow somewhere?" I suggest. "Cell service out here's spotty. Worse in a storm. I've got a friend with a plow truck on the way, but I'll finish the driveway that Paul started and work my way around the house."

He studies me again with that quiet, assessing look of his. "Thank you, Jensen."

I return the nod, solid and simple. No need to make it awkward.

What kind of asshole would I be if I just sat around and watched my girlfriend's family struggle to do a task I can easily handle?

Now that it's gassed up, I shouldn't have a problem starting the snow blower again. I shut it off and follow Mr. Cedarwood up the front steps into the house.

Sweet, suffocating heat wraps around me as I step inside. Margot's waiting to the side. Her dad stops to have a word with her, and she nods.

Someone laid thick, plastic runners over the carpet; even so, I don't want to track more snow over the house than necessary. I quickly unlace my boots and pop them out on the porch, then step into the coveralls. I shrug my jacket off and Margot tugs it from my hands.

"Thank you," she says. "You don't have to do this, you know."

"Well, I can't sit and watch your dad and cousin do it, when I know I can help them get it done quicker." I lean down and kiss her cheek. "Besides, don't you and your dad have to get ready for a consultation?"

She nods quickly. "We moved the time back an hour, but yes."

"So, you do that. And let me worry about the snow."

CHAPTER TWENTY-THREE

MARGOT

The snow didn't stick around for long.

But Jigsaw has.

No more waking up alone.

He was right about being clingy.

But he was wrong about how much I'd love it.

He spends his days doing whatever it is he does for his club, racking up a lot of miles between my place and his home charter. When he's not doing that, he's at his friend's gym, getting to know Cain, or setting up a new business for his club.

But almost every night, he's at my place. When I'm on call, he gets up with me, no matter how late. Offers to drive me, even though I always say no. Paul and I do that on our own. But Jigsaw always waits up for me. I'll find him in my living room working on his laptop or in the theater room, watching a movie with Gretel curled up in his lap. Waiting for me.

Tonight, I'm done early. Still on call but done for now.

I find him in my apartment, sprawled out in my lounge chair, working on his laptop. He sets it on the side table, and I jump onto the chair and straddle his lap.

"Guess who has the whole weekend off?"

He rests his hands on my hips, squeezing lightly. "I hope it's you, otherwise this is the worst game ever."

"It's me!" I laugh and lean in, pressing my lips to his.

Movement from the corner of my eye catches my attention.

Frowning, I pull away and glance at his screen.

A pale, thin woman with black hair and zero clothes on fills the screen. Hand between her legs, rubbing something against herself. Her mouth open on a silent moan.

"What the hell?" I scoot back. "Are you watching *porn* in my apartment, while I'm working?" Worse, is that the kind of women he likes to watch? With her thin frame, small breasts, long legs, and pin-straight black hair—she's pretty much the exact opposite of me.

"Fuuuck." He closes the lid. "No, I wasn't *watching* porn. I was troubleshooting an issue on one of the websites the club owns."

"That has to be one of the most creative cover stories I've heard."

He rolls his eyes. "If I was watching it for pleasure—which I'm not —I'd tell you." He points to his crotch. "Trust me, nothing happy was going on in my pants until you got here. I can't stand her." He jerks his chin toward the now-closed laptop.

"Wait, you know her personally?"

He lets out a long, heavy sigh. "Unfortunately. Our last president was...I don't know what you want to call it—dating her? Fucking her behind his wife's back? He was basically obsessed with her. Bankrolled her website and some of her other business ventures. So now we run everything and take a cut of her earnings. We maintain a couple of sites for other girls, too. But she's the club's biggest earner."

That was a lot of unpleasant information to absorb all at once. "I thought you ran a laundromat. And you're opening one in Johnsonville?"

"I did and I am. Well, technically the club's going to *own* it." He spreads his hands out wide. "I told you I do whatever the club needs me to do."

"Yes. I didn't realize *the club* was such a multi-faceted corporation, though." I tilt my head. "When were you going to tell me you're a porn king?"

"Uh, never? *I'm* not. It's a *club* business. I've been trying to extract myself from dealing with her for, well, ever. But Rooster does the main—"

"Wait. Rooster's in on this too?" Why does that feel like some sort of betrayal? "Does Shelby know?"

"Of course, Shelby knows." He frowns like it's an absurd question. "She's friends with one of our girls in Virginia."

The way he says "our girls" unleashes something unpleasantly feral and possessive in me.

He jerks his thumb at the laptop. "She can't stand Stella either, though."

Stella. Stella. "Why does that name sound familiar?"

He shrugs. "Are you a fan? Her stuff's supposed to be 'for the female gaze,'" he says in a mocking falsetto that sounds more B-movie villainess than feminist icon. "Although, ninety percent of her subscribers are men."

Is he nuts? "Ewww, no. I'm not a fan."

"She writes feminist essays or something too. I think Hope knew who she was from that. Liked her...until she actually met her." He chuckles.

"That's it!" I scamper off the chair and hurry over to my bookshelf. "She wrote a piece about *Feminism and Female Serial Killers.* As someone who identifies as both, naturally I was intrigued."

Jigsaw breaks into harsh laughter, and I grin at him.

"Anyway," I continue, "it examined whether female serial killers kill as a response to violence and oppression they've experienced *or* if it's a challenge to patriarchal structures in society."

"That was a lot of big words all in a row," he says with an amused smile. "What was her conclusion?"

I pull a tattered magazine from a stack on one of the bottom shelves and flip to the page I marked with a red tab.

"Well, honestly, I thought it was mostly navel-gazing nonsense wrapped in a lot of academic buzzwords," I say, glancing at the notes I'd scribbled in the margins. "She tried so hard to sound neutral and intelligent, that she forgot to actually make a point."

He bursts into laughter. "Jesus, that describes her perfectly."

I glare at him, still annoyed he seems to know this woman so well.

"Anyway," I say, voice crisp, "I only kept it because—" I shoot him a wicked smirk. "The subject matter is obviously close to my heart."

He flashes an amused grin. "Obviously."

He holds out his hand, and I pass him the magazine, already open to the article.

"She had a few decent points," I admit. "That violence can be empowering and how women kill for different reasons and use different methods than men."

He glances at the article, flipping through the pages but only stopping to squint at my notes. "Well, if you'd like to have her autograph it for you, she'll probably be at the clubhouse this weekend. Downstate." He snorts. "Rock would skin us alive if we brought her to Upstate's clubhouse."

"No, I don't want her autograph." I snap the magazine out of his hand and tuck it back on the shelf.

When I turn, he's watching me with that unreadable look of his. The one that sees more than I want him to.

"I meant what I said." He holds my gaze. "I'm not a fan. It's just work."

"Some work," I grumble, crossing my arms over my chest. "Would you like me working with naked dudes all the time?"

His lips twist into a playful grin. "You kinda do."

"They're dead. It's not the same!"

He reaches for me, and I let him pull me into the chair with him again. My body against his, the warmth of his arms, the steady beat of his heart—it settles some of my unease. But not all of it.

"So, were you just never going to tell me about this?"

He sighs and runs his fingers over my hair. "To be honest, I hadn't worked on the site in a while. But something came up, and Hustler needed me to fix it. I knew you'd find out eventually. I wasn't sure how to bring up the subject, though."

I lift my head and find nothing but sincerity in his eyes. My nose wrinkles. "Yeah, I guess it's an awkward subject to approach. I already knew your club owns a strip club. Tacking on 'Oh, and we produce porn too,' might've been a bit much."

He nods and blows out a breath. "She dances too sometimes. But like this highbrow artsy stuff."

"Awww." I pull a mock sad face. "She doesn't rip off her clothes and grind her bits on customer's faces?"

"No." He shakes with laughter.

"How rude of her." Now, I kind of feel bad that I made fun of the woman's article. And I don't *want* to feel bad for a woman my boyfriend's seen naked multiple times apparently.

"Can we not talk about this anymore," I say, resting my head on his chest again.

"Yes, pleeease." His voice rumbles through his chest, followed by a dramatic sigh that makes his whole body sink beneath me. "I'd rather talk about literally anything else."

My brain won't stop turning over the situation, though. If she's the club's "biggest earner," whatever that means, he won't be able to walk away from working with her as easily as he makes it sound.

Not when his loyalty to his club is stitched into every part of him —even the parts I wish were just mine.

CHAPTER TWENTY-FOUR

JIGSAW

NOW THAT MARGOT KNOWS ABOUT THE CLUB'S PORN EMPIRE, I MIGHT as well take her to a party downstate. Not exactly a dream date, but it's been a relief not having to hide that detail from her any longer.

"So what are they celebrating tonight?" she asks, settling herself into the passenger side of my truck. She carefully gathers the skirt of her dress—black with big, splashy blue flowers—and drapes it over her knees. Shiny blue heels. Matching cardigan. The whole look is pure class, way too refined for the kind of party we're headed to. But the second I saw her, I lost the ability to say a damn word. The dress hugs her in all the right places, especially that low neckline teasing the soft swells of her tits. Made me want to bury my face in her cleavage and say fuck the party.

I should be taking her out somewhere nice. On an actual date. Not a party for…"Stella just passed five hundred thousand monthly subscribers to her site," I explain.

She twists to face me as I pull out of her driveway, her red lips parted, forming an adorable, shocked O. "Five. Hundred. *Thousand?*"

"Yup. She's been close for a while now, so it's a big deal."

And since Stella's still salty that we turned her down for her one-hundred-and-one-men-in-one-day fuckfest project, Z said to host a party in her honor to celebrate this milestone and stroke her ego.

Of course, he had zero intention of attending the party. So, as an officer, now I *have* to be there.

Rooster promised to bring Shelby and meet us at the party.

"Subscribers? Like, paid subscribers?" Margot asks.

Whatever fragrance she's wearing fills the cabin. Sweet like expensive candy and flowers but warm like vanilla, and a little woodsy. The urge to pull over and lick her all over keeps me on edge. "Yup."

"How much does she charge?" Out of the corner of my eye, I catch her press her hand to her lips. "Sorry, that's rude, isn't it?"

"Not like you can't look up the information if you wanted to." My tone's flat as I flick the blinker on and take the turn for the ramp to the Thruway. "She has a couple of different tiers. From five-ninety-nine to twenty-five-ninety-nine."

"Wow." She fusses with her dress some more. "Boy did I go into the wrong line of work."

Even though I think—*hope*—it's just a throwaway comment, if I turn it over for too long, my head will explode. "Don't even joke about that."

"Who says I'm joking?" She laughs softly. "And your club takes a percentage of that for maintaining the website and stuff?"

A large percentage. Between the investment money and my cut of the porn cash, I've been the beneficiary of several large bonuses recently. Still haven't figured out what I want to do with all that cash yet.

"Sorry," she says again. "That's club business, isn't it?"

"Yes, the club takes a percentage." I squeeze the steering wheel harder than necessary. "And even though it's club business, I want you to understand, when you catch me on my laptop fiddling with porn sites, I'm not jerking off. It's *work*."

"I guess so," she mutters, clearly not thrilled but still curious. "And that's only one of the sites that the club manages? You take a percentage from all of them?"

If only she asked me this much about riding, the laundromat, the racetrack, or almost anything else.

"Yup. Hers is the most…elaborate. And profitable. She produces a lot of different content and engages with her fanbase a lot." *Engage is one way to put it.* I can't believe I'm going to say this to my girlfriend. "As much as I don't like her personally, she's a smart woman. Very driven."

"Guess you'd have to be to have half a million people pay to see you do…" She wiggles her hands in the air jazz style. "*Stuff* every month."

She rests her hand on my thigh and gives me a playful squeeze. "Think there's a niche market for porn starring a cute mortician?"

What she's suggesting makes my eye twitch.

"I'm sure there's a market for everything." I cut a sidelong glance her way. "But that's absolutely the fuck not happening. Unless you're asking for a friend."

"I'm joking. I could never." Her voice quiets, and she turns her attention to the windshield. "Will there be lots of… muffler bunnies attending this party tonight?"

"Probably."

"Good thing I brought the knife you gave me." She pats her side, where I assume the knife's resting in a pocket. "How will they feel about all this attention being lavished on Stella?"

Not quite the question I expected from Margot. "Most of them won't go near her. She's not hooked up with a brother and they know she brings money into the club—which enables them to attend the parties at all—so I think they're too intimidated to pay much attention to her. She'll have her own entourage with her tonight anyway."

"Other porn stars?"

"Most likely."

Margot hums, letting that settle.

Dying to change the subject, I nudge the volume on the radio up a few clicks, letting the haunting hum of Amy Lee's hypnotic voice fill the cab. "You excited to finally have a weekend off?"

"Yes!" She lets out a girlish squeal that's endearing as hell. "I'll probably have next weekend too." Her enthusiasm seems to fade. "Winter's usually the busiest time for us."

"Bad weather accidents?"

"That, and illness—flu and pneumonia."

"If that's slowing down, it's worth celebrating."

"Yes, spring brings something else. Prom season. Graduation. Young people getting drunk and thinking they're invincible, and those are always depressing."

"Even in such a small town?"

She nods, eyes still on the horizon. "You'd be surprised."

After that, we move on to happier topics and before I realize it, I'm taking the exit for the road leading to Downstate's clubhouse.

"Uh, I know Upstate set a high standard but readjust your expectations. Downstate's a lot less pretty."

She reaches over and pats my thigh. "I have no expectations. I'm just happy to finally see your home club. And spend time with your friends again."

Damn, that does something to my insides. I'll have to start being less of a prick to my brothers to thank them for making Margot feel welcome.

When I roll up to our gate, it's standing wide open. A prospect standing guard.

I roll down my window. "What's up, Fiddle?"

"Hey, Jigsaw. I didn't realize that was you." The kid slowly walks over to my window. His short, curly mop of hair flopping in his eyes. "Grinder says he wants the gate closed in an hour."

"You and Stitch monitoring it after that?"

"Yes, sir."

I reach over and rest my hand on Margot's arm. "Fiddle, this is my ol' lady, Margot."

He leans in the window but doesn't smile or look all that welcoming. "Evening, ma'am."

Margot waves and murmurs hello.

"Eyes open, Fiddle," I say.

"You know it." He taps his fist over his heart and steps back.

"So, he's a not a full member, right?" Margot asks, once I've rolled my window up again.

"Not yet. Normally we just refer to them as 'prospect,' but I wanted you to know his name, just in case."

"Is he even allowed inside the clubhouse?" she teases.

"Not without a good reason." I laugh. "Yeah, someone will relieve him of gate duty later, let him come in and enjoy the party for a minute."

"Sounds like code for 'give him enough time to receive a blow job.'"

Margot's so adept at reading between the lines. "When you put it that way, it sounds so seedy."

She chuckles but sits forward in her seat. "Oh, there's Rooster! Shelby must already be here too, then, right?"

Warmth spreads through my chest, pleased they seem to like each other. "Yes."

A group of guys from Upstate are standing in a loose circle in our parking lot in front of the clubhouse entrance. I back into a spot on the far side of the parking lot near Rooster's truck and help Margot out of the 4Runner.

"I feel bad you didn't get to ride with everyone," she whispers to me, casting a nervous glance toward the guys.

"It's not a big deal." I jerk my chin toward Rooster's truck. "Rooster didn't ride either." Farther out in the parking lot, I spot Rock's big blacked-out Yukon. "Rock didn't either."

"Oh." She blows out a relieved breath.

Rooster breaks away from the pack and jogs over to me. "Hey, was wondering when you'd get here." He pulls me in for a quick hug, slapping my back like we haven't seen each other in months instead of a week.

"Miss me, motherclucker?" I squeeze his face between my hands and tap my forehead to his.

He laughs and pulls away. "Not that much." He glances down at Margot and smiles wider. "Welcome to Downstate."

"Hi, Rooster."

"Where's your little songbird?" I ask Rooster.

"Inside with Hope, Serena, Trinity, and Emily." He wags his hand in front of his face. "Doing makeup."

As we cross the parking lot to join the group, several of the guys glance in our direction.

"Look who it is!" Ravage shouts. "Our favorite collector of fingers and his adorable collector of creepy objects."

My lips curl into a snarl but Margot bursts into laughter and lifts her arm in an enthusiastic wave. Her heels click faster over the pavement, like she's eager to join the circle.

Guess Rav gets to live another day.

I nod to or shake hands with each brother in the wide circle. "What're you all doing hanging around outside?"

Grinder cocks his head toward the gate. "Keeping an eye on fuckwad over there."

"Fiddle," Suds corrects.

"I said what I said," Grinder grumbles.

Margot suppresses a snort-laugh, her body quivering.

"Waiting for you," Rooster answers, waving a hand at Rav, Dex, Butcher, Hustler, and the other guys. "Not sure what these other chucklefucks are up to."

"Awww, you two are so adorable." Hustler makes obnoxious kissy-face noises. "Margot, I hope you're aware that Rooster is Jiggy's number one love."

She flicks an amused glance at Rooster, then Hustler. "I can understand why." She presses her hand to her chest and lays on the drama in a breathless Marilyn Monroe voice. "I've learned to accept it."

Everyone—even Grinder—bursts into laughter.

Butcher steps up and slaps Dex's shoulder. "So, your brother here was just telling us how he met his ol' lady because he was stalking her."

"What?" I laugh.

"That's *not* what I said." Dex throws a punch at Butcher's boulder-sized bicep.

Ravage leers in Margot's direction.

"Margot, you've never told us exactly how you and Jigsaw hooked up." He ambles over to us, grinning like a kid in a candy store with a credit card and no adult supervision. "Did he ask you out?" Rav wiggles his fingers in my face, and I slap his hand away. "And you looked at his junkyard dog face and thought to yourself, 'yeah, this seems like a smart life choice?'"

A sharp flare of anger flashes in her eyes. Brief, but I catch it. Margot's as protective of me as I am of her.

"Well, actually." A heavy edge of sarcasm wraps around her words. "My last relationship was so desperately unsatisfying. When I met Jigsaw, I found him so physically appealing, I asked if he'd be so kind as to tutor me in the fine art of sex." She tilts her head and stares up at me from under her lashes. "He's an *excellent* teacher. I couldn't help falling in love with him."

Cold shock seizes my body. Did she just basically lay out our origin story in front of my brothers?

Somehow, I follow Margot's lead and keep a straight face.

She spoke the truth in such an absurd way, no will know it's the truth, right?

Ravage blinks, his mouth hanging open for a beat before he throws his head back and laughs like a drunk donkey. "See, now I *know* that's false."

Laughter spreads through the group like a slow burn. I exhale, the knot in my gut loosening—everyone assumes she's joking.

Except Dex, standing off to my left, his heavy gaze zeroed in on me.

At first, I can't decipher the weird expression on his face. Then it hits me. The dumb, awkward convo I initiated when I was worried about "tutoring" Margot.

Dex has too much tact to ever say anything that would embarrass Margot, so I'm not worried he'll ask me about it in front of everyone.

The double doors sweep open. Suds holds one side and Grip the other, the two of them standing at attention like two gruff doormen for royalty.

"Thank you," a soft, familiar voice says.

"Ladies." Suds dips his chin as Trinity, Hope, and Emily step outside.

I don't normally pay attention to what the ol' ladies are wearing, but I shouldn't have been worried. Margot fits in well tonight.

Trinity strides out first, in a knee-length, body-hugging royal blue dress with black beading around the plunging neckline. Don't-fuck-with-me attitude radiating from her rigid posture and calculating eyes.

Emily follows, more reserved in a light purple dress with lines of silver sparkling things down the front that emphasize her generous rack while still hiding all the goods.

Hope emerges last, and for a second, I think she's wearing nothing but some strategically placed flowers. Up close, I catch the illusion— bright red roses embroidered into sheer nude mesh. Riskier than what I'm used to seeing her wear, but somehow, she makes it look elegant instead of suggestive.

No one will mistake any of them for muffler bunnies and not just because they're all wearing property patches.

"Looking lovely tonight, ladies," I say with my most charming smile.

Hope leans in, brushing a quick kiss on my cheek. "Good to see you, Jigsaw."

Then she wraps Margot in a more informal and enthusiastic hug that plucks any reservation I had about tonight out of my chest. "I'm so happy you were able to join us tonight, Margot." She pulls back, holding Margot at arm's length and giving her a warm smile. "It's your first time visiting Downstate, right?"

Margot nods quickly, her lips curving in a shy smile. "I've been looking forward to it ever since Jigsaw invited me."

Rock and Wrath step out, Wrath stopping to give Suds shit.

"Jigsaw." Rock nods at me, then shifts his attention to Margot. "Good to see you again, Margot."

"Thank you," she says softly.

Hope curls her arm around Margot's shoulders. "Can I borrow you for a moment?"

"Uh, sure." Margot's gaze pings between Hope and me but Hope gently guides her over to Trinity and Emily.

With Lilly absent tonight, Hope seems to be stepping in as the unofficial queen of Downstate's castle. Normally, Lilly would be the one out here greeting guests. Seeing Hope take her place, calm and composed but clearly on duty, drives home just how messy this whole situation is.

For the first time ever, all the complications caused by where we stick our dicks prickles at my conscience.

Why the hell didn't we host Stella's celebration somewhere else tonight? Rent a ballroom, a hotel suite, hell, an abandoned factory with decent lighting and enough parking. We throw enough money around, someone would've looked the other way while we did our dirty deeds.

But I've been in the MC world too long to kid myself. That's not how it works.

Besides, it's not like Z left Lilly home alone. He ain't here either. He's doing the presidential thing by lettin' Stella have her moment, while sending her a clear message—*congrats, enjoy your moment, I'd rather be home with my wife.* A silent—but effective—fuck off. Some of the brothers will probably hassle Z about it later. But I respect him more for putting his wife above club protocol bullshit.

"Hey, Rock. Shelby still in there?" Rooster asks, lifting his chin toward the clubhouse.

"She's filming a thing with Serena for her channel." He holds up his hand, mimicking someone recording with a phone.

Grinder joins us. "Serena had a whole 'glam look' in mind for Shelby."

Rooster snickers into his hand. "I love that Grinder's saying 'glam' now."

Laughing, Grinder elbows Rooster's side.

Rock's lips twist with amusement as he casts an affectionate glance at his wife. "Hope said she wanted no part of the filming, although I think Serena tried to talk her into it."

Still chuckling, Grinder nods at me. "Pretty sure she might try to talk your girl into a video."

I glance over at Margot. She's slipped into her professional pose— head up, hands clasped in front of her, attention focused on whoever's speaking. The same way she carried herself at Whisper's funeral. Maybe she's not as at ease here as I thought she'd be.

Tearing my gaze away from Margot, I focus on Grinder. "I know she was looking forward to picking Serena's brain about makeup-y stuff."

Wrath stalks up behind Grinder and attempts to hook his arm around his neck. Grinder's hand shoots out like a rattlesnake, grabbing Wrath's wrist mid-air. "Nice try, fucker," Grinder says.

Wrath grins, then points at me. "See? Situational awareness."

"One of these days, I'm gonna sneak up on you and choke you unconscious, big guy. Just wait," I warn.

"Never gonna happen." Wrath grins. "But I look forward to your weak-ass attempts."

Rock, Grinder, Wrath, and Rooster start talking about our last trip to Deadbranch. I'm listening but not really adding to the conversation, when someone taps my shoulder.

I turn to find Dex who jerks his head to the side. I follow him a few feet away from the group.

"What's up?" I ask.

"I feel like I'm gonna regret it if I don't ask," Dex says. "And probably regret asking if I do."

"You got a damned if you do, damned if you don't situation brewing, Dex?" I ask, already anticipating what's about to come out of his mouth.

"You could say that. Is Margot...the woman you wanted to help 'gain confidence' and 'teach some skills' to?" He frowns. "Why'd you say she was a virgin?"

"That's not *quite* what I said." I raise my hands in a helpless shrug. "Besides, I don't know what you're talking about."

He nods slowly, like he's proud of me for keeping the details to myself instead of bragging like a lot of guys would do. "She just told all your brothers she loves you. I'm impressed you didn't run screaming down the road."

I drop my cocky smile. "Brother, I'm so fucking in love with her and also wildly obsessed with her."

Dex snorts. "A little healthy obsession's good for the soul. With the right woman, anyway."

"I think you'll find joy in knowing that she calls me out on my bullshit."

His lips twist with amusement. "Those must be some fun conversations."

"They're both terrifying and arousing."

Dex presses his hand over his mouth like he's trying to keep something from escaping—amusement or disbelief, it's hard to tell. His shoulders shake once before he drops his hand. "You worried partying with porn stars might be too much for her?"

"You heard how she pulled a knife on Dee-Dee at the bonfire, right?"

"That seals it. She's definitely the right woman for you." There's nothing but approval, maybe even admiration, in his tone.

"I think so too."

"Good." He reaches out and slaps my shoulder. "Gonna make it official?"

"In due time." He's been so helpful, I figure I owe him the same. "Are *you* worried about Emily partying with the porn stars?"

"I warned her ahead of time." He shrugs. "After Swan and some of the other dancers pulled their crap, I think she can handle Stella and her crew." He holds up both hands. "And I never had any serious ties to any of these women."

A twinge of guilt pokes at me. I could've been more welcoming to Emily when they first got serious. "That situation with Swan get any better?"

He tips his head side to side. "I don't think they'll ever be besties, but they're civil. For now."

"Swan's tight with some of the other ol' ladies. That causing any tension?"

He opens his mouth, then hesitates. "I don't know," he finally says. "She hasn't said so. Serena was her best friend before Grinder or I came along. So, they're fine."

"Maybe we should swap charters," I joke.

Dex gives me a long stare like he's trying to decide if I'm the dumbest motherfucker alive—or a fucking genius.

Margot

"Ready to go inside?" Jigsaw slides his arms around my waist, pulling me back against him.

His solid body surrounding me finally helps me draw my first full breath in minutes. The steady weight of him quiets the static in my head.

I'm not new to people. I talk to grieving families for a living. I navigate strangers' worst days with steady hands and a gentle voice. Small talk and surface-level connection? I can do that all day, every day.

But tonight is different. It's personal. These people matter to Jigsaw. And I want them to like me. I want to fit in and be accepted.

Wanting something I've only experienced once before—at the bonfire—keeps me wound tight with anxiety. They accepted my weirdness then. Surely, they'll notice how awkward I am this time?

No, these nerves twist my insides with a different kind of tension. Why?

The porn stars? Maybe. I have zero experience or knowledge about that industry. Coffins, embalming, formaldehyde ratios, flower arrangements, grief management—those I can handle in my sleep. I can sew a shattered jaw shut and make it look like it never happened. But sex on camera—lighting, angles, what positions look the best for an audience? Nope. That's a whole different universe. One I have no map for. No script. Just insecurity and a lingering fear that I'll be the weird, awkward outsider who wandered onto the wrong set.

My creepy doll story probably won't help me at this party.

Hope reaches out, giving my arm an affectionate squeeze. "Go ahead. We'll be in soon." She flicks her gaze to Jigsaw. "Wait until you see what the guys did to your clubhouse."

"Oh, for fuck's sake," he groans. "I'm afraid to ask."

"It has to be seen to be believed," Hope promises.

As we step inside the doors, a black curtain blocks our view. Red glows around the edges. A biker standing to the side pulls the curtain back, motioning for us to move forward.

"What the fuuuuck?" Jigsaw mutters.

Rooster leans in and shouts, "It gets worse, don't worry."

We step into a large room glowing with bloodred lights. The furniture to the right appears to be all black leather couches, chairs, and ottomans. At least seventy inches of television screen takes up the wall behind one couch. *Congratulations, Stella!* scrolls over the screen with *500K* underneath.

"Why does it look like the devil's darkroom in here?" Jigsaw asks Rooster.

More like vampire's whorehouse.

A low, sensual beat thrums from hidden speakers. Loud enough to add to the ambiance but not drown out conversation. Gasping, thumping, and grunting comes from one corner, and I crane my neck, looking past Jigsaw toward a pool table being violated by at least three people.

"Oh my," I gasp and quickly look away.

Jigsaw curls his hand around mine. "Do you want something to drink?"

I eye the bar straight ahead of us against the wall. Two girls in what looks like red lingerie are behind the long wooden counter, serving drinks to people. "Uh, sure."

Rooster follows us over to the bar.

"What's with all the red?" I ask Jigsaw. "I thought your colors were blue and silver?"

"I have no idea." Jigsaw pauses. "No, I have an idea." He slides a look Rooster's way. "Stella's 'theme' for the night?"

"Got it in one." Rooster points at Jigsaw, then nods to a hallway on his left. "Other rooms have purple lighting," he adds in a sarcastic tone, "blue, green, and I don't know what else."

We stop at the bar and one of the girls slides over to us. "Hi, Jiggy!" Her bright gaze lands on me. "Hi, Margot, right? We met upstate."

She looks familiar. The only club girl who'd been decent to me up there. Unusual name. L something..."Lala, right?"

Her smile widens even more, pleased I remembered her name. "That's me."

"Hi, again." I lift my hand in a quick, dorky wave. Lala responds with a similar gesture, helping me feel less goofy.

"What can I get you?" She turns slightly, the movement shifting the lace covering her breasts enough that one almost falls out. What an uncomfortable outfit for serving drinks.

I glance up at Jigsaw but his grim stare's focused on the shelves of bottles on the wall, or maybe the mirror behind it.

"The selection's not bad tonight," Lala says. "Pretty much any soda you might want, some fruit juices, lots of different beer, and I can do some mixed drinks. Our signature drink for the night is what we're calling the Velvet Crown—it's champagne with a splash of blackberry liqueur."

"Oh. That sounds interesting." I glance up at Jigsaw. "I'll try that." My voice comes out almost like a question.

Why am I asking his permission to have a drink?

One corner of his mouth tips up and he brushes his knuckles over my bare arm. "Have anything you want."

"Coming right up!" Lala says.

I'm so focused on watching Lala make my drink, I don't notice the other woman sliding over to Jigsaw.

"What do you want tonight?" she asks in a raspy tone.

I glance over and she's leaning on the bar with her boobs pushed so far out of her lacy top I spy areola.

"Just a beer, Bonnie. Thanks," he answers without looking at her.

Lala passes me a champagne glass. Under the strange red lighting, the bubbly liquid takes on a muddy hue. Lala garnished it with a plump, fresh blackberry on the rim. I pop that in my mouth first, then take a sip.

Bonnie slides down closer to me. Mean-girl eyes focused on my face.

I take a sip, blinking against the unexpected rush of sweetness.

"We named it that after that really smooth, velvety sensitive spot on the head of a guy's dick," the girl says, her red lips tilting into a smirk as she peers up at Jigsaw.

I almost gag on the small sip.

Behind Bonnie, Lala shakes her head.

Clearing my throat, I set my glass on the bar top with a sharp clink loud enough to get Bonnie's attention. "You named a drink after the corona of the glans penis? Bold choice." I tilt my head, keeping my voice sugary sweet. "Fun fact, did you know the glans and shaft shrivel postmortem?"

"Ewww." Bonnie sneers. "What?"

A strangled snort escapes Jigsaw. Shoulders shaking, he glances down at me. "Warn your man when you're about to get clinical."

"Weirdo," Bonnie mumbles, storming off to harass her next victim.

Coming from her, I'll consider that a compliment.

Lala rushes forward, bracing her hands against the bar. "That's not true. Or if it is, I didn't know that's why they named it that when I offered you the drink."

"It's okay." I twirl the stem of the glass between my fingers. "It's good. Thank you."

Trinity wedges herself in next to me, resting her hand on my shoulder. "I swear this clubhouse doesn't always look like the bordello from hell," she says against my ear.

I huff a soft breath of amusement and give my glass another twirl. "My first thought was 'vampire whorehouse.' Bordello sounds so much classier."

She lets out a quick laugh, points to my glass, then holds up two fingers to Lala. "We'll have to make a T-shirt to mark the occasion. *I Survived the Vampire Bordello*." She twirls her hand in the air. "We'll ask Shelby to come up with the slogan—she's better with words."

Jigsaw leans closer, his warm, solid body pressing tight against my side. "Thank you for letting Margot know it's not always like this, Trinity."

Her gaze flits around the room. "I mean, besides the lighting and big screen o' porn nailed to the wall, it's not *that* much different."

"Not helping." He flicks his hand at her in a mock shooing motion. "Get outta here."

She grins. "Hey, I'm not knocking it. Upstate built a whole new clubhouse for their deviants."

Lala hands Trinity two glasses. "Thanks, Lala." She nudges me with her elbow and tilts her head to the side. "We claimed one of the rooms down there if you want to come join us later."

I nod quickly, not sure I'm comfortable leaving Jigsaw's side yet. "Okay."

"Text me, I'll come find you."

"Thanks, Trin," Jigsaw calls after her.

She melts into the crowd, carefully holding the glasses to avoid spilling on her dress.

A low murmur of excitement races through the room and someone pulls back the curtains by the front door with a dramatic flourish.

A tall, painfully thin and pale woman with jet black hair, red lips and what looks like a see-through slip of a dress walks in and lifts her arm, waving like a queen acknowledging her subjects.

"The guest of honor must've arrived," I say to Jigsaw.

He grunts an affirmative sound and turns away from the door.

Applause breaks out, whistles and cheers following in her wake. Someone yells her name, and a group of men near the bar surge forward like she's a celebrity—which, I guess she is to a certain demographic of people.

I glance up at Jigsaw, but his expression is unreadable—flat, detached, as if he's already checked out of this part of the night.

That should comfort me. It doesn't.

Compared to what I've seen in this clubhouse tonight, asking Jigsaw to teach me the joys of sex seems positively demure.

Now that I've witnessed what he's usually surrounded by, he clearly had all the right qualifications for the job. No wonder he's so good at sex.

But watching the way the women behave—how freely they touch, how little they wear, how shamelessly they offer themselves and how eagerly some of the men lap it up—ties my stomach in knots.

If this is the world he's used to...

How long before the quiet girl who works with the dead starts to bore him?

How long before he craves a woman who's bolder, louder, and more daring?

Someone who's more comfortable surrounded by all this sexual chaos?

CHAPTER TWENTY-FIVE

JIGSAW

As I always suspected she would be, Margot's scandalized by what's going on around us.

And fuck, who can blame her? Between the hideous red lighting, bodies grinding on every available surface, and the screen now playing a loop of Stella's greatest hits, my club ain't exactly giving "girlfriends welcome" energy.

I could've come to the party alone. Showed my mean mug around and then bounced. I thought having the other ol' ladies here would make Margot more comfortable. She's trying. Making an effort not to cringe every time someone shrieks or grunts through an orgasm. I can tell.

Am I a sick fucker for *wanting* her to see this? The raw, vulgar side of club life. The stuff I've grown numb to and bored with? Will she understand that *this* is why I crave being with her so much? Or is she worried I'll feel like I'm missing out?

It's not the time to ask.

Am I testing her? Trying to find out if she'll still love me after stepping into my world?

She handled herself well with Bonnie. Margot's good at giving the same energy she receives. Like outside when she joked around with the guys. That goes a long way here.

She's so damn quiet, her gaze darting around like she's afraid to look at anything or anyone for too long. Or like she's waiting for the next wave of deviance to wash over her.

Like a tsunami of raunch, Stella sweeps toward the bar, trailed by several girls and one guy. I recognize him from other parties—and a few of Stella's films. *Gabe? Gavin? Garth?* Whatever. I nod in his direction as a greeting since I can't remember his name.

Stella tilts her head like she's motioning for her minions to scurry away.

And they do.

I slide off my stool and help Margot off hers. "Want to meet her and get it over with?" I say against her ear.

Her shoulders tremble with a short laugh. "Sure."

"Jigsaw!" Stella says, a smile barely touching her lips. "I've been searching all over for you."

The fuck you have.

"Hey, Stella." I nod to her but keep my arm around Margot's shoulders. "This is my ol' lady, Margot."

Stella's spent enough time around bikers to know the significance of that term and that she better not fuck with my woman.

Stella's wine-red lips part, as if she heard my silent warning and has something worse in mind than flirting with me in front of my girlfriend.

"Oh wow," Stella purrs, raking her gaze over Margot in a way I don't care for at *all*. "Aren't you *adorable*," she says, dragging out the word in her usual pretentious way.

Margot edges closer to my side and tries for a polite smile, but it lands more pained than pleasant. "Uh, thanks."

Stella inches next to Margot like she's trying to line up with her for inspection. "We're such opposites." She pets Margot's hair like she's assessing a kitten at the pound. "The visual contrast would be stunning on film."

Margot tips her head back to stare at me, eyes wide, silently begging me to make it stop.

Stella steps away from Margot and slides her hand onto my shoulder, her fingers drifting down my arm. "Actually," she purrs, "a three-way would be beautiful. You're such an attractive couple. The three of us together would be very popular."

Before I can flick her off, Margot reaches out and clamps her hand around Stella's bony wrist and not-so-gently peels it off me.

"No thank you," Margot says in that sweet but deadly way that gives the same vibe as a southerner saying "bless your heart" when they mean "fuck all the way off."

The only thing getting my dick hard in this conversation is Margot's quiet ferocity and blatant possessiveness.

At this point, Stella's used to hearing "no" from members of my club. She dips her chin at Margot, all fake politeness, but the tight line at the corner of her mouth gives away her irritation at our refusal.

Too fucking bad.

"Of course." Stella lowers her lashes in a sultry sweep that probably works on ninety percent of the male population. *Not me.*

"If you ever change your mind..." Her gaze slides to Margot, then back to me. "Jigsaw knows how to reach me."

The way she says it—low and loaded—makes it sound like we've got personal history. Which we absolutely-the-fuck do not.

Fucking she-devil.

Stella slinks away, hips swaying under her see-through dress like she wants to let us know what we're missing out on. Margot's territorial gaze follows her to the other side of the room. Then she turns her furious eyes on me.

"What about me says, I not only want to have a three-way," she seethes, "but I want it filmed and thrown on the internet for the whole world to watch and jack off to?"

"You're not flattered?" I deadpan.

She jabs her fist in my gut. "No!"

"She's asked a lot of us to 'star' in her films. For a while she had this biker series—"

Margot's eyes narrow. "Has she asked *you* before?"

"Lots of times. And Rooster. And Rock—although she backed off when he told her he's married. Z actually dated her for a while, before Lilly, but she didn't get to capture anything for posterity, and I think she's still salty about it."

"I'm sorry, *what?*" Margot bobs her head, her gaze pinging around the room. "How can Lilly stand that?"

"If you'll notice, Z and Lilly aren't here tonight."

"That's ridiculous," she fumes. "Why can't Stella fuck off to one of your other charters?"

"I ask myself that all the time. But—"

"She's the club's biggest moneymaker," Margot finishes for me.

"Yup." My lips twist into a wry smile. "If it makes you feel better, I think we're the only ones she's pitched a three-way concept to."

"Uh, no. No, that does *not* make me feel better at all." She lowers her voice. "I hope that's not a fantasy of *yours*, because it doesn't appeal to me. At all." She grazes her hand over my crotch. "I'm only into dick. And only one in particular."

It's such a wild thing to come out of Margot's mouth, I choke on a laugh. Maybe she'll survive spending time here after all. She's fifty kinds of fired up now.

"Is it?" she persists.

Been there, done that, found it more work and drama than I need in my life. "No."

Margot smooths her hands over her dress. "Well, I guess I should be thankful she didn't call me fat. Since she went out of her way to put us side by side and point out our *differences*."

I grab her hand, tugging it away from her dress. I lean in, mouth brushing her ear. "I fucking love your body. Every curve. Every inch of you drives me crazy."

Pink floods her cheeks; even the tip of her nose is red. "Thank you."

"No, thank *you*. I liked the way you removed her hand from my arm."

Fire simmers in her eyes. "She's lucky I didn't snap her wrist like a potato chip for touching you that way."

"Easy, killer." I run a finger under the top edge of her dress, grazing the swell of her breast with my knuckle. "Do you remember what I said I wanted to do the next time you wore one of your cute little dresses?"

She blinks up at me. "What?"

Is she fucking with me or does she really not remember?

I turn her and nudge her toward the bar, pressing her against the wood and trapping her there with my body. I gather the hem of her dress in my fists, lifting it a few inches, grazing her thighs with my fingertips. Fuck me, those heels she's wearing put her at almost the right height. "Is this ringing a bell?"

She glances over her shoulder, eyes wide, fear and desire flickering over her expression. Her gaze strays to the crowded room. "Don't you dare."

I drop her dress and coil my arms around her waist. Leaning in, I brush a kiss against her neck. "Careful throwing out a challenge like that, little lady death."

She braces her hands against the bar and pushes into me. I can't tell if she's trying to escape or grind her ass onto my dick. Either way, it feels too damn good to stop her.

Her gaze darts around the room, taking in all the filthy deeds happening around us—Tara grinding in Eazy's lap over on the couch, Grip and Brew tag-teaming some woman over the pool table, couples slow dancing and practically fucking in the center of the room.

"Please don't," she whispers.

Escape.

Damn.

It's for the best. If one of my brothers sees too much of Margot, I might gouge out his eye and ask her to seal it in resin for me, then wear it around my neck like a trophy.

I step back and gently turn her to face me. But her attention's locked on the pool table. All my doubts about tonight return. For a woman like Margo, so many degenerate acts in one place might be more than she's willing to tolerate.

"Unfortunately, that rarely gets used for its intended purpose," I joke. "Doubt any of them even know how to play pool."

Her eyes narrow. "Is that the awful woman who pestered me upstate." A wicked grin lights up her face. "The one I pulled the knife on?"

I squint. The girl's face is buried in Grip's crotch, so... "Can't tell."

She peers up at me. "If we weren't together, would you be partaking right now?"

"Uh..."

So this is what "deer in the headlights" feels like. Not a fan.

Her head tilts. Waiting for an answer.

Just say "no," you stupid fucker!

"No." I work a cocky smirk onto my lips. "Grip's O-face would probably shrivel my dick."

She curls her lip in disgust.

"There ya are!" Shelby shouts. "Been lookin' all over for you two."

Thank you, songbird. Perfect timing to get me the hell out of this conversation.

"And we've been wondering where you were," I answer.

Margot's tense expression relaxes into something happier as Shelby pulls her in for an enthusiastic hug. The steel band around my chest loosens. I really want them to get along. And maybe Shelby can ease Margot's mind about all of this. Hell, all Shelby needs to do is tell Margot about our Virginia chapter's pussy patch challenge, and everything Margot's witnessed tonight will seem quaint in comparison.

No, that story probably won't help my cause.

"You have no idea how happy I am to see you," Margot says.

Shelby's concerned eyes meet mine. "Everything okay?"

"Stella stopped by to spread her special brand of cheer," I answer.

Rooster rolls his eyes.

Shelby bares her teeth and makes a snarly sound that's more cute than scary. "What'd that snotty little bag of hair say to ya?"

"Ahhh." Margot blushes and casts a quick glance my way. "She wanted to know if we'd be interested in filming a threesome with her."

Shelby blinks and stares.

"Is our little songbird speechless?" I tease.

"Dang." Shelby whistles. "I sure am. That's, uh, that's pretty special." She turns her head, glancing around the room. "The three-way offer's bad enough, but I guess I see why she might think y'all were open to it. Offerin' to film it, and I assume, throw it on her website? That's a whole 'nother level of audacity."

"Thank you!" Margot pats her hair and twirls a long wave around her finger. "She ran her hands over my hair like I was a dog she wanted to adopt from the pound."

Shelby's eyes go wide. "She *petted* you?"

Rooster frowns at me and I shrug.

Shelby gives her a reassuring squeeze. "She won't try that again. Not if I'm around."

Margot's lips curl into a wicked expression. "What if she wants *us* to have a threesome with her." She wags her fingers between herself and Shelby but she's staring up at me. "For the 'visual contrast' and all."

Shelby snort-giggles. "Lordy, my PR gal would murder me."

Rooster clears his throat.

Shelby narrows her eyes at him. "You know good and damn well where I stand on such matters."

Margot's eyes widen. She flicks a look my way, then turns to Rooster. "Jensen neatly dodged a question earlier. Maybe you can help me out, Rooster?"

Sensing where this is going, I straight-up glare at Rooster to keep his mouth *shut*.

Ignoring my death-stare, he grins at her. "Anything. Ask away, Margot."

She curls her finger, inviting him to lean closer. "Before I came into the picture, is that the sort of thing Jigsaw would do at these parties?" She jerks her chin toward the pool table where Grip and

Brew have switched places and Kristen's now screaming around Brew's cock.

Shelby bursts into giggles and claps her hand over her mouth.

Rooster flashes a *payback's-a-bitch* grin my way. "Absolutely not," he answers in a grave tone that doesn't quite hit a sincere note.

"Uh-huh." Margot side-eyes me.

"Girl, come with me." Shelby links her arm through Margot's. "We'll be right back," she tosses over her shoulder.

Taking Margot by the hand, Shelby expertly weaves through the crowd, keeping Margot close behind her. Shelby's a good friend. I trust her to look out for Margot.

This motherclucker in front of me, though.

I slam my palm against Rooster's shoulder, shoving him. "You couldn't have just worked some sincerity into the word 'no,' asshole?"

"Be thankful I didn't tell her you were a virgin before you met her." He cocks his head, inviting me to remember the snarky answer I gave Shelby the time she asked me a similar question when they first started getting serious.

"Point taken." I dip my chin in apology. I cast a worried glance down the hallway. "What do you think Shelby's gonna tell her?"

Rooster strokes his hand over his chin. "Probably that you're a deviant fuckboy? Maybe how you tried to nail all the groupies when we were out on the road? Your MILF theory? Don't know. Could be anything."

Not liking any of those options.

"Shelby wouldn't do that to me." I wish I felt as confident as I made that statement sound.

"No, she wouldn't. She likes Margot too much to hurt her feelings." He leans in closer. "She likes you two *together.*"

"Good." I jam my hands in my pockets. "I like us together too."

Rooster bumps his shoulder into mine. "Then don't fuck it up. You're in control of your destiny."

The way he says it sounds more like, "you're in control of your *dick.*"

Which I am.

But damn, did he make some bad past decisions.

CHAPTER TWENTY-SIX

THE FEW SIPS OF CHAMPAGNE I TOOK HAVE ME LIGHTHEADED, FEELING like a balloon bobbing along as Shelby grips my hand tight and leads me through the crowd.

Her emerald-green dress clings to her curves, shimmering with hundreds of beads and sequins that swing with every step—like a modern-day flapper gone glam, hypnotizing me as she pulls me into a long hallway. Although they're dim, at least the lights are a normal color at this end of the clubhouse. The hellish red was starting to give me a headache.

She turns to the left and some of the noise from the party mercifully fades.

"Phew, that's better!" Shelby slows her pace. "Sorry it took me so long to get my makeup done. Serena did Hope and Emily first. But if I'd known you were gettin' propositioned by Stella, I would've come an' grabbed ya sooner."

"It's okay."

She releases my hand and stops in front of a door. I glance up and down the corridor, noting several doors. Some have little plaques tacked to the wall outside. The one we're standing in front of says *Sergeant-at-Arms*.

"Knock, knock!" Shelby taps her knuckles against the door twice, then three times, then once. "So she knows it's me." She tugs at a fob dangling from a stretchy band around her wrist, presses it to a pad near the door. The lock clicks and Shelby twists the handle.

The door swings open, revealing a spacious bedroom. The tall blonde I only met briefly the night of the bonfire hurries toward us, motioning for us to come inside. In her hand, she's holding an iPad with a video of a cute, chubby baby on the screen. She's flawlessly made up—hair in a low, sleek ponytail and full makeup—but still wearing a button-down shirt and loose shorts. Goodness, it's not the lighting that makes her so pretty in her makeup videos. Even in the harsh light of the room, Serena's stunning in person.

Next to her I feel like a vampire who escaped her tomb.

"Sorry," she gushes. "I had to check in with Lilly and make sure Lincoln was okay."

"Hi, girls!" The video swings away from the cute baby and onto Lilly's smiling face. "Hi, Margot!"

Feeling silly, I wave back. "Hi."

"Oh, we've got a doozy for ya tomorrow, Lilly," Shelby says.

Lilly snickers into her hand. "I can only imagine."

Somewhere out of view of the camera, a deep male voice says something to Lilly.

She closes her eyes and shakes with laughter. "Z wants to know if the clubhouse is still standing?"

"Yeah, but it looks like the inside of a devil's butthole out in the common room," Shelby says.

Serena and I sputter with laughter.

"Wow." Lilly's eyes widen. "All right, then. Thanks for the visual, Shelby."

"You're welcome!" She gives us a sheepish shrug. "What? It does."

"I may have used the words *vampire whorehouse* before." I shrug. "But devil's butthole works too."

Serena walks over to a long vanity table with two chairs and several ring lights stationed around it and asks for one more peek at her son before disconnecting the call.

"Okay." Serena sets the iPad down. "Sorry about that."

"Don't apologize," Shelby says. "I knew you were worried about Link."

"Hope said goodnight to Grace earlier," Serena says. "So I got a peek at him then too." She turns her pretty blue eyes my way and holds her arms out, inviting me in for a hug. "Hi, Margot. I'm so happy to see you again."

"It's good to see you too," I say, giving her a quick, hello squeeze. "How's the party?"

"Honestly?" *No.* I don't know her well enough to complain too harshly. Her man's the SAA here. Keeping my opinions to myself, I settle for, "Um, it's been an eye-opener."

"I bet." Serena snorts. Her shrewd gaze lands on me again. "I love that red gloss. It compliments your skin tone well."

My face heats. "Thanks." I duck my head. I was too nervous to tell her this the last time we met but now seems like a good time. "I'm actually a big fan of your channel, so that means a lot."

"No way! Really?" Serena squeals, like she's shocked to meet a fan out in the wild. "Thank you so much." She turns and gestures toward the vanity. "Shelby and I were filming a tutorial before."

"Oh, I can't wait to see it."

On the way over to the room, I'd been too distracted by nerves and dazzled by Shelby's dress to notice her makeup. But now, up close, I can't stop staring. Her eyes are framed in a smoky blend of charcoal and deep plum, a razor-sharp cat-eye in metallic gold adding some shimmer. Warm blush sweeps over her cheekbones in a soft, sculpted arc, highlighting her perfect skin. And her honey-toned satin lipstick? Perfectly applied. Not a smudge in sight.

"It came out beautiful." I hope that doesn't sound like I'm trying too hard. I mean every word.

"Thank you." Serena beams at Shelby. "She's a pretty perfect canvas."

Shelby ducks her head and shimmies her shoulders.

"I've always admired your contouring skills," I add. "I picked up a few tricks from watching your videos."

Regret slams into me half a second later. Why did I say that? She's going to think I'm a freaky fangirl—or worse, realize I mean that I used her tips to contour sunken cheeks, flattened noses, and postmortem eye sockets.

"Margot, you're the cosmetologist at your family's funeral home, right?" Shelby asks.

More heat sears my cheeks. I nod quickly. "It's not the same as what you do, Serena, obviously but—"

"No, but it's deeply meaningful," Serena says. She doesn't seem uncomfortable or weirded out by me. Doesn't tilt her head in polite pity or awkward confusion. She meets my eyes with soft understanding. "What you do must give people a little peace in the worst moment of their lives."

"Yes!" I answer a little too enthusiastically. That's a topic I could talk about all day. "Sorry. I just—sometimes people bring reference photos from, like, twenty years ago. Glamour shots or their wedding day photos. And they want their mom, or grandmother, or whoever to look exactly like that. It's hard. But we always try."

Serena presses a hand to her chest. "Wow. I never thought about how difficult that must be."

Why would she?

I shrug, trying to downplay how much it matters to me. I don't want her to remember me as *weird lady who wouldn't shut up about makeup for dead folks.*

"Sometimes all they need is something small to hold onto—a hairstyle, or a favorite lipstick shade," I say. "It's those little things that matter more than people think."

Shelby lets out a low whistle. "Dang. I never thought about how much pressure that must be."

"Anyway." I hold up my hands like I'm tapping out of the morbid talk. "I think your channel is fabulous, Serena. I've learned a lot."

"Thank you." She glances at the vanity, then back at me. "You know, I've actually had morticians reach out and ask me stuff I didn't have answers to. Would you maybe want to do a video with me sometime?" Her voice rises to a pleading lilt. "We could give tips, demystify what you do a little. Make it less scary."

"I'd love that!" *Breathe, Margot.* "If you think it won't turn your viewers off."

She shrugs. "If they don't like it, they don't have to watch." She flicks her gaze to Shelby. "I'm trying to give fewer *flocks* about what other people think of me these days."

"Dang right. Other peoples' opinions about us ain't our business." Shelby pumps her fist in the air. "That's why Rooster and Jigsaw get to monitor all the comments on our socials for us now. I'm settin' clear boundaries and protecting my peace."

"Okay." Serena claps her hands. "Let me squeeze into my party dress and then we'll do a group selfie."

"Do you mind if I borrow your mirror with the good lighting?" I ask.

"Nope. Help yourself."

I sit and pull out my tube of gloss from my pocket, quickly dabbing it over my lips.

"I have testing applicators if there's anything of mine you want to try, Margot," Serena calls out. "Actually, I have this electric blue gel liner that would look amazing with your dress."

Behind me, Shelby chuckles. "You're in it now, Margot."

I smile at her in the mirror.

"Okay, what do you think?" Serena asks. "Is this too Cinderella-ish for a biker clubhouse?"

I turn as Serena steps out of the bathroom—and instant jealousy sets in. What a stunning dress. Tea-length in a soft powdery blue that shimmers with every step she takes. The fitted bodice hugs her curves like it was molded to her body, the delicate spaghetti straps barely noticeable against her shoulders. The skirt flares out in a dramatic swirl, catching the light with a thousand tiny sparkles.

She twirls, just once, and the fabric fans out in a perfect circle around her knees—equal parts fairy tale and glamour.

"Wow," Shelby breathes out. "It's too nice for *this* clubhouse tonight, that's for sure. With those weird-ass lights Stella insisted on, no one will be able to even see that pretty blue color."

"It's breathtaking, Serena," I add.

Serena grins and smooths her hands over the skirt. "So, not too much?"

"It's perfect. Don't you dare change," Shelby warns. Her lips curl into a teasing smile. "Murder Daddy is going to lose it when he sees you."

Serena bursts into laughter. "Stop it."

"Oh my God." The nickname clicks. "Yes!" I squeal. "You said Murder Daddy, and Grinder immediately jumped in my head. Good one."

"Right?" Shelby grins.

Serena laughs but her cheeks flush. "You have no idea."

A little murder doesn't scare Serena. Good to know.

Serena slips on a pair of strappy, silver high heels, then hurries toward the vanity. She clicks on several of the ring lights, then shuffles through the assorted jars, palettes, and tools spread over the table.

"Here!" She thrusts a tiny pot of bright, royal blue gel liner toward me. "Just a thin line above your upper lashes. It'll make your eyes pop. Can I?"

Uh, turn down Serena of Tranquil Sparkle and her offer to line my eyes? Never. "Sure, why not?"

She works fast and carefully, and when I blink into the mirror, I have to admit—I love it.

"Thanks," I murmur, unable to stop smiling.

"Yay!" Serena claps her hands. "Selfies."

Shelby shrugs off her leather vest with the *Property of Rooster* patch on the back and lays it on the bed.

I squint against the blast of all the ring lights as Serena clips her phone into a mount, sets a timer, and pulls us into a huddle.

As the tallest, Serena stands in the middle. We pose and smile for several pictures before she's satisfied.

"Let's all wave!" She holds her phone up high and takes a short video. Shelby hams it up, blowing a kiss, while I awkwardly squint at the camera. God, I hope Serena can edit me out of that.

Before we separate, I pull out my own phone and snap one last shot of us. It buzzes in my hand a second later.

Please don't be a work emergency.

Jigsaw: Everything okay?

"Awww," Shelby sighs, leaning over to peek at the screen. "Jiggy checking up on you already, huh?"

A flush creeps up my chest. "Yes."

I send the selfie of the three of us as my response.

Outside the room, Serena checks that the door's locked, then points to a room across the hall labeled *Road Captain*, and the one next to it marked *Vice President*. "We're all neighbors."

"And we've made a solemn pact to *never* mention any noises we hear coming from each other's rooms," Shelby says in a sacred tone, lifting her hand toward the ceiling like she's swearing an oath in church.

"No—" I gasp, laughing despite myself. Then the thought hits.

Wait.

Did they have that pact with Jigsaw, too?

Before me?

My gentle slide into their chaotic, affectionate world screeches to a halt.

Don't do this.

You're making a big deal out of nothing.

It doesn't matter what he did—or who he did it with—before we were together.

Even if my brain knows that, my stomach continues flipping as we make the long trek back to the main room.

The three of us link arms, taking up the width of the hallway. Since I'm not wearing one of the property patches, they squeeze me in between them.

"Who's your friend, Shelby?" A biker leers at us as we pass.

"This is Jigsaw's ol' lady, Vegas," she warns without slowing her steps. "Keep your hands to yourself."

"Noted." He laughs.

Grinder, Rooster, and Jigsaw are waiting at the entrance to the main room. Grinder notices us first. The harsh lines of his face soften into a warm smile as his eyes land on Serena.

"You went with the blue one, buttercup." He nods with approval and holds out his hands to her.

Rooster slips an arm around Shelby's waist and Jigsaw practically knocks Grinder down to get to me.

"Easy, Jiggy." Shelby laughs. "We were in Grinder and Serena's room the whole time."

"I know." He comes up behind me, wrapping his arms around my waist. He leans over and whispers in my ear, "I missed you."

"Same." I rest my hand over his arm and lean back against him.

"I like the blue stuff on your eyes," he murmurs. "It's pretty."

My breath catches. I can't believe he noticed so quickly.

"What'd we miss?" Shelby asks, gesturing toward the red room.

Rooster lets out several slow, sharp huffs of laughter.

Grinder cuts him a murderous stare. "Don't."

"What?" Serena asks with wide eyes.

Behind me, Jigsaw's body starts to shake. I tip my head back and find him biting his lip, trying not to laugh.

"What's so funny?" I ask.

"You two, keep your damn mouths shut," Grinder snaps.

"We're not special anymore." Jigsaw flicks a finger under his eye, pretending to wipe away a tear.

Rooster shakes with silent, full-body laughter.

Serena, Shelby, and I all share confused looks.

"Stella has an age gap niche she wants to…fill," Rooster says between chuckles.

Understanding washes over me. Not finding it as funny as the guys do, I elbow Jigsaw in the stomach.

He laughs harder.

"You guys are terrible," Shelby scolds, scrunching her nose. "Wait— are we the only ones who didn't get the three-way invite?"

"Serena wasn't invited to *that* production," Jigsaw says.

 290

Serena's eyes narrow. "Excuse me?" She cranes her neck, swaying from side to side to peer around Grinder's large frame. "She asked my ol' man to do *what*?"

"Don't worry," Rooster adds. "She had a project in mind for you too." His laughter dies mid-sentence.

The icy blast of Grinder's stare ruffles the hairs on the back of my neck. "Keep on cluckin' and I'm gonna beat the disrespect right outta you."

"She has a right to know," Rooster protests. "So she can be prepared in case Stella ambushes her."

Serena's eyes widen like she's trying to hold back tears. "What did she say about me?" she asks in a small voice.

Grinder throws another frosty glare at Rooster, then Jigsaw—who thankfully took the hint and shut his mouth. Finally, Grinder leans down, whispering something in Serena's ear.

Whatever he says must be worse than a three-way. Serena dry heaves. "What the...*ewww*."

"Yup." Rooster nods. "I heard and I judged. Harshly."

Jigsaw reaches out and slaps Rooster's shoulder. "Don't tell Dex, but I'm absolutely yucking that yum."

Shelby raises her hands. "Nope. Don't wanna know."

I pull out my pocketknife and hold it out. "Do you want to borrow this, Serena?"

She blinks at the knife resting in my open palm, then bursts into giggles. "Yeah, kinda." She leans in and kisses Grinder's cheek. "But I won't."

"I told her where to go with her request," Grinder says.

Considering how much money Stella brings into the club, whatever she asked must've been really offensive.

We migrate toward the bar again. I never finished my drink earlier, and I doubt it's still waiting for me—probably claimed or cleared.

"You need something to drink?" Jigsaw asks.

"Yes, but no more champagne." My head's still a little floaty from the first one. Now that we're in the thick of the party again, I need to stay sharp, not start giggling like an idiot.

Our stools are now occupied, a pair of nearly naked women draped over them like blankets. Jigsaw steers me around to the other side, settling us near a pair of tall, silver swinging doors that catch the light every time they flap open.

"What's in there?" I ask, nodding toward them.

"Kitchen. Big dining room off that," Jigsaw answers. "We'll all have breakfast in there tomorrow."

Breakfast with the bikers. The last one at Upstate's clubhouse had been fun. I'm looking forward to that more than what's happening around me tonight.

I climb onto one of the bar stools. The man who came in with Stella earlier walks up and taps Jigsaw's shoulder. Keeping one hand on my back, he turns to talk to the man. He doesn't bother introducing me to the guy—who I assume is also a porn star—and given the way our conversation with Stella went, I'm fine with it.

The bar's slammed and it takes a while for Lala to make her way over to me. "You want another Velvet Crown?" she asks, lifting an open bottle of champagne.

"No, maybe just sparkling water? With lime, if you've got it?"

She ducks behind the bar—then pops up like a waffle out of the toaster. "We're out back here, but I know there's a case of those little San Pellegrino bottles in the big fridge." She jabs a finger toward the double doors. "Or I can grab you seltzer from the soda gun."

She points to a battered black-and-silver machine. My nose wrinkles. Who knows the last time they pulled that thing apart and cleaned it?

"That's okay. I'll try the kitchen."

"I'd do it, but—" She waves a hand toward the packed bar.

"No problem." I offer her a warm smile. She shouldn't have to worry so much about serving me. "I got it."

I slide off the stool.

Still mid-conversation, Jigsaw whips around. His eyes lock on mine, a *where are you going* scowl on his face.

Charmed by his protectiveness, I point to the kitchen doors. "Grabbing a water. Want one?"

He frowns, eyes flicking from the door to me, then nods.

The second the door swings shut behind me, regret claws up my spine.

Five women. Early twenties, maybe younger. Heads cocked like rabbits trying to decide if I'm a threat or a snack. Three perched on the high stainless steel counters, whispering and laughing. One by the stove. One elbow-deep in an industrial dishwasher.

Their chatter stops.

They all have one thing in common—a whole lot of skin on display.

Too many clashing artificial scents—buttery vanilla, coconut lime, cheap musk—crash into me like a mall kiosk ambush.

The two women actually doing something go back to their tasks, ignoring me. The other three continue staring.

I paste on a polite smile like armor and head straight for the large, stainless steel refrigerator on the far wall.

I'm fine. I belong here. My boyfriend's right outside those doors. He's an officer of the club. I've got my trusty little knife.

I might not be wearing one of the property patches, but people have seen me with Jigsaw tonight, right?

The whispers start again. Softer. Meaner. Ignoring them, I yank open one of the heavy fridge doors.

The murmurs grow louder, conniving and smug.

No longer gossiping…plotting?

Lala was right. One whole shelf is full of nothing but short green bottles. I grab two and shut the door. I'd kill for a lime, but I don't want to stay in here longer than necessary searching for one.

I turn and two girls are blocking my escape.

"You're Margot?" one of them asks. She's all angles and eye rolls, arms folded tight. *Huh, must be the leader of the mean-girl gang.*

The one beside her was definitely at the bonfire. My lips tug into a shaky smile. "Hi. Bonnie, right?"

Bonnie matches her friend's hostile stance. "Yup. That's her, Nikki."

Nikki drags her gaze down and back up like she's measuring me for a fight. "So you're the reason Dee-Dee got suspended from Upstate's clubhouse?"

Seriously? They're blaming me? "I'd argue *Dee-Dee* is the reason Dee-Dee got suspended."

"What are you even wearing?" Nikki sneers. "That dress is so cringe. You look like you're dressed for a church picnic."

"Awww, thanks," I say, matching her snotty tone. "We can't all wear stuff from this year's 'desperate for attention' collection. I'll leave that to you."

Ignoring the dig, Bonnie looks down her nose at me like I'm a cigarette butt stuck to the bottom of her tacky plastic high heels. "You won't last long. You look way too innocent to take the rough poundings Jigsaw enjoys."

They cackle—loud, grating, and painfully performative.

She flicks a look at Nikki. "Bet she doesn't even know what he *really* likes."

"Oh." Nikki gasps and bites her lip like she's auditioning for one of Stella's films. "Unless you're into being thrown onto the bed, flipped over, and wrecked six ways from Sunday, you might wanna cut your losses now. Jigsaw loves to give a harsh spanking, fuck hard, and yank a ponytail good."

This is starting to feel oddly familiar. Dee-Dee all over again—only worse. Much worse. And much more…descriptive.

Is it true?

He's never been rough with me in bed. Demanding and growly in the best ways, sure. Rough—never.

"Apparently, none of you got the memo from your friend with the tragic haircut. I'm not interested in opinions on my relationship." I stare them down even though I'm trembling. "Especially from a bunch of raggedy muffler bunnies."

The one left sitting on the counter hops down and slinks closer, joining the two already in front of me.

Great, they're multiplying like...well, bunnies.

"What did you say?" the new one asks, the cheap, rhinestone-studded belt holding up her ratty Daisy Dukes flashing under the kitchen lights. It draws attention away from her bare breasts trying to escape her cut-off white tanktop.

"No one's talking to you," I snap.

"Oh, you're like Serena is now," she says, curling her lip. "Think you're too good for us?"

"Well, if this is how you treat her, I'm not surprised she doesn't want anything to do with you."

She laughs, low and nasty, like she's savoring this moment. "Oh, honey. You think she's your new bestie? That's adorable. Did she forget to tell you she used to fuck Jigsaw?"

I blink.

Serena? Really?

No.

"She's... she's engaged to Grinder," I stammer.

Her lips twist into a cruel smile. "Yeah, but before that old man got outta prison, she fucked all these guys. Same as we do." She lifts an eyebrow at Nikki. "Right?"

Nikki nods quickly. "Yup. And Shelby? That little Walmart Taylor Swift knockoff might like to pretend Rooster wasn't as dirty as the rest of 'em but everyone knows that man would stick his dick in every girl who walked in this clubhouse."

The others titter like it's the funniest thing they've ever heard.

Then Bonnie's eyes narrow on me again. "But hey—maybe we're wrong about you, Margot." Her voice drips with cruelty. "You definitely have the padding to handle Jigsaw," she says, stepping closer and tipping her head as if she's appraising a cow at the county fair.

"She needs all that cushion. I swear that man fucked me so hard, he bruised my spleen one time," Dollar Store Daisy Dukes snort-giggles and clutches her stomach.

That's nowhere near your spleen.

But I'd be happy to slice you open and point it out.

And also, *ewww.*

"I never knew Jiggy was into asses that big, though," Nikki says loud enough for the other two girls to swivel around. "He's so buff and hard all over. I figured he'd go for someone hotter. Not some fat chick."

How original.

I shift both bottles of water into one hand. If she comes any closer, I'm pulling out my knife and demonstrating how quick I can turn all that lip filler into scar tissue.

"Well, he's definitely an ass man," Bonnie purrs, giving her behind a smug little pat. "He's always loved going to town on mine."

The three of them burst into more fake-giddy giggles. Even the girls on the other side of the kitchen chuckle.

I'm going to vomit.

"That's riiight," Nikki says. "I forgot how much Jiggy and Steer used to love tag-teaming new girls out on the pool table. Pretty sure Jiggy always called dibs on ass."

My stomach lurches.

He did avoid my question about the threesomes...

They're being vile on purpose—lining up their nasty stories like knives, sinking them in to see which one cuts the deepest.

I let out a loud, dramatic yawn, patting my hand against my lips. "Your hair isn't as ugly as your friend's, but your story is just as boring."

Nikki's pout twists—too much filler to form a real sneer.

"We're trying to do you a favor. You should say 'thank you.'" She leans closer, face hovering in prime slashing range. "You're not into what he likes. You can't give him what he needs. So maybe don't get too comfortable, babe. On the nights he's not with you?" She gestures around the kitchen. "He's probably with one of us."

I snort. "You wish."

Great comeback, Margot.

She's lying through those overinflated lips. He's been with me most nights for months.

But there were those few times he disappeared on me...

A few times he said he crashed at the upstate clubhouse.

Other times, he didn't say where he'd been.

I didn't ask—because I trust him.

"She's right," Bonnie snaps. "Where's our thank you for trying to warn you?"

I give her a cold, dead-eyed stare. "Cool story, thanks. So if it burns when I pee, now I'll know why."

Nikki's eyes flash with rage. The girl next to her rolls her eyes like this is all beneath her.

But Bonnie? She pulls a mocking sad face, her voice laced with pity. "Let me guess—he tells you you're different?" She tilts her head, fake sympathy oozing from every syllable. "Honey… aren't you old enough to know they *all* say that?"

A million comebacks flood my brain.

But before I can line one up and spit it out—

The doors slam open.

"What the fuck?" Jigsaw's voice slices through the air like a machete. "Get the fuck away from my ol' lady."

The girls scatter—but not fast enough.

I didn't even get to pull my knife this time.

In his rush to reach me, Jigsaw shoulder-checks Bonnie, sending her crashing into the edge of the counter.

She screeches and clutches her side, staring at the angry red line blooming across her exposed stomach. "That's going to bruise!"

I lean in, close enough to choke on her strawberry pound cake–scented body spray.

"You said how much you enjoy taking a pounding," I whisper. "That's the last one you're ever getting from *my* man. So, enjoy."

Jigsaw grabs my hand, rough and possessive, and hauls me out of the kitchen behind him.

My pulse stutters. Is he mad?

Disappointed that I let myself get dragged into another altercation?

Trouble seems to find me every time I step into one of his MC's clubhouses.

Maybe I'm not cut out to be an ol' lady after all.

CHAPTER TWENTY-SEVEN

JIGSAW

THE SERIAL KILLER FACE PEOPLE ALWAYS JOKE ABOUT MUST BE WORKING overtime. Bikers, porn stars, hangers-on—they all part like I'm Moses storming through the damn Red Sea. No one meets my eyes. Even the drunkest hangarounds flinch and stumble back, giving us space.

Good.

I keep my arm clamped around Margot, her body close to mine, guiding us through the noise, lights, and sweat-slick chaos of the common room toward the back hallway.

She's trembling.

Every step we take, she stiffens—like she's bracing for an attack.

My stomach burns.

Grinder slips out of one of the side rooms—eyes scanning the room for trouble. He spots me barreling toward him and throws up both hands like he's trying to calm a wild animal.

"Whoa, slow down. What's wrong, Jiggy?"

Margot clings tighter to my side, like she's trying to crawl under my cut for safety or hide herself from everyone.

Grinder's gaze drops to her. "Margot, what's wrong?"

"Nothing." She pulls away from me just enough to lift her chin. Her voice comes out too calm and flat. "Nothing. I'm fine."

A disapproving, but somehow gentle, scowl settles over his face. Grinder reads people too well. He knows she's lying and putting on a brave face. "Are you sure, honey? You were all smiles and cheer a few minutes ago," he coaxes.

Margot shrugs, shrinking into herself. No more words. Just a slight shake of her head.

The creases between Grinder's brows deepen, and there's nothing gentle about the scowl he turns on me. His arms cross over his chest, biceps straining his sleeves, eyebrows lifted in a *what the fuck did you let happen to her* glare. All of it demands an answer. *Now.*

I don't flinch away from his silent judgment. I deserve it.

"Bonnie, Nikki, and Amanda need to be thrown the fuck *out*," I seethe. "They were in the kitchen last I saw."

He jerks his chin in a sharp nod. Doesn't ask questions. Doesn't need to. Grinder knows I'd never make that call without a damn good reason.

"Anyone else?"

I rake a hand through my hair, pressure building behind my eyes. There were other girls in there, but I didn't recognize them. Those three were the ones specifically in Margot's face. "I don't think so."

"All right." He settles his concerned dad eyes on Margot again. "You all right, sweetheart?"

"I'm fine. Just tired." Her voice is thinner now. Faded. She tilts her head, peering around Grinder. "Can you tell Serena I'll talk to her in the morning? You guys will still be here, right?"

"We'll be here for breakfast," he confirms.

"Okay."

I don't wait for another word. I keep my arm tight around her waist and lead her down the hall. Past the guest rooms. Past anyone still watching. I don't care.

I slam into our room and close the door behind us. My heart's thundering. My chest's tight. My jaw aches from grinding my teeth.

Gripping Margot's arms, I search her body for any signs they hurt her.

"Did they touch you? What happened?" My voice comes out

sharper than I mean it to. "Jesus, you were gone for less than five minutes."

Her lips part, but no sound comes out. Her eyes are wide and shiny with unshed tears.

From the confrontation? Or from me yelling at her?

Calm the fuck down.

Deep breath. Try again.

"Margot, baby—hey." I lower my voice and reach for her again, gentler this time. "I'm sorry. Please. Tell me what happened back there?"

She sniffles, then breathes deep. She lifts her chin and stares at me. Something seems to shift in her. Her eyes aren't filled with tears anymore. They're wary. "Well, for starters, they all seemed eager to tell me how much you enjoy rough sex."

A sharp, unhinged bark of laughter explodes out of me. "What?"

Her mouth flattens into a tight, humorless line. The weight in her stare pins me to the floor, like she's dissecting me with her eyes, searching for a truth she's scared to find.

I scrub my hand over the back of my neck, trying to shake the unease crawling up my spine.

She's dead serious and staring at me like she's trying to puzzle out whether I'm the man she thought I was—or someone entirely different.

They must've told her some fucked-up shit.

"Is that true?" she asks quietly. "Are they telling the truth? Because… that other girl said something similar at the bonfire."

Is it? I don't think so. There are only one or two women in my life I actually cared about pleasing. Felt comfortable enough to let my guard down with.

The rest? A release. A fun time. Boredom chaser. I never wanted to be seen or understood by any of them, so I just fit myself into whatever version of "Jigsaw" they wanted. Played the role. Got them off. Got myself off. Got gone.

So if that's what one of them was into…*maybe?*

Yeah, no way in hell do I want to explain *any* of that to Margot.

"I'm not stupid." Her voice is steady but soft. "You had a life before me." She arches a brow. "A very active life with lots and lots of variety, apparently."

That stings like a motherfucker. Not because she's wrong. But because those jealous little vipers threw it in her face to hurt her. And I wasn't there to stop it.

She tucks her hair behind one ear and almost smiles, but it's fragile. "I know when I first asked you to...help me, I said I just wanted basic instructions." Her lips form a weak smile. "No master-level sex classes."

My chest squeezes and I groan. "Margot, we are so far past sex lessons now."

"Yes. We are," she whispers. "I want you to be yourself with me."

The rawness of her voice curls around me in an almost physical way. Barbed wire wrapped in satin.

She's not angry.

She's scared I've been holding back. That I don't trust her enough to give her all of me.

Fucking hell, why can't I be better with words? Why can't I explain how perfect she is for me? How with her, I feel whole for the first time in my life.

I reach for her, curling my hand around the back of her neck, grounding both of us. "I'm exactly who I want to be when I'm with you." That's a truth I feel deep down in my bones. "I *like* who I am with you. Who I am *because* of you."

She stares up at me like she wants to believe every word.

"I love you," she says, her voice strong and sure. "but I want you to be...happy. Not feel like you're missing out or you have to hold back." Her lips tremble into a brave smile. "I'm a sturdy girl. I can take it. Teach me anything you want."

Fuck, the brave way she says that hits me hard—like she's offering me some sort of weapon and daring me to use it.

But what she's implying leaves me...unsettled.

"Margot." I tip her chin up, forcing her eyes to meet mine. "I don't know what those evil little bitches told you, but I don't enjoy *hurting* my partner to get off. Never have."

She frowns, still unsure.

The weight of what I need to say turns my tongue to lead.

I swallow hard and force the words out. "I've survived enough beatings and punishments in my life. Nothing about hurting someone I care about does it for me."

Pain flickers across her face and it damn near guts me.

I can't breathe seeing that ache in her eyes.

I shift her in my arms, curling myself around her from behind. My arm sweeps over her chest and pulls her tight until her back is pressed to my front.

That's better.

She wiggles, trying to turn around again. But I slide my arm around her waist, trapping her in place.

Leaning down, I brush my lips against the curve of her ear. "Have I ever given you the impression I have trouble asking for what I want from you?"

"I don't think so," she whispers.

I gather the hem of her dress in one hand and slowly drag it upward, the fabric whispering against her thighs until my knuckles graze soft skin. "Aren't you always saying how demanding I am?"

She laughs softly, her breasts jiggling with the movement. "I think the word I've used is *bossy*."

"Same difference." I trail my lips along the side of her neck, enjoying the way her chest rises and falls faster. "So if there was something I wanted to do with you…" I pause, kissing just below her ear. "Don't you think I'd say so?"

"I guess." She hesitates. "Unless you thought I couldn't handle it."

"Margot, there is nothing I want to do with you that I think you can't handle." I close my eyes and tip my head back, searching for the right words to end her fears for good. "Please. Whatever those girls said? Put it out of your mind. It has nothing to do with *us*."

Finally—*finally*—the tension melts from her body. She rests her head against my chest. "Okay."

"I'm sorry this happened again." Sorry doesn't begin to cover it. Furious and murderous are much closer. "I'm angry at myself for not protecting you better. Fuck, I was only ten feet away."

"It's weird," she whispers. "I can't imagine someone coming up to me and saying such horrible things anywhere else. But in your world, that's common?"

I swallow hard. "Unfortunately, it happens more than it should." Her words sink deeper, and I gently turn her to face me. "Wait. What other *horrible things* did they say to you?"

She fiddles with the snaps on the edge of my cut and won't meet my eyes. "They were sort of specific about your past interests...rough sex, ass play, hair pulling, threesomes. One claimed you fucked her so hard, you bruised her spleen." She frowns and purses her lips. "But I don't think that girl actually knows where her spleen is located."

Her gaze lifts, eyes shining with wicked intent. "I was going to use my knife to show her, if she didn't shut up."

My eyes bug. I choke on a laugh. Jesus. Only my girl would say something like that...and mean it.

I'll fight every one of my brothers on this if I have to, but those three bitches are never setting foot in this clubhouse again.

"They all seemed to agree on your love of threesomes with... Steer?" She frowns since the name isn't familiar to her. "So that offer Stella made...is that something you'd want to do? Not the filming it part but..."

"No." I snap the word too hard and force myself to soften. "Christ, Margot. You've seen me come unhinged when a guy so much as breathes in your direction. You really think I'd let someone—male or female—touch you?" I snort and shake my head, searching for something—anything—to move away from this topic.

"And one of them said I need to accept that on the nights you're not with me, you're probably with one of them."

"That's absolutely *not* true. Not since we've been together." I rub my knuckles against her cheek. "Not since you asked *me* to be your sex coach."

She frowns. "But we didn't agree to those terms until—"

"Margot." I meet her eyes, holding her there, needing her to see the truth etched into every word. "I've been more than a little obsessed with you since the day we met."

She stares at me with wide eyes. "I believe you." The corners of her mouth turn down. "I really want to."

That cuts deep. But it might be an easy problem to solve.

I've got nothing to hide.

"Here." I pull my phone from my pocket. "Give me your phone." I hold out my hand and back my way toward the bed, dropping onto the mattress, thrilled to finally be able to *do something* that might fix this.

She follows, cautious but curious, and reluctantly places her phone in my palm. "Why?"

"I'm adding an app. You'll be able to see where my phone is anytime you want." I don't look up as I swipe through her screen. "And my watch. You'll have access to my location. My heartbeat. Everything."

"Why?" She wrinkles her nose. "So I can watch your heart rate spike in real time when you're having sex?"

"No. Jesus, no." I stare her dead in the eyes, needing her to hear this. "You'll feel when *that's* happening, because I'll be doing it with you. No app required."

"This is ridiculous." She holds out her hand, asking for her phone back. "I'm not going to track you down like a jealous lunatic."

"I *want* you to be able to find me, no matter what. I've got nothing to hide." It's taking forever to log in to my accounts. Back and forth between phones. Email codes. Security questions. What a pain in the ass.

Finally, we're linked.

She sits next to me, peering at my screen. "Can you track me too?"

I turn, studying her expression. "You want me to?"

"It only seems fair."

Given her favorite hobby, I probably should've done this sooner.

I side-eye her. "This way I can make sure you're not out hunting anyone without me."

Her cheeks flush, but she lifts her chin, pure defiance. "That's a solo hobby."

"The fuck it is," I mutter.

I check that both ends are working, then hand her phone back.

"No more worrying about anything those girls said. If I'm not with you, I'm thinking about being with you." I lean down and drag my lips over her shoulder. "And if I want something from you, I'll ask for it."

She hums and leans into me, finally relaxed.

We've been awfully focused on me and my supposed needs tonight. I shift, brushing her hair away from her face. "And if you want something from me, you'll tell me."

She pulls back, a wrinkle forming between her eyebrows like she's giving this a lot of thought. "I *really* liked when you chased me through the woods."

Now we're talking.

A slight shiver ripples through her. She bites her bottom lip, eyes flicking up to meet mine.

"I've thought about doing that again with you," she says. "A lot. I think I want to find a wrap dress, so you can just untie it, instead of ripping off all the buttons." She twists a piece of her hair around one finger. "Although the button ripping added an extra thrill."

This woman might be what finally makes me believe in God.

"I'm glad you said that." And I absolutely love how much thought she's been giving it. I flick my phone open and pull up the photo Rooster sent me. "Rooster's place has a whole lot of woods surrounding it." I tilt the screen toward her.

"Oh my God." She laughs and bumps her shoulder into mine. "What if he catches us?"

"We'll wait until he's out of town."

"Okay."

"Anything else?"

She hesitates, glancing toward the door. "Well, there is one other thing I wanted to ask you."

A sense of doom tightens my chest. "Did those girls make up some other shit I'm supposedly into?" I run a hand down my face. *What else could they have possibly said?* "Okay, just so we're clear—no, I don't ever want you to call me Daddy. I'm not into having you dress up like a schoolgirl, nun, or anything else. No, that's not true, you're definitely wearing my property patch and nothing else when I give you one."

She shakes with laughter. "No, nothing like that."

"You're right." I gesture toward her heels. "You can wear those heels with the patch, and nothing else."

She stops laughing. "Oh, I'll definitely do that for you."

One corner of my mouth slides up. "Yeah?"

She nods quickly.

"So what is it? What else do you want to ask?"

She takes a deep breath. "The one in the tacky shorts—"

"Amanda?"

She turns and glares at me. "I never got her name."

Christ, now she's definitely going to think I used to yank Amanda's ponytail. "She was a friend of Serena's," I explain.

"Some friend." She scowls. "Well, Amanda said you and Serena... and implied Rooster and Serena too..." Her brows pull together. "I guess it's none of my business, but I'd like to know. I don't want to—I don't know. How does that work with her being engaged to Grinder?"

It takes a second to piece her choppy explanation together and find the question.

"I've never slept with Serena." I really need to give her more context. I shift closer and lower my voice. "Please don't repeat any of this, and don't bring it up to her unless Serena wants to talk about it. But yeah...she used to be a club girl here."

Margot's eyes widen. "Really? But she's so nice."

"Exactly. She never behaved the way those girls did tonight. She's always been a sweetheart."

Her eyes narrow, just a little.

"I used to *talk* to her a lot when she was hanging out here. She was trying to go back to school, and we'd talk about that kind of stuff." I press my lips together, hating that what I'm about to share is even part of my club's history. "Our old VP was an absolute garbage human.

Even though he had a wife outside the club none of us even knew about, Serena was his girl here toward the end."

"End of what?"

I hold up a hand. "Let me get there."

She nods but keeps frowning.

"He was always kind of a jerk. Even as a brother—the loyalty wasn't there. And our old president was an asshole too."

"The one who had Stella as *his* side piece? What a surprise," she mutters.

That earns a small smile from me. "Anyway. None of us realized how bad it had gotten with the VP. Serena used to be a lot quieter. Had a hard time standing up for herself. When Z took over, some things happened. He saw what was going on and put an end to it."

I hate being so vague, but I don't want to utter Shadow's name and have Margot accidentally repeat it one day.

She lifts an eyebrow. "End to it how?"

"Serena had left the club by then."

"End to it *how*?" she repeats, slower this time. With an edge to her voice.

"He put his hands on Lilly one night." I grit my teeth at the memory. "And it's the *last* thing he ever did."

She stares at me, mouth open. Then a slow, savage smile curls her lips. "Did he die hard?"

"Very. And at the hands of the whole club."

"Good." She nods, satisfied.

I knew she'd approve.

And that's one of many reasons she's so perfect for me.

CHAPTER TWENTY-EIGHT

JIGSAW

THE NEXT MORNING, I'M EAGER TO ROLL THE FUCK OUTTA DOWNSTATE.

Z had us up early for church. I didn't waste any time pleading my case for Bonnie, Amanda, and Nikki to be banned from the clubhouse.

Grinder couldn't agree fast enough. Since they're just club girls— or ex-club girls—Z didn't even bother calling for a vote. No one asked for one, either.

Last night's fuckery was too much.

The sun's already high, the air thick with diesel and dew, but it feels damn good on my skin as I head across the parking lot to grab a bag out of my truck. Looking forward to the long ride to Margot's after breakfast. Just the two of us. No more club drama. No one trying to fill her head with lies.

A baby's wail carries over the parking lot. I turn, seeking the source. Serena's long, blond ponytail whips in the wind as she struggles to balance Lincoln on one hip and drag a large bag from the back of her SUV with her other hand.

I jog across the lot, hurrying to her side.

"You need help?" My gaze darts from the bag in the SUV to the baby in her arms. I reach for the bag.

Her face lights up. "Oh my God, Jiggy. You don't know how happy

I am to see you." She takes a step back to give me room. "Is Gray here?"

"You just missed him. Z and your ol' man ran over to the laundromat. Said they'd be back in ten."

The corners of her mouth pull down. Just a little. Does she think I'm lying? Covering for Grinder while he taps some club ass? Nah, she knows better.

"I told him I was on my way back," she says, adjusting Lincoln against her chest.

"They're not supposed to be gone long." I glance at the full cargo area. "All that stuff coming in too?"

She gives me an apologetic half shrug. "It can wait." She hoists Lincoln higher in her arms and leans closer, rubbing her nose against his cheek. "My little chunk's getting heavy."

"He definitely looks well-fed." *Oh shit, she's gonna think I'm insulting her kid or worse that I'm referring to the lactation porn Stella suggested last night.*

But Serena laughs. "Oh, yes he is," she coos.

"How've you been, sweetheart? I barely got to talk to you last night."

"I'm good. I had fun getting to know Margot better." Her lips curve in a knowing smile. "You two disappeared on us early."

Another way those girls ruined things for Margot. The whole point was for Margot to get to know the other ol' ladies better, not hear lies and half-truths from bitter club girls with big mouths.

"She liked hanging with you too," I say. "She's looking forward to seeing you this morning."

She blows out a relieved breath. "Oh, good."

"Some of the girls hassled her," I explain, reaching into the back to grab a folded-up playpen and two giant tote bags. "Between that and Stella, I figured she'd had enough for one night." I slam the tailgate closed.

"Don't blame you." She walks ahead of me, shaking her long, blond ponytail off her shoulder. "I'm leaving some of that here in our room so I can stop schlepping it back and forth. I left my other travel stuff at Emily's place since we've been staying there when the club's on a run."

"You know Grinder's grumpier than usual when he's away from you for more than an hour, right?"

Serena blushes and shakes her head. "I know."

She reaches the clubhouse doors first and opens one for me. I motion for her to go in first, but she pauses, glancing over her shoulder.

"I like Margot," she says quietly. "A lot. She's really sweet. I think she's a great match for you."

You have no idea. I nod once. "Agreed."

She smiles wider. "I'm so happy for you."

"Thanks."

She pushes the door open wider and steps through, holding it long enough for me to follow.

Margot

Not even the scent of freshly brewing coffee wafting through the hallway could drag me out of our room this morning. Not until Jigsaw returns.

He promised those girls would be gone but I'm not taking any chances.

I don't want to face anyone else yet. Not Serena, or even Shelby. I'm not ready to see his brothers, either. Surely by now Jigsaw's told all of them about last night. So now they'll all know that when Margot comes to a club party, trouble follows.

While Jigsaw's gone, I take a long shower. I packed all my favorite curly hair products to bring with me this weekend and spend time drying and shaping my hair into long, glossy curls. I brought lots of hair products but not much makeup. Part of me longs to run across the hall and ask Serena for help. But I'm too embarrassed.

I dress in a simple pair of jeans and a sweatshirt. Hopefully no one will be all done up at breakfast this morning.

There's a low murmur of voices, then a thump in the hallway. A man's voice. I cock my head. Jigsaw?

A few seconds later, the lock clicks and the door swings open.

As soon as our eyes meet, his serious expression softens. "Hey, you're up." His gaze sweeps over me, and his mouth curves into a smile that melts straight through me. "Already so pretty this morning."

The warmth in his voice sends a flush over my skin. "Thank you."

He crosses the room in two strides and dips his head, brushing his lips over mine—soft, reverent. The suddenness steals my breath, and I gasp against him. His hand slides into my hair, fingers curving around the back of my head, holding me still as his hot, silken mouth deepens the kiss. Heat flares through me as his tongue slides against mine, unhurried and possessive.

I sigh into him, threading my arms around his neck. He hums with approval and gathers me close, one arm banding around my waist, the other still tangled in my hair, like he doesn't want to let go.

A quick burst of knocking rattles our door.

He breaks the kiss with a frustrated growl, resting his forehead against mine. His breath fans my lips, and for a second, I think he's going to ignore whoever it is.

"You ready for breakfast?" he asks, like choosing food over kissing is a punishment he's forced to accept. "Everyone's headed down to the kitchen."

"Are...are those girls still—?" I hate the way my voice quivers. I'm not scared of them—my knife rests heavy in my jeans pocket this morning—but last night was humiliating enough. I'll melt into the floor if they embarrass me in front of the whole club that way.

"Gone." His voice is firm and leaves no room for doubt. "Prospects know not to let any of them in the gate."

I let out a shaky breath of relief.

He scrubs a hand over his face, then shakes his head. "We ended up banning our old president's wife last year—"

"Really?" I blink up at him. "Wow. Why?"

"She pulled a nasty trick on Serena." He frowns, jaw working side to side. "Tawny had been a problem no one wanted to deal with for years. She got to hide behind her old man's president patch. But what she did to Serena was the final straw." His lips curl into a cruel smirk. "I pushed hard for that ban and G had my back today."

"Wow." I hate that I'm about to ask this, especially after what he told me about Serena's ex last night. But I can't help it. "So, I'm not the only one who's run into trouble with other women in the club?"

"No." He frowns. "Those women weren't 'in' the club. Just—club girls who hang around here sometimes. But yeah, I told you it happens. It shouldn't, but it does." He says it like it's a fact of MC life he's had to accept even though it pisses him off.

For a few seconds, neither of us say anything. I study his hard, but handsome face. How many other stories are there? Is he giving them to me in drips so that he won't scare me away?

As if flipping an internal switch, he turns and walks over to his closet, sliding the door open. "Hey, you look really good, but will you wear this for me instead?" he asks, his voice low and so achingly sweet I couldn't say no even if he handed me a pillowcase.

Thankfully, it's a soft, faded blue hooded sweatshirt. I take it from him, fingers brushing his for a second too long, and hold it up to inspect the design. The skull and crown are printed in blue on blue. A subtle design. A whisper of his club's insignia instead of a declaration.

"Am I allowed to wear it?" I tease, peeling off my own sweatshirt and tossing it onto the bed.

"Yes," he answers in a slow, teasing tone. "Only thing you *can't* wear is my cut." His tone dips lower. "But I love you so damn much, I'd probably break that rule for you."

"Wow, that is love," I tease, pulling his sweatshirt over my head. It's huge on me, but so soft and snuggly. "You know you're never getting this back, right?"

"Fine by me." He reaches out and adjusts the hood, his fingers slipping beneath to free my hair from the collar. "I like you in my club's colors." He brushes his knuckles along my jaw, and I lean into him, helpless against the gravity of his touch. "Looks good on you."

"Thank you," I whisper.

He curls his fingers around mine, his palm warm and steady. "Ready? We don't do the elaborate buffet like Upstate, but Lilly brought muffins and pastries from this bakery she loves. They're actually really good. And there's coffee, of course."

"Oh, Lilly's here?" That makes me feel better. Lilly seems to have such a kind, calming presence. My nose wrinkles. "Is Stella gone?"

"Eh, she's still lurking somewhere. Lilly gets along with her." He wobbles his free hand in the air. "Like, they're cordial. I think it was really Z who didn't want to be here to celebrate Stella, you know?"

He respects his wife too much to put her in that situation. I like Z even more now.

Outside our door, Rooster's leaning against the opposite wall with his arms wrapped around Shelby.

Jigsaw stops short, squinting at him. "What are you, my guard dog?"

"Shelby didn't want to head to the dining room without you guys." Rooster's amused gaze slides from Jigsaw to me. "Morning, Margot."

"Morning."

Shelby wiggles loose from Rooster's hold and gives me a quick embrace. "Lost sight of ya last night."

Her sympathetic tone suggests she already knows what happened. My cheeks warm and I shrug.

"We're still waitin' on Serena too," Shelby says.

"You bang on Grinder's door like you did ours?" Jigsaw says to Rooster.

Rooster sweeps his hand toward the door. "Be my guest."

Jigsaw takes a step forward, then hesitates. "Nah. They've got Link with them. I don't want to scare the little guy."

"Exactly," Rooster says, in that slow, exaggerated tone that sounds like a verbal pat on the head.

My lips twitch with laughter I'm holding back.

Shelby catches it and gently bumps her elbow against my side. "They're always like this. Worse, if you can believe it."

"It's fun." The smile slides from my mouth as I glance at Rooster again. From what Jigsaw's told me, Rooster's been an important part of his life—probably even saved his life more than once—for a long time. "There's a lot of love under all that teasing."

Shelby nods, slow and thoughtful. "Mmmhmm. They'll never admit it, but it's there."

"Yes." Rooster throws a patient look in Jigsaw's direction. "Don't know why, though."

Jigsaw widens his eyes and waves his hand toward Rooster's face. "Who else is going to tell you when that collection of tumbleweeds on your chin is out of control?"

Rooster strokes his hand over his impeccably groomed full beard. "All I hear is jealousy, brother. Keep eating your veggies. Maybe that scruff will turn into a big boy beard one day."

Jigsaw rumbles with laughter, not the least bit offended. They know exactly how far to push each other, always dancing close to the line but never crossing it. Their teasing always seems wrapped in affection, not malice.

Grinder's door clicks open and the older biker steps into the hallway. With his broad back to us, he half-turns and glances into the room, one arm casually braced against the doorframe, waiting patiently. A few seconds later, Serena emerges, cradling a chunky baby in her arms, her long blond ponytail swaying as she balances his weight against her hip.

Grinder leans in, brushing a kiss over Serena's cheek, then another against the top of the baby's head. He murmurs something to her, too low for me to make out. When he turns toward us, all softness disappears. His expression sharpens, posture shifting—shoulders squared, chin lifted, eyes scanning with quiet intensity. The change is subtle but unmistakable. Yup, it makes sense that he's the club's enforcer. It's hard to reconcile this commanding, quietly protective man with the way those club girls dismissed him last night—"that old guy who got outta prison." Casually cruel. So far off the mark, it's almost laughable.

I'm so happy he kicked their asses to the curb. I only wish I'd been able to watch.

"Morning," he says, voice calm but clipped.

His eyes zero in on me. "How're you doing today, Margot?"

"Much better." I reach for Jigsaw's hand, squeezing his fingers to anchor myself.

"Hey, lil' mama." Shelby hurries to Serena's side, giving her a gentle one-armed hug while peeking at the baby. "And good mornin', lil' butterbean."

Serena giggles and Lincoln gives a soft, squawky protest, squirming in her arms.

"I'll take him, buttercup." Grinder slides the baby from her hold with practiced ease, tucking him against his chest. He tips his chin toward the hallway. "Why're we all standing around here? Let's go."

"Uh, we were waiting for you, Grumpy." Jigsaw coughs into his fist. "I mean, Grinder."

"Keep that shit up," he growls, cutting a sharp glare at Jigsaw. "You and Z, with the grumpy shit."

"To be fair, I think Wrath started it," Rooster says in his most helpful tone. "And you're kind of proving their point."

Grinder mutters something low and threatening.

While the guys continue their back-and-forth, Serena slips between them and hooks her arms around Shelby and me, tugging us forward with a conspiratorial grin. "I'm starving. Every calorie I take in, Lincoln sucks right out of me."

Shelby titters with laughter. "From what I heard, it's a big ol' carb fest in there this mornin'."

The main room's packed again, but thankfully the giant-screen TV is dark—no pornos playing on a loop this morning. No garish red lights either. Just weak sunlight sneaking through the tinted windows and the white glare of the overhead lights.

Serena edges behind the empty bar and motions for us to sit at the short side of the counter, near the wall. The corner's cozy and out of the way, which I appreciate after last night. The guys sort of form a loose circle behind us, talking in low tones.

Serena pulls three bottles of water from somewhere under the bar and I accept one gratefully. The condensation chills my fingers as I twist the cap open and take a long sip, enjoying the cool rush down my throat.

Serena glances around the packed room, then rests her elbows on the counter, leaning closer to me. "Gray said you had some trouble last night. I'm so sorry we got separated."

I set down the bottle, grateful it's only the three of us tucked into this corner. "It all happened so fast, I'm not sure you could've done anything."

"Bonnie's been askin' for trouble lately," Shelby mutters, picking at the label on her water bottle. "She used to be okay. I dunno what crawled up her butt."

"Well, Gray assured me they won't be coming back." Serena pats my hand, her tone firm and big-sisterly.

"Uh, one of them, Amanda, said you used to be friends?" I wince. "I'm sorry if I got her in trouble."

Serena stiffens at the name. "We haven't been friends in a while, unfortunately."

"Oh."

"No, no." She reaches over and squeezes my hand. "I'm sorry if she said something awful to you."

"Eh." I shrug, then remember how awful it actually got. I stick out my tongue and gag. "She bragged about..." I swallow hard. Seriously? Am I really saying this out loud? "Jigsaw fucking her so hard he bruised her spleen."

"Ewww, what the hell," Shelby groans. "Who says that?"

I pat my stomach. "Well, she was pointing to the wrong organ. I was five seconds from pulling my knife and giving her a splenectomy."

Serena lets out a sharp huff of laughter.

"Should be a lobotomy since she clearly ain't usin' that organ, either," Shelby says with a dramatic eye roll.

Serena's gaze flicks past me. Probably checking if Jigsaw's listening. "I'm not sure if this helps or not, but I don't even think that's true." Her cheeks turn pinker underneath her carefully applied makeup. "Way before I met Gray, when I used to..." She glances around, voice dipping. "Visit here—she wanted to hook up with Jiggy." She shifts her gaze to Shelby. "And Rooster. But she never did. That I know of."

I shrug. "I'm not worried about anything that happened before me." I hold up one hand. "I don't want to hear about it in graphic detail, but I don't care. That wasn't the worst anyway. Bonnie and Nikki were much nastier in the personal attacks."

Serena rolls her eyes. "I can only guess. Don't believe any of the trash they said."

The quick squeeze of her hand lingers. I don't know what I expected—maybe a polite smile and generic apology. But she's warm. Genuine. Like we're already friends, not two women thrown together because our boyfriends wear the same patch.

Shelby leans in. "I'm sorry I wasn't with you this time." Her lashes flutter as she glances over her shoulder. "Jiggy's been on the market so long, I guess some of the bunnies are losin' their dang minds."

I snort, then dissolve into full-on giggles behind my hand. "Yes. He made it clear that he didn't 'do relationships' when we first started..." I clear my throat delicately. "Seeing each other."

Shelby angles her body slightly and shoots a slow, deliberate stink eye at Jigsaw.

"What'd I do, songbird?" he asks, cocking his head in exaggerated innocence. He leans over and taps her shoulder with the tip of his pinky.

She ignores him, smiling sweetly at me instead. "He'll deny it, but he needs someone with steel in her spine to tell him when he's actin' a fool."

Jigsaw slides his hand over my hip and squeezes lightly. "You do call me out when I need it." He leans down and kisses my cheek. "I love that about you."

For him to say that in front of his friends—not that I think they heard his low murmur—means a lot. I turn and press my lips to his. "Anything I do is out of love."

"I know."

"Awww!" Shelby squeals, grinning like she might explode from secondhand happiness.

Jigsaw rolls his eyes at her, but he's smiling as he eases away and drifts back to join the guys behind us, his hand trailing off my back as he goes.

Our conversation shifts, light and easy.

As we move on to talking about other things, I discover that Serena and I share a mutual obsession with Pretty Pout lip glosses.

"We need to get together soon," Serena says, excitement bubbling in her voice. She leans closer and squeezes my arm. "They just sent me a box of their whole spring line."

My mouth drops open. "I would *love* that."

"You have to come see our house," she says, practically bouncing. "I have the studio where I film—"

"Oh my God, I love those shelves you have in the background!" I say, remembering one of her recent videos. "With the backlighting and the acrylic risers? Gorgeous."

She beams, glowing with pride. "Gray found the house and knew I'd love that room for filming."

I swivel on my stool a little, sneaking a glance toward Grinder. The older, gruff biker who practically growled at Rooster earlier had picked out a home for his fiancée with the perfect filming room for her beauty videos? It doesn't get any sweeter than that.

"But," Serena adds with a gleam in her eye, "I have my own private makeup room, totally separate. I never show it in videos."

"You have to see it," Shelby chimes in. "It's spectacular. And I say that as someone who has her own makeup room—thanks to these two." She jerks her thumb at Rooster and Jigsaw over her shoulder.

Jigsaw holds up his hands and turns them over for us to see. "So. Many. Blisters."

Rooster smacks Jigsaw's arm. "I told you to wear gloves, chucklefuck."

A completely unwanted sliver of jealousy slides under my skin. Not over what was said—just the way they all fit together so easily. The shorthand. The history.

Before I can unpack it, the air behind us shifts—charged and heavier somehow.

"Hey, Wrath," Serena says with a quick nod and smile.

Shelby and I both spin our stools around.

Wrath's joined the group. He claps Grinder on the back, says a surprisingly sweet greeting to baby Lincoln, then slings one arm each around Rooster and Jigsaw's necks, dragging them into a tight huddle. "Got my security team for Vegas?"

Jigsaw flicks an annoyed glance at Wrath.

"Ooo!" Shelby says, waving her hand in the air. "I can't wait to talk to Griff at his party. Dawson wants to sponsor him, and he offered his private jet for Vegas."

"Nice." Wrath nods with approval. "Thanks, Shelby."

"No problem. He was pretty tickled that I had a personal connection to a hot, new fighter he can brag on."

I frown at Jigsaw. "Griff, my mechanic?"

"One and the same," Jigsaw confirms with a weary sigh. He shakes loose of Wrath's grip and steps closer, wrapping his fingers around mine. "I was going to ask if you'd come to the party with me." His thumb brushes over my knuckles. "And Vegas."

"Oh." My heart performs a wild stutter. He wants me by his side at more events. Not only around his club brothers but other friends outside of his MC. And a trip to Vegas? Traveling together seems like a big step as a couple.

But my rush of excitement is quickly smothered by reality. The party? Maybe. Vegas? Not likely. I can't fit a trip like that into my schedule on short notice.

"Oh." Shelby slides a look toward Jigsaw. "Jezzie wants to come to Griff's party too."

"What?" Jigsaw scowls. "Why?"

Shelby shrugs. "I have no idea." Her mouth twitches with amusement, suggesting she knows *exactly* why.

"How does she even *know* about the party?" Jigsaw asks, suspicion clear in his voice.

A smile sneaks over Shelby's lips. "I mighta mentioned it last time we talked."

Jigsaw really can't seem to wrap his head around this.

But that's a problem for another day.

Right now, I'm excited there's another party to look forward to.

Since it's not technically an MC party, hopefully I won't get myself into any trouble this time.

CHAPTER TWENTY-NINE

JIGSAW

THE THROB IN MY TEMPLES WON'T GO AWAY.

I glance at my watch, checking the time. I should call Margot and tell her not to bother meeting me here at Remy's bar when she's finished with work. I'd rather be alone with her—no crowd, no noise, no interruptions.

But she's been looking forward to this night out.

Said she wanted to see my sister. Spend time with Jezzie and get to know her better.

The party's in full swing. Music scraping my nerves raw, lights low, and the place packed tighter than a cage on fight night. Most of my brothers are here. A bunch of fighters from The Castle. Friends of Remy and Griff's. A few familiar faces from Zips. Even some cartel guys showed up to welcome Griff home. A regular gangster party in our little corner of Bumfuck, New York.

After Rooster, Wrath, Dex, and I not-so-subtly explained we'd help Griff train for his Vegas fight, he finally seemed to grasp the stakes. We're not only doing it out of the kindness of our black hearts, we're backing him to win. Big.

No pressure or anything.

With my good deed for the night done, I plant my ass at the end of the bar. Elbows on the polished wood, boots planted wide, eyes locked on the front entrance.

My sister's behind the counter, tossing smiles and pouring drinks like she runs the place. Remy's little sister, Molly, handles the rest of the crowd like a pro. Shelby's bouncing between patrons, laughter bubbling from her lips, Rooster watching her every move.

Jezzie seems way too comfortable here. Like this ain't her first visit to Remy's bar. That worries me more than I want to admit. But I don't want to pick a fight with her tonight.

Having Jezzie here, so close to Cain when I haven't introduced them yet, spins a knot of guilt behind my ribs.

A glass thunks against the counter beside me.

"How've you been, Jigsaw?" A low, raspy voice cuts through the crowd noise.

Irritated someone dared to pull my attention from the door, I swivel on my stool—eyeing the tall, tattooed Latin guy dressed like a cartel accountant. Black sweater. Slim black pants. Leather jacket that probably cost more than my first Harley.

Quill.

The last person I feel like shaking hands with.

I slide off my stool and hold out my hand out of habit and respect. "Quill. What're you doing here?" My tone comes out as more of an accusation than a question. *Ooops.*

He clasps my hand with a quick shake—no grip, no warmth. "Eraser said it was open invite."

Of course he did.

If it wasn't for the ink crawling up his neck and the lethal glint in his eyes, his voice might fool someone into thinking he's harmless. But I know better. Son of a cartel king. Half-brother to a club president. Because of that, we let him drift through our territory on whatever business he claims is family-related. Mostly, he haunts Zips like a ghost, challenging people to race with an endless supply of cash.

"Had to welcome young Griff home from his…battle." He rolls his shoulders in a lazy shrug.

"Battle," I scoff. "You mean that clown show on TV?"

"You watched it?" he asks.

"Hell no. Sounded embarrassing as fuck."

"He handled it with class, though." Another lazy wave of his hand. "Well, as much class as one can under those circumstances."

I arch an eyebrow. "Didn't take you for a fan of reality television."

"I'm not. But my mother is." He drops his gaze like it's a private joke. Or maybe he doesn't want me to know too much about his family. "She was rooting for Griff the whole season."

Given how sideways the show went, that'd probably make Griff wanna crawl into a hole. "You tell him that?"

"Nah." His gaze skims the room, detached. "He seemed preoccupied with his girl. Didn't want to interrupt."

"He's always preoccupied with Molly." I wave it off. "Nothing new there."

"Young love." He sighs, all fake wistfulness.

Demons give me strength to deal with this smug asshole.

His gaze drifts toward the entrance. Lingers.

"Ah, now *that's* grown man's work," he says, a slow, appreciative smile spreading over his arrogant face. "What's that boy doing?"

Is Quill having a stroke? "The fuck you talking about?"

"Don't judge. I like my ladies a little more on the ample side." He licks his lower lip like a vulture. "That orange-haired kid isn't equipped to handle all that."

"No one gives a fuck about your preferences," I mutter.

Talking to Quill has my back to the door. I shift slowly, following his line of sight—

And three realizations hit me at once.

Margot's arrived.

Torch is talking to her.

Quill's admiring her ass.

My blood shoots to boiling.

"You better avert your eyes and watch your tongue, motherfucker." I lean in close to Quill's ear. "Or I'll slice them from your skull. That's *my* woman you're talking about."

He blinks.

Surprise, then amusement flickers over his lips.

"Whoa." Rooster's hand clamps down on my shoulder, dragging me back a step. "What's going on?"

Quill holds up both hands in surrender, eyes still lit with smug delight.

"Nothing." I shrug Rooster off and shove away from both of them, their low, tense voices fading behind me.

Margot turns away from Torch, her anxious gaze searching the crowded bar. The second her eyes find me, her whole face lights up.

Her lips form the words "Excuse me," as she squeezes past a group of Molly's giggling friends.

Margot's eyes stay locked on mine as she weaves through the crowd like I'm the only man in the room.

Every step she takes sends heat thrumming through my body.

I meet her halfway, curling a hand around her waist and tugging her closer. "There's my little lady death."

She throws her arms around my neck. "Sorry I'm so late," she says in a breathless rush.

I bend down, sealing my mouth over hers for a quick, hungry kiss. But the second she groans a needy little sound and strokes her fingers against the back of my neck, I lose track of everything else. Her lips part and I sweep my tongue against hers, tasting peppermint.

She drags her nails against my scalp, sending shivers of pleasure down my spine.

A splash of cold hits my cheek.

Then several more. *The fuck?*

I pull away, seeking the source.

Jezzie grins at me, twirling her fingers in a glass of water like she's about to launch round two. "Cool off, lover boy."

"You do that?" I swipe water off my cheek.

"Sorry, I was trying not to soak Margot," Jezzie says, not sounding sorry at all. "But I didn't want the room to catch on fire."

Margot lets out an embarrassed laugh but keeps her arms around my neck. "Hi, Jezzie."

"What can I get you?" Jezzie holds her arms open wide.

 328

"Um, just a club soda and lime, please"

"You got it."

Jezzie hurries to the other end of the bar and Margot returns all her attention to me. "How's the party? Talk to Griff?"

"Yeah. I think he understands the assignment."

"Good." She reaches up and kisses my cheek. "I'm so happy to see you."

"Same. Been watching that door all night."

I step back just enough to admire her. Short-sleeved purple dress hugging her curves. High collar but a cut-out dips down low, leaving her chest and the tops of her breasts on display. "You're stunning."

"Thank you," she whispers, cheeks pink.

"Well, who knew there was a Mrs. Jigsaw?" someone says behind me.

That better not be fucking Quill.

I turn slowly, arm still around Margot's waist.

Quill's disrespectful mouth slides into an appreciative smile as he runs his gaze over her. "This your lady, Jigsaw?"

"Yes," I growl. My hand tightens on Margot's hip.

Behind Quill, Rooster looms, hopefully ready to help me gut Quill and throw him out back.

Quill holds out his hand to Margot, all polite, civilized gentleman now. "Quill. Friend of your man's club."

"Friend is stretching it," I mutter.

Polite but cautious, Margot takes his hand. "Margot."

"I'd say it's nice to meet you." He holds her hand longer than necessary. "But your man just threatened to slice out my tongue and eyes a moment ago."

Margot pulls her hand away and snuggles closer to me. "What'd you do to provoke him?"

Quill lets out a hearty laugh, hand to his chest like he's enthralled with my woman. "Clever and beautiful. You hang onto her, Jigsaw."

"All right." Rooster claps a hand over Quill's shoulder, pushing him around us. "Let's go play darts."

"I feel like you're looking for a way to poke sharp instruments in me." Quill laughs but goes without a fight. Must want to keep his tongue.

Margot tilts her face up, eyes searching mine. "Did I miss something?"

"No, just a guy who needs to learn some manners."

She frowns. "Was he…making fun of me? Of us?"

I let out a sigh, frustration still simmering. "No. He…clocked you the minute you came in. Saw you talking to Torch." I grit my teeth because I still haven't addressed that issue. "He definitely wasn't making fun of you. But he was trying to piss me off just now."

Her brows pinch together. "Oh."

"What'd Torch say to you?" I ask.

She rolls her eyes. "Just said hello and asked me how I was."

"Want to cash in that rain check for your date?"

She pokes me in the stomach. "No. You can't seriously still be jealous."

"Not jealous." I lean down, nose her hair out of the way, and kiss her neck. "Just want my hands"—I kiss another sensitive spot—"and mouth"—I drag my tongue over her pulse—"all over you."

She shivers and slides her hands under my T-shirt, soft fingers stroking my sides and lower back.

"Do I need to get the water gun?" Jezzie says.

Groaning, I drag myself away from Margot.

"My goodness." Jezzie laughs. "Let the woman breathe." She pushes a short glass of bubbling soda with a lime wedge perched on the rim toward Margot.

"Thank you." Margot grabs it and takes a long sip.

Shelby joins us, hugging Margot fiercely. "I'm so happy you're here! Come on, let's go hang with the girls."

Margot glances at me.

As much as I want her all to myself, I want her to hang out with the ol' ladies of my club. Have fun.

But this place is loud, crowded, and crawling with people I don't trust. She's just going to have to do it with me standing guard.

I nod. "Yeah, let's do it."

Shelby loops her arm through Margot's and leads her to the end of the bar, already chatting a mile a minute.

I follow a step behind, scanning every face, every movement, every shadow.

CHAPTER THIRTY

JIGSAW

I'VE BEEN SWINGING BY STRIKE BACK MOST MORNINGS WHEN MARGOT'S tied up with work. Not to hover. Just to check in on Cain.

So far, he's holding it down. Making me proud. Not that I'd say those exact words to him. Don't wanna make it weird.

Kid's been through enough.

Jezzie's got finals wrapping up soon. Once that's over, I think I'll finally pull the trigger and get them together.

They deserve to know each other.

But I need to be the one who decides when and how that happens. If Jezzie ends up mad about it, I'll take the hit.

Cain's wiping down one of the benches when I walk in, sweat darkening the collar of his shirt. He's got a solid rhythm going—cleaning each piece of equipment with the preciseness you'd find in a medical lab.

And it looks like he's put on some muscle working here. I make sure his fridge is stocked every week. But this? This is his own doing. He's been filling out. Building strength. Absorbing tips from Sully and Jake.

"Damn," I say, nodding at the weights. "Look at you bulking up."

He glances over, pushing his sweaty hair off his forehead. A grin tugs at the corner of his mouth. "Gotta get ready to humble you in the cage one day."

He's got a sense of humor too. "You wish."

He tosses the towel on the bench. "You come check in on me every day just to talk smack?"

Before I can answer, Sully steps out of his office, arms crossed, expression unreadable. "You harassing my employees, Jigsaw?"

Look at him. All protective over my brother like he's known him forever.

Shit, I'm glad this is working out.

Even if it means I have to admit Wrath was right.

"Nope." I clap Cain on the back, the sweat on his shirt seeping into my palm. "Just checking in. Making sure everything's running smooth."

I meet Sully at the front desk and lower my voice, leaning in closer to him. "Seriously. Everything good?"

"Yeah." Sully exhales like I just asked him if gravity's still a thing. "He's a hard worker. Was shy at first but he's warming up to the regulars." He rolls his eyes. "Especially the ladies."

I duck my head, laughing under my breath. "Naturally."

"Follows directions. Doesn't half-ass anything. Never late." His gaze shifts to Jake, who's in front of the mirror knocking out a clean set of Romanian deadlifts—form locked in, shins vertical, face unreadable. "Unlike my own brother."

"To be fair," I laugh, can't believe I'm defending him, "Jake's commuting from Empire. Cain's walking four blocks."

Sully lifts one shoulder. "Still. I haven't hired anyone in five years who hasn't bitched about weekends, cleaning, hours, something. Cain's a good kid."

Guilt tangles around my throat, paralyzing my vocal cords. I bob my head up and down a few times before saying, "Thanks."

He crosses his arms over his chest and widens his stance. "You could thank me by telling Wrath to stop poaching my best walking advertisement for this place."

I duck my head, dragging a hand over the back of my neck. "Bro,

we both know I don't control Wrath. Or his business. Or his mouth. He's just trying to help Griff win that fight."

"Uh-huh. And soak up some free publicity from that dumbass show."

"Honestly, I have no idea." I shrug. "I'm going to Vegas to watch Griff's back. That's as deep as my involvement gets." I cross my arms over my chest, mirroring his stance. "Jake and Wrath work together—have your brother talk to him."

"Eh." He waves it off. "I don't want to put Griff in an awkward position. He's still been doing some promo for us."

Then why are you bustin' my nuts about it?

He lifts his chin toward Cain. "He says he might be interested in learning to fight."

Great, just what my brother needs—cauliflower ears and brain damage.

I curl my arm and thump my bicep. "What can I say? It's in his blood."

"You still taking fights at The Castle?"

"Not recently." I shake my head. "Remy hasn't been hosting any, far as I know."

And I've been too busy wrapped around my little lady death to give a fuck about cage fights.

Has she managed to tame the violence right out of me?

"Griff's a talented fighter," Sully says. "Had a once-in-a-million shot with that show. Now every kid who walks in here thinks they're gonna be the next *Supreme Underground Fighter* pick. No clue what a clusterfuck it actually was."

"Ain't that true of just about everything?"

"What I meant was, I don't mind training Cain if he's interested. But…" He hesitates, then lifts an eyebrow. "He says he's planning to go to JCCC in the fall?"

"Far as I know, yeah."

"Good. I told him I'll work around his schedule." He glances toward the weight room, lips twitching into something damn near fatherly. "Told him fighting's fun, but he needs a stable fallback in case he doesn't hit the big time—or, God forbid, gets hurt."

This prick just keeps serving me emotional gut punches.

If only Cain and I had a decent father who gave half the shit Sully seems to give about a kid he barely knows.

The buzz of my phone saves me from spiraling too deep. I check the screen. "Ha. Look who it is—our favorite *SUF* star."

Sully snorts. "Tell him to stop fuckin' around at the garage and get his ass down here on the treadmill."

"Will do."

"Thanks, I appreciate it."

He slaps my shoulder—firm and final—then disappears into his office.

I thumb the green button. "Royal, what's so important you couldn't put it in a text?"

Griff lets out a shaky breath that's supposed to pass for a laugh. "Trust me, you don't want this in writing. Can you and a few of the guys come to Jerry's garage? There's an urgent...situation I could use your club's help with."

Fuck.

Griff doesn't rattle easily. And he sure as hell doesn't ask for help unless he's out of options.

"I'm on my way."

CHAPTER THIRTY-ONE

JIGSAW

I TURN INTO THE PARKING LOT OF JERRY'S GARAGE, UNSURE OF WHAT we're walking into. I roll my bike into a spot on the side of the old brick building, not visible from the road. Wrath stops his bike next to me.

We stare at each other for a minute, then shut off our bikes.

"Murphy's on his way with the van," Wrath says.

"You know what's going on?"

"Guy tried to rob him?" He shrugs and nods toward my saddlebag. "You got your bolt cutters in there?"

"Hell yeah, I do." I pull out a slightly smaller pair than the ones I keep in my truck. Still sharp enough to lop off a finger or two.

Remy meets us at the corner of the building. I've never seen him anything but cocky around the ladies or ruthless in the cage.

Today, he's...rattled.

Wrath stops and frowns. "What's going on, Ruthless?"

At Wrath's grave tone, Remy seems to compose himself. He takes a breath and pulls his shoulders back, slipping into his confident don't-fuck-with-me attitude. "This guy...some tweaker, I don't know. He came after Griff and my sister."

"They all right?" I ask.

He jerks his thumb over his shoulder. "Yeah. They're in the garage. They got the guy tied up but..."

"Let's go meet him." Wrath sweeps his hand through the air in a move-it-along gesture.

The sharp stink of motor oil and burnt rubber hits me as soon as we step into the garage.

Griff's standing next to a half-finished classic car, with Molly slightly behind him. Like he's shielding her from us.

The tension's thick enough to crack a socket wrench on.

Wrath stops short and crosses his arms over his chest, throwing a disappointed scowl at Griff. "Stonewall, don't you have a fight you're supposed to be training for?"

Griff's eyes widen for a second, then he lets out a sharp laugh. "Trust me, this isn't how I wanted to spend my afternoon."

I choke on a laugh.

Wrath nods to the old Chevy. "Nice car. Is it yours?"

I side-eye Wrath. We didn't rush over here to yap about cars, did we?

"It's Molly's." Griff wraps a protective arm around her shoulders. "We were finishing up some work on it when that greasy little weasel over there showed up and pulled a gun on us."

I peer around Wrath's big ass and take a few steps back. Tucked up in front of the car, away from the view of anyone outside, a scrawny man's zip-tied to within an inch of his life, a filthy rag shoved in his mouth.

He doesn't move or look at us but seems to be breathing.

"What'd he want?" Wrath asks in his *get to the point* tone.

Griff drops his gaze, wraps his hand around a fist, and works his jaw from side to side. Then he lifts his head and meets Wrath's stare head on.

"My mom's got...issues. She moved down to Jersey to start over a few months ago. I haven't been in contact with her since I got home. She left me some messages looking for money while I was on the show but..." Griff shrugs, clearly uncomfortable sharing all this personal info. "I tried helping her out and taking care of her when she was here. And fuck knows she's drained a lot of money out of me over the years, but this is the first time someone's ever showed up to collect from *me*."

Remy steps closer to his sister's side, glances at Griff, and then Wrath. "We don't know who he works for."

That's what I'm here for. I lift the bolt cutters in the air. "He's got ten chances to give up a name."

Wrath smirks. "Twenty if you start with his toes."

"This isn't my place," Griff says, holding out his arms in a slow-down gesture.

They go back and forth about where to take the guy while I study the scene in front of me. Molly trembling but trying her hardest to look tough. Griff keeping her close.

The guy on the floor peers up at me, eyes wide. He jerks his shoulder like he's trying to free himself. His leg's at a fucked-up angle. Wrists raw and bleeding. Face already bruising.

"You need to go home," Griff says to Molly, drawing me back to the conversation.

"Not so fast, little girl." Wrath cocks his head and studies her. "What'd you see today?"

"Leave her out of it," Remy snaps.

Molly takes a deep breath and flicks an irritated glance at her brother. "I was *in it* when that guy pointed a gun at me. And even deeper *in it* when I smashed his leg with the crowbar."

Molly's the one who fucked that guy's leg up? Well, goddamn. "Guess that ruthless streak runs through your blood." I laugh.

Remy sighs and side-eyes me.

"Griff had him," Molly continues, clearly wanting to defend her boyfriend's status as her big, bad protector. "But I already had the crowbar in my hands, and I was afraid he'd try to run." She lifts her gaze and meets Wrath's stare without flinching "But if anyone outside of the four of *you* asks, all I saw was the inside of this garage while Griff and I were working on my car."

I glance at the tweaker again.

As much as I thoroughly enjoy giving Griff shit, I won't tolerate someone else fucking with him. He's like another little brother. Someone I enjoy putting in a headlock from time to time. But if anyone *else* puts their hands on him, they're not getting them back.

And threatening Molly—pulling a gun on a teenage girl? Absolutely the fuck not. He signed his death warrant the second he threatened her. How hard he gets to die, though, that's up to him.

When Wrath seems satisfied Molly won't breathe a word of any of this—with Remy and Griff knowing damn well they'll pay the consequences if she does—we send her on her way.

She peels out of the parking lot in Griff's car, tires squealing, dust billowing behind her, taillights flashing red as they disappear down the road.

I crouch next to our new friend, leveling my eyes with his.

His sweat-slicked face twitches as Wrath leans over and yanks the gag free with a sharp snap.

The guy still won't look me in the eye, but he starts whining right away, voice cracked and high-pitched.

"Untie me, man. I think he broke my wrist. And my ankle—she shattered it. I'm in pain, man."

"You fucked with the wrong people." I hold up the bolt cutters, slow and deliberate, until the cold steel hovers inches from his face. "Are you talking, or are we snipping?"

"I...I don't know. Guy I used to answer to was Rio. But...new guy, just gives orders. Come on, my wrist hurts."

I cut my eyes to Wrath. *Rio's dead*, I mouth.

He nods once, his jaw clenched tight.

"I just needed to collect the money," the guy whines again. "His mom took off. No one could find her. I was told this kid was good for it. Come on. It's not my fault."

His voice grates against my nerves like sandpaper. *If I snap his other wrist, would he shut the fuck up?*

Finally, Murphy arrives with the club's van. The low rumble of the engine silences us as he slowly backs into the garage and hops out.

"What's up?" Murphy asks, going full gangster as he pulls on a black knit hat and slips on a pair of black leather gloves.

"I'll fill you in," I promise.

Wrath orders Griff and Remy to get rid of the guy's truck.

Griff scowls at the guy and then our van, as if the reason we're here finally dawned on him. "This is my situation. I'll handle it."

Aw, isn't that cute. "So strong and yet so wrong," I rhyme.

Griff bursts out laughing. "What?"

Wrath's having none of it. He pokes Griff in the chest. "We need you focused on training for that fight. Not gettin' distracted with a side quest. Dump the truck. That's all I need from you."

Heh. Side quest.

Every day feels like a side quest lately. Maybe that's all life is—one long chain of fucked-up detours.

Griff exhales hard and nods. "I'll get it done."

"Now wouldn't it be easier if you just did what we asked when we asked?" I tilt my head and widen my eyes to a dickish degree.

"So glad you're coming to Vegas with us," he grumbles under his breath.

After the two of them leave, Murphy grabs the chain and rolls the garage doors down with a clatter of metal and finality.

For a few seconds, it's quiet. The air's heavy with oil, sweat, and the sound of this guy sniveling.

The passenger side door of the van creaks open.

I frown, shifting to get a better look.

Boots hit the ground.

Finally, Rock steps around the back of the van. Determined presidential expression in place.

"What were you doing, waiting for the bat signal?" Wrath jokes.

"No." Rock shakes his head, his lips flattening into an irritated line. "Didn't see the need to get them more wound up than necessary. What'd you learn?"

"Come on, man," the tweaker whines. "I told you. Rio was calling the shots."

"Rio's been dead for at least two years," Rock snaps. "Try again."

"If he says SOS, I'm gonna blow something up," Murphy grumbles, pacing behind the van.

"They're not local," the guy blurts. "This crew's in Jersey."

Fuck me. I glance at Wrath, then Rock. "Vipers?"

"They *do* hire the worst and dumbest," Wrath mutters, pure disdain curling off each word.

Rock crouches next to the guy and grabs him by the shirt, jerking him up with one hand like he weighs nothing. "How long have you been movin' stuff into New York?"

"I wasn't! I don't. Just collectin' money. I swear!" His gaze latches onto Rock's chest, locking onto his MC patches like they might be his salvation. "Come on, man. I used to hang out with one of your guys back in the day," he whines. "I know LOKI! Really. I do."

Oh, no the fuck he didn't.

Rock hauls back and drives his fist into the guy's jaw. The hit lands solid, dulled only slightly by the leather glove. "The fuck name did you use?"

I cough-snicker into my fist. *Big mistake, dude.*

"You ain't part of our crew," Rock growls. "Show some fucking respect."

The guy's face crumples in confusion, brows knitting as he fumbles his bound hands up to his swelling cheek.

I kick him in the shin—just hard enough to get my point across. "Lost Kings MC, motherfucker. You haven't earned the right to call us by any other name."

"Right, right, right. Lost Kings. Lost Kings. I know."

Murphy frowns. "Wait, *who* was the patch holder you used to 'hang out' with?"

"Bro, he's obviously desperate and full of shit," I say.

Wrath sniffs the air with exaggerated disgust. "Smells like he took a shit, too."

"Jesus Christ," Rock groans, pinching the bridge of his nose.

""S…sh—Shade?" the guy stammers. "I think it was Shade. Or maybe Shadow—something like that. Shadow, yeah."

"So, *way* back in the day." I laugh.

"We're not gettin' anything useful here." Rock stands and dusts off his gloves. "Let's take him to our friend's house." He slants a pointed look my way.

Cedarwood's.

My internal *fuck no* alarm clangs.

I don't want to involve Margot in our business more than she already has been. Not to dispose of some low life scumfucker.

"Shouldn't we leave him somewhere he can be found? Send a message to whoever sent him," I suggest.

Rock tilts his head and studies me, then turns to Wrath and Murphy, like a judge waiting for arguments to be made.

Wrath shakes his head. "Guy's gotta have a record. A *long* one. But if anyone knows he was in our territory, and he just disappears, they might question us." He pauses, lips twisting into a cold grin. "But I also kinda like Jiggy's thinking. If it's New Jersey Vipers testing the waters— we need to send a stronger message than just makin' their guy vanish."

He lifts his hand, fingers wiggling in the air like a magician—*poof.*

"You wanna hang him from a bridge like we're in fuckin' Juárez?" Murphy says with a dry laugh. "I thought that was the whole point of having the Death Palace on speed dial."

He cuts a glance at me, grinning like the smartass he is.

When I don't respond to the dark humor, his smile fades. "What's wrong? You don't want us asking your girlfriend for favors?"

I could fuckin' punch Murphy right now. "I didn't say that."

Rock's steely glare swings my way.

Great.

When I don't elaborate, he finally asks, "What's wrong?"

"Nothing." I force a smirk that tastes like ash. "Margot will be more than happy to fire up the oven for us." I glance at Wrath. "It's like I said, we haven't had any issues in our territory for a while. Maybe we should make an example of this guy."

"He's a low-level tweaker," Murphy points out. "No one's gonna give a fuck what happens to him."

We all glance over at the guy, who's suddenly silent.

He's unconscious.

Wrath slides his gaze to the door Remy and Griff exited through. "That's a good point about not having any issues in this area…"

"Don't even go there, bro." Murphy takes a step closer to Wrath, voice dropping. "Griff's mom is the addict. He's got no control over that. Trust me. You heard him, she's not even living around here anymore."

Wrath's punisher expression dials down a few degrees. "Yeah, okay."

"All right," Rock says, his tone final. "While I agree with you to a certain extent, Jigsaw, I think it's better if we don't call more attention to this guy than necessary."

Fair enough. At least Rock considered my suggestion before shooting it down. "I'll call Margot. Make sure we've got privacy. They've been slammed this week."

Rock nods. "Thank you. That's good to know. We'll wait until dark."

I step away from the group and fish out my phone.

Margot answers on the first ring. "Is everything okay?"

Damn, even when I'm about to make myself an accomplice to murder her voice still tickles my ears and turns my chest cavity all gooey.

"Yeah," I murmur. "Things still busy there?"

"No. Dad's at the church. Paul's helping me grab a few things, then he's heading out." She pauses. "He has a date," she adds in a cheerful tone.

Go, Paul.

"How do you feel about us baking some fresh bread tonight?" I ask, hoping she understands the *us* is my club and the *bread* is a body.

She pauses long enough to suggest she hears what I'm asking. "That sounds good. Let me pre-heat the oven so it's ready when you get here." Her voice finishes on a questioning lilt.

"That works." I glance back at the guys. "We're, ah…not too far from your place."

"Great. See you in a bit."

We hang up and I tuck the phone back in my pocket.

"Bread, huh?" Murphy's ginger-bearded face breaks into a grin. "That's a good one. She knows we're bringing a body, though, right?"

"I'm ninety-nine percent sure she understood my code." I reach out and pat his cheek a few times. "But thanks for asking, Ginger Yeti."

"Stop fucking around and get this asshole loaded in the van," Rock orders.

Wrath jogs over the garage floor like a jolly Viking heading to battle.

Margot. Damn, she was so steady and calm. Understanding my code—willing to "preheat the oven" for us on a moment's notice. Sure, it's the deal her dad made with my club, but she didn't even hesitate.

I squeeze my eyes shut, trying to push out the image of Margot flipping switches and prepping the crematorium—like she's preparing to host a bake sale for demons.

It isn't right.

Dragging her into our mess. Making her dispose of our garbage.

I shove that thought away. She can handle this. She's handled way worse. On her own. Griff's her mechanic. She likes him a lot. She met Molly at the party and loved her. Once Margot knows this guy tried to hurt them, she'll be more than happy to help us toss his worthless body in the fire.

Wrath lifts the guy as if he weighs nothing more than a few bags of salt. The tweaker wasn't that out of it. He squirms and struggles, snapping his teeth at Wrath's wrist.

"Ow! Fuck!" Wrath flings him into the back of the van and stares at the red crescent marks denting his skin. "I better not get rabies from you, fucker."

"Let's move," Rock barks, slapping my shoulder. "We'll all go in the van. Less noise at the Cedarwoods."

Good. The fewer people who see us there or hear us rumbling through their parking lot, the better.

"I'll drive." Wrath plucks the keys from Murphy's hand. Rock returns to the passenger side.

"Whatever," Murphy grumbles. "Guess we're riding in the back with this prick." He jumps into the cargo area.

I follow, ducking my head as I step inside. The back of the van's clean and organized, probably how Dex keeps it. A couple of heavy-duty tarps are folded and strapped down along one wall. A shiny, neon green toolbox sits secured behind the driver's seat—probably a few things in there we could use to make this guy disappear.

No benches back here. Murphy and I take the floor, backs to the wall, sitting across from the prick who thought he could terrorize friends of my club.

The van growls to life; its low rumble thrums in time with the unease churning in my chest. The garage door hums and rattles as it rises.

We sway with the motion of the van as it rocks onto the road. Wrath's up front, bitching about his wrist while he guides the van toward Margot's place. I lean back and close my eyes for a second.

The tweaker mumbles and mutters to himself. We should've put his fucking gag back in.

Snick. Snick.

A grunt of effort. The unmistakable scrape of metal against metal.

My eyes snap open.

The tweaker lunges at me like a rabid vulture out of a fucking horror movie.

"Shit!" I twist to the side.

A flash of silver.

Something sharp and cold punches into my thigh.

White-hot pain sears through my leg.

"Motherfucker!" I roar, grabbing his wrist too late to stop the blade from plunging into my flesh but fast enough to keep him from twisting it deeper.

Murphy launches forward, slamming him against the wall of the van. "You stupid son of a bitch!" He knees him in the gut, driving him to the floor.

"What the fuck's happening?" Wrath shouts.

The van fishtails, gravel spitting underneath us.

"What the fuck?" Rock's voice booms from the front.

"We're fine," Murphy answers, struggling to subdue the guy. "Just get us there."

"We are *not* fine," I seethe through my clenched jaw. "That fucker stabbed me."

"Fuck." Rock turns. "Jiggy. You all right? Where?"

Hot, wet blood soaks through my jeans.

"My leg," I groan.

"Stabbed you with what?" Wrath barks, already flooring it. "How'd he get loose?"

I shoot a glare at Murphy. "That's an excellent question. Where was your situational awareness, jackass?"

He winces. "This." Murphy holds up a short, stubby blade. "He sawed through the ties at his ankles and wrists. Lucky he didn't snap the one under his knees."

Fuck, this burns like hell. A deep, searing throb that pulses with every single bump in the road.

Murphy shoves the bloody knife in his pocket and wraps his arm around the guy's neck. The tweaker struggles and fights but Murphy finally chokes him unconscious.

"You good?" Murphy tosses his knit cap to me. "Put pressure on that."

"Thanks." I grunt, pressing my palm against the wound. "Fucker got me good, but I don't think it's that deep."

Just another fucking scar to add to my collection.

CHAPTER THIRTY-TWO

THE SHARP TANG OF LEMON SOAP AND FORMALDEHYDE CLINGS TO MY skin. No matter how many times I scrub, the chemicals linger, soaked into my pores. Not that odd scents are my biggest concern tonight.

I duck into my closet and peel off the demure navy dress I wore for the service. The fabric sticks to my arms as I tug it off. I toss it toward the dresser—sorting can wait—and grab a pair of black leggings, a black tank top, and a hooded, zip-up sweatshirt with deep pockets.

After I've changed, I check my phone and pull up the app Jigsaw installed. It shows him about half an hour away. Near the garage where I take my car. Odd.

I'm ninety-nine percent sure the *oven* Jigsaw wants to use is the crematorium and the *bread* is a body. But I'm feeling cheeky and have a few minutes to kill before they get here.

Gretel trots into the kitchen and twines herself around my legs, purring like a fuzzy little black Harley. "I should've named you Harley," I murmur, rubbing the top of her head. "You sound like one."

"*Me-row.*"

She settles on the tile beside the cabinets, tail curled neatly around her paws, bright green eyes focused on me like she's expecting another dinner.

"You already ate," I remind her.

"*Mraw.*"

I crouch and hook a finger into the edge of the bottom cabinet shelf, dragging out the wide rolling tray loaded with appliances I never have time to use. Even less since Jigsaw showed up in my life. I heft the heavy, black-and-silver bread maker onto the counter. The lid creaks when I flip it open. I wrestle the bread pan free from its stubborn metal clamps and set it beside the sink with a satisfying thump.

Gretel slaps her front paws on the cabinet and stretches, her tail flicking from side to side with interest.

"Don't you dare," I warn. "Just because Jigsaw let you near the counter once doesn't mean I will."

She drops her feet to the tile, letting out an indignant chirp.

I grab my glass measuring cup and fill it with warm water from the sink, then pour it into the bread pan. I scatter a tablespoon of sugar into the water, then sprinkle a packet of yeast in a loose spiral. I return the pan to the machine and search for the oil, flour, and salt I need. The recipe comes back to me easily, but I still pause now and then to double-check the small breadmaking book propped open on the counter.

What kind of trouble did Jigsaw get into? Who is going in the oven?

I click the lid of the bread maker shut and punch the buttons. The machine kicks into gear with a low hum. I peer inside the small clear window in the bread maker's top. The paddles twist through the ingredients in a rhythmic motion.

Perfect.

I pat the top of the machine.

Gretel's curled up on my lounge chair, tail flicking once. She barely lifts her head as I slip on my sneakers and head downstairs. As I reach the bottom floor, a wave of anxiety sweeps over me. What if the person he's bringing is dangerous?

No. He wouldn't do that. Whoever it is probably isn't even still *breathing*.

What if it's Daniel?

No, last I checked he was still sitting in the county jail.

Besides, Jigsaw promised me he would let justice take its course.

Still, the gnawing in my chest won't stop. It claws behind my ribs as I cross into the quiet dark of the funeral home. I pad down the hall, the chill of the tile seeping through my socks as I step into the prep room.

I'm not even sure what I'm looking for.

My fingers hover over the metal drawers built into the prep table. I slide one open and sort through the neatly organized packages. I pluck out a sterile scalpel, still sealed in its wrapper, and tear it open with a quiet snap. The blade glints, catching the faint glow from the nightlights plugged into each outlet.

I slip it into the pocket of my sweatshirt.

Just in case.

I return to the back door and slip on my sneakers.

Outside, the night air cools my heated skin. The last rays of sunlight streak the sky with deep oranges and pinks. Jigsaw said they'd be here *soon*. It feels too stalkerish to keep checking the app.

I tilt my head, straining to catch any sound of engines.

Nothing but the usual small-town silence—crickets, a far-off car, the occasional bark of a neglected dog.

I cross the parking lot to the brick building that houses the cremation chamber, punch in the code, and open the door. I hurry to the stainless steel control panel, flip the protective cover, and press the sequence to preheat the retort. The burner kicks on with a low whoosh, followed by a deeper rumble as the system roars to life. Heat pulses against my cheeks, and the air in the crematory thickens with the faint scent of scorched metal.

Hopefully things will be nice and toasty by the time the guys get here and this will be quick.

By the time I'm done, sweat slicks the side of my face and trails down my spine. I unzip my sweatshirt and tie it around my waist, leaving me in a black tank top, the fabric clinging to my skin.

I turn all but one of the lights off inside the building and make sure the outside lights are also off.

A low engine hum cuts through the stillness. I freeze, listening.

I crack the door and step outside.

Headlights sweep across the lot.

A black van creeps around the corner of the house.

I swipe damp hair off my forehead and force a small, steady smile as it slows to a crawl over the pavement. The driver backs the van close to the building, almost right into one of the tall bushy rows of lilacs that grow between the funeral home and my father's property.

Unsure of what to do, I step into the crematorium and wait, leaving the door ajar. I don't want to go into the house until I'm sure they have everything they need. Maybe they trust me enough now and won't mind if I stick around?

Low, tense voices go back and forth outside.

A door creaks. Someone groans. A scuffle and a thud. A string of muttered curses. Muffled pleading.

My heart thunders but I stay still. Waiting.

"Ow! Fuck," someone growls.

Is that Jigsaw?

I nudge the door open. Four hulking men, mostly in black clothing, stand in a loose circle, staring down at a heap on the ground. The back van doors are wide open, but no light shines out.

I open my door wide. The hinges squeak.

One of the men turns around. In the shadowy darkness, I make out Wrath's dark blond beard. He lifts his chin in a silent hello, then turns and murmurs something too low for me to hear.

One of the dark figures breaks away.

Jigsaw.

He stares straight at me, an affectionate smile tugging at the corners of his mouth.

He crosses the short distance between us, walking slower than usual. His jaw's tight, shoulders stiff, but he still slides his gloved hands over mine when he reaches me. They're vaguely damp or sticky against my skin.

"Evening, little lady death," he murmurs, voice warm despite the coldness of the occasion. He leans down and brushes a quick kiss over my cheek. "Thanks for doing this tonight," he whispers against my ear.

The warmth of his kiss lingers on my skin. "Of course."

Someone else breaks away from the circle, walking closer.

"Margot." Even hushed, Rock's commanding voice demands my attention. "Thanks for letting us borrow the facilities on short notice." He casts a glance Jigsaw's way. "I understand business has been brisk this week."

He says it lightly, but something about the way his gaze lingers on Jigsaw gives a different feel—like he's verifying information.

Did Jigsaw try to get out of coming here tonight by telling him we've been busy? Would he defy his club, thinking he's protecting me?

"It has," I answer. "But this was good timing. We finished our last service of the day, and nothing's scheduled tomorrow. Dad's still at the church and my cousin's out."

"That's good. Thanks," Wrath adds, turning toward us. Despite his size and Viking appearance, there's something almost comforting in his presence.

"Hey, Margot." Murphy lifts a hand in greeting. His mussed hair and bushy ginger beard make him look more like the friendly neighborhood lumberjack than a biker about to burn a body.

I bump the door open wider with my hip and step aside. "Everything's already going. So hopefully this will be quick..." My gaze flicks toward the van. "Depending on how many 'loaves of bread' you have in there."

Murphy rumbles with laughter and slaps his leg. "Jigsaw knew you'd get it."

I lift my shoulders in a bashful shrug.

"That's good. Thank you." Rock studies the crematory a second, then returns to Wrath, the two of them speaking in whispers.

"I'll let you guys..." I step back into the building.

Rock murmurs something I can't quite catch, and a second later,

Jigsaw follows me inside. His steps are quieter this time. A little uneven.

"You all right?" Jigsaw's voice is soft, but his posture's rigid.

"I'm fine." I smile, small and unsure. "Don't want to get in the way." *Or see something I'll never unsee.*

He glances through the crack in the door. I can't see past him but low voices going back and forth reach me.

"Busy afternoon, huh?" I ask.

Jigsaw lets out a jagged huff. "You know Griff?"

Terror crackles through my chest. "What? No."

I sway sideways, trying to get a better look. That's Griff? No. Can't be. Griff's much bigger. He's a friend of their club. We just went to a party in his honor. *They wouldn't...*

"Shit. No, Margot." Jigsaw wraps his hand around my arm, trying to hold me still. "It's not Griff. Jesus. He's a friend of the club. We don't...no. The guy went after Griff and his girlfriend Molly."

"Little Molly?" I stop trying to look over his shoulder. "Is she okay?"

"She's not *that* little. Caved the guy's leg in with a crowbar." His mouth twitches with pride.

"Oh my God. Are they okay?"

"Yeah. Griff used his martial arts skills on this fucking tweaker. Then, Molly whacked him." He lowers his voice. "*Now* we need him to disappear. We're just trying to get more info about who sent him."

"Okay."

He shifts his weight from one leg to the other and winces. "We wouldn't call on you...lightly. That's all I'm trying to say."

"I know that." From everything I've learned, it's a big deal for Jigsaw to share that much with me—his ol' lady. Especially with his brothers only a couple feet away. "Thank you for being honest with me."

"You're taking a risk too. It's only fair."

I lean up and brush a kiss against his bristly cheek. "You're worth all the risk."

His brow furrows, almost like my words hurt.

"I'm glad you're here," I say.

"Planning to stay if you think you can give me a ride to Jerry's garage to grab my bike in the morning."

"Yeah." A smile lifts my cheeks. "I can do that." I widen my eyes. "Are you sure you really want to leave your bike somewhere overnight?" I tease.

His eyebrows knit into a scowl. "Griff knows I'll kick his ass if anything happens to it."

"Wait, so *you* can threaten him but..." I tilt my head toward the crematorium.

A tired smile curves his lips. "Exactly." He touches his finger to his temple and then mine. "I love the way you just get me."

"Oh, I get you."

He nods slowly, almost like he's not quite paying attention.

The door nudges open and Murphy pokes his head in. "Jiggy, you wanna...?"

He shakes his head quickly. "I'm fine."

Wrath shoulders Murphy out of his way, pushing the door open wider. "Is this ready, Margot?"

"It should be soon." I turn away and walk over to check out the controls.

From the corner of my eye, something rust-colored sticks out.

I freeze. Roll my shoulder forward to peer down at my arm.

A sticky red smear on my biceps. "What the...?"

"Oh shit, Margot. Sorry." Jigsaw limps to my side.

He reaches for me, brushing at the flecks of dried blood on my arm with the back of his gloved hand—already dark with a reddish sheen.

My gaze drops to his jeans.

A dark circle blooms around his upper thigh. Black fabric, a torn T-shirt maybe, wrapped around his thigh, tied tight. Also dark and damp looking.

"Jensen! Oh my God." My voice comes out sharp, too loud, too full of panic. "You're bleeding?"

He grits his teeth and lies, "I'm fine."

My stomach drops. I sway on my feet, but I don't look away.

He's not fine. He's bleeding!

"I'm fine." Jigsaw's voice is slow and calm. "We'll be done soon, and I'll get cleaned up."

"How? Who?" I stammer.

He cocks his head toward the door. "Fucker had a knife stashed in his boot. Stabbed me." His lips twist in a wry laugh. "Lucky my reflexes are so good, he was aiming for my throat."

Everything narrows. My breath comes fast. A high-pitched whine buzzing in my ears.

"Margot?" Jigsaw sounds a thousand miles away. "I'm okay."

Murphy pops his head in again. "I don't think we're gettin' anything else out of him." His gaze shifts between Jigsaw and me. "What's wrong?"

"Nothing." Jigsaw shakes his head and gestures toward his leg.

Wrath elbows Murphy out of his way and kicks the door open wide. A second later, he drags their prisoner inside—the man's bloody fingers clawing at Wrath's arm around his neck.

Jigsaw's blood.

White-hot, stomach-knotting, heartbeat-screaming rage explodes through me.

"How're we doing this?" Murphy asks. "We can't just toss him in."

"I'll help you there." I dig the scalpel out of my pocket and quickly cross the small space.

Wrath drops the guy on the floor with heavy thud and frowns at me. "What the hell are you doing?"

I kneel next to the prisoner, cradling his head in one hand. He stares up at me, eyes wide, mouth slack, shaking his head in frantic denial.

"You stabbed my boyfriend." My voice is calm. Robotic. Detached. "Tried to hurt his friends."

I grip the scalpel tighter.

"I drain blood from the jugular all the time," I murmur. "Tilt the head, nick the vein, let gravity do the rest."

The man shakes his head violently.

"This might be a little messier."

I grip his skull in my palm, fingers digging into his scalp to hold him steady. Bodies on my table are much more compliant. This one still squirms and reeks of sweat and fear.

"Margot." Jigsaw's voice slices through the fog. "Don't!"

Too late.

I drag the blade across the man's throat, firm and smooth. The scalpel glides through flesh. A surge of blood much warmer than I'm used to bursts free.

No cannula to guide it. No drain to catch it.

It sprays across my chest and forearms—wild, chaotic, and hot.

Probably the messiest kill I've ever made.

Because I didn't plan it. This was all instinct. Reaction.

His body twitches. Spasms. Then stills.

Silence floods the room.

I lift my head.

All four men stare at me with wide eyes and stunned mouths.

I hold up my hand with the scalpel; blood drips off my fingers, runs down my arm and patters against the floor.

"Can someone hand me the paper towels?" I nod to the roll hanging by the sink. "This one was messier than I'm used to."

CHAPTER THIRTY-THREE

JIGSAW

Wrath yanks a long roll of towels free and hands them to Margot.

The rest of us stand there staring.

Margot's confused gaze slides from me, to Rock, then Murphy.

"What?" She lifts the scalpel, blood still dripping. "I'm the one who knows how to make precise incisions. You didn't want to spray blood everywhere."

"Uh, I was going to just snap his neck." Wrath shrugs and waves his hand at the body. "But this works. Dead is dead."

He's finding this way too fucking amusing.

Am I hallucinating?

I've lost a lot of blood.

Did she really just slit a man's throat in front of us?

Demons below, how did I get so lucky?

If I didn't have so much blood seeping from the hole in my leg, it'd probably be going straight to my dick.

That's *my* woman. Holy fuck. She did that because the guy attacked *me*.

A wave of lightheadedness knocks me sideways.

There's a clatter and scuffling. Something soft touches my elbow.

"Jensen," Margot's low voice pleads.

I blink and she's at my side. "You're really pale."

"No shit." I sway, my vision tunneling for a second.

"You need to sit down and let me look at your leg."

"Rooster's coming with supplies," Murphy says. "We didn't know what you might have here."

He must be talking to Margot. My eyes are closed again.

"I can suture the wound." She hesitates. "But I don't have anything to numb the area..."

Because she's usually stitching up dead people. Who don't need numbing.

"Help me get him inside the house," Margot says.

Oh, man, the thought of those three flights of stairs to her apartment is brutal.

"Jigsaw." Something not so gentle taps my cheek. "Stay with us," Rock says.

"I'm here." I blink and Rock's right in my face.

"Come on. We need to get you inside," he says. "Get you off your feet. Take a look at that hole in your leg."

"That sounds great." I grin at him. "Margot takes my pants off."

He blows out an irritated breath and slings my arm around his shoulders, locks his arm around my waist, and barks at Murphy to get my other side.

"I got this," Wrath says from behind us. "Go."

"Jesus Christ." Murphy huffs. Another arm wraps around my middle, flings my arm over his shoulder and helps take the pressure off my leg. "You're heavier than you look."

"All muscle." I bear as much weight as I can on my uninjured leg, and we start the long journey across the parking lot.

"We got you," Rock says. "Come on. Few more steps."

My eyes open, tracking Margot hurrying ahead of us.

Then headlights sweep around the side of the house.

Shit.

The four of us freeze.

What looks like a station wagon jerks to a stop. The driver's side door flings open.

"What the fuck happened?" Rooster's heavy footsteps thunder over the pavement.

I lift my chin. "The fuck you driving?"

On my left, Rock shakes with laughter. "It's Hope's car. Told him to take it. Thought it'd attract less attention out here."

"We need to get him inside," Margot says. "Get him on the ramp."

"Where's he hurt?" Rooster asks, marching alongside us.

"Thigh. Fucker stabbed me in the thigh." I side-eye Murphy. "I'm kicking Griff and Remy's ass for not searching that dude better."

He lets out a strained laugh. "I'm sure you will."

"Murphy can you...?" Rock's voice trails off. "Rooster, get his other side."

Murphy transfers my right arm to Rooster.

I turn my head. "Hey, buddy."

"Come on. Let's go," Rooster coaxes. "I brought all sorts of stuff to make you feel better."

"Margot'll make me feel better."

He chuckles. "I'm sure she will."

"Don't be so sure," Margot says in a strained voice.

Something clicks. Metal on metal screeches.

Finally, we're inside. I flick my gaze at the long staircase in front of me. "I don't know guys..."

"Where do you want to stitch him up, Margot?" Rock asks.

Margot bites her lip and stares at me with apologetic eyes. "The best place would really be..."

Realization of what she's suggesting hits hard.

"No way." I struggle to free myself from Rock's iron grip and almost crumple to the floor. "No. You are *not* putting me on the table where you...no."

"It's sterile. The lighting. The right height for me to work and see what I'm doing," she pleads.

"She's right." Rooster starts turning me to the left. "Unless you

want to sprawl your big ass on that narrow little couch in there and bleed all over the furniture."

"Wait." I try to dig my toes into the carpet, but these two big fuckers keep right on moving. "What about the kitchen counter?"

"We could…" Margot hesitates like she's considering it. "But it's not really big enough."

"Come on." Rooster grips me tighter, lifting me higher. "Let's give Margot the best conditions possible to work with. You don't want her to accidentally stitch your nutsack to your leg."

Rock's body jerks with laughter.

"Why do you hate my nuts so much?" I ask Rooster, then turn to Rock. "He wished ticks on my balls the other day."

"Jesus Christ," Rock mutters. "Keep moving, chuckles."

Blinding light sears my eyes as we cross the threshold into the large, white room full of cabinets and four separate metal tables.

"This one," Margot says. She presses a button. A motor whirs and the table lowers.

"Guys, really don't—" I protest.

"Got everything," Murphy says, barreling into the room, holding up a large black duffel bag.

"I grabbed whatever I thought might help from the clubhouse, then stopped at the pharmacy for the rest," Rooster explains. "Sparky sent a bag of weed gummies and cookies for you."

"Perfect," I mutter. The backs of my legs hit something solid.

"Come on, sit down," Rock encourages, slipping my cut off my shoulders and handing it to Murphy.

Another wave of dizziness threatens to take me out. I sit on the metal table, then lie down, stretching out on my back. The spinny sensation slows and I exhale a long breath. "That's better."

"Good." Rock squeezes my shoulder.

Three grim faces stare down at me like I'm already stretched out in a casket.

"Where's Margot?" I rasp.

"Right here," she calls out, though I still can't see her. "This is good. Thank you, Rooster."

 364

She comes to my side. "I'm going to raise the table." She rests her hand on my shoulder. A second later the motor whirs and the table jerks under me, *rising, rising, rising.*

My stomach lurches and horses tap dance inside my skull again.

"Can you guys get his boots?" Margot asks.

Rock and Murphy move to my feet and start unlacing my boots.

Margot reaches for my belt. I wrap my hand around hers. "You know damn well you don't know how to work that buckle."

Her shoulders shake. "Then hurry up."

She watches my hands in a detached, clinical way while I work the buckle loose, then arch my back and pull the belt free and hand it to Rooster. "We're burning these jeans," I explain.

Margot nods and unties the bandage around my thigh. I bite back a scream from the pain. Then she carefully unbuttons and lowers my zipper.

I roll my head toward her. "This isn't very arousing."

Margot flicks her finger against my side. "It's not supposed to be."

She unfolds a small, white sheet and drapes it over my groin before carefully easing my jeans down my legs. *So professional.*

I hiss a pained breath as the denim scrapes over the wound. She's gentle as she peels the sticky material away from my skin, doing everything not to cause more pain. Cold metal chills the backs of my legs and feet.

"How's he doing?" Wrath's big voice echoes in the room.

Margot turns her head. "Haven't quite gotten there yet. He's still cracking jokes. I think that's a good sign."

"It's something," Rooster mutters.

I close my eyes again.

The sharp snap of rubber breaks the air. Then another. Soft fingers press into the meat of my thigh. I flinch but try to stay still.

"I need to irrigate this. See how deep it is." Margot's voice—low, clinical, but shaking at the edges.

"Need one of us to help?" Rock asks.

"If you don't mind scrubbing up and putting on gloves, sure."

Water runs. Plastic rustles. Rubber snaps again and again.

"Hand me that," Margot says.

A second later, something cold and sharp blasts over the burn in my leg.

"Fuck!" My body bows off the table. White explodes behind my eyes.

Strong hands clamp down on my shoulders.

I crack open one eye. Rooster. Murphy. "Your beards are even uglier from this angle."

Rooster applies more pressure to my shoulder. Murphy just snorts.

I swing my head toward Margot. She's not looking at me. Her eyes are on Rooster. Wide. Focused. She gives him a tight nod.

He sets a firm palm on my chest like I'm a deer about to bolt into the woods.

"What's—"

"I'm going to sterilize this. It might burn," Margot says. "Keep him still."

Might? Oh, that definitely means it'll burn. Every muscle in my body tightens.

Rock steps in and plants both hands on my good leg. Not pushing yet. Just waiting.

Fire licks my side.

"Fuuuck!" I twist, muscles spasming, trying to get away.

"Stop." Her voice wraps around me.

The pain fades. Or I black out. Hard to say.

I drag in a breath. Blink hard. Margot comes into focus through the heat and static buzzing over my skin.

A single tear cuts a clean track down her cheek.

"You know I'd never hurt you on purpose, Jensen," she whispers.

I nod. Quick and jerky. Can't form words.

She leans over me again, fingers returning to my leg. Searching. Face blank, except for another tear sliding from the corner of her eye.

"If this had been six inches in the other direction, he would've hit something vital," she murmurs.

I can't tell if she's referring to my dick or my femoral artery. Either way, it sounds like good news.

"The tissue's angry," she murmurs. "But not gaping. I think I can close it."

"Goody," I mumble.

"Relax," she says in a calming tone. "I promise I'm good at this. Dad started having me suture any visible wounds. Says I make them look like nothing ever happened."

I meet her eyes again. "I trust you."

No ER doc would give a fuck about getting this right as much as she does.

"Rock, can you hand me that white can Rooster brought?"

There's a rustle. Clink of metal.

"This might sting," Margot warns. "But not as bad as before. Then it should help numb the area while I close the wound."

"Okay." Not like I've got a choice.

She leans over, spraying a fine mist over my upper thigh. Cold. Sharp. Then a low, spreading numbness. Not painless, but less fire.

Snap. Another pair of gloves. The sharp chemical scent of disinfectant stings my nose.

"Gauze," she says, and someone—Rooster, I think—places it in her hand without a word.

Another sting of antiseptic, milder this time. Then pressure. Damp warmth. My leg twitches. I grind my teeth.

"You okay?" she asks without looking up.

"Just ducky." My voice scrapes out of my throat like gravel.

She picks up something thin and silver. My vision tunnels on it.

Needle. Thread. Probably what she uses to stitch dead faces into their final, peaceful expressions.

"This will pull," she warns. "I'm sorry."

The needle bites through my skin. I flinch hard, fingers curling into fists.

Rooster squeezes my shoulder. "Try to stay still."

I grunt a noise of agreement.

Each tug of the needle pulls. A dull, dragging sort of flame.

Her breath ghosts over my skin as she leans in, focused,

determined. The corners of her mouth pulled down, brows drawn tight.

"You got this," Murphy says, squeezing my other shoulder.

My body's coiled tight, bracing for the moment whatever Margot sprayed wears off and hell kicks in.

"Breathe," she whispers, her voice a soft tether pulling me back. "You're doing great. Almost done."

I drag in a breath that doesn't quite reach my lungs.

Another couple minutes go by in a haze. Then she steps back, staring at her work. "Done. Let me put an antibiotic ointment on it, then cover it with some gauze."

She moves to the counter. I track her for a second, then let my head thud against the table.

"Feel better?" Rooster asks.

"My head stopped spinning, so yeah."

"Good."

Margot returns, dressing the wound with steady, practiced hands. When she's done, she takes a step back, still staring like she doesn't trust the bandage to behave.

"You're staying here," she says firmly. "I'll check it and change the dressing tomorrow." No room for arguing with my girl.

I groan and push up on my elbows. "Not sure how I feel about going up all those stairs."

"We'll get your big ass up there," Rooster promises, way too cheerfully. "One way or another."

"I'm thinking we might run over to the urgent care clinic in the morning. Have an actual doctor look at it," Margot says, still focused on my thigh. "Maybe give you antibiotics."

"I'm sure it's fine," I grumble. "I don't need to drop my drawers for some doctor."

She crosses her arms over her chest, bunching up the blue scrub top she'd put on at some point. "You lose your leg, you won't be riding again any time soon, so you'll go if I think you need to."

Rooster huffs and snorts.

Wrath actually cackles.

"Can he put pants on?" Rooster asks. "I brought some loose athletic shorts and a pair of sweats."

Margot meets my eyes. "The shorts should be okay, if you think you can tolerate them."

"Yeah." I stretch toward the counter. "Gimmie."

Rooster sets the duffle bag on the table next to me. I paw through the stuff—Gatorade, shiny black shorts, sleeveless shirt—

"You brought me a pair of fuckin' Crocs?" I hold up the giant, black clown shoe and whap his arm with it.

"Ow." He laughs and covers the spot I nailed. "I did the best I could on a moment's notice. Figured you'll be recovering for a few days."

Margot fishes the other shoe out of the bag. "We can put some of my pins in the holes to dress them up if you want." Her lips curve into a wicked smirk.

That gets the guys laughing again.

Fuckers. Every one of them.

Except Margot. Can't get enough of her. Even if she's poking fun at me and ordering me to go to the doctor.

"Where's Rock?" I ask.

"Checking the oven," Murphy says.

Margot's eyes widen. "I better go. I need to burn all these clothes." She gathers my ruined jeans, digging into the pockets. She empties everything onto the counter—wallet, keys, loose change...

And one gold foil square that must've escaped my wallet.

Murphy doubles over, howling.

Rooster—*asshole*—chuckles.

Margot slants a look at me and tucks the condom back in my wallet. "You won't be needing that for a few days."

Wrath loses it, snickering like an idiot.

I glance from the gauze taped on my thigh to Margot. "We'll figure out something."

She snorts and rolls her eyes, scooping up the clothes into the sheet and bundling it into a massive ball.

"I can take that, Margot," Wrath offers.

She glances at the bundle, then Wrath's cut. "I've got it. I'd rather not risk transferring any DNA onto your leather, since I *know* you won't toss *that* in the fire."

"Good point." Wrath tips his chin in approval.

I tilt my head toward the door. "Go with her," I say to Rooster.

"Yup." He dips his chin. "On her."

Murphy taps his fist against my shoulder and follows Rooster out.

I cock my head at Wrath. "Guess that makes you the lucky bastard helping me into my shorts."

"For fuck's sake," he groans, but he's already holding them out, letting me use his shoulder for balance and keeping his cranky jokes to himself.

I wiggle my feet into the fucking Crocs and shuffle into the hallway.

Not bad. I can put weight on it. Doesn't burn as much now. There's a tug-and-pull sensation, but it's tolerable.

At the staircase, I stop, grip the banister, and stare at the long road ahead.

"All the way to the third floor, huh?" Wrath asks, resting a hand on my shoulder.

"Yup."

"All right. We've got this. Slow and steady."

Wrath slipping into encouraging cheerleader mode is almost the most unnerving thing about tonight.

Wrath hooks an arm around my waist and jerks me to his side.

"Lean on me," he grunts.

I drape my arm over his shoulders, careful not to twist the wrong way. "You know, this might be easier if you carried me up bridal-style." I fight to keep a grin off my face.

"It'd be easiest to leave you outside in the parking lot." He nods. "Let's go. One at a time."

We take the stairs slow. My leg throbs with every step, but Wrath's bulk makes a solid wall to lean against and he's surprisingly patient.

Not sure if I'm grateful for the help or annoyed for needing it.

"Awww, you two are the cutest," Murphy snarks from below.

I pause at the second-floor landing, catching my breath.

Murphy jogs up the stairs like he's Rocky, just to show off.

"Careful, ginger, or I'm gonna toss you right back down those stairs," Wrath warns.

"Wouldn't it be easier if you carried him?" Murphy grins and holds out his arms like he's cradling a baby.

Wrath shoves his shoulder, sending him ahead of us.

"No playing on the stairs," Margot calls out from below.

Behind her, Rooster's laughing.

She hurries up to meet us. "Are you okay?"

"Yeah." I gesture between Wrath and Murphy. "They were deciding who's going to carry me the rest of the way."

She snorts and crouches beside me, gently lifting the leg of my shorts to check the bandage. "So far, so good. But I grabbed extra supplies in case you pop a stitch."

"Thanks." I wave toward the stairs. "Can everyone else move ahead instead of gawking at me?"

Margot trails her fingers against the back of my knee, just a second, but it sends a pleasurable shiver over my skin, motivating me to move my ass.

She stands and tucks her hair behind her ear, maneuvering around us. "I'll get the door."

Murphy follows her, but Rooster lingers, keeping a few steps behind Wrath and me—backup in case I go tumbling down the stairs or something.

After what feels like a three-mile climb on one leg, we finally reach the top. That tug-and-pull sensation from earlier has graduated into a deep, grinding throb that sets my teeth on edge.

"Fuck," I mutter, drawing in a ragged breath. "That sucked ass."

Inside Margot's apartment, Murphy's already sitting at one of the stools at the counter.

"Make yourself at home, jolly ginger," I grumble, kicking off the Crocs and hobbling over to claim the other stool.

He spins and flashes a smug grin. "Margot *actually* made us bread."

"What?" I lower myself slowly, careful not to jolt my leg.

Margot turns, all sweetness and sheepish smiles. "Well, I didn't know the intense turn the evening was going to take." She stares pointedly at my outstretched leg.

Sure. Me getting stabbed is clearly the shocking part of the evening. Not her calmly slitting a man's throat in front of my brothers.

"I thought it'd be funny," she explains, lifting the lid on what looks like a small stainless steel spaceship. "Since Jigsaw's code was using the *oven* to bake some *bread*." She slips on potholders and wrangles a silver pan out of the machine. "If I actually made bread."

Murphy leans in like a kid watching a magic trick, grinning from ear to ear as she flips the loaf onto a cutting board.

Margot glances up, her gaze flicking between Wrath and Rooster. A faint blush creeps into her cheeks. "Sorry I don't have more chairs."

Rooster lifts a hand in a don't-worry-about-it wave.

"We're good," Wrath says, angling his head to get a better look at the bread.

Margot tilts her head, checking the apartment door. "Where's Rock?"

"Waiting in the van." Murphy checks his phone. "We better hurry."

"Take this to go, then." Margot drapes a towel over the loaf and slices through it slowly with a long, serrated knife. Each slice peels away from the blade, soft and steaming.

My mouth waters. Can't remember the last time I had bread fresh out of the oven. The scent alone's enough to make me forget about the throbbing in my leg.

"Hey, kitty," Rooster calls in a hushed voice.

Gretel hisses her displeasure and slinks around the corner, belly nearly scraping the floor, tail tucked tight and ears flat. She darts a suspicious glare toward Wrath, then Murphy, then makes a beeline for me.

"C'mere, girl," I murmur.

She sniffs at my foot, her whiskers tickling my ankle. With a pained grunt, I lean down and scoop her up. My thigh protests the motion with a sharp twinge.

She headbutts my chin once, then freezes, eyes sharp and alert, her

head darting from side to side as she scans the room. No motorboat purring tonight. Just coiled tension and twitching ears.

Wrath jams his hands in his pockets and ducks his head, a smirk forming on his lips. "You have a black cat, Margot?"

If he brings up the Virginia charter's pussy patch challenge, I'm going to push him down those three flights of stairs.

"Yes." Margot's tone walks a fine line between proud and patient. She slices another piece of bread with practiced ease. "She's a rescue. Not usually friendly but—" She flicks the knife toward me without looking. "For some reason, she's a shameless hussy for this guy."

The guys chuckle. Gretel presses tighter against my chest, and I lean down, running the tip of my nose over her soft head. "That's right, she's got good taste, don't ya, girl?"

She wiggles, so I set her down gently. Instead of bolting, she stays low to the ground, tail swishing. She creeps toward Murphy, pauses out of reach, then finally stretches up, her spine arching with slow confidence. When he doesn't move, she straightens fully and flicks her tail high like a banner of disinterest. She checks out Wrath next, gives him a long, assessing stare, then detours to rub her cheek against Rooster's leg.

Then, like a queen who's surveyed the riffraff and found them tolerable, she saunters off—tail held high.

Margot arranges the bread slices on the cutting board, sets down a stack of napkins and two sticks of butter, then gestures for the guys to help themselves.

I reach over and snag a slice first, claiming one of the butter sticks and a knife while I'm at it. Warmth seeps into my fingers as I tear off a chunk and slather it with butter.

Margot places a bottle of water and a few Advil in front of me. "Take that after you eat a little."

"Thanks." I crack the seal and take a long swallow, cool water easing the dryness in my throat.

"Coffee should be ready in another minute," Margot says as she opens a cabinet. She taps Wrath's arm and points inside.

He grabs a package of paper travel cups and sets them on the counter without a word.

Murphy loads up—two thick slices of bread, a generous smear of butter, and two cups of coffee. "Gonna run this down to Rock." He pats my shoulder. "Take it easy, brother." Then he tips his head at Margot. "Night, Margot. Thank you."

I glance at the now-empty cutting board, then shift my most pathetic puppy eyes her way.

She doesn't miss a beat. "I'll make you another one later," she promises in the tone of someone humoring a demanding child.

Once everyone's got a coffee in hand, Rooster and Wrath thank Margot and head for the door.

I trail after them, easing the door halfway shut behind me so Gretel doesn't try to escape.

"I'm gonna ride in the van back to the garage," Rooster says. "I'll get your bike and bring it here."

"Ah, shit." I pat the empty pockets of my loose shorts. "I think my keys are downstairs."

He holds them up and dangles them in front of my face. "Already got 'em."

"There's no way you're riding any time soon," Wrath points out.

"Gee, ya think?" I drag the leg of my shorts up to flash my patch job.

"We'll have someone come pick you up for church. Day after tomorrow maybe?" he says. "Give you a day to rest."

"How generous of you."

Ignoring my sarcasm, Wrath tilts his head to the side, peering into the apartment through the crack in the door. "See if Margot can come with you."

I nod quickly.

"I'll drive your 4Runner up to the clubhouse. So you have it," Rooster says.

"Thanks. I was planning to leave it here when we're in Vegas anyway."

They both stare at me with odd expressions I'm too tired to

decode. "Is that all?" I arch a brow. "I'd kind of like to sleep for the next ten hours."

"Yeah, get some rest." Rooster grips my shoulder and pulls me in for a quick one-armed squeeze, careful not to jostle my leg. "You've earned it."

"Earned it," Wrath scoffs. "He's earned an intensive training program on situational awareness once that leg's healed."

"Are you blaming *me*?" My eyes widen with outrage. "The victim in the stabbing?"

He tilts his chin and stares pointedly at my injured leg.

"I was situationally aware, you dick." I rap my knuckles against his chest. "I rolled before he jabbed it into my jugular."

"I'm just fuckin' with you," Wrath says. As close to an apology as I'll ever get from him. "You gave us a scare tonight."

"Look at Wrath admitting how much he loves you," Rooster says, grinning as he slaps Wrath's shoulder and starts down the stairs. "Night," he calls over his shoulder.

Wrath's gaze follows him for a second, then he pivots like he's leaving too.

I press my palm to the door.

"Wait." Wrath grabs my arm. "One final thing, Jigsaw."

I turn and he's right in my face.

Exhaustion sweeps over me, every inch of my body aching. "What now?"

His eyebrows knit together, and he jabs a thick finger into my chest. "Bro, if you don't protect that woman at all costs, I'm gonna personally strip your patch." His eyes blaze, not a trace of humor in sight. "You need to lock her down for life."

CHAPTER THIRTY-FOUR

JIGSAW

After all the punishments I survived as a kid, I never thought I'd be able to stand someone hovering, tending, and fussing over me. Sure, I've been knocked around in plenty of fights and stupid shit. Had club girls tend to me with their fake concern and ulterior motives.

But Margot taking care of me with her soft hands, sharp tongue, eyes full of fire and concern—it's not just bearable.

It's fucking intoxicating.

I haven't stopped thinking about what Wrath said.

Lock her down for life.

Giving her my property patch? That's a no-brainer. But that's only a commitment on *my* end. Lets every biker we meet know I'll yank their spine out through their mouth if they so much as touch her.

Outside the club, it doesn't mean shit.

If I want her for life, Margot will expect a ring. A wedding. Marriage. Shit I never thought I'd want.

But now?

Every time I think about it, there's no fear, no revulsion.

Just peace.

The way she slit the throat of the guy who stabbed me—Next.

Fucking. Level. I know what she's capable of, seen the evidence hanging in her closet. She's told me all her dark secrets.

Seeing it in person?

Watching her glide that blade across his throat like it was nothing —calm, precise, controlled. Like she was buttering toast, not taking a life.

Didn't flinch.

Didn't care that my brothers were watching.

It did something to me.

Something primal.

Possessive.

She took a risk. A big one.

Now my club knows—without question—what lengths she's willing to go.

For me.

Then she served us homemade bread.

She's violence wrapped in sweetness.

"How's my favorite patient?" Margot's warm voice pulls me from my dark thoughts.

She's leaning in the doorway, still dressed in the soft gray blouse and slacks she threw on earlier to meet a client downstairs.

"Better now."

"Um, what have you been thinking about?" Her gaze drops pointedly.

I glance down at the tented sheet covering me from the waist down.

"Huh." A huff of a laugh escapes me. "I was thinking about you, actually."

"Really?" She toys with the top button of her blouse, slipping it loose with a flick of her fingers.

I push my palms into the mattress, shifting upright until I'm sitting. "Get those clothes off."

Laughing softly, she finishes unbuttoning her blouse, then turns around, dropping it slightly, giving me a glimpse of bare shoulder.

"Off," I growl.

 378

She still moves too slowly. Teasing the hell out of me. Stripping piece by piece until she's down to just her bra and panties.

My blood's on fire. Cock at full attention now.

She slides over to the side of the bed, standing just out of reach.

"I should look at your leg first."

"It can wait." I flip the sheet back. "Get in here."

She climbs in carefully, every movement cautious but deliberate, as if she's afraid one wrong move will rip open my stitches.

She kneels beside me, eyes locked on mine. "Now what?"

Margot

"Make out with me." His voice is low, rough, and the warmth of his palm gliding up my thigh has the power to unravel me.

So gentle yet commanding.

My heart kicks harder at his simple request. I lean in, brushing my lips over the stubble on his cheek.

"Little more," he murmurs, voice even raspier now. One strong arm hooks around my waist and his hand curves over my butt in a possessive squeeze that sends heat straight through me. "Come here."

"Where?" I whisper, my gaze flicking down to the bandage on his thigh. "I don't want to hurt your leg."

"You won't." His fingers tighten at my waist, dragging me closer with the kind of strength that makes my stomach dip and flutter. "Straddle me."

I shift with care, my knee brushing the edge of the bandage. My weight settles across his hips, and heat flares between us, low and deep.

"Better?" I ask, anchoring myself with my hands on his shoulders.

His lips quirk in that devilish half-smile that always melts me. "Getting there."

A low, gravelly hum vibrates in his chest as he cups the back of my head and pulls me down. His lips crash into mine, stealing my breath and sparking a wildfire under my skin. Heat surges through me, deep and urgent. I slide one hand to the nape of his neck, leaning in, careful to keep my legs steady and avoid bumping his wound.

His hands roam over my back, confident and warm, until he finds the clasp of my bra and pops it loose. I laugh softly against his mouth, breaking the kiss for a second to rest my forehead against his. My breath mingles with his, and the heat between us simmers higher.

"What do you want?" I whisper, not because I can't guess—but because I love hearing it from him.

He presses a kiss to my cheek. Then my lips. His mouth is soft, but his fingers are sneaky, sliding the straps down my arms with deliberate ease.

"Your tits in my hands."

The blunt honesty sends a zing through me, sharp and sweet. The cool air kisses my bare skin just before his hands replace it—hot, rough, greedy.

He groans low in his throat and palms my breasts, thumbing my nipples until I gasp.

"Much better."

I hiss in a breath and reach behind me, wrapping my hand around his length through the thin fabric of his shorts.

"Fuuuck." His hips twitch beneath me. He sucks one of my nipples into his mouth, tongue flicking over it in slow, reverent strokes. A low groan rumbles in his chest and his eyes squeeze shut like he's hanging on by a thread. "Take me out. Please."

I cup his face between my hands and tip his head up, forcing his gaze to meet mine. His eyes are glazed with need—but still so focused on me.

"Will you behave?"

He frowns, as if it's a foreign concept. "How?"

"Let me take care of you."

He cocks his head, breath ragged. "Be my guest."

I ease off his chest, kissing and licking my way down his stomach, slow and unhurried. He's all mine to explore. When I reach the waistband of his shorts, I run my tongue along the edge, teasing the sensitive skin just beneath.

His abs tense. "Stop fuckin' teasing me, woman."

He hooks his thumbs under the waistband and lifts his hips, a challenge in his eyes.

I sit up straighter, placing a palm on his stomach. "You promised to behave."

He lets out a low, frustrated growl and lets his hands fall to the bed, fingers curling into the sheets. "You want to taste me?"

"Mmmhmm." I trail one finger along the waistband, slipping it just beneath the fabric, watching the way his muscles tense and jump in anticipation.

"Then do it," he rasps, voice low and wrecked with need. For me.

A thrill shivers through me. This strong, powerful man is trembling under my hands.

"You want to rub my cock between your tits?" he asks, voice sharp and jagged.

"I will if that's what you want." I ease the waistband down, letting the elastic drag against his skin. His cock springs free, thick and hard. I wrap my hand around him, drinking in the way he shudders under my touch. "I'd do anything for you."

Our eyes lock. He cradles my chin and strokes his thumb along my cheek. "I know."

He's so solemn, I don't think we're only talking about all the ways I'm willing to please him anymore.

"Get these off," he pants.

He arches his hips just enough for me to slide his shorts down. I keep my grip on him, one hand stroking slow and steady as I work the fabric past his legs. He kicks them away, gaze never leaving me—like I'm the only thing that exists.

I wet my lips and lower my mouth, swirling my tongue over his tip.

"Fuck, yes," he hisses.

I suck just the tip inside, and his hips jerk, seeking more. A moan escapes me as I take him deeper.

"Yes, yes, yes," he pants between choppy breaths. "Come here."

I pull off slowly, hand still stroking, spreading the wetness from my mouth over his length. "I'm right here."

He slides down on the bed and taps my hip. "I want your pussy in my face." His fingers curl under the band of my underwear, tugging hard.

Laughing, I sit up and shimmy out of them, letting them fall to the floor. "Better?"

"Perfect." His eyes are wild, hungry. He licks his bottom lip, then grins. "Come on. Let me eat your pussy while you suck me."

When I hesitate, his grip tightens on my hips, dragging me closer. "It only seems fair."

"Okay, okay." I laugh, breathless with heat blooming under my skin. "How do you want me?"

"Put your legs on either side of me." He shifts beneath me, guiding me into place. "There ya go."

His hands splay across my ass, thumbs parting me. "Fuck," he groans, lips grazing my inner thigh before sweeping his tongue between my legs.

My thighs tremble. "Oh—"

"C'mon," he urges, voice full of desire. "Let's see who comes first."

I already know I'm going to lose. Every stroke of his tongue sends jolts through my body, and I'm shaking, gasping, barely keeping upright.

Still, I wrap my hand around him again, determined to try. Bracing myself on one arm, I crawl forward, careful of his leg. No teasing this time—I lower my mouth, open wide, and take him in.

He lets out a muffled groan that vibrates against me, sending a shiver straight through my core. I tighten my grip around him, sliding my hand down his thick length, following with my mouth.

Another desperate sound escapes him, buzzing against my skin. His hips jerk, pushing more of himself into my mouth.

He flattens his tongue against my clit, dragging it side to side in a steady rhythm. I gasp around him, the sensation too much and not enough. Still, I keep stroking, stretching my mouth wider to take more of him.

His fingers slide along my slick skin, teasing, circling, then finally pressing inside.

I gasp, choke, and pull off, resting my cheek against him while still lazily sliding my hand up and down.

"What're you doing?" he rasps, his lips brushing the sensitive skin of my inner thigh as he keeps moving his finger in and out of me—slow, steady, relentless. "Keep sucking."

"I...can't." Pleasure shudders through me like a thousand sparks beneath my skin. I squeeze my eyes shut, desperate to hold on, trying to focus on anything but the sharp edge building inside me.

"Now who's not behaving?" His voice is a dark tease. He bumps his hips, and I take him in my mouth again, deeper this time, driven by his voice, his hands, *him*.

He groans, low and filthy, and adds another finger, curling to hit the spot that scrambles my thoughts. I whimper, gag, and pull back, then push forward again with a broken moan.

His hand tightens on my hip, anchoring me in place while his tongue circles my clit with diabolical precision. I buck against him, a gasp caught in my throat, then freeze, afraid I'll hurt him. He answers with another firm squeeze, then sucks harder.

God, he *knows*. Every inch of me. Every trigger. Exactly what to do to unravel me, while I'm struggling to keep rhythm with my hands and mouth, too overwhelmed to return the pleasure.

"Jensen." His name spills from my lips in a broken gasp.

He doesn't stop. Doesn't slow. Just holds me there and devours me like I'm his favorite meal.

Pleasure crashes over me, sharp and blinding. I shatter against him, and all I can do is cling and ride it out until I collapse, limp and shaking.

He pats my ass with a smug, satisfied grunt. "I win."

Breathless, I try to reclaim a shred of dignity after losing so easily. I wrap my hand around him again, stroking slow, savoring the way his body tenses, how his groan vibrates all the way through me.

"No." He flips me off him with an ease that makes me gasp. "Come kneel next to the bed for me."

I scramble off the mattress, eager and already aching for more. He shifts with a grimace, gingerly sitting up and tossing a pillow on the floor at his feet.

I drop to my knees, bracing one hand on his uninjured leg for balance. My other hand wraps around his cock, firm this time, no teasing. I lick my lips and lean in, mouth wide, determined.

"That's my girl." He brushes his knuckles over my cheek, then gathers my hair in one hand. "Get me nice and wet."

The way he watches me, focused and darkly reverent, sends a shiver down my spine. I work harder, trying to force a reaction, wanting to earn his groans of approval.

"Good girl." His voice turns rougher as he tightens his grip and pulls me off with a wet pop.

"What?" I blink up, lips swollen, chest heaving.

He surges forward and crushes his mouth to mine. A brutal, possessive kiss that melts every worry from my brain. He releases my hair and grabs my breasts, squeezing, molding. "Come closer."

I shuffle forward on my knees, pressing myself against the side of the bed.

"That's it." He slides his cock, slick from my mouth, between my breasts and thrusts. "Fuck, your tits are perfect. Give me your hands."

He slows, guiding my hands over my chest, encouraging me to hold myself for him. I toss my hair over one shoulder and arch my back, presenting myself.

"Fuck, yeah," he breathes out. "Just like that." His hips roll forward, thrusting harder until the head of his cock grazes my chin. I squeeze my breasts tighter, pushing them around him, and open my mouth, licking him each time he gets close enough.

"Fuck, that's it," he growls. "Stick your tongue out."

Breath tearing from his lungs, he pumps faster, more erratic. An animalistic groan rips from his chest as he comes, hot and thick over my breasts and neck.

I blink my eyes open and find him watching me with a lazy, satisfied half smile. "Thank you," he says, voice rough but full of affection.

His gaze drops to where I'm still holding my breasts. A crooked grin tugs at his lips. "I like you like that."

He threads his fingers through my hair, pulling me into a slow, tender kiss. "Thank you."

Leaning over, he scoops his shorts off the floor and wipes the cooling mess from my chest. His touch is surprisingly gentle, like he's handling something precious.

I tap his knee. "Let me look at your leg."

"I'm fine." He stands, jaw tightening as he takes a cautious step forward.

"You shouldn't have been thrusting so hard," I scold, using the nightstand to push myself up from the floor. "At least it looks like no blood seeped through the bandage."

"See? Told you I'm fine." He grins, cocky as ever, but there's still a flicker of pain in his eyes he can't quite hide.

"You don't have to be all macho with me, you know." I swat his butt.

"I'm not. I felt fine...until I stood up." His grin fades into a frown. "What's wrong?"

My eyes drift to the bed, heat creeping into my cheeks. "Am I not good at that? Why didn't you let me finish?"

His brows knit. "Good at what?"

"You know..." I wave a hand vaguely. "That."

"Sucking my cock?"

"Yes."

He cradles the back of my head with his hand and pulls me closer, kissing my forehead. "Margot, you're fucking incredible. Your body's like Disneyland; I get so crazed I can't decide which way I want to dirty you up first."

I blink, then hold his gaze. "I don't feel dirty with you."

His teasing expression softens into something reverent.

"I love *doing* dirty things with you, though." I force a bright smile, holding back all the other things in my head.

Dirty—never. I feel whole, seen, understood, cherished. A whole lot of things I never thought were even possible until we met.

CHAPTER THIRTY-FIVE

JIGSAW

Wrath: Church 11:30. Officer meeting first.

I DON'T NEED MORE THAN ONE GUESS TO KNOW IT'S ABOUT THE tweaker.

I toss the phone onto the nightstand and shift, curling around Margot's warm, sleepy body. The scent of plums, sugar, and sin clings to her soft skin—sweet and lethal. Makes me want to stay right here, wrapped up with her, and forget the world exists.

"Think you'll come up to the clubhouse with me today?" I ask, dragging my lips over the curve of her shoulder.

"Mmmm." She sighs and rolls to face me, eyes half-lidded. "Can't. Appointment at eleven."

Fuck.

"Someone's coming to pick you up, right?" she asks. "You won't try to ride, yet."

"Yeah, Rooster's coming." My fingers trail down her arm.

She bites her bottom lip and searches my face like she's bracing for bad news. "Are the guys going to tell everyone what I did the other night?"

My whole body stills.

Yeah, probably. "Maybe just the officers. We're gettin' called in first. Usually, Rock and Z just keep us after."

She squints as if she's trying to remember who the other officers are. "Besides you, Rooster, Murphy, Rock, and Wrath…your other officers are…Z, Grinder, Dex, Teller, and…"

Impressed she remembered almost everyone, I kiss the tip of her nose. "Hustler. Downstate's treasurer."

"Hustler," she repeats. "Well, I assume Teller won't care. Neither will Murder Daddy."

"I'm sorry." I laugh. "What?"

"Grinder." She shrugs, a playful glint in her eye. "That's what Shelby calls him."

I squeeze my eyes shut and shake my head. "Great." Then I realize why she's puzzling this out. "No one's going to care, Margot. They'll be impressed. Trust me."

"Oh, all the other ol' ladies slice and dice people too?" She raises an eyebrow, but her voice is tight, uncertain.

I chuckle—can't help it—but keep my tone firm. "No. But Heidi's clocked a few guys with a hammer when they came after Murphy."

That gets her attention. Her eyes widen with more curiosity than concern. "Really?"

"Yes. All of them would protect their men, in their own ways. Your way is just more immediate and visceral."

She bites her lip and drops her gaze. "It wasn't protective, though. It was reactive. Revenge for hurting you."

That lands hard in my chest. I trace her jaw with my knuckles. "Look, I know you have a certain code for how and why you end people, but don't lose sleep over this one. Sooner or later, he would've hurt someone else. Either in a drug deal gone bad or out of sheer stupidity. He came close to shooting Griff. Threatened to hurt Molly. He was scum."

She lets out a slow breath. "I don't want your brothers to be… afraid of me. Think I'm nuts."

"Trust me, they respect the hell out of you."

Her lips twist into a wicked smile. "Ah, just what every ol' lady dreams of—her boyfriend's outlaw biker brothers impressed by her murder skills."

"Yeah." A flicker of pride burns through me. "Now they know exactly how far you'll go to protect your man. And the club."

A COUPLE OF HOURS LATER, Rooster and I pull into the upstate clubhouse's parking lot.

On the way up the stairs, he side-eyes my outfit. Again. He'd given me the same *dying to crack a joke* face when I'd met him in Cedarwood's parking lot this morning.

"Shut up," I grumble.

"I didn't say anything." He offers his shoulder like I'm a fragile grandpa who forgot my walker at home, but I make it up on my own.

"Your face says plenty."

Inside the clubhouse, it's quiet and clean. A lot fewer wild parties being thrown up here these days. Sparky and Stash are still passed out on the couches—some things never change. Although today it looks like Willow's sound asleep on top of Sparky—his own human blanket.

I slap Rooster's arm and point at the trio.

He shrugs and keeps heading for the war room. "Not my business."

"What in the gangbanger-turned-suburban-dad fuck are you wearing?" Murphy cackles the second I limp into the room.

Short on options that wouldn't irritate my Franken-leg, I'm wearing the ridiculously loose black sweats Rooster brought the other night, a plain white T-shirt, and the Crocs. Still ugly as sin but surprisingly comfy. Of course, my cut on top. I wouldn't dare show up for church without it.

Rock shoots Murphy a shut-the-fuck-up look. "You're fine, Jiggy. Come in. Have a seat."

I land a solid punch on Murphy's arm as I pass his chair.

"You all right, bro?" Teller asks.

"I'll live." I lower myself into the chair beside him. "Think you've

had worse. At least no one put a bullet in my ass or splinters in my side."

"Or ran you off the road," Teller mutters. "Don't remind me."

I lift my head and nod at Dex across the table.

"How're you feeling?" he asks.

"Eh." I shrug. "Still stings like a bitch. But Margot says it looks okay. Stitches have held so far." I try to flatten the smirk forming on my lips. Been testing those stitches by asking Margot to ride my face a couple times a day—which inevitably turns into something else not medically advised.

Wrath holds out his arms as if he wants to silence the chatter. "Glad you're okay, brother." He pauses and looks around the table. "But can we all take a moment to appreciate how Margot *slit* that guy's throat without even hesitating?"

Teller's eyes bug. "I'm sorry, what?" He glances at Murphy. "I thought you were exaggerating."

"Nope."

Rock's mouth twists into a smirk. "You two are one hell of a match."

"Agreed." I swallow hard. This would be the time to mention her favorite...hobby. I won't get a better opportunity.

But it feels wrong. Private.

Her kills don't have anything to do with the club.

"She was rattled when she saw me bleeding," I offer instead.

"Didn't look rattled to me." Murphy makes a slicing motion through the air. "She handled business like a boss."

"Sorry I missed it," Dex says.

"Same." Rooster nods. "I got there right after, apparently."

I lean in, voice low. "Can we maybe not talk about it too much? She's worried what people'll think."

"Uh, that your ol' lady has more balls than most men?" Wrath arches an eyebrow.

"She just..." I scrub my hand over my jaw. "She doesn't want anyone thinking she's a psycho."

"You mean awesome?" Murphy throws in.

I let out a short laugh. "I told her that'd be everyone's reactions."

Rock stares at me for a beat. "I get what you're saying, Jiggy. That's why we called officers in first." He shoots a glare toward Z's empty end of the table. "You know Z and Grinder will be impressed too."

I nod. No doubt. No one's ratting her out. Even if they did, the guy's nothing but ashes now. Not a trace left. No proof he was ever in upstate New York.

We discuss the bits of information we did get out of the tweaker. While we're going back and forth on that, Z, Grinder, and Hustler join us.

"Well, good morning," Wrath says, pointedly staring at his wrist.

Z rolls his eyes and pulls out the chair next to Dex, instead of his normal seat. Grinder stands behind him and Hustler paces between his usual chair at the end of the table and one closer to the middle.

Wrath gives them a short, quick version of events and when he's finished, Z and Grinder are staring at me slack-jawed.

"That's some woman you found, Jigsaw." Grinder nods with respect. "Now I'm even more impressed she didn't slice those girls up after the way they went after her at our clubhouse."

"She's not...she's not like that," I say carefully. "I mean, *if* they'd laid a hand on her, they might not have gotten it back, but otherwise..."

"She's a sweetheart," Dex finishes.

"Yeah." I nod.

"She actually baked us bread." Murphy shakes with laughter as he goes over that portion of the story again.

"You got a crush on Jigsaw's girl?" Wrath jokes.

Still smiling, Murphy shakes his head. "No, I'm thinking we should ask her to prospect."

Unlikely, since she doesn't ride.

Wrath throws me a look, arching a brow.

I nod at him and raise my hand to catch Z's attention. "I doubt she wants to prospect, but I want to give her my property patch."

"Who didn't see that coming?" Hustler cackles and rubs his hands together.

"Her father going to be okay with that?" Teller asks.

I turn and glare at him. "I don't know. I didn't ask." I shrug. "What the fuck's it matter, anyway? She's only gonna wear it when she's at one of our clubhouses."

"True."

"Obviously, she has my vote," Rooster says.

"Big surprise." Hustler covers his mouth and laughs between his sausage fingers.

"Shut up," Grinder snaps, then focuses his stern gaze on me. "I'm ready to vote her in too."

Well, look at that. Grinder's such an ornery old goat, tweaker kill or not, I thought for sure he'd request a fifteen-point presentation on why Margot's ol' lady material.

Hustler grins and bobs his head up and down.

"Hell, yeah," Dex says. "If she's not your soulmate, I don't know who is."

Wrath snorts. "You already know where I stand on this."

I point at Wrath but lift my chin at Rock. "He threatened to take my patch if I don't marry her."

Rock snorts but nods as if he agrees. "She's a formidable woman."

"Tiny but terrifying," Murphy adds.

"And." Wrath leans forward and throws his arm over the table, grabbing my hand. "Five minutes after she slit that guy's throat—in one clean cut I might add—she's got Jiggy up on a table, sewing him up like she's operating on the Pope." He slaps my hand again and settles back into his chair. "Unbelievable. We should call her next time one of us gets a bullet in our ass, instead of Doc."

Not liking the sound of that. "Yeah, but she doesn't have access to meds and stuff. I mean, the shit she used on me is usually for *corpses*."

"Eh, details." Wrath waves his hand like he's batting away my words.

Z's sitting back with a pinched expression.

"What's wrong, Prez?" I ask.

"Nothing." He shakes his head. "I'm sorry I missed it. I hate that I'm so fuckin' far away when you guys need something."

"We had it covered," Murphy says. "In other mighty-girlfriend news—Molly clocked the guy with a crowbar before we even *got* to the garage."

Z bursts out laughing. "Little Molly? Remy's sister?"

"Yup." Murphy nods. "Not so little anymore."

"Christ." I shake my head. "I was threatening to stab drunk assholes for grabbing her at the bar last summer. Now she's out here knee-capping motherfuckers."

"They grow up so fast," Wrath says in a mock-wistful tone, clasping his hands together like he's about to shed a tear.

"Same vibe, though." Murphy jerks his thumb at me. "Guy came after Griff. She did what Margot did—protected her man."

"Love to see it," Dex says.

The door opens again and more brothers start filing into the war room, grabbing seats and settling in. Z and Hustler shift to the far end of the table.

Once everyone's in place, Rock gives a stripped-down version of the tweaker incident. No mention of Margot's role. Just that the body's been disposed of.

"And now for the really bad news," Z says, tipping his hand toward Rock like he's passing off a loaded weapon.

Grinder steeples his fingers in front of his mouth, probably to physically hold his inside thoughts *inside*.

"Brace yourselves." Rock's jaw shifts from side to side, like he's got something unpleasant resting on his tongue he needs to spit out. "Priest's planning to visit this summer. I don't think it's to shoot off fireworks and roast marshmallows around the fire."

"Aw, fuck," Ravage moans and stabs a finger against the table, "is he staying here?"

"Probably," Rock confirms. "I don't think he and Valentina want to stay at the clubhouse next to CB."

"Valentina's coming too?" Dex asks. "Then it's more of a social call?"

"Doubt it," Rooster says, glancing at Rock, then Z. "She'll probably try to sweet-talk whatever information she can out of Hope and Lilly."

"Good luck to her," Rock mutters.

"So what you're saying is," Z's lips curl into an evil grin as he glances around the table, his gaze finally landing on Rock. "We better get ourselves on an all-broth diet after the Fourth of July?"

Rock raises an eyebrow.

Grinder frowns at Z.

Wrath chokes on a laugh.

"Christ," Rooster mutters.

"Since," Z adds, wagging his hand in the air in an *isn't it obvious* gesture, "it sounds like he plans to crawl up our asses and conduct a thorough inspection."

Rock lets out a disgusted groan. "The fuck's wrong with you?"

Z grins even wider.

"Proud of that one, are you?" Grinder says.

Wrath's still shaking with laughter.

"I'm not getting the joke, Prez," Murphy says, his gaze pinging between Rock and Z.

Wrath reaches over and pats the top of Murphy's head. "Of course you don't."

Teller quickly shakes his head. "Now that we're all aware you spend way too much time watching porn, can we discuss this visit like adults?"

"Whoa, look at mini-me with the attitude this morning." Z throws his head back and laughs. "Who said anything about porn, you pervert?"

"Yeah, Prez could've just been letting us all know he likes a good colon cleanse before gettin' pegged by his ol' lady," Hustler says.

Z's eyes narrow to slits as he slowly swivels his head in our treasurer's direction. "Careful, or *you'll* be on an all-broth diet because you're eating all your meals through a straw."

Hustler raises his hands in the air. "Come on, I was just fucking around."

"How many times do we have to explain this," Dex says, exasperation coiled around his words. "Crackin' jokes on each other is fine. Bringing our ol' ladies into it is not."

Hustler seems to sit with that for a moment, then lifts his head. "Yeah, but—"

"For fuck's sake," I mutter, pinching the bridge of my nose.

"I'd argue it's still aimed at Z," Sparky pipes up from the couch in the back. "Lilly's got all the power if she's doing the pegging, so it's a compliment, really."

"Thanks for the riveting TED Talk, Professor Powerbottom," Dex quips.

Birch starts slow-clapping. "I feel enlightened and empowered now. Thanks, Sparky."

"You're welcome." Sparky throws two middle fingers in the air and kicks his feet up on the coffee table.

"My worldview has truly been shifted," Hustler adds.

Rock heaves a long breath. "If I *do* take Priest's place at National, does that mean these charming clusterfucks are all yours, Z?"

"Hah!" Z claps his hands and points at Rock. "I knew you'd come around. Fuck, yeah."

"Simmer down," Rock says. "No one knows what Priest actually wants."

Once the laughter dies down and Rock reins everyone back in, he goes around the table, asking for updates.

Dex mentions needing help at Crystal Ball.

I stare at the table like it's the most fascinating thing I've ever seen, praying someone else speaks up first.

Thank fuck, Ravage, Butcher, and Eazy volunteer before I have to say a word.

Hustler pipes up next. "Stella just cracked six hundred thousand subscribers."

"Already?" I blink. "Good for her." I groan and rub my hands over my face. "But please don't tell me we're throwing another party at our clubhouse."

"Not yet," Hustler says, pointing between Rooster and me. "But I need one of you to get that site update done this week and her new photos uploaded. Banner's still showing pics with her 'old hairstyle' and I'm sick of listening to her bitch about it."

"We'll get it done," Rooster promises.

Rock nods at Teller.

"We're getting ready to open up the drive-in for the season," Teller says. "I could use some help cleaning the place, hiring some folks and getting it ready."

"I might be able to help out there," I volunteer.

Teller nods. "Thanks. What about your brother? How's he like it at Sully's?"

"So far, so good. But I'll ask if he wants a second job for the summer."

Once all regular business is done, Z stands. "As some of you know, our favorite chucklefuck has taken an ol' lady."

I roll my eyes and sit back in my chair.

"And he's asked to patch her."

My brothers start slapping their hands against the table.

"So, I ask, do we need to take a vote on Ms. Margot Cedarwood to wear Jigsaw's patch?"

"No." Wrath laughs like it's an absurd question.

Z goes around the table anyway. Every officer—upstate and downstate— says yes to giving Margot their patches as well.

Z nods, pleased with his performance. "I'll try to have it ready for you by the time you get back from Vegas," he promises.

"Thanks." I nod once, a little slower than usual.

No twist of anxiety. No second thoughts.

Just the low, steady hum of anticipation buzzing under my skin.

Margot's mine. And I want the world to know it.

CHAPTER THIRTY-SIX

JIGSAW

By the time I land in Vegas, my leg's mostly healed. Still twinges if I twist the wrong way, but nothing I can't handle. I didn't come here to whine.

I came to watch Griff's back—before, during, and after the fight.

Then I'm getting my ass home to see my girl.

Until then, I check into my fancy-ass room in the hotel where all the fighters are staying. Unfortunately it's in a suite, with Griff and Molly in the room next to mine. Ella and Eraser are on the other side, and Remy's room is next to theirs.

Great. Two couples and a hound dog that likes to jump on everything in sight. These fancy-ass walls better be thick.

First thing I do—before unpacking, before even sitting down—is call Margot.

She answers on the first ring.

"Hey," she answers, all soft and almost sleepy sounding.

Fuck, I needed to hear her voice.

"Hey, little lady death."

A soft laugh rustles over the line. "Did you land okay?"

"Yeah. Just got to the hotel."

"How is it?"

"Nice. Real fuckin' nice. Glad I'm not the one paying for it."

Another bit of laughter, then hesitation. "How does your leg feel after all that walking?"

"Fine. Little sore." I ease back against the stiff hotel chair, stretching my leg out. "I miss you already. Really wish you'd been able to come with us."

"I miss you too," she answers, a bit clipped. "How was the private jet?"

"Fuckin' nice. Kinda sucks 'cause I think I have to fly back commercial."

"Awww, you've been spoiled."

"You miss me?"

"Of course," she answers immediately. Matter-of-fact. No hesitation. Even though I'd been a bit of a dick, pestering her to take the time off and come with me to Vegas.

"Miss you too."

"I really do wish I'd been able to go with you guys," she says softly. I picture her curled up in her lounge chair with Gretel in her lap and a stack of books next to her. "You know that, right?"

"I know. Sorry I've been a prick about it." I need to get it through my head, not everyone can just fuck off to Vegas for a week whenever they feel like it.

Silence hums for a beat. Did she hang up?

"It's okay," she finally says.

"How was your day?" I ask.

She sighs. "Helped a cantankerous family plan a memorial service. Handled two cremations with Paul and probably have a pickup later tonight."

Jesus, that's grim. "Sorry."

"It's what we do. But I feel better now that I've heard your voice."

Damn that fucks me up. "Me too."

"Be careful. I know you're there to watch Griff's back but—"

"Honestly," I hope this will ease some of her concern, "it sounds like I'll be tagging along with Rooster, Shelby, and Molly so the girls can do some dress shopping."

She breaks into giggles. "How fun for you. Well, tell the girls to send me pics."

My chest squeezes. No jealousy. Margot knows I belong to her.

"I will." We talk for a few more minutes, then hang up.

I sit there and stare at the screen.

I roll my shoulders, crack my neck, and grab a bottle of water from the stocked fridge.

The ache in my chest won't go away.

Probably won't until the next time Margot's in my arms.

A FEW NIGHTS LATER, I'm missing home more than ever. This isn't my kind of city. Too loud, too bright, too many annoying fucking people.

I miss Margot, my club, my bike, the open roads and trees of upstate New York—hell, I even miss Gretel.

The guy Griff is fighting, Mike "Magic" Everson, is every bit the asshole I expected. Every presser he's made nasty, out of line comments to Griff, trying to get him to throw some punches. Griff's handled it like a pro. I'm starting to think the club bettin' so much money on him to win was smart.

At least scaring the shit out of "Magic" and his annoying entourage after the press conferences has been entertaining. For me, anyway.

I told Margot I'd be careful, not that I wouldn't have a little fun while I'm here.

But it doesn't fix the pit in my chest that's been growing since the second I stepped off that plane.

Every slinky, half-naked girl with a fake smile and dead eyes reminds me how far from home I am. How far from her I am.

Margot.

My little lady death.

Tonight, I'm at a diner with most of our crew. Jammed into a booth with everyone. Shelby got wedged between Rooster and me. Griff, Molly, and Remy are packed in tight on the other side.

Under the table, I slide my phone out of my pocket and fire off a quick text.

Me: You up?

It's almost ten here, but back home it's later. Doesn't stop her from texting back three seconds later.

Little Lady Death: On call. You okay?

Fuck. I love that she always asks me that first. Not *what are you doing,* or *where are you.* She hasn't cracked any *what stays in Vegas jokes.* She trusts me completely.

Me: Miss you.

The dots appear immediately.

Little Lady Death: Miss you too.

Little Lady Death: Where are you?

Me: Out with the whole crew.

Shelby nudges me and peers over my shoulder. "Are you texting Margot?"

"Who else, songbird?"

She holds her phone out and snaps a quick photo of Rooster, herself, and me. She flashes the screen my way.

Jesus, I really do look like a serial killer.

"Would it kill ya to smile?" she teases.

"Would it kill you to warn a guy?"

She taps her fingers over the screen. "There. Sent it to Margot."

I side-eye her. "She knows she can trust me." Something worse occurs to me. "Wait, did she ask you to…keep tabs on me?"

"No!" She slaps my arm. "I just know you won't send her any pics."

How wrong you are, songbird. I've sent Margot dozens of pics while we've been here.

Little Lady Death: Cute pic.

I had sent a check-in text to Jezzie and Cain earlier today. Both of the little shits answered back with emojis.

Looking at their messages, one after the other, twists a knife of guilt in my chest. When I get back from Vegas, I need to have my sit-down with Jezzie and have her meet Cain. It's time.

"Molly, you speak this age range, what the fuck does this mean?" I lean over the table and flash the screen with Jezzie's straight-faced emoji, dramatic-sigh face, and heart.

Molly flicks her gaze between the screen and my face, her lips forming a small "O."

That can't be good.

"My sister's telling me to fuck off, isn't she?"

Molly snort-giggles. "No." She sits up straighter and tosses her long, shiny brown hair over her shoulder, like she's preparing a presentation. "Given the context of your text to *her*, I think she's responding with, 'I'm exasperated with you checking on me all the time, but I love you.'" She nods, quickly, like she's confirming her interpretation. "Yup. That's it."

I glance at the screen again. *Maybe?* "What's the emoji combo for 'you're a pain in my ass?'"

Remy leans sideways over Griff. "Eye roll and donkey. You're lucky. All Molly sends me are middle finger emojis."

Molly playfully slaps his arm. "Only when you're being a jerk."

"So, all the time?" I add, helpful as ever.

Remy laughs but Molly gives me a mild stink eye.

How cute. She doesn't like anyone *else* making fun of her big brother.

Remy leans back and stretches his arms across the back of the booth. "Saw your brother at Strike Back last week, Jigsaw."

My spine goes stiff.

"Cain?" I say stupidly, just to make sure he doesn't mean someone from my club.

Remy nods. "Kid's quick. Showed him how to roll out of a choke. He picked it up fast."

Pride flashes hot through my chest before I can stomp it down. "Glad he's got good instincts," I mutter.

"He's a funny kid. Kinda quiet. Shy at first." A flicker of a smile cuts across his face. "Totally opposite of your sister."

Something twists so hard in my chest, my ribs might snap.

I smooth my expression, even though my jaw's grinding behind it. He doesn't know our history. All the shit we've been through. And if he thinks he's ever dating—or whatever the fuck he does—my sister, he's dead, fucking wrong.

"Different moms," I say in a tone designed to shut him up.

He'd have to be suicidal to pull at that thread with me.

He nods quickly and shifts his gaze to Griff. "You're out way past your bedtime, Stonewall."

Griff, bleary-eyed and heavy-limbed, nods. "Yeah, I think we're heading back now. Coach'll kill me if I'm draggin' ass tomorrow."

The three of them slide out of their side of the booth, collecting phones, wallets, and half-finished drinks.

Wrath and Trinity stop Griff and Molly, talking about logistics for tomorrow's afternoon press conference.

Griff? He's barely present—arm draped around Molly, eyes fixed on the door like he's already halfway out of it.

Remy hangs back, drops into the booth across from me. "Hey, Jiggy?"

I raise my eyebrows, not fond of him shortening my road name. "Yeah?"

He cuts a quick look toward his sister. "Griff's worried Molly might freak out at the fight. If he..."

"Starts bleeding all over the canvas?" I offer.

"Yeah." His mouth twists with annoyance. "Will you help me hustle her out of the arena if I have to?"

"Maybe she shouldn't go?"

He tilts his head. "Yeah, I'm not even gonna try to stop her."

The girl *did* take a crowbar to someone's leg. "I think she'll be fine. But yeah, you got it. Just say the word."

"I'll have her sit next to me, Remy," Shelby offers. "She's dyin' to see Magic get knocked on his ass after all the trash he's been talkin' this week."

"I know." Remy nods. He knocks his knuckles against the table and stands. "Thanks, Jiggy."

"No problem."

Why does Remy bug me so much? I respect him—he works his ass off. He's a damn good fighter. He's loyal to his friends and his family.

My gaze lands on his sister, Molly. Talk about spirited. She reminds me a lot of Jezzie, except unlike my sister, Molly actually seems to *like* her brother. Worships the big goof, really.

Maybe that's what bugs me? They had a shit family too. I don't know details, except Remy was out of his dad's house and living with his grandparents by the time he was fifteen or sixteen. After they passed, Molly moved in with him instead of staying with their alcoholic father.

He took his sister in. Made sure she was safe. Looked out for her.

He didn't ship Molly off to another relative like I did to Jezzie.

Didn't abandon her like I did to Cain.

Well, Cain had a mother. Still, I tried to pretend the kid didn't even exist.

Christ, I'm not this deep. Don't usually give this many fucks about untangling my issues. Never have.

I take another pull from the bottle, shake my head, and stare through the open door like I might find an answer out on The Strip. I should head back to the hotel. Tomorrow's gonna be a long one.

"What's up, bestie?" Shelby drawls. She elbows me, bumping her hip into mine, warm and insistent until I shift over.

"What's up with you?" I ask, grateful for the distraction.

"I want to get out of the booth." She fans her hand in front of her face. "It's hot as blazes in here."

"You're from Texas."

"Yeah, but this is *dry* heat." She sticks her tongue out. "Ain't the same."

"Fair enough." I stand and help her out of the booth.

Rooster slides out next. "I can't wait to be done with this," he says against my ear.

"Same, bro."

Fight night can't come soon enough.

Margot

Am I really going to the clubhouse by myself?

Jigsaw promised tonight was strictly family. Then Lilly called early in the morning to make sure I was coming. She offered a guest room in their cabin on the club's property so I wouldn't have to drive all the way home after the fight ends.

Older or not, Jigsaw's 4Runner handles better than my Thunderbird. Especially up the steep driveway leading to Upstate's secluded clubhouse.

The parking lot's full. Big trucks. SUVs. Motorcycles.

Seeing all of them makes me miss Jigsaw even more.

I pull my phone out and send him a quick text.

Me: At the clubhouse.

Sparky greets me as I step down from the truck. A big grin on his placid face. "You made it."

"I did. I can't believe I found the place without Jigsaw."

He holds up a thin, brown paper bag. "Treats for the fights." His forehead scrunches. "Fights are really bloody. You might want to be high to watch."

I take the bag and slip it into my purse. "I don't know if I'm falling for that again."

Last time I ate one of Sparky's THC-laced masterpieces I had Jigsaw to protect me while I floated in and out of consciousness at Teller's wedding.

He nods solemnly. "That one was, uh, nuclear. This? Just a little kick." He waggles his hand. "Maybe save it for when Jigsaw's back, just in case."

I squint at him. "Define 'little kick.'"

He shrugs, already turning toward the clubhouse.

Laughing to myself, I open the back door and pull out the long Tupperware container of THC-free inside-out chocolate chip cookies I made.

The low thump of bass and muffled crowd noise from the big-screen TV hits me first. The clubhouse living room's been transformed—extra recliners, beanbags, blankets spread out on the floor, all angled toward the massive flat screen on the wall. Snacks and drinks at the bar by the door.

On the screen, two men are circling each other inside a cage. One's already bleeding, a red river streaming down the side of his face.

"Wait, did I miss it?" My voice comes out more anxious than I intend.

"Oh, Margot!" Hope appears like the fairy godmother of the clubhouse—graceful, composed, and welcoming. A warm smile lights up her face as she hurries over and pulls me into a soft, reassuring hug. "I'm so glad you made it." She waves a hand at the television. "No, this is one of the early fights. They're going all day. Griff's is last."

"If you want something more mellow, let me know," Sparky says to me, then wanders over to a nest of blankets piled on the floor with a couple of the other brothers I vaguely recognize. He flops down flat on his stomach like a teenager at a sleepover. His gaze locks on the screen, already half-lost in the action.

Hope throws a fond smile his way and shakes her head, her dark red hair sliding over the shoulder of her cozy purple sweater.

I hold up the container in my hands. "I brought inside-out chocolate chip cookies."

Her green eyes light with genuine interest. "Oooo." She rubs her hands together. "Thank you. I only got to try one at the bonfire. They were so good."

She takes the container, nudging aside a few items on the bar to make room. Without hesitation, she plucks a few cookies out, setting them on a napkin.

Warmth shoots through me. Silly as it is, now I'm ridiculously proud I remembered to make them last night. At least I brought something one person will enjoy.

Lilly walks down the long hallway from the dining room, spots me, and waves.

"There you are." She crosses the room with a warm smile, pausing just long enough to hold out her arms in silent question. When I step forward, she wraps me in a soft, full-body squeeze.

Overwhelmed by all the affection. I pull back and yank my face into a smile.

"We've got more food set up in the dining room if you're hungry." Lilly leans in slightly, lowering her voice. "A lot of us are hanging out down there with the kids. This," she waves a hand toward the screen, "is a little much for them."

"Yeah, I can, uh, see why." The guys on the screen are now wrestling on the floor of the cage. The two men are tangled in a violent knot on the mat. Their bodies so tightly pressed together it's hard to tell where one ends and the other begins.

Hope turns, her gaze scanning everyone in the living room. "Oh, Teller's placing bets if that's something you're interested in."

My gaze lands on Teller's long frame, folded into one corner of the couch, a laptop balanced on the armrest. Charlotte's curled up next to him, legs tucked beneath her, calmly watching the chaos unfold on-screen while talking to her husband. Rock's settled in the chair beside them, eyes fixed on Teller's screen. Every so often, he nods or shakes his head, quiet approval or a subtle veto, I can't tell.

"Margot!" someone calls from the far corner of the living room. A hand shoots up, waving wildly.

Lilly laughs and rests her hand on my shoulder. "Serena's been looking for you since she and Grinder got here."

"Really?" My voice comes out higher than I intended, threaded with a pinch of desperation I hate that I revealed.

"Of course." A slight frown pinches between Hope's eyebrows. "We were all so happy you could join us."

Now that Serena's called attention to me, the room shifts. Every face turns my way and offers a greeting. I wiggle my fingers in response, my skin heating.

Charlotte pats her husband's leg and rises, weaving through the guys with an unapologetic grace. A few groan that she's blocking the TV, but no one stops her.

"Hi, Margot." She pulls me into a hug. The scent of baby powder and something tart, but pleasant—like grapefruit—fills the air between us.

I don't think I've been hugged this much since my grandmother's funeral.

My eyes sting.

Get it together, Margot.

I'm not used to this many people caring about my presence. Not even my own family. It's nice...in an overwhelming sort of way. Jigsaw's not even here, so they're not just being nice for his benefit.

"Hi." I smile at Charlotte. "I hear your husband's the one I should take my bets to?"

Charlotte's mouth turns up in an affectionate grin. "Oh yeah. He's in full bookie mode today—placing parlays, over-unders, knockouts by round... I think someone even asked if there was a line on how many times some guy bleeds." She waves a hand toward Teller. "Honestly, I think he enjoys the bets more than the fights. So far, he's won more than he's lost, so it's all good."

"But the big one's tonight!" Murphy calls out as he strolls over and joins us. "No pressure or anything, Teller!"

Without missing a beat—or lifting his eyes from his laptop—Teller flips him off.

Charlotte snorts.

"Hey, ginger twinny." She taps her knuckles against Murphy's shoulder. "Where've you been hiding?"

He tilts his head toward the dining room. "Playland. Hoping if we wear 'em out enough, they'll all crash before Griff's fight starts."

Lilly gives my shoulder a gentle squeeze. "I need to check on Chance. I'll see you in a bit."

Hope offers me another reassuring smile before following her down the hall.

I trail after Charlotte, weaving around the recliners and stepping over a couple of blankets.

From the far side of the couch, Serena waves again. She nudges a stuffed-to-bursting diaper bag off the seat and pats the cushion beside her.

"Come sit," she whispers.

Baby Lincoln's nestled against her chest, his tiny body rising and falling in a soft, sleepy rhythm.

My heart does that weird, achy flutter again.

I'm not used to people making space for me.

"Sorry," she says as I ease into the seat beside her. "I would've come over to meet you but…"

"Your hands are a little full?" I lean over, peeking at Lincoln's round cheeks and perfectly pursed lips. "He's, uh, grown a lot since last time."

"I know." She smiles down at him and snuggles him closer.

"Hi, Margot," a deeper voice rumbles.

I glance up at Grinder—looking especially murder daddy-ish tonight—seated in the corner of the opposite couch, angled ninety degrees from Serena and their baby. Quiet menace radiates off him. His intense gaze settles on me, and he gives a slow, respectful nod.

Oh, lord. Jigsaw must've told him about the guy I helped into the crematorium express lane.

Of course he did. The whole club probably knows.

But no one seems afraid of me. Or even seems concerned.

Yeah, no kidding. They've all probably done much worse.

Instead of terrifying, it's comforting.

Everyone in this room would probably kill to protect their loved ones.

That, I can relate to.

Feeling more settled, I let my gaze wander around the room, noting not everyone's here.

"Where are the other guys?" I ask Serena. "Ravage? Birch? Dex?"

Serena laughs softly. "They're either watching the fight at Crystal Ball or Remy's bar." She pulls her phone out from under her thigh, expertly thumbing the screen, like she's used to doing everything one-handed. "Well, Dex and Emily are running things at Remy's bar while he's away. Em says the place is absolutely packed."

"That's great." Except for Griff's party, Remy's bar has been slow when I've been there. Hopefully the boost in business helps.

"Oh! I brought you something—" Serena stretches her free arm out, straining to reach for the bag on the floor without jostling Lincoln.

"Let me take him for a while, buttercup." Grinder stands and scoops his son into his arms.

Serena throws him a soft, grateful smile. "Thank you."

She digs around in the bag, pulling out diapers, wipes, toys, blankets, extra baby clothes—so *many* extra clothes. Finally, she unearths a sleek, black, sparkly case shaped like a coffin.

"A-ha!" She holds it in the air like a trophy. "The company sent me two of these limited-edition kits. I thought the bag was so cute. I brought one for you."

She hands it to me, and I blink in surprise. The name stamped in silver across the front jumps out immediately—an expensive brand I've admired but never dared splurge on.

"Wow. Really?" I unzip the case. "Are you sure?"

"Yes, yes. It's their fall line. Not available yet. I have to post my videos by the end of the summer. Oh! Maybe you can come down and we'll swatch everything together. Their new liquid liners are insane—super pigmented, zero flake, and the precision tips? So, so clean."

Serena's cheerful enthusiasm finally cuts through my anxiety. We geek out over the kit, comparing shades and formulas. She helps me test one of the lip colors, gently swiping it over my lips like a pro.

I snap a quick selfie and send it to Jigsaw.

No death talk. No sideways glances or whispered gossip. I'm not the weird girl who touches dead people for a living.

I'm…a friend. A guest. Someone who belongs here.

Heidi and her daughter stop by for a few minutes. But after Alexa watches the screen for a bit, she tries to mimic one of the fighters' moves on Z's son, Chance.

"That's our cue to go back to the dining room," Heidi mutters, while Murphy scoops up his mini menace before a full toddler cage match breaks out.

The rest of the afternoon and evening is just as pleasantly chaotic.

Then, the television screen goes dark except for thousands of twinkling lights in the arena.

"This is it!" Teller shouts. "It's starting!"

A low hum of anticipation zips around us.

The theme song to Halloween starts playing.

"What the fuck? The guy's using the Halloween theme song as his walkout?" Sparky shouts. "What a doofus. I hope Griff rocks that dude into next year."

"Who knew Sparky was so bloodthirsty," Serena titters.

While Griff's opponent takes a lap around the entire arena, the screen splits, showing a full hallway of jittering men.

Stash jumps up off his blanket and points at the screen. "There's Remy."

Hope squeals. "There's Wrath. Oh my God, he looks ready to chuck people left and right."

The camera zooms in on Griff squinting into the light and Molly handing him a pair of sunglasses.

"Awww, they're so cute," I sigh.

"There's Dawson." Heidi elbows Murphy's side. "I'm *so* jealous we couldn't go with them. Shelby said the private plane was a-maze-ing."

"Next time," he promises her.

The screen shifts to just showing Mike "Magic" Everson again. Sparky's right, the guy looks like a doofus, hurling insults and talking trash about Griff.

The camera switches again.

The whole parade of people backstage starts walking down the long hall into the arena. A loud, grinding country song blares from the speakers. Lights flash everywhere.

"I never realized it was such a spectacle," I murmur. "It's all so... theatrical."

"Right?" Lilly flashes a grin. "Men are *so* dramatic."

I shake with laughter and nod.

The announcer's voice booms, rattling off betting stats—how the odds are laughably against Griff. Making it sound like he's a charity case.

Indignation flares in my chest. "That's rude. Why would he be there if he has no chance of winning?"

Teller turns and grins at me. "Let 'em keep underestimating him." He rubs his fingers together in the universal sign for money. "Only benefits us."

"Is it too late for me to place a bet?"

"Nope." He rattles off a bunch of different options—which mean nothing to me, finally promising to place fifty on Griff to win by knockout.

"Oh!" Heidi jumps out of her chair and points at the TV. "There's Shelby and Molly."

"Shelby looks so cute in that jumpsuit!" Serena gushes.

A microphone gets shoved in Shelby's face. "Who are you rooting for, Shelby?" someone off-camera asks.

Shelby's pretty face screws into an *are you stupid* scowl. "Stonewall! Who else?"

The camera slides to Molly's anxious face. "You think your boyfriend's going to win this fight, Molly?"

Like a baby deer caught in the headlights, she blinks several times. My heart squeezes at her obvious discomfort. Finally, she lifts her chin and glares right into the camera. "Of course he will."

If Shelby's on the screen, Jigsaw shouldn't be far away, right? Searching the people in the background, I finally spot him. My heart kicks. He's so focused and serious, standing next to Rooster, glaring at the cage. Even in a sea of shouting fans, my eyes go straight to him.

I shoot a quick text.

Me: I see you.

The camera pans away just as it looks like he dips his hand into his pocket.

Next to me, Serena's phone dings. She quickly checks the screen and frowns. "Aww, some jerk asked Shelby if she's pregnant."

Lilly's eyes narrow. "People are such assholes." She gestures wildly at the screen. "She looks adorable."

The screen goes to the inside of the cage.

"Ladies and gentlemen, welcome to the main event tonight! Reigning champion Mike 'Magic' Everson out of ME Army Gym right here in Las Vegas with an impressive record of eleven wins and one loss, versus the up-and-coming *Supreme Underground Fighter* Griffin 'Stonewall' Royal out of Furious Fitness all the way in Empire, New York! You're here to witness history as Stonewall steps into the cage for his first professional fight tonight."

"Yes!" Murphy claps. "Shout-out to Furious Fitness!"

Z walks over and high-fives him.

I glance to my right. Teller's abandoned his laptop, standing next to Charlotte and Rock.

The bell rings.

And all hell breaks loose on the screen.

Fists fly. Kicks land. They're spinning, grappling, throwing each other into the cage wall. The force behind their movements feels violent and intimate all at once. It's hard to track everything—they move fast, and the commentary is a blur—but the sound of the crowd roaring inside the arena? That cuts through loud and clear.

Magic throws a punch that Griff ducks, throwing the guy off balance.

Cocky as all hell, Griff walks right up and slaps the guy across the face.

"Yes!" Murphy laughs maniacally. "Stonewall Slap."

More punches and kicks are thrown. Griff goes flying into the cage wall.

"Oh my God." I squeeze my eyes shut. "I can't watch." How do people do this? How is Molly sitting right there in the front row, watching the man she loves get punched? Repeatedly. And kicked. And choked.

I force myself to open my eyes and watch, afraid it's bad luck to miss a moment.

Hope clasps my arm. "Jeez, no wonder he needed me to write up a will for him." She winces but can't seem to look away from the screen either. "This is brutal."

"Yeah, I can see why he'd need a will."

Every so often, the camera glides over the front row, catching Molly and Shelby's anxious faces, Trinity's stillness, Wrath's coiled

tension, and if it lingers long enough, I catch a glimpse of Rooster and Jigsaw's stone-cold stares too.

Each time, my heart squeezes.

I miss him so much.

I don't know if I could stand to be in the arena, though. It's hard enough watching on television.

By the third round, sweat beads at my temples, and my nerves are wound tighter than a garrote wire. Magic plods across the canvas like a half-dead zombie, while Griff stays light on his feet, bouncing and sharp.

A spark of hope lights in my chest.

"Don't get cocky," Murphy says in a low warning tone, as if Griff can somehow hear the advice all the way on the other side of the country.

The same crowd that booed Griff now chants his name—"Stonewall!"—echoing through the speakers.

Magic ducks. Griff's knee crashes into his face. Blood sprays.

My stomach flips.

A few brutal punches later, Magic hits the canvas like a rumpled blanket.

"That's it!" Murphy jumps up, hands over his head, clapping wildly.

The front row on-screen erupts. I lose sight of Shelby's glittering jumpsuit in the blur of movement.

Fans and team members crowd the steps to the cage. The camera pans over them.

"Looks like Stonewall's crew is first on the steps. There's his young girlfriend," the announcer drawls with a dirty chuckle. "Look at that dress."

"What a bunch of pigs," Charlotte mutters.

"Winner by knockout in the third round," the arena announcer shouts. "Griffin 'Stonewall' Royal!"

Seconds later, the broadcast announcer echoes the words.

"Yes! Fuck yes!" Teller jumps up, punching the air.

Charlotte whoops, clapping as he pulls her into a kiss.

I turn back to the screen.

Jigsaw and Rooster stand close, cocooning Molly as they wait to be let into the cage.

She's finally waved in and bolts straight into Griff's arms. Jigsaw, Rooster, and Remy hover behind them. Jigsaw glances down at something in his hand, flicking his gaze up every few seconds.

My phone buzzes.

Jigsaw: He won.

Me: I know. Still at the clubhouse watching. I see you.

A few seconds later, he lifts his head, gaze scanning the area as if he's searching for me.

My throat tightens.

Serena leans over. "Are you texting Jiggy, now?"

Laughing, I tilt my screen toward her. "Yes."

She turns back to the TV screen, smiling. I do too, but the ache in my chest stays.

He's thousands of miles away.

Even though tonight was more fun than I expected, I miss him more than ever.

Jigsaw

I'm going to need a month at a secluded cabin to recover from this trip. Away from noise, dumbfuckery, and people. Way too many people in my face, crowding around us in the hallway outside the room where Griff's supposed to sit down and answer questions from every dumbass sports "reporter" with a podcast. Rooster, Remy and I do our best to keep a circle of protection around Griff and Molly while fans push and shove to get his autograph or ask him obnoxious questions.

How can he stand this shit?

Griff's already wobbly from the fight. He's probably exhausted but he keeps a tired smile in place while he talks to people and signs stuff. Molly keeps tugging on the hem of her dress and swiveling her head like she's searching for the nearest escape route.

"You all right, kiddo?" I ask her.

Her mouth pulls to the side. "Just tired."

Griff glances at her, concern darkening his expression. "Almost done, muffin. Promise."

Finally, we're let into the room. Griff's whisked away by a team of people. I plop into a chair out of the way and dig out my phone.

A flood of notifications lights up the screen—messages from damn near everyone I know, asking about the fight.

Nothing new from Margot.

I hope she had a good time at the clubhouse. Not sure the fight was her kinda entertainment but at least she got to hang out with everyone. Lilly and Charlotte had each sent a text letting me know Margot was okay.

My thumb swipes open the tracking app—her blip's still parked at the clubhouse. Good. She's supposed to crash at Z and Lilly's place tonight.

Shelby rests her hands on my shoulders and peers over my chair at my screen. "I'm startin' to think you believe *Every Breath You Take* was a love ballad and not a stalker anthem."

Damn, I love this woman and her random music references.

I tip my head back and widen my eyes. "It's not?"

"Quit playin'." She taps my arm and settles into the chair next to me.

"As if you and Rooster aren't obsessed with each other."

She grins wider. "Absolutely true."

I glance at the screen again and close out of the app. "I really wish she could've come with us."

Her smile fades. "Me too. Next time, hopefully?"

"I hope so." I tap my phone. "She knows about the app, just so you know."

Her expression softens. "I was only kiddin' about the stalker thing."

"After the girls said that shit to her at the clubhouse," I explain, "I gave her the apps for my phone and watch, so she can always tell where I am. And she said it was only fair…"

"Jiggy." She squeezes my arm. "That's so sweet—in a kinda unhinged way." She blows out a breath. "But with the twists and turns our lives seem to take, it's probably smart." She covers her mouth with her hand. "Not that I think Margot's gonna get kidnapped or anything."

"You okay?" I ask her.

She tosses her hair back, like she's collecting her self-esteem. "I'm Shelby Frickin' Morgan, I'm flockin' fabulous."

I shake with laughter. "Yes, yes, you are, songbird."

She lets out a loud yawn. "Actually, I'm plum tuckered out. Thought my heart was gonna leap outta my throat watchin' them two go at it. I've seen y'all spar and mess around, but that was next level."

I jerk my chin toward Dawson, who's holding court with some reporter in the corner. "How's he feeling?"

"Pretty dang good. Won a buttload of money, I'm sure—" Her eyes widen, and she lowers her voice. "Oh, shoot, Teller must've crapped a brick. Whole club was throwin' down heavy on Griff, right?"

"Hell yeah." I nod. "So did I." I glance at Rooster and Wrath. "Them too."

"Dang." She twists around, catches Rooster's eye, and he nods back at her.

After what seems like hours later, Griff's finally up on the small stage, squinting into the lights, keeping his cool while reporters lob stupid questions at him.

The rest of our crew filled out the seats around me. Somehow Remy ended up next to me. Shelby moved to sit with Molly.

"Griffin, over here. Brett from Tridant True Media."

Next to me, Remy groans. "This guy's a clown. You ever listen to his podcast?"

"Fuck no. I try to avoid any and all dudebro content," I answer.

Remy snorts.

Griff turns his head, his eyes scanning the crowd until they land on the reporter. He picks up his microphone and nods for him to ask his question.

"You were the underdog in this fight," Brett says. "This was a stunning victory—"

"I wasn't stunned." Griff cuts him off.

The room erupts in laughter. *Good one, kid.*

Griff lazily points in our direction. "None of my crew was surprised that I won, either."

"Fuck yeah!" I jump out of my chair and throw my fists up, daring the reporter to say something else stupid.

Other reporters stare at us wide-eyed and give us more room.

Remy's silently laughing when I sit back down.

Griff grins at the reporter and lifts his eyebrows. "Anything else?"

Not smart enough to keep his mouth shut the guy asks, "Well, actually yes. Since you won, will you be proposing to your girlfriend this weekend?"

Remy groans. "What the fuck is wrong with these people? Some asshole asked her that in the cage too."

"Fucking creeps," I growl, clocking this dude for later. Maybe a four a.m. blanket party in the parking lot will cheer me up.

Griff blows off the question. "My personal life is personal. Let's keep the questions fight-related."

Since I can't punch any of the reporters right now, needling Remy seems like my next best option. I lean over and whisper, "You're not worried they're going to get hitched once your plane takes off?"

He snorts a laugh. "No. Molly wants *me* to walk her down the aisle." A more serious expression falls over his face. "Griff wouldn't do that to me."

"You're good with them together now?" Because he sure seemed to have a problem with it last year.

He cocks his head and stares at me for a moment. "Yeah. Royal will turn himself inside out to make my sister happy. That's all I care about." He shrugs, then laughs. "Not that my opinion matters. They're going to be together whether I approve or not. I'd rather be *in* their lives than..." He trails off and shrugs again. "Whatever the alternative is."

That's a more mature answer than I expected from Remy.

Not that I have room to judge.

I've got my own little sister problems.

Jezzie's gonna breathe hellfire in my face when she finds out Cain's been living near me all this time and I haven't told her yet.

Will she understand I just wanted to make sure she'd be safe?

That I needed time to figure it all out?

I scrub my hand over my face.

Once I get Margot in my arms, I'll sort through the complicated web.

She'll help me make sense of everything—help me form a plan.

She always does.

CHAPTER THIRTY-SEVEN

JIGSAW

PHYSICALLY, I'M WRECKED. RUNNING ON FUMES. BUT EVERYTHING ELSE? Wired. Buzzing with the need to get home. To see Margot.

So desperate to touch her, I dropped a fuck-ton of cash on the next first-class flight out.

Don't think I've ever wanted to see someone so bad in my life.

Every muscle in my body strains, silently begging the plane to move faster.

Even the extra legroom in first class isn't enough—still feels like a cage, leaving me cramped, twitchy, and ready to crawl out of my skin.

Six goddamn hours of white-knuckling the armrest and trying not to throttle the chatterbox next to me who won't shut the fuck up about how much he won in Vegas.

I bet I won more.

Teller was sure Griff would take it in the third, so I put that porn money I've been earning from the club to good use.

Pretty sure I'm going car shopping when I get home.

"Good afternoon and welcome to Empire, New York. The weather—"

Thank fuck.

I blow out a long breath and gather my shit. Phone, earbuds, backpack. Shoulder's stiff, back's aching, but I'm moving like someone lit a fire under my ass.

Could've hugged the annoying fuck next to me when he stepped back and let me grab my shit out of the overhead compartment first.

The second my boots hit the jet bridge, I'm already reaching for my phone. No new texts from Margot, but that's fine. I can see where she is on my phone.

Right where she's supposed to be.

Where I'm headed now.

There.

On the other side of the security gate.

The second my gaze lands on Margot, I'm done. Absolutely feral to get my hands on her.

No more. I can't be away from her this long again. I can barely function like a normal human.

She's wearing a black long-sleeved shirt underneath a black-and-pink plaid dress. The dress is tight up top, showing off her perfect breasts, but the skirt's loose and flowy, only hinting at her curves underneath. Her shiny black heels give her a little height.

I throw my bags on the floor and scoop her up into my arms immediately.

She lets out a happy squeak of surprise and throws her arms around my neck. "Welcome home!"

I answer by smashing my lips against hers.

"Oh," she sighs and melts into my body.

"I missed you." I pull away long enough to look into her eyes. "I don't want to be away from you again that long."

"I missed you too." She slides down my body and I release her. "How's your leg?"

Fuck my leg. Did she hear what I said? "Fine."

"Good." She loops her arms around my neck again, inviting me to pick her up.

Fuck yes. I lift her and seal my mouth over hers, licking at the seam of her lips, sucking on her tongue. She tastes like mint and something sweeter.

Home.

A few nervous, awkward chuckles ripple past us. Someone mutters, "Get a room."

Don't care.

She pulls back, her gaze darting to the side. "Let's go," she says against my lips. "Before security grabs us for a pat down."

I follow her line of sight to two airport security agents, watching us with too much interest. Nosy fucks. I snarl in their direction, then pick up my bags, curl my hand around hers and start marching for the exit.

"Where'd you park?" I ask.

Her heels click over the concrete as she hurries to keep up with me. "Straight through here. In short-term parking."

"Good."

Once we're in my truck and out of the garage, she flicks the blinker on. I reach over and tap her leg. "Go right."

"Okay."

"Here." I point straight ahead. "Turn left at the next light."

"What?" She laughs. "Why?"

"I can't wait until we get to your place."

She peers out the window. "This is a hotel."

Smart woman. "Exactly."

"Jigsaw, we don't need to waste money on a hotel. We're an hour from my house."

"I told you, I can't wait that long. It's not a waste."

"But—"

"Margot." I angle my body toward her. "I won enough money on the fight. We can afford a hotel room for one night."

She throws me a sidelong glance, teeth sinking into her bottom lip. "Okay."

That's more like it.

We're like newlyweds in some dipshit rom-com, holding hands and half-running into the hotel lobby. And I don't even care.

Margot blushes and won't look at the woman behind the counter who takes my credit card and slides two keycards across the desk.

"Enjoy your stay, Mr. and Mrs. Killgore."

I like the way that sounds too much to bother correcting her.

Margot

I can't believe we're actually in a hotel.

Just to... have sex? In the afternoon?

It feels so illicit. Wild. Maybe a little impractical.

I'm mortified checking in with no luggage, just my purse swinging from my shoulder like a neon announcement—*just here to fuck!*

The elevator doors whisper shut, and Jigsaw crowds me against the wall, cupping my cheeks and sealing his mouth over mine. His lips are hot, insistent, impatient. I melt into him without hesitation.

Someone clears their throat.

Jigsaw growls low in his chest but peels himself away, straightening without even glancing back at our unwanted audience. He curls his hand around mine, protective and reassuring.

The elevator dings.

My pulse skips as he tugs me into the hallway, his grip firm around my hand.

A rush of excitement floods through me.

Outside the room, he pins me to the door with his entire body, heat radiating off him like a furnace. I try to slide the card into the reader, but there's no space between us. I'm plastered to the door—flushed, breathless, burning.

Finally the lock beeps and we stumble into the room.

I barely manage to step out of my shoes before he grabs me under the thighs and lifts me, setting me on something solid—maybe the dresser, maybe a table, I don't care. His mouth never leaves mine. His hands are everywhere, shoving up my dress, fingers ripping my tights.

"You look so fuckin' pretty," he murmurs, kissing my jaw, my cheekbone, the hollow under my ear. "But these—" he hooks a finger in the ruined nylon, and yanks hard, "—these are in my way."

The rough tug rips them even more.

His hips thrust against me, hard and frantic, not close to being inside me, but desperate. He groans against my throat, the sound low, needy, and close to a whimper.

"Awww," I trace my fingers over his cheek, "you're like a puppy who hasn't been taken for a walk all week."

"Puppy. No." He growls, forehead pressed to my temple, hips grinding in a frantic rhythm. "I'm a man who hasn't been inside his woman in a week." He brushes his lips over my cheek. "Why aren't you helping me get these fucking panties off?" His fingers close around the elastic and he yanks hard.

Using his shoulders for leverage, I lift my hips, giving him room to drag my underwear and what's left of my tights down my legs. The tension in his muscles, the heat rolling off him, the impatient way he shoves the fabric down my legs leaves me desperate.

He breathes a satisfied sigh. "Finally."

"If I'd known they were going to cause you so much trouble, I wouldn't have worn them."

I grab his belt buckle and work it loose, fingers fumbling against the metal.

His eyes flare, mouth curling into a slow, wicked smile. "You want me just as much."

"Of course I do." I press kisses to his chest, flick my tongue against one nipple.

He groans—loud, guttural, grateful.

"Come here." He hauls me off the dresser and spins me around where I'm facing a mirror, already smudged from me leaning up against it. I stare at my wild hair, reddened lips, and flushed face. I barely recognize myself.

Behind me, Jigsaw kicks off his boots and shoves his jeans down.

"Fuck."

"In my purse," I manage to whisper. If I move, I'll collapse. My legs are liquid.

He bends, grabs my purse off the floor, and rifles through it.

"Inner pocket," I gasp.

He yanks out an embarrassingly long strip of condoms I'd grabbed at the last minute on my way to meet him.

"Margot?" He dangles the strip in the air and arches a brow.

"I thought…maybe we'd stop and play in the back seat of your car or something." I grin at him, not even a little bit sorry to reveal that. "Not go to a hotel."

Laughing, he tears into one with his teeth and, watching me in the mirror, rolls it on. "I fucking love you."

He drops my heels next to me. "Put those back on for me."

I wiggle my feet into the shoes.

Heat shoots to my core as he flips my dress up and slowly pushes inside me. His eyes close and he throws his head back. His fingers tighten on my hip. "Fuuuck, told you how long I've been wanting to do this."

"Oh my God." Now I'm the one whimpering. I rest my cheek on the dresser and arch my back to accept more of him.

"You okay?" he asks, hips pressing forward again, slower this time.

"I'm very…full." I gasp. "Please don't stop."

A shiver travels over his body, as if he's holding back from pounding into me.

"More," I whisper.

He slides one hand around my hip between my legs and strokes my clit. My heart thunders.

I squeeze my inner muscles around him.

He pushes deeper, rolls his fingers over my clit over and over, amplifying my pleasure. Finally he thrusts harder. Moves faster.

"Yes," I encourage, praying he won't slow down again.

Fingers tugging and pulling at the zipper of my dress, he finally drags it all the way down and shoves my shirt up, skimming his fingers along my spine.

Heat races over my skin, radiating out in waves. My knees threaten to buckle.

He drives into me harder, slamming the dresser into the wall with a steady thump.

He grips my hips again, digging in, quickening his thrusts.

I spasm and clench around him.

Pleasure barrels down on me, fast and brutal. I cry out, sharp and broken, not even caring if the whole hotel hears us.

"Ah, fuck." He comes with a groan, shuddering through his release.

After a heartbeat, he collapses on top of me, pressing me against the dresser, covering my hands with his. "Thank you."

He kisses along my spine, then slips out of me.

"You okay?" he asks.

"I'm wrecked." I kick my shoes off. "Can't move. I live here now."

He chuckles and pats my behind as he steps into the bathroom.

A minute later he returns, chuckling when he finds me in the exact same position.

"Poor lady death," he teases, pulling me into his arms. "Got fucked hard, huh?"

I'm still shaking—with aftershocks, with laughter—as I trace my fingers over the stubble on his cheek.

His smile softens.

He carries me to the bed and helps me peel off my clothes.

The light goes off and he settles into bed behind me, skin to skin, one arm around my waist.

"Are we staying?" I whisper.

He strokes his fingers over my belly then lower. "I'm not done with you yet. This is just an intermission."

Jigsaw

Margot's slow, rhythmic breathing should settle me into sleep. Should quiet the noise in my head.

Instead, my thoughts won't stop ricocheting around.

I shouldn't say this. Not now.

I've never been good at keeping the thoughts in my head out of my mouth. Not the important ones, anyway. "Margot?"

"Hmmm?" she murmurs.

"I meant what I said before." I roll to my side and trace my fingers over her shoulder. Why can't I let her rest and tell her this later?

 429

She shifts, leaning into my touch. The sheet slips down, baring most of one breast.

No. Don't get distracted.

Fuck it.

I flick the sheet with my pinky, exposing one nipple. "I meant what I said," I repeat.

"You've said a lot of things." She yawns and blinks up at me. "What specifically are you referring to?"

"That I missed you."

Her expression softens. "I missed you too."

"I know your job is stressful and unpredictable...but I want you to come with me next time I have to go somewhere. Anywhere."

Her lips flicker into a patient smile. "What would I have done in Vegas while you were busy being a bodyguard?"

"Hang out with the girls." I shrug. "I wasn't standing around guarding Griff twenty-four-seven."

She nods softly. "I'd like that."

"I didn't want to keep blowing up your phone, but I missed you." I never thought I'd admit this level of neediness to a woman. *I did* try to *warn her I was a clingy motherfucker, though.* "A lot."

"You can call me anytime you want. I loved hearing from you. Getting all your texts and pictures. It was nice knowing you were thinking of me."

"I'm always thinking about you."

Her forehead wrinkles. "What's really...what are you trying to say?"

"I..." How the fuck do I put this into words? "I never expected...I don't know. I used to make fun of Rooster...the guys if they missed their ol' ladies..."

Pretty sure I used the word "castrated" a few times to describe their lack of interest in pursuing other pussy while on the road. "And didn't want to..."

Her eyes narrow. "Hook up with random women on the road?" she finishes for me.

She understands me a little too well.

Why couldn't I just let her sleep?

 430

I dug myself into this hole. Either I'm going to bury myself deeper or claw my way out.

"Something like that," I admit.

"Is this your twisted way of telling me women were throwing themselves at you in Vegas?"

"What?" I frown. "No. Not really."

Her lips push into a thoughtful pout, silently calling bullshit.

"Okay. Yes," I admit. "There were women circling us all the time. It didn't matter. The only woman I wanted was *you*."

"You sound surprised." Her forehead crinkles and she squints at me. "Or proud of yourself."

The corners of her mouth twitch and laughter glints in her eyes.

"All right. I guess I deserve that." I blow out a breath. "I don't know how to tell you—"

"Tell me what?"

"That I want you so bad. So much. All the time. I can't even fucking breathe sometimes when you're not with me." There. I said it. Most of it.

She snuggles closer. "I want you too. I missed you terribly. I hope you know that."

"I do." She'd sent me as many messages as I'd sent her. Always answered me too. "Still like hearing it."

"Mmmm." She sighs against my shoulder.

A few quiet minutes pass.

"Margot," I whisper again. Why can't I let her rest? We can talk about this in the morning.

"Hmmm?" She wriggles closer and throws her leg over mine.

Just fucking say it. Margot's nothing if not honest. If she's not feeling it, she'll say so. It'll rip my heart out, but she will.

"I want to marry you."

"What?" she gasps, coming fully awake, and sits up so fast, she elbows me in the chin.

"Ow." I wiggle my jaw.

"Sorry." She presses her palm to my cheek. "Were you talking in your sleep? Or do you mean that?"

"I…" Christ, I'm in it now. *Just say it.* None of the dumb shit that comes out of my mouth seems to scare her away. Why should this? "I never thought I'd want to do that. I'm not sure I'm really husband material. But for you, I'd like to be."

"Jensen," she whispers, a slight catch in her voice. "You're all the best kinds of husband material. I'd love to be your wife."

"Yeah?" I slide my hand over her hip and trace my fingers along her spine.

"Are you proposing?"

"Uh." *Fuck, see, I knew this wasn't the right time.* "Officially? No. I guess not. Just putting it out into the universe."

"Testing it out?" she teases.

"Maybe." I capture her hand and brush my lips against her knuckles. I'm supposed to get her a ring, aren't I? Shit, Rooster just saw a ring in a window one day and *knew* it was the right one. Did he ask Shelby what she liked ahead of time, or did he just wing it?

Instead of making fun of him, I probably should've paid attention.

Except I never thought I'd give a shit about something like an engagement ring.

"What kind of ring do you want?" I ask.

She hesitates, staring at our linked hands.

How could I forget? She's been engaged before. I bet that murdering asshole gave her a huge fucking diamond. She probably thinks I can't afford something nice.

"You know me well. Better than anyone's ever known me." Her breath hitches like she's fighting off tears. "I trust you."

"You're going to wear it for the rest of your life, so I think you should give me some inkling." I brush my thumb over her cheek. "Are you crying?"

"No." She sniffles and shakes her head, her hair sliding over the pillow. "You really want to know?"

"Uh, yeah. That's why I asked."

She holds out her hand and wiggles her fingers. "Nothing too big —I work with my hands so much. But I once saw this white gold, art deco-style ring once. Emerald-cut diamond in the center, halo of blue sapphires around it, and little diamonds in the band."

I'm not sure what some of those words mean but that's what Google is for. *Wait.* "So basically, blue and silver? Lost Kings colors?"

She ducks her head against my chest and shakes with laughter. "Yeah, I guess so. Makes sense, right? I feel like if I'm marrying you, I'm marrying your club too."

Glad she understands that. "Yeah, kinda. Speaking of, I'd really like to give you my property patch. That's like a ring in the MC world. Would you wear that for me?"

"Of course." She doesn't even hesitate. "At your club events, right?"

"Yeah." I kiss her forehead. "You won't be offended?"

"Not at all," she whispers. "Should I be?"

"It's a little…outdated, I guess." I trace lazy circles on her hip with my thumb, grounding myself in the feel of her skin. "But it's an important tradition in our world."

"I like belonging to you."

The words gut me in the best way. I shift closer, tuck her tighter into my side. "I like belonging to you, too."

She's quiet for a beat, then asks, "Does that mean you're going to get *Property of Margot* tattooed on you somewhere?"

"If you want me to."

Her laugh is soft but full, warming the space between us.

"Charlotte keeps joking that she had Teller get *Sunshine* tattooed on his dick. Is that where you want me to get it?"

"Well, you have enough room for all three words." She snickers, and her whole body shakes against mine. I missed this—her laughter, her spark, that sharp tongue of hers.

"Think you're funny, huh?"

Her laughter stops. "I had fun with your club. Hanging out with everyone, watching the fight." She stretches slightly, her heel nudging my shin under the blanket. "I thought it would be weird being there without you. But it was nice. I was nervous at first, but everyone's so… kind and down-to-earth."

"I'm glad you went."

"Me too." Her voice softens again, like she's drifting, but not ready to let go yet.

A quiet beat stretches between us, and I almost leave it there.

Almost.

"I thought a lot about Jezzie and Cain while I was gone."

"What about them?" There's a hopeful note in her voice she tries to bury, but I catch it anyway.

"I'm gonna talk to Jezzie," I say, the words scraping on the way out. "She's catching a ride home with a friend this weekend. I need to make things right. Tell her Cain's here. Let them meet if she wants to."

Margot shifts, cupping my cheek. Her palm is warm, anchoring. "Good."

A slow smile pulls at my mouth. "Will you be there when I talk to her?"

Her whole face lights up. "Of course."

"I'm not expecting you to do the hard work. Or make excuses for me. I just…" My chest tightens.

"Yes," she says quickly. "Whatever you need."

CHAPTER THIRTY-EIGHT

JIGSAW

A FEW DAYS LATER, I'M PACING THE CRACKED SIDEWALK OUTSIDE A REST stop off the Thruway.

"I should've just gone to pick her up myself."

Margot brushes her fingers along my arm, like she's trying to calm me. "She'll be here."

I glance at my phone for the third time in a minute. "They're close."

A red Honda slows, blinker ticking, then swings into the lot. The passenger door flies open before the car even stops, and Jezzie jumps out, backpack slung over one shoulder, her grin so big my heart squeezes. Like she's actually happy to see me.

"Hi!" Jezzie squeals, running so fast, she stumbles over the curb.

I catch her, locking my arms around her just in time. She crashes into me with a grunt and throws her arms tight around my neck. "Hi, Jensen."

"Hey, kiddo." My voice comes out rougher than I want it to.

She pulls back, eyes bright, then throws herself into Margot's arms with even more force. "You came with him?"

"Sure did." Margot laughs, hugging her back. "I was looking forward to seeing you too, Jezzie."

"So, I finally get to see your place, Margot?"

"Yup." Margot tosses me a quick glance. She'd been worried Jezzie might get creeped out, but my sister practically bounces with excitement.

If everything goes the way I hope, we'll head to Cain's place afterward. One thing at a time.

She talks nonstop the whole drive to Margot's. Barely comes up for air.

"Oh my God, I love the new 4Runner," she says, running her hand over the seat like she's appraising it. She leans in and takes a sniff. "Still smells brand-new. When'd you buy it?"

"Picked it up yesterday."

"What're you doing with the old one?"

My grip tightens on the wheel for half a second. I glance at her in the rearview. I was planning to give the truck to Cain so he had something to run around in besides his crotch rocket. But if Jezzie wants it…"I have a buyer for it, I think. Why? Do you want it?"

She wrinkles her nose. "Nah. Too big for parking where I live."

I blow out a relieved breath.

"So are we all going to Zips to celebrate Griff's big win?" Jezzie asks.

"That's the plan."

"Did you watch the fight, Margot?" Jezzie asks.

"I did." Margot half turns in her seat. "Did you?"

"Yeah, some guys Erin is friends with had a big party for it."

I scowl into the rearview. "What guys?"

She flicks the back of my head.

"Don't mess with the driver," I warn.

"Sorry." She sits back and stares out the window. "Jensen?"

"Yeah?"

"Do you remember…" Her voice falters. In the mirror, I catch her glancing at Margot before settling her eyes back on me. "When we drove cross country? When I moved in with Aunt Angela?"

I swallow hard, gripping the steering wheel tighter. "How could I forget?"

"Meeting at the rest stop today kinda reminded me of that trip." She rolls her eyes. "We stopped at *so* many, remember?"

I almost choke and drive off the road. We stopped at so many because I was scattering my father's bones in as many different locations as possible. There's no way Jezzie knows that, though.

"And you took me shopping," she adds, softer now.

I nod slowly, not sure where she's going with this. "Is that a hint you want me to take you shopping again?"

She smiles faintly. "No." Her gaze shifts to Margot. "Has he told you about where we grew up? On a farm. Very religious parents."

Margot nods slowly. "He's told me."

In a way I'm glad it's on her mind today. I just don't know *why*. "You okay, Jezz?"

She doesn't answer right away. Just keeps staring out the window. Finally, she nods. "Yeah. Just thinking."

Half an hour later, I ease into the driveway and pull around to the back of the funeral home.

"Wow, this place is huge," Jezzie says. "You really live here?"

"My whole life," Margot says. "I have an apartment on the third floor now."

"Okay, this is actually amazing." Jezzie steps out of the truck, staring at the house. "You could like film a whole creepy mini-series here or something."

"Jezzie," I warn.

"What? I mean it in a good way. It's a whole vibe. It's giving haunted but elegant."

Margot chuckles. "I like that."

We head inside. Jezzie slows down just inside the back hallway, eyes scanning everything like she's stepping into a museum.

"Whoa," she murmurs. "It's even cooler inside."

After a quick tour of the upstairs—everywhere except the prep room—we stop in the kitchen.

"Want something to drink?" Margot asks, already opening the fridge. "We keep refreshments down here for clients."

"Sure. Water's great," Jezzie says, eyes still roving over the dated kitchen.

"I've got cookies and brownies too."

"Oh, yum. Yes, please."

We settle at the small table in the corner.

Neutral ground.

Margot said the house should be empty today. Paul might be home but unless Jezzie and I get into a screaming match, it should be fine.

Jezzie tears into a brownie while I try to remember how to breathe.

Margot leans against the counter, watching us. Jezzie turns in her seat, raising an eyebrow at Margot. "What's up. Why do you two—oh! Are you guys getting married?"

Margot ducks her head with a laugh, brushing her hair behind one ear.

"Not yet," I say.

Jezzie blinks. "Wait, what? I thought you never wanted to take a wife."

I bite back a smile. Sometimes she still slips into those antiquated phrases.

Jezzie finishes the brownie and grabs a chocolate chip cookie, biting into it like a little savage. "So, what's with the weird faces?"

I rub my palms over my thighs. The words are right there, but they catch in my throat.

"I have something I need to tell you," I say.

She freezes, mid-chew, then slowly sets the cookie down. "Are you sick?"

"No. Shit—no. Sorry. It's not like that." I glance at Margot. She gives me the smallest nod, like she's willing me to go on. "At least, I don't think it's bad."

Not anymore.

Rip off the Band-Aid. Just say it.

"Cain came and found me."

Jezzie's whole body goes still. Her breath catches. Eyes wide, locked on mine.

"Cain?" she whispers.

I nod.

A dozen emotions flash across her face—shock, disbelief, something like hope. "Really? How is he?"

"Uh, okay. Good."

"How's his mom?" she asks, picking up the cookie again, though she just holds it now, forgotten in her hand.

"She actually passed away." I hesitate. "That's why he wanted to find me... us."

"Shit." Her voice drops. "That's awful."

I nod slowly, giving her space, watching closely. Waiting to see where she wants to go with this information.

She sets the cookie back down. Doesn't look at me.

"Where is he now?"

"Not far. I've got him set up in an apartment." My thumb taps against the side of my thigh. "Friend of the club found him a job. He's planning on sticking around and going to school here in the fall."

Silence stretches between us—heavy but not angry, yet.

"Did he ask about me?" Her voice is so soft I barely hear it.

"Yeah. He... asked about you right away." I clear my throat. "He wants to see you."

She finally looks up, eyes shining, jaw tight, like she's holding back a flood of memories. "I didn't think I'd ever see him again."

I nod again, swallowing past the lump in my throat. "Yeah, I know."

That had been my plan back then. To forget he even existed.

"Is he mad at us?" she asks, voice cracking on the last word.

"I don't think so."

She frowns, maybe considering how much I've revealed. "You got him an apartment? And a job? How long has he been here?"

My chest tightens. There it is.

"Not long," I say carefully. "Couple weeks." I cough and glance at Margot. *Couple months.*

Jezzie leans back in her chair and stares at me.

"A few *weeks?*" Her voice doesn't rise, but her disbelief hits hard. "And you're just telling me now?"

"I wanted to wait until your semester was over." I shift in my seat, the words thick in my throat. "And I wanted to make sure... he wasn't dangerous."

She lets out a short, bitter laugh. "Oh my God. Are you kidding? He's like the shyest, sweetest kid—"

"He's not a kid anymore."

Her mouth opens—ready to fire back—but nothing comes out. She clamps her lips shut, nodding slowly, breathing hard through her nose. Her eyes go glassy again, jaw working like she's chewing through anger and heartbreak all at once.

"It's not an excuse." My voice scrapes up from somewhere low and ragged. "But I've never forgiven myself. For leaving you there. For what our father..." I can't even say the words. I swallow hard. "For what he did to you."

"Jensen." She lets out a strangled sob. "But you...saved me."

"I should've done it sooner."

"But you were...shit, you were younger than I am now." She frowns, blinking fast. "Wow, I really need to get my act together."

A muffled laugh huffs from Margot.

Jezzie shakes off the moment of self-reflection. "I never blamed you. I was just thankful you got me out of there."

"Yeah, but then you were mad at me for leaving you with Aunt Angela—"

"No, I wasn't."

I blink and stare at her.

"I was mad you didn't *stay* there with us." She shrugs. "I thought we were going to all live together. I realize now, that would've been weird for you *and* her. But I was mad you wanted to live with a bunch of bikers instead of us."

It's a subtle difference—but it changes everything.

I glance over at Margot. No smug *I told you so* in her expression— just soft eyes, glistening with tears. She brushes them away and gives me a quiet, wobbly smile.

A chair scrapes over the tile and Jezzie approaches me slowly. I stand and pull her into my arms. She sniffles against my chest.

"Were you really worried Cain was a threat?" The words are muffled against my shirt, but I make them out. She tips her head back. "He used to hide under my bed when it rained."

I rumble with laughter and squeeze her tighter. "Like I said, he's not a kid, anymore. He's still kinda shy. A little mouthy. Resourceful."

"Can we go see him?"

"Yeah, let me see if he's around." I release her and pull out my phone.

"Wait, you didn't tell him I was coming today?"

I hesitate. "No. I didn't want to…get his hopes up if *you* didn't want to see *him*."

"So…you were trying to protect *both* of us?"

"I guess."

"I love you, Jensen. You're a good brother. Even if you're a pain in my ass sometimes."

"Right back atcha."

Instead of wasting time texting, I dial Cain's number.

While the phone rings, Jezzie approaches Margot and gives her a hug. "Was this your doing?" she whispers.

Margot shakes her head.

Cain answers. "Bro, who still calls people, like ever?"

"I do," I growl. "Are you home?"

"No, but I'm headed there in like ten minutes."

"Great, you mind if I meet you there?"

"Yeah," he answers cautiously, like he's hopeful. Fuck, I really have been neglecting this kid. "Sure."

"I'm bringing someone with me who really wants to see you."

CHAPTER THIRTY-NINE

I ALMOST SPLATTER INTO A THOUSAND TEARS WHEN JEZZIE HUGS ME.

"Was this your doing?" she asks.

No, he would've done it weeks and weeks ago if I'd had my way.

I shake my head. "No."

She pulls back, eyes narrowing slightly. "You sure? You're probably one of the only people he listens to about this kinda stuff."

A shaky laugh slips out of me. "Yes, but it takes him a while to realize I'm right."

She chuckles.

"All right." Jigsaw tucks his phone away in his pocket. "He's heading home now. Let's go."

Jezzie hurries ahead of us, out the door and into the parking lot.

"I guess she's eager to see him," I whisper.

He stops me with a hand on my shoulder. "Thank you. You sure you don't mind coming with us? I shouldn't—"

"I want to finally meet him." I lean up on tiptoes. "My future brother-in-law and all."

His eyes widen like he hadn't thought of it. Cain doesn't quite fit into those pockets of his life yet.

He will.

I'll help him make space.

JEZZIE'S quiet on the way to Cain's.

I don't think she's nervous. Just thoughtful. Processing. Or maybe it's bringing up memories she'd rather leave buried.

She's in the back seat, staring out of the window again. Remembering more of that long drive she took across the country to start a new life?

Jigsaw reaches over and laces his fingers through mine, his grip firmer than usual. Like he needs the contact.

I'm proud of him for facing those shadowy parts of his past. For trying to protect both siblings the best way he can.

We pull into the parking lot of a boxy building. A tall, lanky guy is out front, leaning against a motorcycle that looks like it was built for speed and danger. Neon green with streaks of white and black—sleek, and flashy. Much different than Jigsaw's bigger, heavier, darker Harley.

The guy's arms are crossed over his chest, head bowed, the hood of his sweatshirt pulled up, covering his face.

He tips his head up as we slide into a parking space, the hood falling back, revealing his features. His hair's darker than Jigsaw's and he's a bit skinnier, but the resemblance is strong.

This has to be Cain.

Jigsaw

It feels like my past has come full circle as Cain lifts his head and watches me pull into the lot. I kill the engine, the silence anything but peaceful. Margot gives my hand one last squeeze, then lets go.

I step out first. The door shuts behind me with a clean, solid thunk that cracks through the still afternoon like a warning not to wake old ghosts.

"I thought that was you." Cain pushes away from his bike and takes a few steps closer. "Sweet ride. When'd you get that?"

"Yesterday." I hesitate. "Actually wanted to talk to you about—" I wave it off. "Never mind. That can wait."

He frowns, clearly confused.

The back door opens with a soft, airtight whoosh.

I step back. I've already stood in their way for too long.

Cain's throat bobs as he swallows hard, eyes locked on the sister he hasn't seen in what probably feels like a lifetime.

"Jezzie?"

"Cain?" She laughs and rushes toward him. "Holy crap. You're so tall!"

He blinks at her. "You have colorful stripes in your hair."

She touches the top of her head and nods. "I do."

Cain's hands stay jammed deep in his pockets. Jezzie inches closer, arms slightly outstretched but not quite committing.

"Can I hug you?" she asks softly, like she knows she needs to give him the option to say no but hopes he won't.

The corners of his mouth lift, dimples popping on his cheeks. "Yeah."

They shuffle toward each other—stiff, tentative—arms out, shoulders hunched, like they're abandoned ducklings awkwardly waddling out of their nest for the first time.

They meet halfway and something shifts.

Cain wraps his arms around her like he's afraid if he lets go, she'll vanish again.

Jezzie clings just as hard, her face pressed against his shoulder, silent but shaking.

Feeling like an intruder, I back away, leaning against my truck. Margot steps beside me, sliding her hand into mine without a word.

Finally they part. Cain scrubs a hand over the back of his neck, his gaze flicking everywhere—me, the pavement, the sky—before finally landing on Margot.

"This the girlfriend you stay with all the time?" he asks, still with that weirdness around the question.

"Yes." I keep my voice steady. Now's not the time for my inner asshole to come out and play. "This is Margot."

"She's good people," Jezzie chimes in, her voice warm and sure. "Best decision our brother's ever made," she adds in a lower voice.

Our brother. Damn, that feels weird.

I don't hate it, though.

Cain rubs the back of his neck again. "You, uh... want to come inside?"

"Yeah, sure."

We follow him all the way to the top floor.

I haven't been to the apartment since before I left for Vegas. And I'm pleased he's keeping the place clean. Teller might've said he wasn't worried about any damage, but I still don't want my brother to trash the place.

Jezzie steps in tentatively, eyeing the kitchen. She throws me a teasing stink eye. "This is bigger than my place." She wanders further inside. "And it's a two bedroom?"

"Club only had this one available, smart-ass."

Cain swings his arms in wide, jittery arcs, like he's got too much energy and nowhere to put it. "So, uh... when can I meet your club? I wanna thank your friend for letting me stay here."

"Some of my brothers will be at the track." I swallow hard, not sure this is a great memory to bring up for Cain. "You remember my friend Logan? The one who…"

Cain nods quickly, sparing me from finishing that sentence. *The one who showed up and helped kick you out of your home.*

"Yeah, he'll be there. Dex too—he's the one who usually manages Crystal Ball."

His cheeks redden at the mention of the strip club.

"Are Heidi and Murphy coming?" Jezzie asks. "Heidi said she'd let me do a lap in her Hellcat."

"Get out of here," I laugh. "You want to get behind the wheel of that beast?"

She smirks and shrugs. "She offered. Aunt Angela would die if she saw me driving that."

Cain frowns. "Who's that?"

"Oh." Jezzie freezes. "Our mom's sister...I lived with her after..."

Cain nods slowly. "We have some catching up to do, I guess."

"We do," Jezzie agrees.

Cain perks up, lifting his chin at me. "Remy said one of his friends has a Mustang?"

Jezzie's gaze snaps to him. "How do *you* know Remy?"

Margot coughs into her hand, failing to hide her laugh.

"He comes into the gym I work at all the time," Cain says, like it's been the highlight of working at Strike Back. "Been teaching me some stuff."

He shifts into a fighting stance—feet planted, hands up, balanced like he's done this more than once. Not just street brawling. More controlled. More trained.

"Cute," Jezzie says. "So how do you like it here? Jensen said you were living in...New Mexico?" She lowers her voice. "I'm sorry about your mom."

"Thanks." He stares at his sneakers, scuffs one against the carpet. "It's a lot colder, that's for sure. Otherwise, I don't know."

"You're going to stay, though... right?" Jezzie asks gently, but she doesn't hide the hope in her voice.

He's quiet for a beat, then lifts his head and looks straight at me. "I dunno. If you guys want me to."

"Yeah." I shrug, unnerved by the questions in his eyes. "Thought you wanted to go to school here?"

He shrugs, still holding my gaze. "I can do that anywhere."

I already told the kid I'd help him with school and pretty much whatever else he needs.

It's not money he's looking for. Not the logistics of getting an education.

It's family.

I chose my club as my family a long time ago. Built a life on that choice. No regrets.

But now that I've found my little brother again...

Maybe I'll choose him, too.

CHAPTER FORTY

MARGOT

"You think they stayed up all night, catching up?" I ask Jigsaw as I finish slipping a rainbow-striped cardigan over my black T-shirt with a picture of a cute, fluffy kitten licking blood off its paws. Underneath the kitten, *Feminine Rage* is written in a loopy, cursive font.

Jigsaw's mouth quirks as I walk into the living room. "If that isn't the most perfect shirt for my little lady death."

"Isn't it cute?" I tip my head down and smile.

He steps closer, eyes dropping to my chest. "Sexiest threat I've ever seen—stretched across the most perfect breasts."

"Oh, you're just full of compliments tonight, aren't you?"

"Yup." He holds out a small white box. "I saw this today and thought of you."

"Really?" I squeal, not even caring what's inside. I pry the lid off and find a glossy red enamel pin—heart-shaped lollipop, devil horns, smug little face, tail curled sweetly around the stick like it's not planning to stab anyone. A ribbon banner across the middle reads: *Sweet as Hell.*

"This is so cute. I love it." I work the clasp loose and poke the sharp end of the post through my sweater, right over my heart. "I needed one to replace my fuckboy repellent pin."

Jigsaw scowls as he helps me fasten the back of the pin. "Why are you replacing it?"

Puzzled, I frown up at him. "I don't need it anymore."

He stares at me.

Heat rushes over my cheeks. "I only bought it to express my frustration with *you*." I cough and glance away to cover my embarrassment.

"Oh." He lets out a short huff of laughter. "Yeah, but you still need it to repel *other* fuckboys."

I reach up and press my hand to his cheek, smiling sweetly. "Why, when you mean-mugging at every man we run into is so much more effective?"

He scrunches his face into a silly version of his get-away-from-my-woman expression. "Excellent point."

"You didn't answer my question," I say, not sure if he deliberately avoided it or didn't hear me. Jezzie said she wanted to stay at Cain's place last night, instead of here. "Do you think Jezzie and Cain stayed up all night, catching up?"

He shrugs, the levity in his expressing vanishing.

"Are you upset she wanted to stay with him?"

"Not really. I get it." He hesitates, his gaze flicking away for a second. "I was more worried she might've hurt your feelings. Not wanting to stay here, I mean."

"Oh!" I step closer and wrap my arms around him. "You're so sweet for worrying about that. But I'm fine. It crossed my mind for a second, yeah—but even if that was the reason, it's okay." I pull back and look up at him. "But honestly? I really think it was more about wanting to spend time with him."

He nods slowly. "You're probably right."

"Well then," I smile, "are we going to pick them up?"

"I think he wanted to ride his bike there," Jigsaw says. "But yeah—we're going to get Jezzie."

THE SCENT OF GASOLINE, scorched rubber, and fried food hits my nose the moment I step down from Jigsaw's SUV.

Cain's bike glides to a stop beside us, sleek and nimble, the neon accents gleaming under the overhead lights.

"That looks so much more nimble than Jensen's Harley," I say.

Cain unleashes a grin as he climbs off the bike. "That's 'cause Harleys are sluggish and built for old dudes." He rests his helmet on the seat and pulls up his baggy pants.

Jigsaw laughs, sharp and amused. "Careful where you speak such blasphemy, kid."

He loops an arm around my shoulders, dragging me close, his heat searing through my sweater and jeans. "Why you out here startin' trouble?"

"I didn't realize I was," I laugh.

Jezzie pulls Cain toward the track, and we fall in behind them.

Near the bleachers, a tall figure lifts a hand in greeting.

"That's Rooster." Jigsaw picks up the pace.

Jezzie stops to give Rooster a quick hug.

"Hey, Jezz." He pats her back, then turns to Cain.

"Cain, this is my friend Logan," Jigsaw says. "Everyone calls him Rooster."

Rooster lifts an eyebrow, like he's waiting for Jigsaw to tack on something obnoxious.

Cain dips his chin. "Hey, Logan. I remember you."

"I remember you too. Glad you found your way here."

Cain's mouth curves—not a full smile, but close.

"Did Shelby come with you?" Jezzie asks.

Cain's eyebrows rise. "*He's* the one engaged to Shelby Morgan?"

"Yeah, I told you that," Jezzie says.

Rooster's jaw shifts like he's fighting off a laugh. "Yeah. She's over by the picnic tables with the girls." He nods to Cain. "She's looking forward to meeting you."

The five of us head toward the track. Rooster drifts closer to Jigsaw, the three of us walking just behind Cain and Jezzie.

"Everything all right?" Rooster asks in a low voice.

"Yeah, I think so." Jigsaw tilts his head, studying his friend. "You?"

"Not really. Torch brought this guy—Buck? He's gettin' sloppy drunk. Mouthy with some of the girls. Pax says if he keeps it up, we're tossing him."

Jigsaw squeezes my hand, the pressure a silent order. "Stay with me."

I nod. "You know if he says something to me, I'll give him the tongue-lashing of his life, right?"

"Yeah, but he might like that."

I snort and roll my eyes.

A group's gathered around one of the food trucks at the edge of the track. Some guys I recognize from the club and a handful of people I've never met. One of them saunters toward the picnic tables. He plops down at a table where Heidi, Ella, Shelby, Molly, and some other girls are sitting.

"Looks like a guy-free zone he just crashed without an invite," I mutter under my breath.

"Noted," Jigsaw growls beside me, his eyes narrowing as he tracks the guy's every move.

Griff approaches with his hand out, still sporting the bruised evidence of his recent win. The dark blotches on his cheekbone and jaw make me wince.

Jigsaw grips his hand, pulling him in for a rough hug and clap on the back. "How you feelin', bro?"

Griff's whole face lights up. "Sittin' on top of the world, honestly."

"Yeah, you are," Rooster adds, tugging him in for a quick bro-hug.

Then Griff's gaze lands on me and drops to where Jigsaw's hand is firmly wrapped around mine. He blinks, mouth parting like he's trying to recalibrate what he's seeing. His expression flickers—shock, disbelief, maybe a trace of awkward amusement.

Jigsaw notices the hesitation. His friendly smile flattens fast.

Griff seems to shake it off. "Margot Cedarwood. Yellow Thunderbird."

"That's me." I tip my head in acknowledgment.

His eyes dart back to Jigsaw. "How the hell did you two get together?"

Jigsaw growls low in his throat, the sound warning and dangerous. "What's that tone implying, son?"

"I'm not implying anything." Griff lifts his chin, all swagger and sunshine. "I'm outright asking," he says with all the confidence of a man who just won his first pro fight after everyone said he didn't stand a chance.

Jigsaw works his jaw from side to side, probably deciding where to punch Griff first.

I jump in before testosterone starts flying. "We met at a wedding," I offer, keeping it simple. "I accidentally ate a pot brownie. It knocked me on my butt and Jigsaw was kind enough to watch over me."

Griff shakes with laughter. "Had to be Teller's wedding and Sparky's brownies, right?"

"That's the one."

Griff glances at Jigsaw again. "You're just full of surprises, aren't you."

"You're about two seconds from getting the last surprise of your young life," Jigsaw mutters, voice low and flat.

Griff rolls his eyes. "I came over to thank you for having my back in Vegas, but I'm starting to rethink my gratitude."

Jigsaw's shoulders lose a fraction of their tension. "You're welcome."

Griff reaches out and clasps Jigsaw's shoulder. "Seriously." He flicks his gaze to Rooster. "Both of you. Thanks for sticking with Molly while I was busy training. Appreciate it."

Jigsaw nods. "Not a problem."

"Griff!" someone shouts.

"Come on. Join the party." Griff waves and jogs toward the picnic benches.

"Why are you so hostile to him?" I ask after Griff's out of hearing range.

"Who?" Jigsaw lifts both eyebrows, the picture of mock innocence. "Me?"

"Yes, you."

He shrugs. "Told you—I'm not a nice guy. Only one I'm nice to is *you*."

Rooster bobs his head in agreement. "And Shelby. You're definitely nicer to her than you are to me."

"Shut your bearded piehole." Jigsaw clamps a clawed hand over Rooster's face.

"Proving my point." Rooster flings his arm out, knocking Jigsaw's hand away.

Shaking my head, I slip my hand from Jigsaw's and march ahead, lifting a hand to wave at Shelby.

Heavy footsteps slap over the asphalt behind me.

Two seconds later, thick arms lock around my waist, hauling me off the ground. I squeal as he spins me in the air.

"Where do you think you're going, little lady death?" he growls against my ear, voice rough with laughter.

I kick and squirm, laughing too hard to put up much of a fight, even as his iron grip keeps me caged against his chest.

He sets me down and pats my ass, taking my hand again.

Still laughing and only a tiny bit embarrassed everyone saw me shrieking like a nutjob, I follow him into the closed-off patio area.

The table Shelby's sitting at is full, so I say hi to everyone, then join Jigsaw at the next table. Shelby extracts herself from the picnic bench and slides into the space next to me, slinging her arm around my shoulders. "How are you?"

"Good."

"Jezzie introduced me to Cain," Shelby says to Jigsaw in a low voice. "He seems real nice. Kinda shy."

"I think that's because you're famous," Jigsaw whispers.

"Oh. No." She frowns as if she's having trouble making sense of her fame.

"I have officially listened to my first country album," I say to her. "And loved it."

She blushes a fierce shade of pink. "Ya don't like *any* country music?"

I don't want to hurt her feelings and tell her what I always thought about country music. "No, but you changed my mind."

Across from me, Rooster huffs a laugh. "Same. I hated it until I heard her sing."

"You like Dawson's music now," Shelby says.

"Ehhh." Rooster lifts one hand in the air, wobbling it from side to side. "It's tolerable if there's no other options."

"Logan!" She slaps the table, laughing too hard to sound genuinely offended.

"I won't *say* that to him," Rooster promises.

"I will," Jigsaw deadpans.

"The heck you will," Shelby mutters. "I still owe his record label a bunch of songs."

Remy stops at our table, gives Shelby and me a quick hello, then leans down to murmur something into Jigsaw's ear.

"Yeah." Jigsaw nods. "Where?"

"Behind the last food shack."

Jigsaw jerks his head toward Rooster.

"We'll be right back," he promises.

Shelby and I watch them swagger off toward the edge of the track, disappearing behind a row of squat white buildings.

"What do you think they're up to?" I ask.

"Lord only knows." She exhales slowly and shrugs. "Probably better not to ask."

CHAPTER FORTY-ONE

JIGSAW

ROOSTER AND I ROUND THE CORNER OF THE FOOD SHACK.

"This guy's been a clown long before tonight," Rooster says.

"Yeah. Puttin' his hands on Libby, though? That's straight up insane. Dex is gonna kill him when he gets back."

We find them in a field beyond the last shack, the grass bathed in a weak circle of light.

Buck's standing there, half-slouched, working his jaw like he's chewing on something foul. Or gearing up to plead for his life. Remy's got his arms crossed, casual but tense, like he's restraining the urge to swing first. Griff's back in the shadows, leaning on the chain-link fence, scanning the area to make sure no one's gonna walk up on this scene uninvited.

Torch is off to the side, hands in his pockets—a pissed-off expression on his face.

I slow my pace, sweeping my gaze over the group.

Buck's voice grates through the humid air. "If she didn't want the attention, she shouldn't be wearing jeans that tight."

Rooster stiffens beside me. My blood boils.

Griff straightens, but Remy beats him to it, stepping forward. "She's a kid. A friend of my sister," Remy says. "Barely out of high school. The fuck is wrong with you?"

"Whoa, whoa, chill." Buck smirks and holds up his hands. "How am I supposed to know that?"

Rooster jerks forward. "You shouldn't be puttin' hands on anyone, asshole. Point-blank."

"Period," Torch adds.

Rooster's fists clench, but I stick my arm out and stop him going any further. Not yet. "Let's wait for Dex."

"Yo, fuck this. You guys are being fuckin' pussies." Buck starts walking, using both hands to shove Torch out of his way.

Mistake.

I might not like Torch all that much but he's a good fighter.

He throws a punch and Buck flies back, landing on the ground with a thud. Out cold. "Nope," Torch says. "I brought him here. I'll clean up my own mess."

Cain steps out of the dark, quick but stealthy, like he's afraid he missed the good part.

Rooster laughs. "What the fuck's he doing?"

At his side, something's swinging. Nothing but a blur of motion.

"Where is he?" Cain asks. "I was with her when it happened. We were just talking, and he came up and—" Cain's face flashes red, his lips thinning to an angry line.

It takes me a second to process what I'm looking at—a white sock, long and stretched thin from something heavy stuffed in the toe, pinwheeling lazily from Cain's hand with quiet, rhythmic menace.

My brow furrows. "The fuck you got there, bro?"

He stops the swinging, gives me a casual, dead-eyed, *are you sure you want the answer* smirk, then bunches up the sock, slowly tugging on it until he pulls out a small can of chicken noodle soup.

Rooster doubles over laughing. "What the...where did you find a can of *soup?*"

"I always carry one with me," Cain answers with a completely straight face. "It's cheap. Got some heft to it. Cops stop and ask me about it, it's just soup for my dinner." He tucks the can back into the sock and gives it a swing. "If someone needs the audacity beat outta 'em, I just take off my sock and…" A wicked smile twists his mouth up.

Rooster, Remy, Griff, and I just stand there staring at him.

Who is this kid?

"My little brother, everyone." I slap my chest and turn in a circle. "Brilliant little fucker."

"Added bonus," Remy says. "They have to smell your stinky sock while you cave in their skull with a can of chicken noodle soup?"

Cain's mouth turns up in a slow smirk, vengeance and menace wrapped in boyish charm. "It's good for the soul."

CHAPTER FORTY-TWO

JIGSAW

Never in a million years thought I'd be doing this.

But now I can't wait another second.

Zips didn't seem "special enough" for this occasion but then I remembered, this is where Margot met my sister for the first time and fearlessly pointed out that Jezzie and I use our dark humor to cover up a lot of uncomfortable feelings.

So given the way she's helped me piece my family back together, maybe this *is* the right place after all.

After I helped Torch toss his unconscious friend Buck out by the road, I stop by my truck and pull a blanket out of the back.

The guys are starting a bonfire. Music's pouring out of car speakers. Stadium lighting brightens up half the track.

My gaze scans the area, finally landing on Shelby, Molly, Libby, and Margot sitting on a blanket close to the fire.

I circle behind Margot and tap her on the shoulder. "I need you."

I hold out my hand, helping her off the blanket. Her worried eyes meet mine.

"What's wrong? Is Cain okay?"

"He's fine." I take her hand, leading her to a quieter area of the field.

I spread the blanket out and pull her down with me.

"What're you doing?" She snuggles close to me, sitting so we're shoulder to shoulder, thigh to thigh.

I gotta get this out before I forget everything I want to say.

"Margot," I start, my voice lower than I mean it to be.

I clear my throat, glance down at our hands—fingers just barely brushing. Then I pull her into my lap, her legs draping over mine.

She wraps her arms around my neck like it's instinct.

"You once asked me to teach you…" I pause, letting my hand settle on her thigh. "A few things."

She ducks her head, silky strands sliding across my cheek.

"And I thought I was so damn clever," I murmur, "warning you not to catch feelings." I tip my forehead against hers. "Then I went and caught the biggest case of feelings a man's ever had."

A soft laugh escapes her. "How do you know that?"

"Because I'd spill blood for you. Burn down buildings. Burn down the whole fuckin' world if I had to."

Her smile falters, eyes locked on mine. "I'd do the same for you."

"I know it." I close my eyes, trying to think of the words that have been knocking around in my skull for months. How to piece them together.

"You're the one who ended up teaching me so many things." My voice roughens. "And I love you so much. I want to keep learning with you—something new, every day—for the rest of my life."

Her fingers skim my cheek. "I want that too."

We just stare at each other, suspended in the moment.

Ring!

Fuck!

I jam my hand in my pocket and pull out the shiny, black box. "Will you marry me?"

"What?" Her gaze slips from my face to the box.

Did she think I was recapping our history for fun?

"I wanted to do something…fancier, nicer, bigger, but—" I say, half apologizing.

"I don't like big spectacles."

"Tonight seemed right." I let out a short laugh. *Shit, I'm nervous.* "And I'm worried I'm going to lose this if I keep carrying it around, waiting for the right time."

"Jensen!" She launches herself at me, lips crashing into mine and knocking me backward.

Her fingers thread through my hair, clutching, desperate. She kisses me like she's starving for it—like she needs to prove I'm real.

In between kisses, I flip us, covering her with my body. "Is that a yes?"

"Yes." She curls her fingers in my shirt and pulls me forward. "Yes, I want to be your wife. It's the biggest yes that's ever been yessed."

I blow out a long, satisfied breath.

The ring.

It went flying when she knocked me over. In the dark grass, it's hard to find. We sit up and I pat my hand around the blanket and finally scoop up the box and hand it to her.

She flips the lid open and squints. Even in the semi-darkness, it glitters and sparkles.

"It's…it's exactly what I described to you." She presses her fingers to her lips. "Even the halo of sapphires."

"I know." I tug it free from the box and take her hand, slipping it on her ring finger. She holds out her hand, wiggling her fingers, admiring the ring.

"Oh, it's perfect." She cuddles close and kisses my cheek.

I feel her eyes on me and turn, staring straight into her eyes.

"You've taught me so much more than sex, you know."

I take her lips in another blistering kiss. "Good."

She kisses me back, clinging to me like she owns every jagged piece of my soul. The ones she's helped stitch back together—every one of them belongs to her now.

EPILOGUE

JIGSAW

Margot pops out of her bedroom, hands tucked behind her back, a nervous smile tugging at her lips.

"Jensen, can you come in here, please?"

"Fuck yes. On my way."

I drop my laptop, push out of her lounge chair, and stride across the room—already half-hard and fully hoping this is about to go exactly where I think it is.

It's not.

It's almost...*better*.

Laid out across her bed is a helmet and riding clothes. Margot-sized.

She twists her engagement ring round and round on her finger. "I'm not saying I want to go all the time. Or long distances." Margot hesitates and glances at the clothes on the bed. "But I trust you." A frown flashes over her face. "I mean if you want me on the back of your bike."

Do I want her on the back of my bike? What a question.

More than anything in the world.

I'm too overwhelmed to speak. Words keep firing through my

brain but fizzling out on my tongue. I never expected Margot to go to all this trouble. To want to ride *at all*. And I never planned to push her into it. That she obviously gave it so much thought—researching what to wear and then buying it all by herself. I can't wrap my head or heart around what a massive gesture this is for her.

"Yes, I want you on the back of my bike. You don't have to if you don't want to, though. No pressure."

She blows out a long breath and slowly nods. "I know. I talked to some of the girls about riding. Hope told me how nervous she was at first, but that Rock made sure she was comfortable."

She squeezes her eyes shut and chuckles softly. "Shelby told me the first ride Rooster gave her she was wearing a wet sundress and afraid she was going to get splattered on the road, but Rooster was so careful with her..." Her voice trails off and she shrugs.

I flick my gaze to the ceiling. *Thank you First Lady and songbird for sharing those stories with Margot.*

Margot must've done extensive research and purchased the most high-end safety gear she could get her hands on. Motorcycle-specific jeans with Kevlar lining and knee armor. She chose a summer jacket with a ventilated mesh lining and elbow armor. Almost exactly what I would've chosen for her.

"You're not fucking around," I say, admiring the gloves and boots. "When did you buy all this?" And where's she been hiding it?

"When you were in Vegas?" She lifts her head and stares at me with wide, worried eyes. "Is it too much? I'm a big nerd, aren't I?"

"Nope." I cup her cheeks and lean down to kiss her forehead. "You're perfect."

Margot

Jigsaw's lips touch my forehead, and my whole body goes still.

He's so patient. And holds me like I'm something precious.

Not fragile. Not weak. Important to him so I know I'll be safe on the back of his bike.

He brushes his knuckles down my arm and nods toward the gear. "You ready, little lady death?"

No.

Not even close.

But I nod anyway. "Let's do this before I lose my nerve."

He helps me gear up without making a joke about how long it takes me to fasten the gloves or adjust the knee armor. Just smooth, steady patience.

Heart thudding in my throat, I follow him outside.

His bike's already waiting in the driveway. Gleaming chrome and matte black metal—intimidating and beautiful. It looks fast even when it's parked. Sturdier than Cain's bike. So maybe that's a good thing. Maybe that means it's safer.

Nope. Don't go there. You're doing this today.

I stop short a few feet away.

It's one thing to say, "take me for a ride." Another thing entirely to willingly climb on that beast.

Jigsaw turns, nothing but concern on his face. "You sure?"

No. But I love you.

So I give him the only truth that matters. "I trust you."

He nods once, serious as death. Helps me fasten my helmet, then swings his leg over and settles into the seat.

He holds out his hand.

I take it.

"Put one hand on my shoulder. Foot on the peg, and swing your leg over."

The leather of his cut creaks as I grip it. My knee scrapes the edge of the seat. I fumble, catch myself on his shoulder, and climb on—heart in my throat, hands trembling, stomach somewhere near my butt.

His voice cuts through it all, steady and low. "Hold on tight. Lean when I lean. I'll take it slow. We'll go down to the end of your street, to the park and back, okay?"

"Okay," I whisper. Then louder so he can actually hear me. "Sounds good!"

I wrap my arms around his waist, squeezing tight, and press my cheek to his back. The engine roars to life, vibrating through my legs, my chest, my bones. It's loud, and powerful, and wild.

I hate it.

But then, I kind of love it.

We start to move.

The bike rolls forward and my heart threatens to claw its way out of my chest. I squeeze my eyes shut, certain we're going to fall to our deaths when he turns out of the driveway. Every breeze feels like it could lift me right off the back. My fingers dig into his leather.

But he rides smooth. Steady. Slow. The way he always is with me.

We're not going far. Just to the park and back. I can handle that.

This isn't about the distance.

It's about overcoming my fear and getting to know something he loves so much.

Trusting him with something I never thought I'd do.

By the time we reach the park, I realize I'm breathing. Not panicked. Not hyperventilating. Just breathing.

And smiling.

Jigsaw

"That was perfect." Margot tosses her hair over her shoulders, then gives me a shy smile. "A perfect introduction. Thank you."

"Thank you for giving it a chance." I clasp my hand over her hip and take her helmet from her hands. "Will you do it again one day?"

Her gaze slides to my bike and back to me. "Yes, I think so." She leans up and slides her arms around my neck. "Maybe that can be our Sunday morning ritual. A ride to the park and back?"

That sounds like my kind of weekly worship. My brave woman on the back of my bike. My chest squeezes with so much love for her. "I'd be honored."

"Thank you." She brushes a soft kiss against my cheek. "For letting that be enough for now."

For now. I like that part.

She's my better half. Soulmate.

I never believed in soulmates. But that's what she is.

She's my quiet girl with a scalpel smile. Violence wrapped in sweetness.

The darkest pieces of our souls were always meant to fit together.

THE LOST KINGS MC® WORLD

**by *USA Today* bestselling author
Autumn Jones Lake**
This is my suggested
suggested chronological reading order
for all of the books in the Lost Kings MC World

1.Kickstart My Heart (Hollywood Demons #1)
2.Blow My Fuse (Hollywood Demons #2)
3.Wheels of Fire (Hollywood Demons #3)
4.Renegade Path (A Lost Kings MC World Novel)
5.Slow Burn (Lost Kings MC #1)
6.Corrupting Cinderella (Lost Kings MC #2)
7.Three Kings, One Night (Lost Kings MC #2.5)
8.Strength From Loyalty (Lost Kings MC #3)
9.Tattered on My Sleeve (Lost Kings MC #4)
10.White Heat (Lost Kings MC #5)
11.Between Embers (Lost Kings MC #5.5)
12.Bullets & Bonfires (A Lost Kings MC World Novel)
13.More Than Miles (Lost Kings MC #6)
14.Warnings & Wildfires (A Lost Kings MC World Novel)
15.White Knuckles (Lost Kings MC #7)
16.Beyond Reckless (Lost Kings MC #8)
17.Beyond Reason (Lost Kings MC #9)
18.One Empire Night (Lost Kings MC #9.5)
19.After Burn (Lost Kings MC #10)
20.After Glow (Lost Kings MC #11)
21.Zero Hour (Lost Kings MC #11.5)
22.Zero Tolerance (Lost Kings MC #12)
23.Zero Regret (Lost Kings MC #13)
24.Zero Apologies (Lost Kings MC #14)

...and many more to come!

ABOUT THE AUTHOR

Autumn Jones Lake is the *USA Today* and *Wall Street Journal* bestselling author of over twenty novels, including the popular Lost Kings MC series. She believes true love stories never end.

Her past lives include baking cookies, bagging groceries, selling cheap shoes, and practicing law. Playing with her imaginary friends all day is by far her favorite job yet!

Autumn lives in upstate New York with her own alpha hero.

www.autumnjoneslake.com

facebook.com/autumnjoneslake
goodreads.com/autumnjoneslake
pinterest.com/autumnjoneslake
instagram.com/autumnjlake
bookbub.com/authors/autumn-jones-lake

www.ingramcontent.com/pod-product-compliance
Lightning Source LLC
Chambersburg PA
CBHW061506020726
47502CB00006B/1961